POINTING THE BONE

Details of Daryl Joyce's previous publications are:

"Crossing Over" available from Balboa Press
"Going, Going, Gone" available at Inspiring Book Shop

POINTING THE BONE

Daryl Joyce

Library of Congress Control Number: 2020915573
ISBN: Hardcover 978-1-9845-0696-2
Softcover 978-1-9845-0695-5
eBook 978-1-9845-0694-8

All the characters in this novel, be they black or white, are fictitious and any resemblance to actual persons living or dead is purely coincidental.

Print information available on the last page.

Rev. date: 10/30/2020

To order additional copies of this book, contact:
Xlibris
AU TFN: 1 800 844 927 (Toll Free inside Australia)
AU Local: 0283 108 187 (+61 2 8310 8187 from outside Australia)
www.Xlibris.com.au
Orders@Xlibris.com.au
816192

Acknowledgements

Firstly, I would like to give my heartfelt thanks to Josie Budge for her invaluable guidance and support during the structural editing phase of 'Pointing the Bone'. Josie you are an inspiration.

Secondly, I would like to thank Mery Stevens from Bangalow for her kind editing support and for the valuable knowledge that she imparted about the Byron Bay Area.

Thirdly, I would like to thank my wife Philippa, who endured the journey from conception to completion, always providing me with unstinting support and encouragement.

About the Author

DARYL JOYCE is the author of two previous books, "Crossing Over" a memoir published by Balboa Press in 2015 and "Going, Going, Gone," a crime novel set in Sydney published by Inspiring Publishers in 2016.

Born in the country town of Kooweerup east of Melbourne, Daryl has previously lived in London and Ottawa, but now resides in Potts Point Sydney with his wife Philippa. The couple have one son Kristian, who lives with his family in Singapore. In previous careers, Daryl was a teacher of special education and a Sydney property agent, but now spends his time as a full time writer.

"Pointing the Bone" is a fictionalised story based on the troublesome relationship that developed after Europeans colonized Aboriginal land in Byron Bay NSW. Joyce has a strong affection for the characters he has created, especially the Indigenous women in his story who are strong role models. Joyce's insights create empathy while questioning the shared identity of 'Country'. The novel which is based on historical facts, personalises the conflict between the traditional owners, whose ancestors had lived on the land for over 65,000 years, and the predatory new colonists who aggressively commandeered their sacred sites and put up fences to shut them out.

Joyce's novel is Australia's answer to 'To kill a Mockingbird,' a classic portrayal of racism, injustice and intolerance in America. Here in Australia, in this age of 'black lives matter' and 'black deaths in custody,' this is a seminal piece of literature demanding to be read.

CONTENTS

Chapter 1 Byron Bay, Australia 1
Chapter 2 North Sydney 19
Chapter 3 The Journey to Byron Bay 37
Chapter 4 Arrival into Byron Bay 52
Chapter 5 Abel's House on Marvell Street 57
Chapter 6 Aboriginal Camp 65
Chapter 7 Marvell Street 70
Chapter 8 Rebecca's House 74
Chapter 9 Archie at the Aboriginal Camp 93
Chapter 10 Secret Family Business 98
Chapter 11 The Bay Café 105
Chapter 12 Wategos Beach 113
Chapter 13 The Fruit and Veg Co-op 118
Chapter 14 Rebecca Stenmark's House 122
Chapter 15 Alkira's Apartment 129
Chapter 16 The Pacific House 131
Chapter 17 The Sands Beer Garden 134
Chapter 18 Marvell Street 144
Chapter 19 Nirvana 146
Chapter 20 Kane and Rebecca Visit Abel's Office 152
Chapter 21 The Tempest 155
Chapter 22 Archie at the Aboriginal Camp 158
Chapter 23 Alkira's Apartment 165
Chapter 24 Ironbark 173
Chapter 25 Alkira's Apartment 180
Chapter 26 Ronnie's Nursing Home 182
Chapter 27 Kane, Alkira, and Archie 186

Chapter 28 Pacific House 190
Chapter 29 Alkira Preparing Her Claim 194
Chapter 30 The Sands Bottle Shop 195
Chapter 31 Byron Bay Police 200
Chapter 32 The Byron Shire News 204
Chapter 33 Alkira on TV 208
Chapter 34 Solicitor's Office 215
Chapter 35 Marvell Street 220
Chapter 36 Boat Trip 222
Chapter 37 Fisherman's Lookout 228
Chapter 38 Alkira's Apartment 233
Chapter 39 Meeting with the Tribe 240
Chapter 40 Alkira's Call 243
Chapter 41 Kane Visits Ronnie's Nursing Home 246
Chapter 42 Ronnie's Interview 249
Chapter 43 Alkira's Claim Is Assessed 259
Chapter 44 Kane's Search for the Truth 262
Chapter 45 Kane Grills Rebecca 265
Chapter 46 Archie and Kane 268
Chapter 47 Archie and Rebecca 270
Chapter 48 Kane Challenges Abel 284
Chapter 49 Kane 286
Chapter 50 Enlisting Jude 288
Chapter 51 Jude at the Grave 293
Chapter 52 Dubay Dancers 303
Chapter 53 Archie at Broken Head 308
Chapter 54 Jimmy at Broken Head 310
Chapter 55 Breakfast at MarvelL Street 315
Chapter 56 Archie Sleuthing in Byron Bay 319
Chapter 57 The Barn in Bangalow 326
Chapter 58 Indigenous Protest 329
Chapter 59 Forensics 333
Chapter 60 Exhumed Bodies 336
Chapter 61 The Pacific House 340
Chapter 62 Kane at the Aboriginal Camp 342

Chapter 63 Kane's Trip Home....348
Chapter 64 The Sands Hotel....352
Chapter 65 Rebecca's Admission....359
Chapter 66 The Barn in Bangalow....363
Chapter 67 Byron Bay....366
Chapter 68 Jude....371
Chapter 69 Lismore to Byron Bay....374
Chapter 70 Byron Bay Police Station....376
Chapter 71 Gallagher Visits Marvell Street....381
Chapter 72 Taking Control....385
Chapter 73 Alkira Visits Felix Barker....390
Chapter 74 Siblings Visit the Jail....393
Chapter 75 The Announcement....399
Chapter 76 Jimmy's Ceremony....403
Chapter 77 The Sands Hotel Beer Garden....408
Chapter 78 The Picnic Table....416
Chapter 79 Historic Broken Head Ceremony....420
Chapter 80 Byron Bay....428
Chapter 81 North Sydney....432

Acknowledgements....435

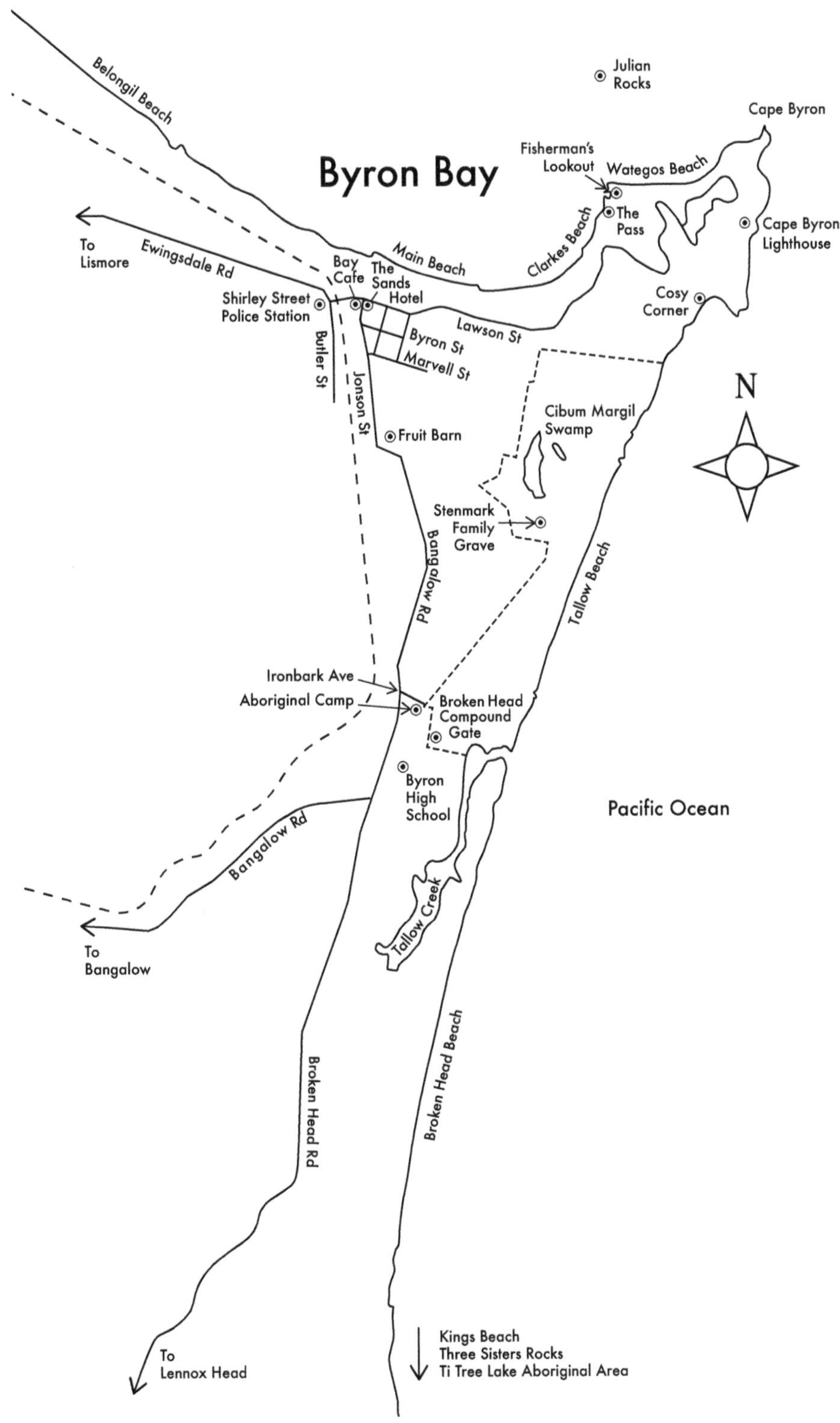
Byron Bay
Belongil Beach
Julian Rocks
Cape Byron
Fisherman's Lookout
Wategos Beach
The Pass
Cape Byron Lighthouse
Clarkes Beach
Main Beach
To Lismore
Ewingsdale Rd
Bay Cafe
The Sands Hotel
Shirley Street Police Station
Cosy Corner
Lawson St
Byron St
Marvell St
Butler St
Jonson St
Fruit Barn
Cibum Margil Swamp
N
Stenmark Family Grave
Bangalow Rd
Tallow Beach
Ironbark Ave
Aboriginal Camp
Broken Head Compound Gate
Byron High School
Pacific Ocean
Bangalow Rd
To Bangalow
Tallow Creek
Broken Head Beach
Broken Head Rd
To Lennox Head
Kings Beach
Three Sisters Rocks
Ti Tree Lake Aboriginal Area

I dedicate this novel to the four women who were the signatories to the original Arakwal National Park Indigenous Land Use Agreement in Byron Bay. I wish to respect Yvonne Stewart, Aunty Lorna Kelly, Aunty Linda Vidler and Aunty Dulcie Nicholls, who all contributed in formulating the actual plan of management, because their efforts inspired me to write this novel.

Chapter 1

BYRON BAY, AUSTRALIA

With her shock of white hair waving uncontrollably in the sea breeze, Ronnie Merinda wanders around her hometown, a jewel of a place located at Australia's most easterly point. The locals of Byron Bay may dismiss her as an idle vagrant with nothing of importance to impart, but should she choose, the proud indigenous woman has the power to throw a grenade into their world.

Like the craggy cliffs of the local coastline, Ronnie's deeply furrowed face is a testament to the unimaginable hardships she's had to face during her forty-nine years of survival. Although she belongs to one of the oldest cultures in the world, these days the local denizens of Byron Bay are refusing to shake her hand for fear of catching a disease. While white people are following the whirligig of modernity, enjoying the things that money can buy, Ronnie has been left behind wondering where her next meal is coming from. Her greatest triumph is that she has persevered enough to survive, and to cushion herself from the constant rejection she receives, Ronnie draws on an inner world of ancestral characters, who speak to her from somewhere deep inside, connecting her with her kin and the natural world.

Ronnie's tribe's long affiliation with the country around Byron Bay was drastically severed in the mid-1800s when white settlers arrived on the scene armed with rifles. These invading Europeans boldly declared ownership of her ancestor's land, and after fencing off large portions of it, effectively expelled them from grounds that they'd occupied for generations. The tribe's songs, dances and customs which were an integral part of their identity, were dramatically interrupted. This land grab had the effect of unravelling the societal bonds that had held them together. Those who were not rounded up and sent off to the missions were left behind to struggle on the margins south of the town, but with little or no means of creating wealth these once-proud people quickly sank into poverty.

Being a curious woman, Ronnie Merinda tried to come to terms with the white men's alien beliefs, but despite her best efforts she could never understand why they felt they had to possess the land rather than become its custodian. Finally, with no real defence against their rabid greed, she became the town vagrant, spurned by all as she hustles for food and cigarettes on the local streets.

Known always as Cavenbah by the original First Nation people, Byron Bay has more recently captured the hearts of global travellers. The celebrated New South Wales (NSW) beachside village has an irresistible allure, and for many the love affair with it lasts a lifetime. The seaside town holds a tightly held secret however, as many of the locals continue to blame one of its prominent sons for abducting an indigenous girl in mysterious circumstances. Although he has never been convicted of the crime, most of the town still consider Kane Stenmark from the powerful Stenmark family, to be responsible for the girl's disappearance. Little do they know that the missing girl's sister, who they see endlessly wandering the town's hot streets, has a potent story to tell.

As it is now the height of summer, the town's temperature has skyrocketed to an excessive forty-two degrees Celsius. Byron Bay's footpaths have turned into scorching hotplates and anyone with any common sense has already deserted them to cool off at one of the town's many magnificent beaches. Undaunted by these soaring temperatures however, Ronnie Merinda is struggling along Lawson Street with the soles of her feet feeling as if they're on fire. Squadrons of cockroaches scurry for cover as as she scoots over the scorching bitumen to a rubbish bin she has seen outside the Bay Seafood Market.

After finding some discarded cigarette butts in the bin, Ronnie rolls them in her gnarled fingers and lines them up in a rusty tin. After collecting about half a dozen of them, she decides to ignite one, but her lighter flares up like a torch burning her thick lips. After ripping the butt away from her mouth, she slides her pink tongue back and forth to relieve the sharp pain

Undaunted by this failed attempt, Ronnie selects another butt from her tin, but this attempt also proves perilous, because after inhaling on it deeply, her head begins to swirl. After stumbling forward, she saves herself from the ignominy of a fall by clinging onto the bin's metal edge at the last minute. Swaying back and forth like a willow in the wind, she remains there gripping tenaciously to the bin with Rawson Street shimmering in front of her like a mirage.

After her head clears, Ronnie deems her 'smoko' to be over and she swivels her head towards the fish shop window to survey the fresh seafood on offer. Inspired by what she sees, she barges through the plastic ribbons dangling at the shop's entry, and after dumping her heavy bags onto the recently hosed concrete floor, lifts her tired eyes in search of the proprietor.

'Hello, Ronnie!' a portly man with a ruddy face calls out from the filleting bench.

'G'day, Freckle,' she answers, recognising her old friend.

'How are you today, love?' he asks as he strips the innards from a whiting.

'Hungry,' she answers.

'Then look around and choose something you like, darlin',' he replies rinsing his hands under a running tap.

Ronnie inspects the various types of fish that Freckle and his assistant have neatly lined up on beds of ice. She recognises her usual choices of red emperor, snapper, and trevally, but today she is after something different . . . something really special.

'I like these crabs here,' she declares excitedly, pointing towards two giant mud crabs.

When Ronnie points to the huge cooked crabs, Freckle observes the rich black Byron Bay dirt permanently residing under her fingernails.

'You've got expensive tastes, Ronnie. These mud crabs are a delicacy,' he chides.

'No, they're bloody not . . . We used to catch 'em at Broken Head when we were kids,' she rebuffs.

'Yeah?'

'Yeah! After we caught 'em, we'd cook 'em over a fire on the beach. They were delicious. Can ya break 'em up an' remove some o' the shells for me, Freckle?'

'I can, darlin'. I certainly can do that for you. Would you like anything else, love?'

'I'll have some of this sushi too,' she answers, pointing to a salmon, avocado and wasabi rice roll located on the top shelf of the refrigerated takeaway section.

Ronnie's face lights up with appreciation when Freckle signals for her to take whatever she wants. Ronnie considers Freckle to be a generous man because he has never asked her to pay for whatever she selects. Their relationship goes way back to when he joined her on a protest march. At the time, Ronnie was protesting against an exclusion zone that the local council had set up banning her people from coming into the town. In those days, First Nation people were excluded from the Byron Bay township, and it was only after this law was repealed that Ronnie could become a regular at Freckle's fish shop. To his credit, from the date of that repeal, Freckle has never failed to gift her with anything she wants.

The duo has built up a strong affinity over the years, strengthened by a shared interest in books. As both of them are avid readers, they like nothing better than to share their knowledge with each other. Freckle has seen Ronnie perched on a milk crate outside the local shops, often with her head deep into a novel and whenever she comes into his shop, he never misses the opportunity to ask her the same old question.

'Read any good books lately, Ronnie?'

'Yeah, I'm reading *Harp in the South* at the moment,' she answers him today.

'Who's the author?'

'Ruth Park . . . It's real good.'

'What's good about it, Ronnie?'

'It's all about the first slums in Sydney. Sometimes it makes me laugh, and then I cry.'

'Oh, I remember hearing about it now . . . It's a classic Aussie novel with a great heart, isn't it?'

'Yes, and I'm loving it,' she adds with a shy smile.

'Guess what I'm reading?'

'What?'

'I'm reading *Burnum Burnum*.'

Ronnie pricks up her ears when she hears the title.

'I've heard about 'im, Freckle. He was one of our mob, wasn't he? Didn't he plant our Aboriginal flag at the White Cliffs of bloody Dover?'

'Yes, you're right, Ronnie. He took possession of England for the Aboriginal people on Australia's bicentenary. It was quite audacious, really. I'll give it to you when I finish it.'

'Good. I'd like that.'

Freckle wraps Ronnie's fish in white butcher's paper.

'That's what you lot did to us, you know!'

Freckle waits for the rebuke.

'You invaded us and then you hoisted up the bloody Union Jack!'

'Steady up, girl. Go easy on us, Ronnie.'

'It's bloody true!'

'Here's your crab meat, love, and here's your sushi roll,' he says, handing over the two packages.

'Thanks, Freckle. I'm going over to my daughter's place tonight for our annual dinner. It's her birthday, and she loves crab.'

'Enjoy it, Ronnie, and please say hello to Alkira for me, won't you?'

Ronnie loads up her swag again and struggles out through the plastic strips at the fish shop door.

'Phew! She's on the nose today,' Freckle sighs to his assistant once Ronnie is out of earshot.

'Yeah, it's a heady mix when her body odour mingles with the smells of our fish,' his offsider agrees.

'I hope she takes a shower at her daughter's place tonight,' Freckle adds before returning to his bench to finish filleting the rest of the whiting.

As Ronnie wanders from the fish shop towards Clarkes Beach, many of the beachgoers who pass her on Lawson Street give her a wide berth. Not completely unaware of their reactions to her, Ronnie decides to ignore them, preferring instead to inhale the salty sea air and listen to the familiar sounds of the seabirds that are calling to her overhead.

When she finally reaches the beach, Ronnie spots a vacant picnic table on the grass and she rushes madly towards it eager to secure it before anyone else can. With an exhausted sigh, she dumps her bags beside the table and slides her tired frame onto the attached seat. Glad to be off her burning feet at last, she impatiently tears open her parcel of sushi and looks out to sea.

Ronnie's eyes immediately light up when she sees a sedimentary formation jutting from the water just beyond the immediate beach. In awe, she watches the waves as they crash onto Julian Rocks – or Nguthungulli, her tribal name for them. With the legacy of ancestral creation flooding her senses, Ronnie stares at them with a wide smile. She has adored these rocks for as long as she can remember, because her creator rests there. Ronnie's mind drifts back to the many ancestral stories her mother had told her about them – how in the beginning, the creation beings came from them to form the land, the rivers, and the mountains.

As a child, Ronnie used to live in an urban camp just off Lawson Street. It was located in the sand dunes at the edge of Clarkes Beach. When she resided there, she loved waking each morning and looking out towards Nguthungulli. At that time, she lived in a simple humpy manufactured from corrugated iron. It sheltered her from tropical downpours in summer, but did little to protect her in winter when the fierce winds whisked their way in from the south. She shudders at the thought of those cold nights.

Spurred by these remembrances, some disturbing thoughts make their way into Ronnie's consciousness, and these thoughts cause her brow to furrow. A frightening incident took place when she awoke on her tenth birthday that caused her world to turn upside down. On that unforgettable morning the local police entered her camp at sunrise, blaring announcements on a megaphone.

'We are dismantling this camp immediately!' a loud voice boomed. 'From this day forth, all Aboriginals will be banned from entering the downtown area of Byron Bay.'

A shiver runs through Ronnie's body as she remembers being herded from the camp at daybreak and ordered to relocate in the impoverished margins south of town. Her heart quickens when she recalls the vicious police dogs that barked at her heels as she fled in terror.

After the desecration of her home, Ronnie felt disoriented and misplaced, but she was soon to learn via the bush telegraph that she was not the only victim of this practice. The banning of Aboriginals from downtown areas was not an uncommon practice at the time, as similar bans had been placed on scores of indigenous settlements throughout Australia.

After hearing these reports, Ronnie made the decision to highlight how these harsh bans were negatively affecting her people, and she organised a number of protest marches from Broken Head to Byron Bay. Sadly her many demonstrations gained minimal traction, and it was only when a group of white civil libertarians joined her cause that the national press finally gave a voice to her protests. Ultimately, however, these protestors were able to shame the local council and they forced it to reverse its racist bans.

Today, as Ronnie sits at the picnic table looking out to sea, she feels a personal pride that she was the original instigator of this movement for change. More than anyone else in this town, she appreciates the pure pleasure of freely wandering the streets without being hounded by the police. These days, she is free to sit at the beach for hours if she so desires, unharried by the local constabulary and their vicious dogs.

From her well-earned position at the picnic table, Ronnie watches the young surfers as they ply their skill against the ocean swell. If she has timed it right, she may even catch sight of her daughter, Alkira, who may be riding in on one of the waves. Ronnie scrunches up her eyes to scan the surf, but when she is unable to decipher which board rider is her daughter, she turns her attention back to her sushi.

The first person Ronnie recognises at the beach is young Corrie Stenmark, who suddenly appears from behind a bush next to her picnic table. Corrie is dressed only in his striped board shorts, clutching onto his new performance shortboard. As Ronnie watches him looking out towards the waves, she admires the boy's lean tanned body and long straw-coloured hair, but she refuses to wave to him. Corrie is a Stenmark and she despises the Stenmarks. Her First Nation people have had a long history of conflict with his ancestors and she harbours a deep-seated grudge against them.

The problem began way back in the mid 1880s, when his great-grandfather Joseph Stenmark took up a settlement grant over a large tract of land at Broken Head, just south of the town. At the stroke of a pen, Ronnie's tribe was dispossessed, and when Joseph Stenmark built a high fence around his new property, they were effectively locked out from their sacred land. From that moment on, the traditional owners were denied access to a site on which they'd conducted their ceremonies for countless centuries.

Corrie Stenmark has heard on the morning radio that the swell is pumping at Clarkes Beach, and from his position just a short distance from Ronnie's picnic table, he checks it out. Under an azure sky, he sees a set of substantial waves barrelling into shore from Fisherman's Lookout. The size of them brings a broad smile to his youthful face and as the sea birds swoop in formations overhead, the boy breaks into a run towards the water's edge. Without a care in the world, he attaches his leg rope to his left ankle and thrusts himself out to sea.

When Corrie Stenmark reaches the break, he notices Ronnie's daughter waiting for the right swell to come along. He has seen the indigenous girl out surfing on several occasions before today, but he doesn't know her name. Even though Byron Bay is just a small coastal town, the two of them seem to exist in completely different worlds and somehow their paths have never crossed on land.

When Corrie looks out to sea, he observes a large wave building, and after deciding to position himself in front of it, he paddles furiously to gain enough momentum to launch into his ride. After straightening up on his board, he elegantly skims across the curve of the wave with his arms outstretched.

Unfortunately for Corrie however, the Aboriginal girl has caught the wave already and as it is surfing etiquette to abort his ride, he calls out 'Sorry!' and swerves out. Feeling quite chivalrous after this act, he reverts to his original position, straddling his board while he waits for the next wave to build.

The act of sitting on his board out in the ocean under a clear blue sky is usually the epitome of absolute joy for Corrie Stenmark, but today his elation quickly turns to terror when he spots a shiny black fin heading straight for him. The boy's body stiffens at the sight of the triangular shape and almost instinctively he lifts his legs onto his board to keep them out of harm's way. With his heart thumping inside his chest, Corrie watches the shiny fin as it glides closer and closer towards him. He becomes spooked however, when the shark's fin disappears beneath the surface.

His alert eyes scan back and forth as he waits for the shark to reappear. He is actually hoping that the predator has retreated into deeper water, but something tells him however, that the man-eater is still circling somewhere directly beneath him.

When a dark shadow appears beside him, the boy watches in horror as the shark opens its jaws, showing two ugly rows of razor-sharp teeth. Its jaws chomp noisily into Corrie Stenmark's fibreglass surfboard, missing his legs by mere centimetres.

With his board wrenched from underneath him, Corrie plunges into the ocean, and frightened out of his wits, he attempts to scramble back onto it. His board is somewhat shorter now, however, and he has a great deal of trouble hoisting his entire body back onto it. He manages to raise his upper body out of the water, but his legs are still dangling behind him in the brine.

'Help! Shark! I've been attacked! Help! Help me!' he cries, but his desperate pleas go unheard. Realising that there is no one around to save him, Corrie Stenmark fears for his life, because at this moment he is perhaps the most vulnerable morsel in the food chain.

As in a horror movie, the ominous shadow appears beside Corrie a second time. Alarmed that the monster of the sea appears to be readying itself to make another swirling lunge, he waits. This time the shark rises up like a Phoenix beside him and its jaws chomp into Corrie's right leg, severing it just below the knee. In a sea of blood, the boy screams in agony, as he flounders in the ocean experiencing the most excruciating pain he has ever known. Resigned to being entirely at the shark's mercy, Corrie can only hope that his severed right leg will be enough food to satiate the predator's voracious appetite.

After her successful ride, the Aboriginal girl returns towards the break and when she hears Corrie's desperate calls, she picks up the pace of her paddling until she is within earshot.

'Are you OK?' she calls out to him.

'A shark got me! Please help me! I've lost one of my legs!' Corrie yells back to her, wincing in agony.

The girl paddles closer, but when she sees the ugly wound where the shark has severed Corrie's leg, she becomes immediately alarmed. After watching copious amounts of blood gush from his injury, she concludes that a tourniquet must be applied to the wounded leg immediately before the boy bleeds to death in front of her.

Throwing caution to the wind, the indigenous girl assists Corrie Stenmark back onto what remains of his board, and after freeing his rope from his left ankle, she gamely winds it around his right thigh. After securing it as tightly as she can, the girl attaches her own leg rope to Corrie's damaged board, and with him moaning in agony behind her, she paddles bravely towards the shore.

'Did you see it?' she asks.

'It was a great white!' he shouts back between moans of anguish.

'Hell!'

'They're the only ones that come out of the water. I reckon the bloody thing was about three metres long!'

Alkira shudders at this revelation.

'All you have to do is stay on top of your board,' she directs firmly, before increasing the rate of her paddling.

Terrified the shark will lunge at him again, Corrie lies still hoping the Aboriginal girl can paddle him to shore before he passes out. By the time Alkira has dragged him onto the sand however, he is quite delirious. After examining the boy's angry wound again, Alkira realises that she has to do more to stem the flow of blood, and in a panic she scans the beach to find a clean towel to wrap around the boy's angry gash.

The person closest to Alkira at this point is her mother, who is sitting at a picnic table up on the grass. Realising that Ronnie is the last person to approach for a clean towel however, the girl searches farther along the expanse of the beach until she spies a couple of sunbathers some way off. Leaving Corrie writhing on the wet sand, she sprints towards the couple at top speed and after panting breathlessly in front of them after her fifty-metre dash, she begs them for a towel. When they offer one to her, Alkira thanks them profusely, but before returning to Corrie Stenmark, she beseeches them to call for an ambulance on their mobile phone.

After carefully wrapping Corrie's wound with the clean towel, Alkira remains beside the boy's semi-conscious body, continually asking him questions in an effort to keep him awake until help arrives. She is all too aware that Corrie has lost copious amounts of blood during the rescue, and she desperately hopes that the paramedics will arrive in time to revive him before he sinks into an unconscious state.

After an interminable wait, an ambulance finally pulls up at the top of the beach. The girl waves frantically towards the vehicle, and soon two female paramedics rush towards her with a stretcher. After observing the blood-soaked towel, they immediately place an oxygen mask over Corrie Stenmark's mouth and nose, and inject him with a strong painkiller. After unwrapping the towel, the paramedics spray a disinfectant on his wound before covering it up again with wads of clean white gauze. Alkira is alarmed when the paramedics repeatedly slap Corrie's face to prevent him from sliding into unconsciousness, but not wanting to be a gawking bystander, she picks up her surfboard and strides towards her mother up at the picnic table.

When Alkira reaches the picnic table however, she is alarmed to find her mother flat on her back on the grass with a nasty gash on the back of her head. Aghast to see her mother lying lifeless in the hot sun, the girl immediately kneels beside her to examine her face and listen for her breath. When she cannot hear any breathing, the girl becomes frantic and she rushes back to the paramedics to alert them of their next emergency. After requesting their assistance, she quickly returns to her mother to begin administering mouth-to-mouth resuscitation.

It is a hideous task for Alkira to perform however, as not only does her mother's body odour overwhelm her, but also when she presses her lips against her mother's mouth, it tastes for all the world like a dirty ashtray.

Alkira is more than thankful when the paramedics finally arrive to take over the resuscitation, and she watches intently as they jolt her mother's chest as they try to revive her. After ten long minutes of severe jolting, Ronnie makes no response and fearing that her mother has died, Alkira becomes extremely anxious. To her enormous relief, she finally hears a deep spluttering cough and then the resumption of her mother's breath.

When the paramedics deem Ronnie to be stable enough, they slide her into the back of the awaiting ambulance beside Corrie Stenmark, and the last thing Alkira sees through the windows of the departing vehicle are its occupants, all wearing face masks in a vain attempt to block out the indigenous woman's pungent body odour.

After the ambulance has gone, the girl looks forlornly around at the three large bags left beside the picnic table. Knowing they contain all her mother's meagre possessions, Alkira makes a half-hearted attempt to pick one of them up. As she lifts it however, a large parcel of mud crabs spills out onto the grass. When she sees the sizeable pieces of crab, the girl suddenly remembers that today is her own birthday and that these crabs would have been Ronnie's offering towards their annual dinner. At that moment, the reality strikes Alkira that she had almost lost her only relative on her birthday. She covers her face with her hands and weeps bitter tears, her sobs welling up from somewhere deep within her.

Alkira knows that in the past, even though her mother had desperately needed the money, she'd always refused to accept any help from the government. Being way too proud to receive welfare, she had preferred to roam the streets of Byron Bay as a vagrant, than to become a welfare recipient. There was no way on earth that she would ever accept charity from the very authorities whom she blamed for her predicament.

'I'll roam the streets forever rather than have that lot pity me,' Alkira remembers her mother voicing on a number of previous occasions.

With her eyes blurred with tears, Alkira struggles with her surfboard and her mother's cumbersome bags along the full length of Lawson Street, not stopping until she reaches her apartment situated a few blocks farther along on Jonson Street.

Ironically, her mother who was known as the local bag lady, used to do the same. She was always carrying things. Even when Alkira was a tiny baby, her mother would carry her around in a dilly bag that was tied around her neck while she fossicked in the scrub for bush tucker. Alkira applauds her mother's resourcefulness during these tough years because despite the considerable odds that were stacked against her, they'd both somehow managed to survive.

With the tragedy of her mother's life clouding her thoughts, Alkira deposits her mother's bags next to the external staircase leading up to her apartment. Unable to lift them any further, the girl rests her exhausted body on the bottom step while she catches her breath.

Some childhood memories flood into Alkira's mind as she sits there recovering her strength. She remembers how proud she'd felt on her twelfth birthday at Ti-Tree Lake, when her mother covered her in black mud at her initiation ceremony. She'd felt so special when the women of her tribe helped her mother pile more and more mud onto her nubile body. As the women sang ancient songs in their own tongue, each handful of mud was evidence that they were accepting her as a fully fledged woman of the tribe.

With her mother's bags still at her feet, Alkira remains seated on the bottom step remembering the past. In silence, she joyfully recalls her mother singing song-lines to her. Ronnie would sing them over and over to her until she was able to sing them for herself. It was the way all the women in the tribe passed on their secret women's business, and over time her mother had successfully transferred a swag of information to her about her heritage, hoping that in turn she would pass on these oral stories to her family. Once Alkira had learned her mother's songs by heart, she felt truly connected to her tribe, equipped to transfer what she'd learned to the next generation.

Alkira's mother had acted quite differently from her tribal sisters however. Unlike them she had a strong ambition burning inside her. This aspiration was not for herself but for her daughter, as she had set her heart on Alkira rising above her station in life. Believing that Alkira's ticket to freedom was receiving a proper education, she sent her off to a private boarding school. No one knew where the money had come from to pay for her tuition fees, but somehow she'd managed to enrol Alkira into a prestigious white man's college, and once registered, she saw to it that her daughter never missed a day of school.

Alkira closes her eyes and silently thanks her mother for her foresight, knowing that she had saved her from the downward spiral of welfare dependency that could easily have become her destiny. Ronnie had sacrificed her own life for her well-being and she was well aware that it was a true act of charity. While she was receiving an invaluable education in an excellent boarding school, her mother was left behind in Byron Bay living in abject poverty. While Ronnie was roaming the streets looking for food and cigarettes, she was finishing off high school and going on to complete a university degree. Her mother's sacrifice had enabled her to finish her law degree and now she was ready to reap the considerable benefits that this advanced education would bring her. Alkira weeps bitter tears at the gross injustice of it all.

The only time Alkira's face brightens during these reflections is when she recalls her recent graduation ceremony at Sydney University. She allows a little smile to creep over her face while recalling her mother trying on her mortarboard while holding up her graduation certificate in front of her as if it was her own. On graduation day Ronnie had been so immensely proud that Alkira had managed to complete her degree.

A deep sadness immediately returns to Alkira when she reflects upon the recent pitiful state of her mother. Few people knew that except for Alkira's graduation day, Ronnie refused to come anywhere near her, agreeing only to meet her on her birthday each year. In the interim, Alkira had attempted to give her mother gifts, especially when she saw her so utterly destitute on the street, but each time she'd slip money or food into her pocket, her mother would dig it out and throw the notes and food onto the roadside. She'd tried to make contact with her on countless occasions, but the impoverished woman would always turn on her heel, ensuring that Alkira was set free from the shackles of her birth.

For the past 364 days, Ronnie had stayed away from Alkira, believing that she'd impede her progress, but tonight as it was her birthday, Ronnie intended to meet up with her like they always did. Tonight they would have eaten mud crabs and talked about the good old days, but sadly, it was not to be. Alkira bursts into loud heartfelt sobs on the bottom step.

With the heavy load of her mother's belongings weighing in each hand, Alkira clambers up the remaining wooden stairs to her apartment. After opening the door, she sighs heavily as she unloads her mother's bags onto the hall floor. Feeling physically and emotionally drained, she collapses onto her bed.

It has been such an extraordinary day, one in which she'd mustered enough strength to haul poor Corrie Stenmark to safety from the jaws of a shark, and in addition, she'd managed to keep her mother alive after finding her collapsed body at the picnic table. Now, however, she is done. She has no more to give.

'I love you, Ronnie,' Alkira mouths into the air above her bed, as she surrenders to the waves of fatigue that flood over her exhausted body.

Chapter 2

NORTH SYDNEY

Some 765 kilometres south of Byron Bay, 24-year-old Archie Stenmark is on a train heading towards his publishing house in North Sydney. As the train crosses the glorious harbour via the celebrated Sydney Harbour Bridge, built of steel in 1932, Archie looks out towards the Sydney Opera House on his right side and then Luna Park on his left. Despite his many journeys back and forth over the celebrated bridge, the dynamic harbour vistas from both sides of the train never fail to excite him.

Opposite him, a young woman looks up from her cell phone, endeavouring to catch his eye, but Archie deliberately ignores her. Although his chiselled good looks and ideally proportioned body consistently attract admiration from strangers, he has little regard for such superficial affection, preferring instead to sit alone relishing his solitude. The magnificent waters of Sydney Harbour are more likely to stir his soul than a casual encounter with a stranger. From experience he knows that if he plunges himself into nature's limpid pools, they are more likely to release an ecstasy inside him that will serve to crowd out the darker shadows that sometimes lurk in the corners of his mind.

As he is late for an appointment with his editor, who is a well-known stickler for time, Archie sprints like a gazelle from the North Sydney train station, and with beads of sweat dripping from his handsome brow, he dashes up the front steps of Aston & Irwin Publishers two at a time.

Initial success has come quite easily for Archie as he has managed to get onto the Australian fiction bestseller list on his first try. When he compares himself with other exceptional writers however, especially those who have struggled for years to attain any recognition, he feels like a sham, seriously doubting he'll be able to replicate this initial success.

As he is keen to keep everything low-key, Archie hopes he can slip into his boss's office unnoticed, but to his chagrin his arrival at the publishing house creates a considerable stir. When they spot him entering the building, his colleagues flock towards him to congratulate him on the runaway success of his debut novel. Although he is gratified to receive this praise from his peers, the ambush only compounds his tardiness and increases his anxiety.

After finally escaping his admirers, Archie Stenmark edges his way towards his boss's glass-walled inner sanctum. He expects Sue Barkham to laud him with praise at his recent triumph, but his boss doesn't even look up when he enters. The editor-in-chief continues to scan through a country newspaper on her computer screen and without any reference to his rocketing book sales, she points to the screen in front of her, showing the front page of the *Byron Shire News*.

'Archie, do you know this Rebecca Stenmark woman on the front page of this paper?' she asks.

'And good morning to you too, Sue,' he responds, edging closer to peer at the newspaper on the screen. 'No, I don't know her Sue, but with that name, she's probably a relative of mine.'

'Yes, Archie, I know you are a Stenmark and that your father originally came from Byron Bay. Don't you know the members of your own bloody family?'

'Sue, I don't know any of the Stenmarks and what's more, they don't know me either.'

'Why not, for god's sake?'

Archie peers at Sue Barkham's glossy fire-engine-red lips. He knows from experience that these lips can deliver intense vitriol and that they're not to be messed with. 'My father was thrown out of the family years ago, Sue. I don't think the Stenmarks even know I exist,' he blurts.

'Why not, for god's sake?'

'My father has kept that fact a secret from them.'

'Why?'

'He's been estranged from the family for decades. They think he's been living out in the wilderness – both literally and figuratively.'

The editor raises one pencilled eyebrow at this admission and with her manicured finger, she beckons Archie to examine the article in the paper more closely. Archie edges in beside his boss, but as she points her red fingernail towards the picture of Rebecca Stenmark, her strong perfume overwhelms him and he wonders why she applies quite so much scent.

'Archie, this woman could be your father's sister and she's saying that there's a curse on the entire Stenmark family!'

Archie's eyebrows go up.

'Do you know anything about it?'

Archie shrugs. He knows nothing.

Archie's eyebrows stay up while he peers at the large photograph of Rebecca Stenmark on the front page. He checks out the woman's features, but when he fails to find a family resemblance, he quickly scans the copy beneath.

'Sue, I've never known the Stenmarks. This woman may be my aunt, but Dad has never mentioned anything about her to me, or anything about a curse either for that matter.'

'Look closely at what she's saying, Archie. It sounds as if your family is in jeopardy, as she's rattling on about a run of disasters. Are you aware of any of these?'

'No.'

'I've googled your father's name, and I've found out that he was a suspect in a possible murder case in Byron Bay when he was a youth. Do you know anything about that?'

Archie's face shows deep concern. 'I know nothing about it, Sue. My father refuses to speak about his past life. It's a forbidden topic in our house.'

'You should look into it, my boy,' Sue Barkham warns. 'Rebecca Stenmark says the curse began way back when her grandfather took over an important sacred site in Byron Bay. When he threw the elders of the local tribe off their land, they were so angry about it that they pointed a bone at him!'

Sue Barkham looks up at Archie quizzically. She requires much more information from him, but Archie just shrugs. He has nothing to impart to her.

'Archie, listen to me. This woman is talking about your family. This curse could affect you one day. She says there's been a long line of family tragedies already. I've just read that she attributes the recent death of her partner to the curse. It's personal and you should be looking into it, Archie Stenmark. I smell a big story here!'

Archie understands that his boss has a nose for these sorts of tragedies, but he displays little interest. When he shrugs again, Sue Barkham raises her voice.

'Up and down the east coast of NSW, everyone knows the Stenmarks, Archie, because they represent the establishment in Byron Bay. I understand they own the major hotel there, plus a large tract of land on Broken Head. Your family has been a pillar of strength in the community for generations. For god's sake, Archie, they're filthy rich and there's a bloody curse on them! It's big news, and I want you to write about it. It will be brilliant fodder for your next big novel.'

'You're bulldozing me, Sue!'

'After all the money we've spent promoting your last book, you do realise that you are still under contract with us?'

Archie steps back from the desk. His back stiffens and he shakes his head. 'Find someone else to write about it, Sue Barkham, because I won't do it. This curse looks like a can of worms to me and I know absolutely nothing about Aboriginal voodoo. I've never had anything to do with the family and I'm sure they won't want anything to do with me.'

'You can't refuse this assignment, Archie. Can't you see it's made for you?'

'No it's not, Sue. I don't want to go. Why don't you send someone else to Byron Bay?'

'Unfortunately, I'm not taking no for an answer, my boy. Now get up there and dig around to see what you can come up with. I have a strong hunch that it will end up as your next bestseller and that will be good for both of us.'

'Sue, all my life my father has warned me to keep away from Byron Bay. He has repeatedly told me that I won't be welcome there. He's always insisted that I should stay away.' Sue Barkham glares at Archie with a death stare.

'To hell with your father! Man up, Archie! Beat the bloody Stenmarks' door down if you have to, but come back with a bloody good novel. Now get up there and don't come back until you have something worthy of publication!'

Feeling railroaded, Archie Stenmark stares at his boss's lips as she summons a literary reference.

'According to Rudyard Kipling, if you encounter triumph and disaster, you must treat these two imposters the same. That's when you'll inherit the earth and everything in it, and what's more, you'll be a man, my son!'

Archie stares back at his boss, thinking that she's a veritable bully.

'When you return, I want to be reading the next great Australian novel. Now get out and get on with it!'

Archie scurries out of the office, hoping to make a quick getaway, but one of his female colleagues thrusts a copy of his recent novel in front of him at the door, asking him to sign his name on it. He quickly scribbles, 'Treat triumph and disaster the same — Archie Stenmark.' Archie then dashes down the stairway to the street before anyone else can catch his attention.

As Archie retraces his steps from the publishing house back to the North Sydney train station, his mind is in turmoil, wondering if he should comply with his boss's wishes by facing the curse head-on, or stay well away from it.

While he travels home in a storm of confusion, Archie's 48-year-old father has just awoken. It is midday by this time and after a night out on the town clubbing, Kane Stenmark is trying to recover from the previous night's massive onslaught of alcohol and drugs. He stands at his kitchen bench trying to convince himself that he's only hammered, not stark raving mad. Aware that his morning malaise is just a hurdle to be cleared, Kane Stenmark decides to cook up some pasta, a dish high in carbohydrate.

With his terry-towelling dressing gown open at the front showing his softening waist, Kane mechanically drops some fettuccine into a pot of boiling water and after rinsing a bunch of fresh basil under the kitchen tap, he places it in a food processor along with some pine nuts, garlic and extra virgin olive oil. When he flips the switch on the appliance however, it emits such a high-pitched whirring sound that it almost lifts Kane's head from his shoulders. After silencing it, he couches his head in his hands until he can muster enough courage to hit the switch again.

Kane Stenmark has always regarded his kitchen as his haven. It is one of the only places in the world where he alone is in charge. As it is his only sanctuary, he has made up a strict rule to protect himself from ridicule. His edict is 'No unkind words can ever be spoken in my kitchen'.

It has been over two and a half decades since Kane fled from Byron Bay and during all of this time he has refused to think about his hometown. He has always made Byron Bay a forbidden topic in his house, but today as he's at such an incredibly low ebb, he has allowed a little introspection to creep in, and his thoughts drift to his kid sister, with whom he hasn't spoken in twenty-five years. A tear wells up in one of his eyes. *If only I could hug my sis*, he muses, recalling the closeness he once enjoyed with her before their relationship blew up like a grenade.

'I love you, Rebecca,' he sobs out loud, as he rubs the tell-tale tear away.

Kane's connection with his sister was a great deal stronger than the one he had with his brother. With Rebecca he had a genuine relationship, one in which each of them could confide to the other about almost anything. In a perfect world, he would have stayed on in Byron Bay just to be close to her, but he was intelligent enough to realise that if he had stayed on, he would have clashed with his brother, Abel.

The brothers had obviously been named after the biblical brothers who were the sons of Adam and Eve, but the reason for this is a story from the family's history books. As the boys grew up, Kane's brother could never quite understand why his brother would choose to play with the local indigenous kids rather than with him. Although Kane had explained to him that he was fascinated by their knowledge of the land, the sea and the sky, Abel could never grasp what he was talking about. Kane would tell him how his indigenous mates were indelibly connected to their surroundings, and he'd often explain to him that they possessed a visceral, animalistic feeling for nature that was bordering on the supernatural, but Abel could not comprehend that Kane's mates were joined to ancient voices in the wind. In Kane's view, Abel would always remain in the formless middle of white society, divorced from any empathy towards the First Nation people.

Kane carefully takes the boiling pot of fettuccine from the burner to strain it at the sink, but before he upends the pasta into a strainer, he reassures himself that under no circumstances will he ever return to his hometown of Byron Bay.

Consumed by the dilemma placed on him by his editor, Archie Stenmark reaches the front door of his house, and after opening it wide he barges down the narrow central passageway. Feeling as if he is in a dark tunnel, he finally emerges into the kitchen at the rear, where he finds his bedraggled father dressed in his threadbare dressing gown straining fettuccini at the sink.

With the window behind him clouded with steam, Kane dumps the strained pasta into a large white mixing bowl and looks up. 'You're just in time for lunch, Archie!' he calls as he stirs his pesto into the bowl.

When Archie smells the fresh basil, garlic and pine nuts, he immediately accepts his father's invitation and drags up a chair to the kitchen table. Glad that his son is joining him, Kane separates the fettuccine into two smaller bowls and after theatrically grating some Parmesan over both portions, slides one of the dishes across the table to Archie.

'Pasta al pesto Genovese,' he declares as he hands him a fork.

'Grazie mille,' Archie replies.

'How did you get on with dragon lady, Son?' Kane asks, not wishing to continue on in Italian.

His question causes Archie to pause before he devours his first forkful of pasta. 'Sue Barkham wants me to go up to Byron Bay, Dad,' he discloses.

'What in the hell for?'

'She says there's a curse on our family and she wants me to investigate it for my next novel.'

'Archie, my advice to you is to stay the hell away from Byron Bay!'

'You always tell me that, Dad, but why are you warning me away?'

'It's not a safe place for you to go, son.'

'Something happened to you in Byron, didn't it?'

'Why do you ask that?' Kane questions.

'Don't you think it's time you let me in on what went on up there?' Archie challenges.

Kane looks down at his pasta while considering his reply. 'I'm just saying that you should stay away, that's all. Don't get involved, son,' he cautions.

'It's easy for you to give me orders, Dad. But you've told me nothing about your childhood. In fact, you've hardly ever mentioned your family over the years. I've been left completely in the dark. I know you grew up by the sea and that you went to school there, but that's about all I know, because you've never talked about it. Don't you think it's time you told me what has gone on?'

'It's all water under the bridge, son. I live in the present now.'

Archie stares at his foster father, wondering if he should divulge to him that Sue Barkham has found out he was a suspect in a possible murder investigation. He pauses for a minute before biting the bullet.

'I heard from Sue Barkham that you were involved in an abduction case way back in your youth,' Archie ventures boldly.

Kane's face pales and he jabs his fork into his pasta and deliberately winds the long strands around it many times before looking up. 'I left all that shit behind, son. What went on in Byron Bay stays in Byron Bay as far as I'm concerned, and there's no bloody need to relive it!'

'You're hiding something from me, Dad. Something dire must have happened to you to make you leave. What was so dreadful that you can't tell me?'

Kane scratches his thinning hair, wondering why Archie is acting like a terrier with a bone. He suddenly rises from his chair to plug in the kettle and after switching it on, he deliberately stands with his back to Archie waiting for it to boil. In the pregnant silence that follows, Archie is left examining the rapidly receding bald patch on the back of his father's head.

'Dad, it's not healthy to repress your emotions,' he finally advises in an attempt to break the silence.

There is a stalemate in the kitchen however, with Archie waiting for his father to reply. Kane remains mute, resolutely waiting for the whistle to blow on the kettle.

'Come back and finish your pasta, Dad,' Archie implores, staring at his foster father's half-finished bowl.

After a while, Kane shuffles back to the table to face the music.

'It looks as if you ran away from something and even though you've wanted to return home to Byron, you can't,' Archie challenges.

Kane dares not look up.

'You don't want to face up to it, do you, Dad?' Archie persists.

'Look, son. The truth is that I'm innocent, but innocent or not, I'm never going back there. I'm not going to put my head on the chopping block for my family ever again. I'm past being the fall guy for them all. I burst free of it long ago and now I live in peace down here in Sydney. I'm glad to be away from the bloody lot of them.'

'Burst free of what?' Archie asks doggedly.

'Free of my bloody family, Archie! Here in Sydney, there's no one to push me around except you!'

The whistle on the kettle blasts into the air and Kane rises again, pleased that tea making will give him a break from the interrogation.

'That's enough about me, son. What is it that Barkham wants you to do?' he asks, keen to switch the topic.

'She wants me to write about this curse that's plaguing the Stenmarks. As I said before, she's insisting I go. She even showed me an article in the *Byron Shire News* about it.'

'Really?'

'Tell me, Dad, who is Rebecca Stenmark?'

Kane slowly places his mug of tea onto the table and looks Archie in the eye. 'Rebecca is my kid sister, Archie . . . That makes her your aunt.'

'I've never heard you speak of her until now, but in the local Byron Bay paper, she is saying that a curse has been responsible for a series of deaths and near deaths in the Stenmark family.'

Kane stares out the kitchen window, thinking about how close he and his kid sister used to be.

'I have always loved my sister, Archie, and I've missed her like crazy over the years, but Rebecca attributes every bad thing that has ever happened to our family on the curse. She may have a point though, because many bloody tragedies have affected us over the generations.'

'So there *is* a history of this curse in action,' Archie concludes.

'Possibly, son. But I still advise you to stay well clear of Byron Bay for your own good.'

'In the article in the *Byron Shire News*, Rebecca said she attributes the recent death of her partner to the curse. Apparently, a deadly brown snake bit him.'

'Yes, I heard about that. I was wanting to comfort her when I heard about it, but I stayed resolute and I kept my distance. Look, there's possibly a curse on our family, Archie, but you definitely shouldn't get involved in it, son. If you want my advice, you should tell Barkham to go to hell.'

'Why, Dad? Do you think this curse could affect me too?'

'Well, it could.'

'Doesn't its power diminish over time?'

'No, apparently not. I managed to get out in time. I've missed my sister, Rebecca like hell, but it's the price I had to pay when I left. I had to cut off all communication with them for my own good, and I haven't heard a thing from any of them since that day.'

'You turned your back on the family!' Archie challenges.

'My brother and his wife and kids are still living in the family house on Marvell Street, Archie, but they're all bloody bigots. I don't like any of them because they perpetuate the curse with their horrific attitudes. Look, it's tragic that a snake bit Rebecca's partner, but you should leave it at that, son. Read my lips, Archie – stay away from Byron Bay!'

Underneath his brusque exterior, Kane Stenmark is a lonely man because his deep-seated mistrust of others continually inhibits him from forming meaningful relationships. Despite the many years that have passed since he was exiled from his family, his feelings of isolation still engulf him like a sheath. With his self-esteem in tatters most of the time, he relieves his deep-seated loneliness and self-loathing by frequenting jazz clubs late at night, often trying to land one-night stands with girls half his age. As he lacks the required social skills that most people use to navigate personal social currents however, his success rate is poor. With his advancing age, most of the young girls whom he encounters, regard him as an aging hippie.

In a reversal of the traditional relationship between father and son, Archie appears to be the more mature of the two. He is the one more likely to be at home reading and writing, while his father is out on the town until the sun comes up.

Before the break of day, Archie descends the stairs with his laptop under his arm, ready to do some early morning writing. Feeling fresh and clearheaded after a good night's sleep, he sets his laptop down on the kitchen table. As the sun is about to make its triumphant arrival over the horizon at this time, Archie decides to wait at the kitchen window to see the morning sun burst through the clouds like a fireball. Its magnificence always fills him with joy. When the show is over, he adjusts the blinds to reduce the glare on his screen.

Aware that Kane has not yet returned home from his night out, Archie settles himself at the table in the diffused light, feeling impotent that he has been unable to stop his father from making these regular nocturnal sojourns. At his advancing age, he wonders why his father isn't staying at home, curled up in front of the TV like most 48-year-olds. After Sue Barkham's comment that in his youth he was involved in the disappearance of an indigenous girl, Archie wonders if Kane's adolescent behaviour could be his way of repressing this traumatic event.

Archie hears the key turning in the front door and listens to Kane as he sneaks furtively down the narrow corridor towards the kitchen.

'Good afternoon,' he greets his father.

'Oh, you're up,' Kane answers, seeing Archie at the kitchen table.

'I've had a night from bloody hell!'

'What happened?'

'The cops strip-searched me on the way home.'

'Why?'

'They thought I was high on drugs.'

'Were you?'

'Yeah, a bit.'

'Dad, this is not good . . . You're going off the rails lately.'

'Not you too, Archie. I've had enough blame for one night.'

'Where's your shirt?'

'I had to dump it. It had puke on it.'

'Were you sick?'

'Yeah.'

'You smell of vomit, Dad! You're out of control. What's going on?'

'If you want to know, son, this time it's all this stuff about you going to Byron Bay.'

'I know you don't want me to go, Dad, but I don't know why.'

Kane walks to the fridge and selects a carton of yoghurt and after grabbing a teaspoon from the kitchen drawer, he begins spooning it directly out of the container. 'I don't want you mixed up in it all, son. Byron Bay is a bloody hornet's nest.'

'Mixed up in what? Is this about the girl's disappearance?'

'Fuck, Archie! I'm trying to put all that shit behind me. Why do you keep throwing it back in my face?'

'What shit, Dad? What are you running away from?'

Kane deliberately remains silent, determined to remain a closed book.

'Your life is out of control, Dad. You should be taking a good hard look at yourself. It's time you reckoned with yourself so you can find some inner stillness.'

'It's my life you're talking about, Archie. I can do with it whatever I bloody well want!'

'You've raised me up and hopefully you've done a good job of it, but lately you've been acting like a bloody adolescent.'

'Fuck off with all this "holier than thou" shit, Archie! Who do you think you are telling me how to live my life?'

'I'm finding I can't communicate with you anymore. Your behaviour is a bloody disgrace and these days I'm ashamed to be associated with you.'

'You're ashamed? You don't know anything about me. You have no idea what happened to me.'

'You're right. I don't know anything because you're hiding it from me. You're too bloody scared to tell me the truth!'

'I can't.'

'Why not?'

'I just can't!'

Realising he has hit a roadblock, Archie decides to throw out a challenge.

'Sue Barkham told me she thinks you committed a crime in Byron Bay. You could be a murderer for all I know!'

Archie's words cut his father to the quick. Kane feels as if Archie has plunged a knife deep into him. Suddenly overtaken by rage, he springs towards Archie and with a single punch, he knocks him off his chair, causing Archie to fall to the floor. With another sweep of his arm, Kane swipes Archie's laptop from the kitchen table and it crashes into the wall before dropping noisily to the floor.

'You're a bloody maniac! You've gone way too far this time!' Archie yells from his lowly position on the kitchen floorboards.

'My kitchen is a no-go zone for criticism, remember? You're the one who has crossed the bloody line!' Kane retorts.

Archie crawls across the floor to inspect his laptop and after picking it up, he hugs it to his chest. He hauls himself up into a standing position and carefully replaces it back onto the table.

'You may have written a bloody successful novel, Archie, but in my opinion you're still a fucking novice. How could you possibly think I'm a murderer?'

'I apologise for saying that, Dad,' Archie responds. Desperate to diffuse the situation he states, 'I know you don't have it in you to kill anyone. Believe me, I'm really sorry for calling you a murderer.'

After a long pause, Kane is eager to check if he has done any permanent damage to Archie's laptop and he approaches the table to examine it. As he approaches, Archie takes the opportunity to hold his arms out towards his father. It is an inviting gesture that shows Kane that he has forgiven him for his outrageous outburst. After a momentary hesitation, Kane accepts Archie's hug and with tears streaming down both of their faces, the son and the father embrace.

There is a sharp ring on the home telephone and Archie interrupts the clinch to pick up the receiver.

Sue Barkham's strident voice is shouting down the line. 'Archie, have you heard the latest news from Byron Bay?'

'No, Sue, I haven't.'

'Another Stenmark has been cursed.'

'What? How?'

'Rebecca Stenmark's son has been attacked by a great white shark!'

'You're kidding me!'

'No, I'm not. I'll read out what it says in the *Byron Shire News*. The headline is "Mystery indigenous girl saves Stenmark Boy" and there is a picture of Corrie Stenmark in bandages taken at the Lismore Hospital.'

Archie listens intently as Sue Barkham reads the article.

'"Eighteen-year-old Corrie Stenmark, the son of Rebecca Stenmark, who is part owner of the Sands Hotel, is lucky to be alive after being attacked on Saturday afternoon by a great white shark at Clarkes Beach, Byron Bay."'

'Bloody hell!' Archie exclaims.

"The youth lost part of his right leg in the attack and may have died had not a brave indigenous girl rescued him."

'An indigenous girl?'

'Yes, and it goes on to say, "The girl tied his leg rope into a tourniquet and hauled him into shore, where she kept him conscious until the paramedics arrived. The boy had seen her out surfing before, but he doesn't know her name. Now he's desperately trying to find her so he can thank her for saving his life." The curse is still very active, my boy,' she concludes.

'It certainly sounds like it, Sue,' Archie agrees.

'You'd better pack your bags and get up there right now, Archie. I want you to find out what in the blazes is going on.'

After Sue Barkham ends the call, Archie turns to his father. 'Dad, Aunt Rebecca's son has been attacked by a shark. Sue Barkham wants me to leave immediately.'

Kane looks back at Archie with grave concern, instantly realising that his sister must be in great distress. He would dearly love to reach out to her, but after cutting himself off from the family for so long, he wonders how he can help her through this tragedy

'Poor Rebecca,' he laments. 'She must be absolutely desperate. First, her partner died and now her son has fallen victim to the bloody curse. I'm seriously worried now, Archie. Maybe I should return to be with her. Bugger it, son … we'll both go to Byron. Let's head off tomorrow.'

Chapter 3

THE JOURNEY TO BYRON BAY

The next morning, Kane is looking very sheepish when he enters the kitchen.

'I'm so sorry for threatening you yesterday, Archie,' he apologises before Archie has a chance to open his mouth. 'I couldn't sleep thinking how disgraceful I was. Please forgive me, son. I was totally out of line. I don't know what came over me.'

'Let's forget it ever happened, Dad. I was aggressive too. I placed you between a rock and a hard place. The best thing that came out of it is that at last, you've made the right decision. You've always had unfinished business in Byron Bay and now you'll be able to face your demons. I'm excited that you're joining me. I can't tell you how much it means to me.'

'Are you sure, Archie? I've become such an arsehole lately, haven't I?'

'As I said before, let's put it behind us. Let's both try to forget it ever happened.'

'Is your laptop working?'

'It's a little bit dented, but it still works. It looks as if I've been writing with it for decades' Archie laughs. 'We don't have a lot of time, Dad. The coach for Byron leaves from the depot in a little over an hour.'

'Shit. I haven't finished packing yet,' Kane replies.

After heeding Archie's words, he heads upstairs to throw some final items into his suitcase. Initially, he cannot find his baseball cap or his sunglasses, but after rifling through a number of drawers he finally locates them. The final item he throws into his suitcase is a carton of Marlboro cigarettes.

'Let's go, Dad! We've got to get out of here right now!' Archie calls from downstairs.

After bumping his battered suitcase down the stairs, Kane finally appears at the front door and with his trusty guitar slung over one shoulder, he locks the front door on his house for the last time.

'Are you sure I'm doing the right thing, Archie?' he asks.

'No second thoughts now, Dad. You're on a journey to your birthplace where you're going to face your demons head-on.'

'And see my darling sister,' Kane quickly adds.

When the coach arrives at the depot, a burly driver who looks a lot like Elvis in his later years, raises the door to the baggage compartment.

'All aboard for beautiful Byron Bay!' he calls before pitching the men's bags into the hold with too much gusto. Noting this low level of care, Kane is pleased he has kept his guitar with him while he strides towards the coach door. Like Dustin Hoffman and John Voight in the film *Midnight Cowboy*, the father and son settle into the very back seat for the twelve-hour journey.

Elvis spirits the pair in air-conditioned comfort through the leafy northern suburbs of Sydney, but the farther the coach wends its way north, the more Archie wonders what life will be like in the subtropics. He hopes he won't encounter any of the well-known predators he'd read about in the travel brochures. Sharks, spiders, goannas and enormous pythons thrive around Byron Bay and its hinterland, and although he's up for a little excitement, the thought of encountering any one of these deadly creatures makes him extremely uneasy. Kane, on the other hand, has no such fear of the local fauna, and in no time at all, he has dozed off beside Archie on the back seat.

While Kane sleeps, Archie reflects on his father's life so far. In his view, Kane is a lone wolf who is trapped in a psychological prison. He seems to exist in a kind of wasteland, refusing to commit to anyone or anything. Most of the time, he acts more like an adolescent than a mature man, but to his credit he has single-handedly brought him up, and Archie imagines that that has been no mean feat. Although he finds his cursing to be abrasive and his nocturnal behaviour to be abhorrent, Kane is important to him, because he is the one person in his life who has always been there for him. In addition to his role as his father, Kane possesses the phenomenal ability to drag him out of the doldrums that have been known to overtake him. A knowing smile appears on Archie's face as he recalls one of Kane's recent quips. *I have two sides to my brain – there's right, and there's left. On the left side, there's nothing right, and on the right side, there's nothing left.* Archie laughs out loud at the recall.

With so many hours at his disposal, Archie also has time to embark on a little introspection about his own career, but unfortunately he contemplates ending up like Harper Lee, who found it hard to write a successful sequel after her blockbuster novel *To Kill a Mockingbird*. Her famous book was concerned with the irrational attitudes of white people towards their African American neighbours in the small town of Maycomb, Alabama. Archie wonders if he will run up against similar redneck attitudes when he gets to Byron Bay. He also wonders if he will end up like Harper Lee and not be able to produce another bestseller.

As the bus roars on through the tinder-dry Australian countryside, Archie notices that the recent lack of rain has caused the grass by the side of the road to become brittle, and he becomes concerned that a carelessly discarded cigarette could easily set off a summer bushfire. The tossing of a burned-out cigarette could be just the thing his father might inadvertently do, and if the wind fans it, vast areas of the national forest through which they are now travelling, could be burned out. As Archie thinks about the potential destruction that a bushfire like this could cause, he makes a mental note to warn his nicotine-addicted father to be careful.

Beside him, Kane is having a somewhat fitful sleep and Archie watches his body shake spasmodically from time to time, as if he is experiencing small shocks. When he finally jerks awake, Archie is staring straight at him.

'Did you have a bad dream, Dad?' he asks.

'Ugh, yeah . . . I was being expelled from school.' Kane yawns, stretching his arms skywards.

'You were expelled?'

'Yeah, I got mixed up with a black kid.'

'We have all the time in the world today, Dad. Why don't you tell me about it?'

'Archie, do you really want to hear an old story about why they threw me out of school?'

'Yes, Dad, I do.'

As it's not a common topic for him to be telling his son, Kane has to think about where to begin.

'Unlike my brother, I refused to be sent off to boarding school because I preferred to attend the local secondary school, where I could play with the indigenous kids. Mostly, that was OK, but there was one particular occasion when the principal hauled me over the coals for hanging out with one of them.'

'I'm all ears, Dad. Tell me why the principal expelled you.'

Kane closes his eyes to gather his thoughts.

'I was fast asleep in my sleep-out at Marvell Street when I heard someone outside my window urging me to wake up. I peered outside to see who it was, but all I could make out was the outline of some kid outside my window. I could see the whites of his eyes and that he was waving a flag, but I could see little else. When the kid asked me to get dressed before the sun came up, I recognised his voice. It was my indigenous friend Jimmy who was giving the orders.

'I flung the sheet off my bed, pulled on a pair of chinos and escaped through the squeaky sleep-out door to join him. The two of us scampered off like wolves in the night through the dark streets until we reached the Byron Bay Secondary School, our bastion of education on Broken Head Road.

'When we found that the main gate was locked, we knew we had to scale the cyclone fence to get inside. Jimmy handed his Aboriginal flag to me and proceeded to climb to the top of the fence, and after making a courageous jump into the school grounds, he asked me to throw the flag over to him. I remember making a couple of feeble attempts to throw it over the high fence, but I failed miserably on each occasion. Finally, after a few more tries, I managed to get it over into Jimmy's waiting hands. Then it was my turn to climb over.

'I grasped the wire to haul myself up, but my hands hurt like buggery. Determined to get to the top, however, I took off my shoes and dug my bare toes into the fence. Somehow I managed to scramble up, and at the top Jimmy told me to swing my legs over, but I was unable to move. In a much more authoritative tone he urged me again and after psyching myself up, I bravely swung one leg over. The movement caused me to overbalance however, and I dropped like a sack of spuds inside the fence.'

'Jimmy asked if I was OK, but I was so stunned by the fall that I couldn't answer him. After several frightening minutes, he noticed that I was trying to make a feeble attempt to sit up and he assisted me.'

'"I nearly killed myself," I whimpered to him while rubbing at my injured leg.'

'Jimmy waited until I became a little more alert before suggesting that we walk over to the flagpole to hoist up his flag. With his arm around my waist, I managed with his help, to hobble over to it, and in great pain I stood there while he attached the flag to the snap hooks on the halyard. When he'd completed the task, Jimmy proudly pulled the red, black and yellow flag to the top of the school flagpole. When it reached the top, Jimmy triumphantly declared that his mob had officially taken possession of the school.'

'"I'm reclaiming it for my people!" he bellowed in full voice, and I remember agreeing with him that it was his tribe's land in the beginning and that he had every right to fly the flag high once again.'

'Jimmy patted me on the back to thank me for helping him, saying that he had wanted to do this for years. Too injured to climb back over the fence, I advised Jimmy that I'd have to wait until they opened the gate up for the schoolkids. Jimmy agreed to remain with me, explaining that it was his idea to hoist the Aboriginal flag up the pole in the first place.'

'When Jimmy asked me if I thought they'd expel us, I answered him with "Yeah, Jimmy, no question!"'

'So I presume the two of you were hauled into the principal's office and kicked out of school for this flag-hoisting offence,' Archie concludes.

'You're bloody right, Archie. The principal was so furious that he expelled us on the spot. From that moment on, Jimmy and I were considered outcasts, but the best thing about the whole incident was that we'd become inseparable. We became like brothers in arms, much to the chagrin of my family.'

Archie smiles at Kane's foolhardiness. Over the years, he's heard so few stories about his father's early days that he's quite jubilant that he is at last hearing about his boyhood adventures.

The farther the coach travels up the coast, the more Archie realises that this bus trip is a one-off opportunity for him to learn about his father's childhood. While he has him trapped on the back seat, he may even be able to find out what caused him to leave Byron Bay twenty-five years ago.

'I've always wanted to know why you were banished from Byron Bay, Dad. Are you ever going to tell me the reason why you were kicked out of the Stenmark family?'

'It's too long a story, son, but I can tell you about the final incident that separated me from the Stenmarks.'

'Yes, tell me that then,' Archie replies eagerly.

Kane strokes the stubble on his chin as he thinks back.

'There were many times I thought of running away, especially when the whole town turned on me, but this particular fishing trip that I'm going to tell you about was the last straw. After this incident, I knew I just had to get out of town.'

Archie is riveted. At last, his father is about to open up.

'It was Jimmy's twenty-first birthday, and to celebrate it, I asked him if he wanted to go deep sea fishing. When he jumped at the idea, I said I'd load up my brother's boat with some of his newest rods and spinner baits. After promising him that we'd go after some big ocean fish, I set off from the Pass to pick up Jimmy and three of his mates. Jimmy, Willy, Dingo, and Mick had no hesitation in swimming out to meet me just beyond the break at Broken Head, and once they'd all clambered aboard the boat, I turned it towards the Three Sisters Rocks, which were situated a little farther to the south.

'At the rocks, we attached Abel's spinner baits and some fresh beachworm baits to our lines. I remember the boys all laughing wildly at my brother's lures because some of them resembled actual creatures like soft shrimp and wobbly witchetty grubs. I tied a brightly coloured lure onto my own line and when I saw its rainbow colours shimmering seductively below the surface, I hoped that it would entice a big ocean fish.

'It wasn't long before Willy had a firm tug on his line. His rod bent in a steep ark and he had to employ short spurts to gradually wind in his catch. It was a large jewfish. It flopped onto the floor with its angry teeth firmly clenched around Willy's spinner bait.

'"What a beauty!" we all whooped as we stared at the fish that was gasping for worthless air on the boat floor.

'Moments later, Mick felt a bite on his line, and when we peered into the water, we observed a sizeable red fish darting back and forth, glimmering in the sunlight. The boys snatched the net from the side of the boat to help out, but they soon found that the fish was far too big to fit into it, and the boys ended up swinging the fish into the boat with it poised precariously on the rim. Everyone let out a collective sigh of relief when the huge snapper finally flopped onto the deck and I remember Mick's smile being as wide as the ocean.

'The indigenous boys reeled in a mighty catch that day. In addition to the jewfish and the snapper, they landed a bag load of tailor, whiting, and bream, and Jimmy was lauded for catching the most fish, which was highly appropriate seeing that it was his birthday.

'I was delighted to see the smiles on the boys' faces when they swam away from the boat at Broken Head Beach, dragging their catch in a netting bag. Waiting for them on the beach were their girlfriends, who, anticipating a feast, had already lit a fire. So impressed were they with the catch, that they offered to clean the fish for Jimmy's fireside dinner later that evening.

'As the fishing trip had been such a sensation, I called out to the boys to invite them to come to the Sands Hotel beer garden for a pre-dinner drink. I explained to them that it would be my shout, as after all, it was not every day that Jimmy turned 21. I returned alone to the Pass, but unfortunately, my angry brother was there to greet me at the ramp, demanding that I tell him what the hell I was doing with his boat.

'"What does it look like, bro?' I answered him. "I've been out fishing."

'This offhanded answer was like a red rag to a bull. "You can't take my boat out without my permission, Kane," he reprimanded.

'I replied that I owned one-third of the boat. I also added that I owned one-third of its equipment, because it was all paid for by the family pub. He retorted that he'd report me to the police for stealing, but when I reiterated that I actually owned one-third of everything that I was using, he faltered. The idea seemed to be a new concept for him.

'"Fuck you, Kane!" he finally bellowed. "You're bloody irresponsible! It's the last warning I'll give you. If you cross me one more time, I'm going to ban you from the hotel!"'

'Abel didn't sound like a happy camper, Dad. What happened next? Did the boys turn up at the pub?' Archie asks.

'Yes, Archie, they did, but it's a sad story. My four freshly scrubbed indigenous mates arrived at the Sands Hotel in Jimmy's old Holden ute, and after parking like rock stars in front of the entrance, they entered the beer garden. As I had a couple of jugs of beer at the ready, I signalled for them to come over to my table, but the boys appeared ill at ease. Being the only black faces in the predominantly white beer garden, they sensed some animosity from some of the regulars as they entered. Some patrons were pointing towards the exit, as if to tell them they were in the wrong place. I signalled again for them to come over to me, but only after a great deal of hesitation did the boys edge their way over.

'I wished Jimmy a happy birthday and handed him the first beer, before pouring each of the boys a glass from the two jugs on the table. When all their glasses were full, I held up my glass to salute Jimmy.

'"Happy birthday, mate!" I wished, and the boys followed up the toast by exuberantly singing the birthday song. At the end of it, they gave him three rousing cheers.

'When the cheering died down, a rough-looking fellow in a navy-blue singlet approached our group from a neighbouring table. He tapped Jimmy on the shoulder.

"It sounds as if it's your birthday, mate, but aren't you celebrating it in the wrong place?" he asked.

'"I'm allowed in 'ere just the same as you are," Jimmy responded, trying to look confident.

'The man turned around to his mates, who looked like a group of "tradies" who were having a beer after work. Eager to enlist their support he said, "Boys, something smells off in this beer garden ... Something's on the nose out here!" The rough man's mates began sniffing. "Yeah, yeah, there's a smell," they all seemed to agree.'

'"It smells like a bloody zoo! There must be some monkey business goin' on," the man continued. Determined to ignore him, the indigenous boys turned their backs on the offensive fellow, hoping he'd take the cue and return to his seat.'

'"Hey, what are the worst three years of an Abbo's life?" the rough man persisted. There was silence.'

'"First grade!" he answered and his friends broke into derisive laughter. Emboldened by this positive reception, the man asked another question. "What's the most confusing day in the Aboriginal community?" Another silence followed.'

'"Father's Day!" he yelled, and once again his mates exploded into laughter. The man was definitely on a roll.'

'"Hey, did you hear about the new black Barbie?" he continued without missing a beat. "She comes with twelve kids and a welfare cheque!"

'Appalled at the bigot's racist remarks, I stormed over to him to reproach him. After explaining to him that I was a part-owner of the hotel, I told him that my friends were welcome here and that they had a right to enjoy a drink without being harassed by racists like him.

Not liking the reprimand, the burly bloke lifted me from the ground until my face was just centimetres from his own.'

'"This place has been my watering hole for ten years and I don't want them in here! Understand?" he boomed.'

'The indigenous boys immediately rushed to my assistance, and on Jimmy's birthday a ferocious fistfight broke out in the beer garden. At the height of it, the aggressive man picked up a glass jug and, after smashing it against the edge of a wooden picnic table, he thrust the jagged edge into Jimmy's face.'

'By the time Abel had arrived on the scene to quell the outburst, blood was gushing from Jimmy's brow and a deep gash was lying open on his right cheek. Abel immediately took the side of the "tradies" and ordered us from the hotel grounds, telling me in particular to piss off and to take my mates with me.'

'"You're banned from the pub for life, Kane! Don't ever set foot in this place again or I'm likely to kill you!" he bellowed.

'After this ultimatum, Abel signalled for the men at the security post to toss us out onto the street. It was the very last time I was seen at the hotel.'

'Wow! I had no idea that was the reason you left, Dad. Is that seriously what happened twenty-five years ago?'

'Yes, Archie, that was the day I left town for good.'

'Was Jimmy's face all right?'

'I hope you meet him when we're in Byron, son. These days, I hear he has a huge scar on his forehead and another one on his right cheek. His face is proof that this is a true story.'

'Now I understand why you left town, but didn't you ever want to come back to Byron? Didn't you want to continue your friendships?'

'No, Archie. I was more than ready to get out of town and stay out of sight.'

'Was there any other reason you left?' Archie asks pointedly.

'Yes, Archie. I think you've heard already that an Aboriginal girl went missing and that I was blamed for her disappearance. The whole town thought I'd abducted her, but Archie, that's a story for another day I'm afraid.'

'Didn't you miss your sister?' Archie persists.

'I missed her like crazy, Archie. Rebecca was very close to me, but I had to get away. I had to cut myself off completely. Abel was a racist redneck with a serious superiority complex. I think he still believes that the local Aboriginals are hunters and gatherers, but back then, the First Nation people were my true friends . . . Archie, my friends were actually all black, not white.'

'What did you like about them?' Archie presses.

'I used to join them at every opportunity. My childhood was spent hunting in the bush, catching fish, or just sitting around a campfire listening to stories with them. They lived their lives as if they belonged to the earth and the sea and I liked that a lot.'

'What went wrong then?'

'My troubles started in earnest when my mates got older.'

'Why?'

'The boys would come into town for alcohol, but my brother wouldn't allow them into the hotel.'

'Did he have one law for the whites and another for the blacks back then?'

'Yes, he did,' Kane confirms. A sorrowful expression takes over Kane's face. He turns his head towards the window and stares at the ubiquitous gum trees that are lining the roadside. 'It was all so unfair back then, Archie,' he laments.

When he closes his eyes, Archie decides to leave him be.

By the time the coach makes a pit stop at the seaside town of Ballina, Kane is so desperate to have a smoke, that after descending the steps of the bus, he immediately lights up a Marlboro. He remains by the roadside chain-smoking, while Archie heads towards the roadhouse to purchase some sweet Danish pastries. Kane has lit up a fourth cigarette by the time Archie returns, and he is still puffing away on it when the coach begins to move off. Worried that it will depart without him, Kane quickly tosses his unfinished cigarette on the ground and he sprints madly towards the moving vehicle.

After stopping for him, the impatient driver closes the coach door behind Kane before he has even finished mounting the steps, and with a deep scowl on his face, he jerkily pulls away from the kerb, eager to complete the final leg of the journey to Byron Bay.

Suddenly, the coach jerks to a stop and Elvis leaps from the vehicle. Like an Olympic sprinter, he dashes beyond the bus to stomp on a patch of grass that had burst into flame by the roadside. After a merry dance, Elvis's studded boots manage to extinguish every last ember of the grass fire, and mission accomplished, he returns to his vehicle. Before driving off, however, he strides down the aisle of the coach to castigate Kane for his cavalier behaviour. Red with embarrassment, Kane shrinks into the corner, having accrued more fuel for his already damaged ego. Feeling very foolish for his careless behaviour, Kane remains silent for the next twenty minutes, while Archie blames himself for not warning Kane about being careful.

Before daring to ask Kane any more questions, Archie prudently waits for the coach to leave the Ballina area, but once they are back on the highway again, Archie feels he has waited long enough to venture another question. 'Dad, when Abel kicked you out of Byron Bay, where did you go?' he asks.

Kane stares at him sullenly. 'So many bloody questions! You know where I went,' he answers impatiently.

'Tell me again.'

'For Christ's sake, Archie. I was twenty-three at the time and I ended up in bloody Nimbin.'

'I've heard about naughty Nimbin, Dad,' Archie replies.

'It sure was naughty in those days, let me tell you,' Kane concedes, his frosty attitude softening with his memory of happier times. 'Nimbin was a perfect place for me to escape to at the time … It's a pretty little village not far from here. It's located on the edge of a rainforest.'

'You make it sound so idyllic.'

'Archie, you are aware aren't you, that in Nimbin the locals live an alternate lifestyle?'

'Everyone knows it's a druggy little town, Dad,' Archie replies.

Kane nods, thinking that it was not only drugs but also sex and rock 'n' roll. He allows a slight smirk to appear on his face. 'They were very accepting of me when I got there, Archie, probably because I joined in with their protests. Their main goals at the time were to liberate hemp and to stop logging in the rainforest. Most days, I was stoned on marijuana and I wore tie-dye clothes. I kept myself busy by painting murals on the town's shops. Nimbin was my version of Woodstock, son.'

'Was I born there, Dad?' Archie asks pointedly.

'Yes Archie, you were. You were a flower child. I think I told you I met your mother at Nimbin's Aquarius Festival, didn't I?'

'Tell me again.'

Kane's face brightens at the memory and Archie listens with great interest.

'When I first saw your mother, she was so beautiful that I couldn't believe my eyes. Her wavy golden hair had daisies in it and it fell over her bare tanned shoulders.'

'She sounds like a hippie, Dad.'

'Yes, your mother was a free spirit. The first time she spoke to me, she quoted the anthem from the Aquarius Festival and I've never forgotten it. "May the long-time sun shine upon you, all love surround you, and the pure light within you guide your way home." I loved her from that moment on.'

'She became ill, didn't she?'

'Yes, Archie, but you and I had two wonderful years with her before she died.' A tear appears in Kane's eye.

'You told me how she died . . . It was breast cancer, wasn't it?'

'Yes. It tore me apart to see her in such pain. She refused to take any medication and she didn't want you ever to know how bad she was feeling.'

'After she died, you looked after me on your own, didn't you?' Archie asks.

'Yes, I did, Archie, but I couldn't bare staying on in Nimbin after she died, so I took you to Sydney.'

'You know, Dad, I have no picture of her. All I have to remember her by are your stories.'

'You look a little like her you know, Archie. You've inherited her good looks.' Kane digs into his pocket, and after some fumbling, he produces a small emerald ring. 'Here, son. You can have this.' Kane hands the ring over to Archie. 'Your mother always wore this ring. I kept it after she died, but it's time you had it.' Archie examines the ring and finds it to be both simple and exquisite.

'I'll always treasure this, Dad. Thanks,' he responds, threading his mother's ring onto a thin chain he's wearing around his neck. After attaching it securely, he reaches over to give his father a heartfelt hug.

Finding the intimacy embarrassing, Kane breaks the mood by calling out, 'Hey, look at the sign! We're only a few kilometres out of Byron Bay.'

Chapter 4

ARRIVAL INTO BYRON BAY

It's been twenty-five long years since Kane's brother banished him from the family hotel after the horrific fistfight in the beer garden. At the time, the conflict was just the catalyst Kane needed to leave Byron Bay for good, as it gave him a strong impetus to escape the furore that was surrounding him. The locals thought he had disappeared into the wilderness, and except for someone reporting that they'd seen him briefly in Nimbin, he managed to stay out of their sight for two and a half decades.

Like the prodigal son in the Bible who came back home to face his fears, Kane is returning to his hometown exactly twenty-five years to the day after he left. When he descends the steps from the coach, he knows instantly that he's back on home turf when half a dozen flies land on his face. From previous experience, he knows the local flies are not easily discouraged, and he continually swipes at them as he retrieves his suitcase.

Between swipes, Kane gazes down the familiar main street. At first glance, his hometown appears almost the same as he'd remembered it, and he's delighted that it has been spared the fate of its philistine neighbours just an hour's car ride farther north. In his view, the neighbouring Gold Coast has developed into a glitzy version of

Miami, with tall glass towers which overshadow the pristine beaches in the late afternoon.

Despite his hometown's lack of champagne views from elevated balconies, Kane is delighted that Byron Bay has retained its laid-back small-town appeal. In his view, it can be compared to quaint New England towns, the likes of which he'd previously encountered on Cape Cod or Martha's Vineyard.

Kane has heard that there is a high demand for holiday accommodation in Byron Bay these days, with the locals capitalising on the booming tourist trade. With holiday rentals skyrocketing, he's heard that the locals can haul in big bickies, especially on Christmas and Easter, and during the various music and writing festivals, not to mention Schoolies Week.

Across the street, Kane sees a few sunburned tourists wearing next to nothing as they mooch about barefoot while they check out the local souvenir stores. He dislikes their casual fashion, however, thinking that they should keep their scanty swimwear for the beach.

'Let's get out of this tourist section, son,' he suggests, signalling for Archie to join him.

The duo head off towards the family hotel and after a short walk in a north-easterly direction, they get their first glimpse of the mighty Pacific Ocean, with Julian Rocks jutting from the water just beyond the shoreline. They are like two emerald jewels, and Kane feels a huge pang . . . It's as if these rocks are welcoming him home.

With his baseball cap on backwards, his guitar slung over his shoulder, and his aviator sunglasses shielding him from being recognised, Kane struts confidently down the familiar street passing eager holidaymakers who smell of coconut oil. As they flip-flop past him endlessly speaking on their mobile phones, Kane knows he is not one of them. Although he has a touristy appearance, he is definitely just a local returning home after a very long absence.

Confident that no one will recognise him behind his aviators, Kane strolls into the Sands Hotel and confidently fronts up to the bar to order two cold XXXX beers on tap. After paying for them, he hands one to Archie, and they both carry their frosty glasses into the noisy beer garden. After dumping their bags under a free picnic table, Kane holds up his schooner to make a toast to a happy homecoming.

When he holds the beer up in the air, it takes on the golden hue of the late afternoon sun, and at that moment Kane realises that he has missed the last twenty-five golden summers in Byron Bay. He'd forgotten how much he loved this place and he joyfully removes his sunglasses so that he can scan the familiar surroundings. After registering the improvements that his brother had made since he was last here, Kane concludes that the beer garden is looking a great deal smarter than it used to.

A woman of about 35 with tattoos down both arms comes straight up to Kane just as he is about to replace his sunglasses. 'It can't be true. It *is* you! You're Kane Stenmark, aren't you?' she asks.

Kane squints his eyes. He has been sprung already.

'You don't recognise me do you, Kane?' she asks.

'Let me see,' he replies. 'I think I do know who you are, but you've grown up since I last saw you.'

The woman makes a coquettish pose, and Kane recalls that she's a friend of Rebecca's.

'You're Roxanne Jarvis!' he exclaims.

'Right you are. You *do* remember me. Where have you been all this time, Kane?'

'Oh, I've been hangin' out.' Kane shrugs.

'Not around these parts, you haven't, because I haven't seen you since that dreaded B&S ball in 1975.'

'You're right, Roxanne. I left town after all the drama that followed that event.'

'That was a bloody good decision, Kane. I still remember all the hoo-ha. Everyone was blaming you for that girl's disappearance, weren't they? Everyone except me, that is. At the time, they were sure you'd done her in, but as far as I could see, you had no motive. Anyway they couldn't find enough evidence to convict you, could they?'

'I guess not.'

'Have you been back in town long, Kane?' she asks.

'No, we've just arrived by coach from Sydney, Roxanne.' To verify this, Kane points to the luggage under the table. 'We only arrived ten minutes ago,' he adds, checking his watch to make sure he's correct.

'What's your name, you handsome brute?' Roxanne asks, turning her attention to Archie.

'I'm Archie.'

'Pleased to meet you, Archie. What a spunk you are!'

Roxanne extends her hand towards Archie, and Archie shakes it shyly.

'Archie's my son,' Kane explains.

'Really? Good for you, Kane.' She applauds, and Kane looks proud.

"I'm so pleased you're back, Kane. I used to fancy you in the old days, you know, but you were a little too old for me then. I used to think you were such a maverick!'

'I still am, Roxanne,' Kane jokes.

'I'm pleased to hear it. If you're going to stay a while in Byron, why don't we meet up sometime, for old times' sake? You haven't lost any of your animal magnetism, you know.'

'I'm not sure if we're staying here for long, Roxanne.'

'Well, I hope you do, both of you. I'm a waitress over there at the Bay Café, so if you ever get hungry, come and see me.' Roxanne saunters off, pointing to where she works.

'What was all that about, Dad?' Archie asks.

'Just old gossip, son.'

'It sounds as if you were a strong suspect in that girl's disappearance. Why haven't you told me more about it?'

'I know why I haven't, Archie. It's because I've been trying to bury it for twenty-five years.'

'Dad, you are going to tell me all about it while we are here,' Archie orders, looking Kane straight in the eye.

Chapter 5

ABEL'S HOUSE ON MARVELL STREET

As Kane is keen to find out where his kid sister, Rebecca, resides, he decides to bite the bullet and call into his brother's house to find out. From the Sands Hotel, the father and son make the short walk to Marvell Street to find the stately weatherboard dwelling that used to be Kane's original family home. It is a place with many childhood memories for him and as they approach the impressive timber dwelling, Kane explains to Archie that the family house is known locally as a Queenslander for its distinctive architectural style.

'It's set high off the ground for ventilation,' he tells him as they approach.

Archie is immediately impressed with the decorative white latticework featured on the front porch.

'When I lived here, the house was a pale lemon colour, but now it's a smart stone white,' Kane states, appreciating the change. 'I'm pleased that Abel has retained the iron hoods over the windows because they help keep the house cool in summer. And look – the old Poinciana tree is still grabbing attention in the front yard, just as it always did. That tree was always a showstopper.'

The pair stops to gaze at the tree's plethora of showy orangey-red blossoms. After reaching the front gate of the property, Archie is alarmed to see a huge reptile sunning itself on the concrete path that leads to the front door. The reptile has a long neck and tail and its skin is rough and speckled. When it makes a hissing noise and starts moving towards him, Archie quickly reels back.

'What in hell's name is that?' he bellows at Kane.

Kane, who has seen countless goannas in his youth, replies, 'It looks like a monster, son, but goannas are more afraid of you than you are of them.'

As he utters this, the goanna sprints towards them on its hind legs, with the skin around its neck inflated. Kane quickly grasps Archie by the elbow to guide him away from the angry goanna, deciding to take a more circuitous route via the Kikuyu lawn to the front door.

Kane is about to rap on the knocker of the old family home when he hears a familiar voice calling to him from next door. When he looks over the fence, he recognises old Mrs Boyle, his former neighbour.

'I remember you, boy! You're Kane Stenmark, aren't you?' she bellows.

'Oh, hello, Mrs Boyle,' Kane replies, surprised that she still recognises him after all these years.

'You've got a bloody cheek coming back here!'

'Why is that, Mrs Boyle?'

'You were the bastard who killed the Aboriginal girl, that's why!'

Kane is taken aback by this accusation, and he calls back, 'What makes you think it was me, Mrs Boyle?'

'Because I heard the ear-splitting shot the night the girl disappeared, that's why!'

'Is that so?'

'Yes! It came from your house and not long afterwards, I saw you drive off in that fancy red car of yours!'

'The Ford Falcon?'

'Yes!'

Archie's eyebrows go up when he hears this, wondering if the old woman actually witnessed Kane leaving the scene of a crime. He watches Kane turn away from her and face Abel's front door.

'You got away with murder, young man!' she barks, lifting her walking stick to poke it in his direction.

'You're mistaken, Mrs Boyle. I wasn't at home that night!' Kane calls back over his shoulder.

'You're a liar, Kane Stenmark! I told the police I saw you leaving Marvell Street in the middle of the night, but the incompetent idiots let you go free!'

Kane resigns himself to the fact that he is back in Byron Bay and that this will be the first of many accusations that he will have to endure.

'It might have been my car you saw, Mrs Boyle,' he rejoins tersely, 'but it wasn't me in it!'

'You've got away with murder as far as I'm concerned!' she decries before retreating inside her house.

Feeling unjustly accused once again, Kane knocks loudly on the front door of the family home before stepping back to wait for his elder brother to open it. When the door opens however, it is not his brother who appears, but his wife, Stephanie. Although somewhat older now than when he'd last seen her, Stephanie stands before him looking every bit the actress he'd remembered. Dramatic as ever, she wears a colourful scarf tied in the style of an African turban. As she stares at Kane in disbelief, Kane has the same reaction to her that he has always had – he can't trust her.

Stephanie immediately turns on the charm. 'Kane, you're alive, darling!' she shrieks, stretching out her arms to embrace him in a theatrical hug. 'I've always wondered what happened to you, Kane. We've heard nothing for decades. What a disappearing trick! Someone told us they saw you in Nimbin at one stage, but then we heard absolutely nothing. It must be twenty years since we've seen you.'

'Twenty-five, Stephanie, and you're right, I did have to get out of town back then.'

'Who's this?' Stephanie asks, looking over to Archie.

'This is your nephew, my son, Archie,' Kane replies.

'My nephew? I never knew you had a son, Kane. I'm delighted to meet you, Archie. My, my, you are a handsome lad!'

'Hello,' Archie replies, offering to shake Stephanie's hand.

'That's way too formal, darling! Let me welcome you properly.'

Stephanie opens her arms wide and hugs Archie tightly, and Archie remains in her grasp for some time before being released.

'Please come on in. We've got such a lot to catch up on,' she invites.

Amazed that Stephanie is so welcoming, Kane enters his old family home, with Archie following close behind. When Kane sees the old ceiling fans, the fancy fireplaces and the wide red cedar floorboards, he has the giddy feeling that he's going back in time. He takes a seat at the family's old dining table and rubs his hand over its smooth surface, just as he used to do as a child. Stephanie offers the men a drink of barley water, but they both politely refuse.

'We've just come from the pub,' Kane explains.

This answer causes Stephanie's eyebrows to rise because she remembers her husband banning him from ever entering the establishment. 'When did you get into Byron?' she asks, deliberately changing the subject.

'Oh, a little over an hour ago,' Kane tells her.

'Where are you both staying?'

'We've booked into the Pacific House guesthouse. It's not far from here.'

'That's a very nice place to stay. I was going to say that you could ask Abel if you could stay at the hotel, or maybe you could return to your old sleep-out at the back, Kane.'

Kane shudders. 'No, please . . . We'll be fine at the Pacific House, Stephanie.

Where is my brother?' Kane enquires.

'Abel is helping one of our sons rent a house in Bangalow today. He'll be back soon if you'd like to stay.'

'No, we won't stay, Stephanie. After we've settled into the guesthouse, I plan to visit my Aboriginal mates. I want to catch up on what they've all been up to.'

'Yes, I'd forgotten about them, Kane. You were always with those black fellas, weren't you?'

Kane remains silent. 'Stephanie, do you have Rebecca's telephone number? We want to contact her while we are here,' Kane asks.

'Rebecca's in a sad state, Kane. She'd only just got over the death of her partner, when a week ago, a great white shark attacked her son, Corrie.'

'We heard about it, Stephanie. Actually, that's why we're here – because we want to call in on her. The poor thing must be in total shock.'

'Yes, she is, Kane . . . She's in a bad way.' Stephanie writes down Rebecca's number in a small ringed yellow notebook and she tears off the page to hand it over to Kane.

Once the number is in Kane's hand, he and Archie make a move towards the front door, but as they stand waiting to be let out, Stephanie appears hesitant to see them go. She's wondering whether she should invite them to a luncheon party that she will be throwing for Abel on Sunday week. Even though she knows Abel will be against the idea, she decides to bite the bullet, because after all, it's going to be a family affair.

'Kane and Archie, I'm throwing a party for Abel's fiftieth birthday on Sunday week. It's a luncheon in the beer garden of our hotel, and it would be a great surprise if you both could come. You can each bring a friend if you like.'

'I'm not so sure it would be a good idea, Stephanie,' Kane warns.

'Look, Kane, you are the prodigal son now. I know there were a lot of rumours going around when you left town, but now that you've returned, the family will support you. I'm sure they'll welcome you back with open arms.' As he leaves Marvell Street, Kane is not so sure.

Once Kane is settled into the guesthouse, he calls the number that Stephanie has given him.

'Hi, Rebecca. It's your brother,' he greets.

Rebecca cannot believe her ears when she hears Kane's voice, and for a moment there is silence on the line as she recovers from the shock.

'Rebecca, are you there?'

'Is that really you, Kane?' she finally asks.

'Yes, it's really me. I'm back.'

'I've been waiting twenty-five years for this call, Kane Stenmark! Where are you?'

'I'm here in Byron. I heard you'd lost your partner and that you almost lost your son. I've come back to see how you are.'

'How kind. I've been despondent, as you can imagine, but hearing your voice has cheered me up to no end, Kane.'

'How is Corrie doing, Rebecca?'

'Corrie is just about ready to come home from the hospital. At the moment, he's trying to get around the ward on crutches, poor kid.'

'What a horrific thing to happen to him.'

'It's tragic, but the kids take a chance every time they enter the ocean, you know.'

'I guess so Rebecca. I hear Corrie has lost part of his leg?'

'Yes he has, and he's very depressed about it, Kane. We both are. Corrie thinks the life he once knew is now over. It's hard for him to come to grips with the fact that his surfing days are now behind him. He was a natural at it, you know.'

'It's just not fair, is it?' Kane sympathises.

'It's the bloody Stenmark curse, Kane! Corrie's its latest victim.'

'I want to talk to you about that, sis,' Kane replies.

'It's all so very unfortunate, Kane, but I'll tell you more about it when I see you. When can you come over?'

'We've just arrived in Byron, Rebecca. So far, we've only had time to call into Stephanie's house to get your number. Archie and I are staying at the Pacific House guesthouse, and I intend to leave him there to settle in while I go out to the Aboriginal camp to see the boys, but maybe we could meet up tomorrow night if you're free.'

'Who . . . who's Archie?' Rebecca enquires.

'He's my son.'

'Kane, you have a boy?'

'Yes, Rebecca. He's a man now. He's 24.'

'What wonderful news! Kane, you've made my day. Why don't both of you come around for dinner tomorrow night then? I can't wait to see you and to meet Archie.'

Chapter 6

ABORIGINAL CAMP

In his youth, Kane was acutely aware of the desperate plight of the local indigenous people who lived on the outskirts of his hometown, but when he had bolted from Byron Bay two and a half decades ago, he effectively severed all ties with them. He'd left town in such a rush that he didn't pay them the courtesy of saying goodbye, but over the years, he'd regretted abandoning them like that. Now that he's back in Byron again however, Kane is keen to re-establish relations with them, especially with his trusty school friend, Jimmy.

After having decided to face his fears, Kane leaves Archie at the guesthouse, and drives a rented jeep along the familiar Bangalow Road. Fearful of receiving a hostile reception after such a long absence, his stomach tightens when he approaches the Aboriginal camp. Kane is concerned that Jimmy may blame him for deserting him right at the time when his young sister had mysteriously disappeared. Although he probably deserves it, he'll be mortified if Jimmy still harbours anger in his heart and sends him off with a simple gesture like an upturned middle finger.

Sweating at the temples, Kane steers his jeep into the parking lot and makes his way on foot towards the entrance. On guard in front of the camp, he sees a large woman with jet-black skin, a broad nose and a wide smile.

'Jingi wahlu widtha,' the woman greets in a raspy voice.

'Witha bayan, Maisy,' Kane replies, recognising the woman from the distant past.

'I'm good, Kanee . . . Long time no see,' she rejoins.

'I've been on a walkabout, Maisy,' he admits.

'Well, it's good to have you back,' she replies, her broad smile welcoming him.

'It's good to be back,' he responds, delighted that Maisy has given him such a cordial reception. 'Maisy, I'm looking for my old mate, Jimmy.'

'He's over there, Kanee,' she answers, pointing towards the community building.

Kane advances nervously towards the camp's circular community hall, where a thin male figure stands at the entrance with his kelpie dog. The man is wearing a familiar red bandana, and from a distance, Kane wonders if it might be his mate. He advances a little closer until he can see the unmistakable scars on his old friend's face. Seeing Jimmy's prominent facial injuries immediately triggers the raw memory of the malicious brawl that took place in his family's hotel beer garden all those years ago. Jimmy's dog begins to bark loudly when Kane approaches.

'What are you doin' back here, you mad bastard?' Jimmy asks as he bends down to settle his dog.

'I've come back to see you, Jimmy,' Kane ventures, attempting to be upbeat.

The dog continues to bark.

'You left us for dead, man. What have you come back for?'

'I thought it was time I showed my face again,' Kane responds, but the dog's bark turns into a growl.

'Ya took ya time about it, you bastard,' Jimmy replies in disdain.

'Yeah, it took me a while to pluck up enough courage to face you, mate,' Kane admits.

White saliva begins to drip from the growling dog's jaws.

'You've been away twenty-five fuckin' years, mate!' Jimmy says, spitting contemptuously onto the dry earth.

'Yeah, I know.'

When the dog continues to growl, Jimmy attempts to settle it down by holding tightly to its collar and reprimanding it sternly.

A silence ensues while both men stare at each other, their eyes flitting up and down as they assess the damage two and a half decades has wrought.

'You left town in a bloody hurry didn't you? You abandoned us, mate, an' you didn't even tell us where you was goin'.'

'I'm sorry, Jimmy. I really am. But at the time, I just had to get out of Byron Bay real fast.'

'Sorry? You pissed off and left me wond'rin' if you had somethin' to do with Matilda goin' missin'!'

'I know, Jimmy . . . I was a coward, a bloody yellow-bellied coward.'

'You always told me to face up to my troubles, Kanee, but you ran for the bloody hills.'

Kane knows he ran away to avoid all the accusations, and Jimmy detects a guilty look on Kane's face.

'I couldn't stand the pressure, Jimmy. Everyone thought I was responsible for your sister's disappearance. The cops tried like bloody hell to pin it on me, but nothing stuck because it wasn't me.'

Jimmy's scarred face remains unconvinced. 'I didn't know who to blame, to tell ya the truth, Kanee. But when you pissed off out of town, I blamed you like all the others. But now that you're back, I want you to tell me what happened to my kid sister.'

'All I know is that it wasn't me. Matilda was a wild one, but she had a heart of gold, and I had no reason to go after her. Now that I'm back here though, I promise you this. I'm going to find out all about it.'

'I loved my sister, Kanee. She had a filthy mouth on her, but she had a beautiful spirit. Do you know what it's like not knowin' if she's alive or dead? It's a bloody riddle that never leaves your mind, mate. Day in an' day out, I think of 'er.'

'Are the cops still searching for her?' Kane asks.

'It's a cold case now, Kanee. The cops told me.'

'There's been no closure for you then,' Kane says, shaking his head in sympathy.

'Do you know what I get hung up on?'

'What?'

'Two of Matilda's mates were with her that night, an' they both say they heard a shot when they was at Marvell Street. They ran for their lives, but Matilda didn't make it. It makes me think you Stenmarks have blood on your hands, mate. If it wasn't you who shot her, then who the hell was it?'

'Jimmy, I wasn't there. Abel and I were at the bachelor and spinster ball until late. I was trying to pick up a girl from Mudgee that night.'

'Oh yeah, Kanee? The cops told me someone saw your red Ford Falcon on Bangalow Road late that night.'

'It wasn't me driving it, mate,' Kane protests.

Jimmy studies Kane's face attentively. His intuition tells him that Kane is telling him the truth, but the vital question remains. If it wasn't him, then who was it in that car? Jimmy feels sure that the Stenmarks are into it up to their necks, but he remains silent.

'Can I come back tomorrow, Jimmy?' Kane asks. 'I want to introduce you to someone.'

'Yeah, bring whoever ya like, so long as it's not the bloody cops. I hate those bastards.'

'Thanks for talking to me, Jimmy. I was dead worried you'd send me away.'

'No way, Kanee. It's great to have me old mate back in town.'

Chapter 7

MARVELL STREET

The next day is Saturday, and Stephanie has invited the immediate Stenmark family to Marvell Street for lunch to announce the party. While the ceiling fan whirs overhead, the family sits around the old cedar table, finishing off their meal of roast lamb and couscous.

Stephanie calls them all to order. 'Attention, everyone! I have an announcement for you concerning the birthday celebrations next weekend.' The noise continues.

'May I have your undivided attention, please?' she calls a little more forcibly, this time tapping her knife against her goblet of cabernet shiraz. 'I want you to know that I have invited eighty people to Abel's fiftieth birthday luncheon. It's an important family milestone, and I plan to set up the tables in the beer garden with white tablecloths. I've even commissioned a string quartet to play under the tree.'

'Sounds like you're pulling out all the stops, Mum,' her son Jude comments.

Jude is a wayward boy of 17 who sports a Mohawk haircut and a silver nose ring in his septum. He has recently spent time in a correctional facility after being involved in armed robbery, but as he's out on probation at the moment, he is able to join in with the family celebrations.

'Who's coming?' he asks.

'I've invited loads of our famous friends, darling, but none of them is as important as our own family,' she answers, careful to include him.

On hearing this, Corrie Stenmark, who has just been picked up from the hospital by his mother, raises his glass in the air. With his long blond hair shaking in disarray, Corrie makes an impromptu toast.

'To the Stenmark family!' he calls.

Overjoyed that Corrie will be with them after surviving his horrific encounter with the shark, the family members eagerly raise their glasses to join him in his toast.

'Cheers to you, Corrie. We're especially glad that you'll be here celebrating with us,' Stephanie responds, and after deliberately placing her goblet down on the cedar table, she picks up a sheet on which she has drawn the seating arrangements. 'Abel and I will be seated at the main table in the centre, and, Rebecca, you will be on our left. On our right will be Kane and his partner, whoever he may bring along —'

'What's this about my bloody brother coming?' Abel interrupts. 'What are you on about, woman? What's going on?'

'Darling, your brother arrived back in town yesterday. I initially wanted to surprise you by having him turn up unannounced, but I've let the cat out of the bag now, haven't I?'

A dark look crosses Abel's face.

'I told him he could bring a friend if he wants to,' Stephanie adds.

'Let me be clear, Stephanie. Kane will not be attending my party, and I'm certainly not having him bring along some floozy to embarrass us.'

'Abel, your fiftieth is an important family occasion. It's been twenty-five years since the entire family has been together. I insist that he attends. What's more, he must sit at the head table with us, with or without a partner.'

With his temple pulsating in anger, Abel thumps his fist on the table. 'In the past, Kane has ruined every bloody birthday I've ever had, and over the years, he's sullied our family name with his actions. If you invite him, Stephanie, the floodgates will be open to the whole native mob. I don't want him here, and I certainly don't want them flooding into the hotel either. It's my fiftieth birthday, and this time, Kane will not be ruining it. I've banned him and his black mates from the hotel forever, and he's the last person I want sitting with me at the main table. For god's sake, woman, why in hell did you invite him?'

The family hovers in trepidation after this outburst and all eyes are glued on Stephanie waiting for her response.

'All members of our family are invited, Abel. Your birthday has somehow morphed into a family reunion,' she replies bravely.

'Bullshit!'

'Stephanie's right, Abel,' Rebecca interjects in support of her sister-in-law. 'I've waited twenty-five years to see my brother again, and now that he's back, there's no question he should attend.'

Rebecca looks over to Corrie, hoping that he will support her, but Corrie appears stunned at the altercation.

'Where will I be sitting, Aunt Stephanie?' he asks.

'You'll be at the cousins' table, Corrie. Darling, you'll be with our boys, Jude and Brett. Kane's son will also be at your table.'

Abel looks across the table at Stephanie, his eyes piercing like daggers. 'Kane's son? That's the first I've heard of him. I didn't know Kane even had a son.'

'I met Archie yesterday, darling, and I've invited him along too. I also told him he could bring a friend.'

'For fuck's sake, Stephanie, they're not coming!'

Having heard enough, Abel rises from his place at the table, throws his napkin onto the floor and storms from the room, slamming the dining room door loudly behind him.

Chapter 8

REBECCA'S HOUSE

When Kane and Archie arrive at Rebecca Stenmark's front door that evening, Archie immediately recognises his aunt from the photograph he'd seen on the front page of the *Byron Shire News*. Although she has a slimmer build and appears slightly younger than in the photo that he'd seen, Rebecca's smile is the same as he recalls. The moment Kane sees his sister, he is overcome with emotion. He immediately realises how much he's missed her over the years, and when he hugs her tightly the floodgates open wide. Tears stream down his cheeks and down Rebecca's too.

'Kane, when I saw you last, you were a much younger man,' she sobs through her tears.

'You were much younger too, sis. You weren't even a teenager when I left,' he responds, and they both laugh.

'You must be Archie,' Rebecca finally acknowledges, trying to extricate herself from Kane's bear hug.

'Hello, Aunt Rebecca,' Archie greets and Rebecca opens her arms to hug him too.

'What a marvellous surprise! I'd lost hope of ever seeing you again, Kane,' Rebecca discloses, dabbing at her tears with her handkerchief, 'and here you are, bowling up with your adult son.'

'When I heard a shark mauled your boy, I couldn't stay away any longer, sis. I just had to come back and see you. Is he OK?' Kane asks.

'Well, let's say he's lucky to be alive, Kane.'

'Are the doctors confident he'll be all right?'

'Oh yes, they've released him already. I brought him home from the hospital this morning. Why don't you both come inside and meet him?'

When Kane and Archie enter Rebecca's house, Corrie is standing tousle-haired in the kitchen with his crutches supporting him. He is wearing cream-coloured cargo pants, with one trouser leg pinned up.

'Corrie, this is your uncle Kane and your cousin Archie.'

'Hi,' he answers.

'Hi, Corrie,' they both chorus to him in unison.

'We hear you've been playing with a man-eater,' Kane jokes.

'I don't think it was playtime. I think it was more like dinnertime,' Corrie corrects. 'I reckon the lower part of my leg became the shark's gourmet meal.'

'How are you managing with the crutches?' Archie asks.

'I'm clumsy as hell, but I guess I'll gradually get control over them.'

'What a catastrophe! Who dragged you away from the bloody thing?' Kane asks.

'An indigenous girl pulled me to safety. She deserves a medal, but I don't even know her name.'

'I'm sure you'll find out soon enough. Byron isn't such a big place,' Kane replies.

'If the girl hadn't been there, Corrie, I'm guessing it could have been much worse —' Archie propounds.

'Oh, he'd be dead!' Rebecca interrupts.

Kane and Archie nod sympathetically.

'Mum, I'm going over to Andy's place. He's picking me up in a few minutes, and I might stay with him overnight, if that's all right.'

'OK, darling. Just make sure you take your medication with you,' his mother instructs.

'I've got everything in this bag,' he replies, holding up a plastic carry-all.

Corrie plants his crutches in front of him and swings his single leg forward. In in an ungainly motion he propels himself towards the front door, where he struggles through to the porch to wait for his friend to pick him up.

After the door closes behind him, Rebecca remarks, 'You know, it's to be expected that something bad was going to happen to Corrie one day.'

Archie considers this to be quite an offhand remark. 'Pardon me, Aunt Rebecca. Why was it to be expected?' he asks.

'You must be from Sydney, Archie, or you'd know about the famous Stenmark curse.'

'I have actually heard about it, Aunt Rebecca. I read about it in the local paper and now that my curiosity has been tweaked, I'm keen to learn more about it while I'm here in Byron.'

'Well, Archie, you'll soon find out that the Stenmarks are never too far away from trouble. In fact, there's a whole tragic history of it. It's a sorry tale to tell, I'm afraid.'

'I'd love to hear more about it,' Archie fields, hoping his aunt will divulge more information.

'If you like, I'll tell you about it while I prepare dinner, Archie. I hope you brought some wine with you. You'll need it.'

Kane holds up a brown paper bag containing two bottles of red wine that he'd purchased on the way over. The trio retreat to the kitchen and they regroup around Rebecca's marble bench where Rebecca assembles her vegetables on one side. On the other side Kane attempts to lever a cork from one of his wine bottles and when he returns the opened bottle to the bench, Rebecca picks it up to examine the label. After nodding her acceptance at Kane's judicious choice of Barossa Cabernet, she directs him to pour it out into three stemmed glasses she's procured from a high cupboard.

'To the curse,' she toasts, holding up her glass.

'I don't think I want to toast to that,' Kane rebuffs.

'To the end of the curse then,' she amends quickly and they all clink glasses.

'Nobody here knows what happened to you when you left Byron Bay, Kane. You've managed to stay out in the wilderness for twenty-five years, but suddenly, here you are, back in town with an adult son in tow. Might I say that's a good thing?'

Kane looks proudly across at Archie as Rebecca gives Archie an approving smile.

'Archie, you don't look much like your father, so I imagine you got your good looks from your mother.'

'I don't remember my mother, unfortunately, Aunt Rebecca. I was told she died when I was only 2. I've heard from Dad that she was lovely, but I don't even have a picture of her. After her death, your brother brought me up on his own.'

'Good for you, Kane. I always knew you were a good egg, despite Abel's view of you. Well then, welcome to the family, Archie,' Rebecca states, holding up her glass of red wine again.

'To our family,' they all toast.

'Archie, you may not want to have anything to do with the Stenmarks after you hear what I have to say.'

'I'm ready to hear it, warts and all, Aunt Rebecca. In fact, I've been sent here to put pen to paper about it. By the sound of things, there's a ripping tale to be told.'

'You're right, there is, but as each year passes and more and more water passes under the bridge, the stories get forgotten. Before they slip away altogether, I'm pleased that someone will be recording them.'

Both men sip on their wine and wait eagerly for Rebecca to begin.

'Well, let me start by telling you about our grandfather Joseph Stenmark, because he was the bugger who started it all.' Archie leans forward, eager to hear precisely what triggered the rift in the first place.

'Joseph was awarded a tract of land on Broken Head in 1880, but he should never have taken ownership of it.'

'Why not?'

'Because ostensibly, it belonged to the local tribe who had occupied it for multiple generations. They shared this particular piece of country with the whole Nation, which was made up of tribes who travelled up and down the coast for possibly sixty-five thousand years. It was a sacred ceremonial site for them all, and the great corroborees they held on this particular headland had an exceptional significance for them. Every year, since time immemorial, they'd assembled there, and over the centuries they'd formed a deep attachment to it, even calling it Cavanbah – their meeting place.'

'I've heard that name before, Aunt Rebecca,' Archie recalls.

'Please, Archie, call me Rebecca,' his aunt corrects.

'Cavanbah was the original name for Byron Bay, wasn't it, Rebecca?' Archie asks.

'Yes, it was, Archie, and it still should be. Originally, there were many different tribes who visited Broken Head from the north, the south and the west, but the local tribe was always the host. They were the custodians of land which was located in a special position at the most easterly point of Australia. Essential to their culture, this particular sacred land was inextricably linked to their spiritual world and was deserving of the utmost respect.'

'I see.'

'When the government awarded the land to our grandfather in a settlement grant, the local tribe was understandably furious. They believed that he had no right to own it, because they had continually conducted their important cultural traditions on it over many centuries. On this spot, a stream of communication had passed from generation to generation, right up to the day Joseph took it over.'

'They must have found it inconceivable that they couldn't continue these traditions,' Archie fields.

'You're damn right! They solemnly believed that this land should always remain completely untouched.'

'What was their philosophy?' Archie asks, intrigued to know more.

'They had an earthbound philosophy, Archie. The earth gave life to them, sustained them while they were alive, and then took them back again when they died.'

Rebecca stops cutting her vegetables, and Archie and Kane detect a faraway look in her eye.

During the pause, they take another sip on their wine, both wondering if Rebecca is experiencing a pang of guilt. Perhaps she is regretting that her grandfather Joseph Stenmark had barged into Byron Bay in the 1880s and had taken possession of the most culturally relevant land in the area, without so much as a second thought about what had gone on over the preceding thousands of years. After the long pause, Rebecca looks back at Archie and Kane with a sorrowful expression. She had actually been reflecting on how the native tribes had lived undisturbed for centuries before European settlement.

'As I was saying, the local First Nation people used to call Byron Bay Cavanbah. It was the unthinking early white settlers who had changed the name of the town. Before they arrived, Cavanbah was a place of plenty, a place where the indigenous people could find shelter by the coast. They ate the rainforest fruits, feasted on the seafood, and shared this abundance with visiting tribes. For centuries, these peace-loving people had drunk from the pure spring waters of the rainforest streams and had swum undisturbed along the pristine sandy beaches, but Joseph took it from them.'

Archie and Kane notice a tear appearing in Rebecca's eye.

'Did Joseph Stenmark respect their interest in the land?' Archie asks pointedly.

'Phewff, no! When he first took possession, there were some cave drawings showing the wildlife that used to sustain the local people. Some of these drawings depicted land animals such as wallabies, goannas, possums, and emus, while others were of fish and crabs, showing that they were a coastal tribe.'

'Did Joseph protect the cave art?' Archie asks.

'He got rid of every last one of them,' Rebecca answers.

'Dear me, that's deplorable!' Archie utters.

'Kane, do you remember Dad telling us that on the land that Joseph commandeered, there were several ceremonial Bora Rings carved into the trunks of the trees?'

'Yes, I vaguely remember something about Bora Rings.'

'They were evidence of the local tribe's continual occupation of the place over the years, but Joseph chopped them down and burned them up.'

'Let's be frank, sis. That happened all over Australia,' Kane asserts. 'The white man has displayed precious little respect for the traditions of indigenous people.'

'We've all been wickedly unaware,' Rebecca agrees.

Archie sips on his red wine, feeling guilty for the first time in his life about the treatment of the First Nation people by white settlers. Up to now, he has known precious few details about how the early white colonists dealt with the First Nation people with whom they encountered. Perhaps he'd heard about the Aborigines having terrible things done to them, but up to this point, he had taken no responsibility for them. Like most white Australians, he'd claimed it was the work of others at other times, but tonight, as he stands at Rebecca's kitchen bench, he is haunted by the underlying motifs of racism that are directly linked to his family.

'Every time I look out to Julian Rocks, I get sad,' Rebecca declares.

'Why is that, Rebecca? Most people find them to be a magnificent sight.' Archie enquires.

'The rocks are indeed magnificent to look at, Archie, but they were a very spiritual place for the local indigenous people. Originally, they were named after Nguthungulli. He was the one whom they believed was responsible for creating the land and the people. Tragically, its name has now been changed from Nguthungulli to Julian Rocks, so we have no link to its initial significance. It's as if we've given its long history a complete whitewash.'

'I've read that the early white officials named Julian Rocks after Lord Byron's "Don Juan,"' Archie adds.

'Yes, that's the unfortunate story. Isn't it deplorable? The early settlers were so ethnocentric that they deliberately threw out any hint of Aboriginal settlement, and now the streets of Byron Bay are named after English literary notables. Instead of the wonderful original Aboriginal names, we now have Jonson, Wordsworth, Browning, Milton, and Byron Streets, for god's sake!'

Archie is keen to steer the conversation back to the Stenmarks.

'If you don't mind, Rebecca, can we concentrate on the Stenmark family? It sounds as if we are the descendants of a man who made a land grab.'

Rebecca swills down the last of her red wine before continuing as the family raconteur.

'Yes, we are,' she continues. 'When the land was allocated to our grandfather, it was benignly called "free selection" under the Crown Land's Alienation Act of 1861. The NSW government at the time encouraged white settlers to develop the land to make it productive, but this directive urged the colonists to eliminate everything that was in any way Aboriginal.'

'It was a deliberate occupation then?' Archie asks.

'Not just an occupation, Archie. It was an annihilation.'

'What?'

'Haven't you heard about the horrific massacres that took place in this area?'

'Not really. Were any of our ancestors involved in them?' Archie asks sensing that there is a story ready to unfold, especially when he notices that Rebecca has stopped chopping the vegetables. After laying her knife down on the bench, she stares directly at him with a stony face.

'After being banned from their traditional hunting grounds, the local tribesmen were sometimes so hungry that they'd steal a sheep to eat. As you can imagine, this type of theft outraged the early settlers who were highly protective of their flocks and herds. Shamefully, our family was known to endorse the witch hunts organised to hunt down the culprits. Kane, do you remember our father telling us that Joseph Stenmark supported a massacre of natives down near the quarry at Suffolk Park?'

'Yes, I do remember Dad telling us about that. It was shameful . . . out and out murder!' Kane retorts, recalling his father's report.

'Whoa . . . Is that so?' Archie sighs with alarm.

'At the northern end of Sussex Park, near the mouth of Tallow Creek, our local Aboriginal people experienced a terrifying massacre. It was so atrocious that it left devastating vibrations that persisted for decades. Even today, the elders talk of disturbed spirits that have not been released from bondage.'

'This is our family history!' Archie exclaims.

'You won't read about it in any history books though, Archie.'

'What else can you tell me?' Archie asks, eager to get more details of the real story.

'Well, before that massacre, the local indigenous people reported that the European police officers stationed in East Ballina forced the native mounted police under their command to fire at a group of First Nation people while they were asleep. The indigenous accounts state that this unprovoked attack killed about forty men, women, and children, but it went unrecorded.'

'That's bloody genocide, literally!' Archie responds in shock.

'That's right. It happened way back in the mid-1800s, but the NSW government at the time refused to make any official record of this massacre. I've heard that some of the Aboriginals who were trying to escape the bullets were driven off Black Head, while another group were left to rot on Angel's Beach.'

'This is utterly shameful – such a dark time in our history,' Archie expresses shaking his head in disgust.

'It didn't stop there, Archie – 150 more died a decade later when they gave them poisonous flour.'

'That's mass murder!' Archie exclaims, raising his hands to cover his face. He is finding these atrocities extremely confronting, and in response, he gulps down more of his wine.

'Archie, one day I hope the land on Broken Head is given back to the poor local tribe,' Rebecca opines.

'Here, here,' he agrees, and all three raise their glasses to this unlikely occurrence.

When Archie's mobile phone rings, he finds that it is his editor, Sue Barkham, on the line. He apologises to Rebecca and Kane by raising his palm before moving away to take the call.

'It's Sue here, Archie. How's the story coming along?'

'Oh, it's actually in process right now, Sue. I'm at Rebecca Stenmark's house, getting the lowdown on the curse.'

'Good for you, Archie. Put her on, will you?'

'Really?'

'Yes, I want to talk to her.'

Archie passes the phone to Rebecca. 'It's my editor. She wants to have a word with you.'

'Hello.'

'Hello, Ms Stenmark. I'm Sue Barkham from Aston & Irwin Publishers. Thank you for speaking with Archie. Has he told you yet that he's your nephew?'

'Yes, he has.'

'I believe he's your brother's boy.'

'Yes. He tells me he's Kane's son, but they don't look at all alike.'

'He's a handsome bugger, and he's a good writer, so I urge you to tell him everything you know. I won't keep you now, but thank you for filling him in on the background to the curse. I look forward to reading about it when he gets back to Sydney.'

'It's no problem,' Rebecca replies, and she hands the phone back to Archie for him to complete the call.

'Archie, I need your manuscript here in ninety days,' Sue orders.

Archie promises her true diligence before switching off his phone.

After the call, Rebecca places some crab and smoked trout dip in front of Archie and Kane. She has mixed the crab and the smoked trout with chives, dill, and lemon from her garden. Archie spreads some of it on Rebecca's home-baked bread.

'This is so delicious,' he compliments.

'Thank you, Archie. I'm glad you like it. I baked the bread this morning.'

'Rebecca, do you know what happened on the day the bone was pointed at your grandfather?' Archie asks, keen to get to the point of the story.

'Yes, Archie. We heard about the incident from my father, Jake Stenmark, didn't we, Kane?'

Kane nods.

'What did he tell you both?'

'One day, when Joseph had left the gate open to his property a solemn group of elders approached him from the local tribe. There had been a history of confrontation between them since he took over their land, but on this particular day, they came onto his property appearing quite friendly.

'They called out, "Jingi wala!" which is an amicable greeting, and one of them told Joseph that he'd had a *baribun*, a dream. He'd dreamed that their sacred land had been given back to them and that it was a definite sign from his ancestors that the land should be returned to them so they could continue *jagi*, their ceremonial rituals.

'Another elder spoke up, proclaiming that the area was very special to the tribe because it was *durebil*, a sacred place. He said their creation myths told of legendary totemic beings wandering over the land in Dreamtime and that it was not just the local tribe who considered this place a sacred destination, but also all the tribes up and down the coast.

'When my grandfather asked the elder why it was so sacred, he told him that after their journey of creation, the creation beings had lain down on this very ground to allow their spirits to sink into it. That's when everything on the land became sacred – trees, animals, and rocks.'

'What did your grandfather do when he heard this?' Archie asks.

'He responded in no uncertain terms, Archie. He advised them that everything had changed, and that now they would have to learn to live with the white man's law, because it was now the law of the land. He told them that according to the white man's law, the land on Broken Head was now legally his.'

'He sounded resolute,' Archie comments.

'He was. My dad told us that on that day, Joseph waved his papers at the elders to show them his pastoral lease.'

'How did it end up then?'

'The story goes that after waving the lease papers at them, my grandfather stood up and bellowed, "Get off my land, the lot of you! I'll have none of this nonsense . . . To hell with your creation beings!"'

'What happened then?' Archie asks, eager to get to the bone pointing.

'Before they left the property, one of the elders was so indignant at being dismissed, that he produced a large bone with emu feathers attached to it, and after pointing it at my grandfather, he waved it up and down, hissing, "Pourri-pourri, me no like you, mugul fella!"

'The group apparently gathered around the man with the bone, and in unison, they began chanting an ancient curse. The men all seemed familiar with the age-old chant, and they sang it over and over until our grandfather had been well and truly "boned". On that day, Joseph Stenmark was officially cursed by the local elders, who had summoned a *durangen*, a diabolical evil spirit, to always follow him and his family.'

'Wowee, that was serious! They officially pointed the bone at him then,' Archie declares.

'It was very dire at the time, Archie, and that curse continues to this day,' Rebecca adds.

Archie raises one eyebrow at her, awaiting proof of the curse in action.

'My husband was killed by a brown snake just recently, and just look at what happened to my poor Corrie in the surf a week or so ago. After all this time, the sacred animals are still after our family . . . That shark nearly took him.'

'I get it, Rebecca. Ever since that fateful day, every bad thing that ever happens to the Stenmarks can be attributed to the boning.'

'That's right,' Rebecca replies, nodding sagely.

The hairs on Archie's arms stand on end.

'Your dinner is ready, gentlemen. Please move over to the dining table,' Rebecca directs, as she lifts a homemade vegetable lasagne from the oven.

Archie has been intrigued by Rebecca's descriptions of how the curse began, and he now has a strong appetite for more of the story. In particular, he is eager to know how it has directly affected the family over the years.

'Rebecca, why don't we start with your grandfather and how he made his money? I'm interested to know how the family's considerable wealth was created.'

'Well, let me see,' Rebecca replies, pursing her lips as she tries to recall what her father had told her.

'When Joseph Stenmark was in his twenties, he married a girl from Ballina called Bella. She was the daughter of a cedar cutter.'

'Bella from Ballina, whose father was a woodcutter,' Archie parrots, thinking that it is like a fairy tale.

Kane follows this statement up by interjecting some facts.

'Cedar logging was one of the original industries in this area in the late 1800s, Archie, and this type of deforestation continued into the first part of the 1900s.'

'Yes, it was a huge industry in the early days around here,' Rebecca concurs. Archie nods to indicate that he is taking in all this historical information.

'Bella's father was responsible for delivering tons of cedar to the dock at Ballina. The logs that his men cut down were then shipped to a sawmill some distance away. There was a great deal of timber around in those days, but the redwood was the most valuable of them all. It was in such high demand that he did very well.'

'After cutting down the huge cedar trees, how did they transport them?' Archie asks.

'Bella's father was in charge of several bullock teams that pulled timber wagons along rough tracks to the port,' Kane explains.

'It sounds like hard yakka,' Archie remarks.

'The men worked tirelessly, and I've heard that he kept them happy at the end of every delivery by providing them with a keg of rum, which they rowdily consumed on the beach,' Kane adds.

'That would keep the blokes happy,' Archie quips, thinking that it's a man's world.

'Rebecca, do you know anything about your grandmother?' Archie asks, keen to get some gender balance.

'I've heard that Bella was a God-fearing girl who never drank a drop and never missed a Sunday church service.'

Archie nods, thinking that she sounds pious.

'When her father died, Bella benefitted from his inheritance, and she moved to Byron Bay with her husband, Joseph Stenmark, who was her father's right-hand man. On arrival, she immediately joined the new St Paul's Anglican Church and resumed her devotions there, becoming one its active founding members. The church opened its doors around the same time as the railway station opened in Byron Bay.'

'That must have been when Byron Bay was about to come alive,' Archie proposes.

'That's true, Archie. Byron was about to boom. Originally, the town was just a small port servicing the whaling industry, but in the late 1800s, when the railway opened up the north coast of NSW, it linked the town to Sydney and that's when Byron Bay began to really prosper.'

'Did Joseph and Bella have any children?'

'Yes, they had a boy called Jake. He was our father.'

'This all sounds very good so far. I don't detect the curse adversely affecting anyone yet. So far, it sounds as if your grandfather and Bella came to Byron Bay at the right time,' Archie proposes.

'Yes. In retrospect, I think they did arrive at the right time,' Rebecca agrees. 'For a while, things went smoothly for both of them. Although there wasn't a lot of money around initially, Joseph occupied himself with odd jobs in the timber industry and in his spare time, he cleared the bush from his newly acquired tract of land on Broken Head. Aiming to convert the land from scrub to pasture, he diligently removed the trees, burned off the scrub and planted paspalum grass to feed his newly acquired herd of dairy cattle.'

'He changed the ceremonial land to make it productive,' Archie paraphrases.

'Yes.'

'Did he remain a farmer?'

'No, he didn't. An opportunity arose for Joseph at the local butter factory, and history tells us that he was an extremely competent employee who quickly rose up the ladder to become general manager. Under his direction, the firm acquired centrifugal separators that could separate cream from milk, and this purchase streamlined the laborious process of making butter.'

'He was a pioneer of modern technology then,' Archie chimes.

'Ah yes. In addition, he encouraged the local farmers to plant his favourite grass in their fields, and soon, paspalum became an excellent fodder for their dairy cattle, enabling him to increase the production at the butter factory. In short order, with the new advances in refrigeration, Joseph was able to expand the factory's output considerably.'

'Joseph sounds very progressive,' Archie affirms.

'Yes, he was remarkable. He not only standardised the manufacture of butter but also used the skim milk by-product as fodder for the farmers' pigs. In time, he cured ham, packaged up bacon and pork sausages, and even began canning foods, which he shipped to Sydney in the refrigerated holds of sailing boats. Some of his products even made their way from Sydney to London via ocean liners.'

'Wow, what an enterprising man! He must have become very wealthy,' Archie surmises.

'Yes, he did, Archie. He was one of Byron Bay's first entrepreneurs, a true captain of industry.'

'I'm not hearing anything detrimental to the family yet, Rebecca. Perhaps the elders' curse hadn't worked, because it doesn't seem to have hindered him in any way at all so far,' Archie baits.

'Wait, Archie. It's about to kick in,' Rebecca warns, as she takes a few bites of her homemade lasagne and sips her refilled glass of red wine. She stares at Archie before launching into the first example of the curse.

'Everything was going swimmingly for Joseph until his wife fell pregnant for the second time. Bella's first child, Jake, was thriving, but a little way into her second pregnancy, she found out she was going to have twins. This news was greeted joyfully, but Bella contracted smallpox during the pregnancy. She became desperately ill and at the age of 30, she tragically died during childbirth, with her twin boys dying along with her. Before her death, she told Jake that if the twins were going to be boys, she was going to name them Kane and Abel, but obviously, this never came to pass.'

'How did Joseph react to their deaths?' Archie asks.

'Joseph was grief-stricken and immediately blamed the death of his wife and twin boys on the curse. He became so incensed, in fact, that he charged into the Aboriginal camp with a shotgun, and he killed two of the elders at point-blank range. "This is what I think of your curse!" he was reported to have yelled at the poor men as he took aim at them.'

'Whoo, murder most foul! Was Joseph prosecuted?'

'He was charged with the offences, but Joseph had a great deal of influence in the community in those days, and with some hefty bribes, he was able to have the charges against him thrown out.'

'That is outrageous!' Archie utters.

'The tribesmen who had witnessed the murders did not like to speak about the dead, so no accounts of the incident were ever recorded correctly. The police papers were doctored to shift the blame for the shootings onto a black man suspected of killing sheep with a shotgun.'

'There was a miscarriage of justice here,' Archie declares, pursing his lips and screwing up his face.

'Yes, Archie, there was. Joseph was able to get away with murder, just like others before him.' Rebecca shakes her head slowly in complete disgust.

'What happened to the first child after that?' Archie enquires.

'Our father, Jake, was brought up by Joseph, but Joseph was a different man after his wife had died. He'd lost all interest in the butter-manufacturing business, and after resigning as general manager, left with a considerable private fortune by local standards. He scouted around for an alternate business, and fortune struck when he was able to buy the hotel by the beach. Archie, if you walk towards the beach from the town along Jonson Street, you come to it right on the water . . . It's called the Sands Hotel.'

'I know it, Rebecca. Everyone does. It must make an absolute fortune.'

'Yes, it's a veritable goldmine. It makes heaps of money these days, Archie, but Joseph had to build it up,' Rebecca explains.

'I heard that Joseph died in an accident.'

'Yes, he did. Joseph was crossing the road outside the pub on his eightieth birthday, and he was run down by a truck driven by an indigenous man.'

'The curse?'

'Yes.' She nods.

'It was to be expected,' Archie parrots, acknowledging Rebecca's logic.

'He was buried on his land, in the same plot where his wife, Bella, was interred with the twins. You can go to it. It's in our compound out on Broken Head.'

'That must be a diabolical burial site,' Archie surmises.

'The local indigenous people are not happy about it being there on their ceremonial land, Archie, that's for sure.'

Both Archie and Kane understand their objection.

'Boys, that's all I can manage tonight. Good heavens, it's past midnight! When we meet again, I'll tell you more.'

As they leave, Archie and Kane both thank Rebecca for the family history lesson, and after kissing Rebecca on the cheek, they disappear into the night.

Chapter 9

ARCHIE AT THE ABORIGINAL CAMP

Keen to introduce Archie to Jimmy, Kane drives out to the Aboriginal camp the following morning. Archie feels as if there is something spiritual about the land over which they are travelling, something deep and abiding. The sky is vast above them and the trees on the side of the road look indolent in the sunshine, some standing tall, some stooped, some bent as if they are beckoning them in. It is an area filled with energy. At the entry to the camp, Maisy is there once again ready to greet them.

'Oh, Kanee, your son looks like a film star,' she ventures, when Kane introduces her to Archie.

'I can assure you, I'm not,' Archie responds, embarrassed by her remark.

Maisy continues to giggle as if she is in the company of a celebrity and Kane has to wait until she settles down before asking her if they can see Jimmy. Maisy explains to him that Jimmy isn't available today because he is conducting some secret men's business with the male tribe members.

'You come here on a sad day, Kanee,' she tells him. 'We don't say the name, but someone in our tribe has gone to be with his ancestors, an' all the men have *nyalar* in their eyes today. They're down on the beach, lettin' their sorrow out at a smokin' ceremony before the burial.'

'Maisy, it sounds as if we've arrived here at a very sorrowful time. Do you think it's OK for us to go and watch them from a distance?' he asks respectfully.

'It's OK for men, but it's not OK for women, Kanee. It's secret men's business, you know. I reckon 'cause you are men, it's OK to let you in, but I don't want you to do no wrong around here.'

Kane detects that Maisy is concerned that she may be transgressing the rules of the tribe by allowing him and Archie in. She doesn't appear to be sure if whitefellas should be allowed to observe the blackfellas' sacred rituals.

'You better behave, Kanee. We don't want no harm to come to this place,' she warns.

The father and son head along a sandy path until they reach the top of a rise, where they take a seat under a pandanus palm. In the distance, they see a group of about a dozen indigenous men on the beach, stomping in a circle around a smouldering campfire. The men have painted their bodies liberally with white paint and each of them carries a tree branch. Archie and Kane watch as the men repeatedly shake the branches above their heads before poking them into the fire, causing wafts of blue smoke to billow out across the beach.

'They are doing *jagi* . . . It's their smudge dance,' Kane whispers. 'The smoking ceremony is one of their traditional dances. They believe the plants they're burning have cleansing properties and that the smoke from them will ward off bad spirits. I've seen them do it before. They're sharing their sorrow and it gives them purification after grief.'

Enthralled, Archie watches the men as they lay down their branches beside the fire and pick up their click sticks. To the rhythm of these sticks, the men make small jumps in a clockwise direction with their legs wide before jumping back in unison in a similar fashion. When this dance finishes, the men pick up their spears and start enacting what appears to be a crab hunting ritual, which ends with them crouching down close to the sand and walking sideways like crabs.

'The crab could be the dead man's totem animal . . . the one that connects him to country,' Kane explains to Archie.

When the ceremony is over, the men gather up their spears and click sticks, and they march in a single line back up towards the sandy rise. Archie waits under the pandanus palm, feeling like an intruder into their world. When the men advance towards him with spears in hand, he wonders what kind of reception he and his father will receive. Will they think that they have been spying on their secret ceremony?

'Witha bayan?' a man with a severely scarred face calls out to them.

'Jinga wala,' Kane answers his friend.

The two men grasp each other's arms in a kind of personal greeting.

'I'm sorry that someone in your mob has passed on, Jimmy,' Kane sympathises.

'Yeah, it's sorry time now, mate. We don't say who it is, but I can tell you I'm a sad man today, Kanee. My mate has gone. When we bury him, he'll rest here in country.'

Kane and Archie remain respectfully silent.

'When ya left yesterday, Kanee, I realised that after all these years, I'm still mad at you. I haven't got over that you didn't even say hooroo to me when ya left. No goodbyes, no nothin'! I was left here for years wond'rin' if you had something to do with my sister disappearin' an' all. I was bloody angry at you because you didn't act like a friend.'

'Jimmy, I'm so sorry. It's true that I didn't treat you with respect, but I promise you that I'll act more courteously from now on. I really value our friendship.'

'Better late than never, I s'pose,' Jimmy replies.

'Jimmy, this is my son, Archie.'

'Your son? Well, blow me down – he's already a man. Bugal.'

Jimmy stretches out his arm towards Archie, but Archie finds the gesture unusual as it is not like a usual handshake. It is more like a touching of the forearms. It's the first time Archie has touched a black man and he is immediately aware of the marked difference between Jimmy's skin and his own. While Jimmy's hands are hardened and weathered, his are smooth and virginal by comparison.

'Your daughter is doin' fine now, Kanee,' Jimmy states. 'She stays somewhere in Byron now, but we only see her in the summer months.'

Archie's eyebrows go up in amazement at this comment, wondering if he has heard Jimmy correctly. It's the first time he's heard mention that his father has an offspring of any kind. *Does Dad have a daughter? Could it be possible that I could actually have a sister?*

'Do you think she'll want to see me?' Kane asks.

'I dunno, mate. She's in the white man's world now. She's been studyin' to be a lawyer in Sydney, an' I heard she just graduated.'

'Where can I find her?'

'The last I heard, she was working at the fruit and veg co-op each summer. You should look 'er up.'

'Thanks, mate. I might. Have you got any family yourself, Jimmy?' Kane asks.

'Yeah, I've got two boys o' me own now.'

'Fantastic . . . I hope we can meet them one day,' Kane rejoins.

'Yeah, I hope so too, mate.'

'Well, Jimmy, we'll be off now. I just wanted to catch up with you and introduce you to my son.'

'Look after yourself, Kanee, an', Archie, keep your ol' man out of trouble, eh?'

'That's going to be a hard task,' Archie jokes.

'Hooroo then,' Jimmy says as the father and son stride back to their jeep.

Chapter 10

SECRET FAMILY BUSINESS

After deciding that he will take over the driving on their way back to Byron Bay, Archie jumps in behind the steering wheel and starts up the jeep.

'What's this about your daughter, Dad?' he challenges as he revs the engine.

'Yep, I have a daughter.'

'You never mentioned her before.'

'There was no need to, son. We were so far away, and I thought you didn't need the aggro.'

'Dad, you've been hiding this from me!'

'It was a long time ago, Archie. It was a youthful indiscretion of mine.'

'That's an understatement. You got an indigenous girl pregnant, and you were too proud to admit the baby was yours.'

'Yeah.'

'Did you abandon her?'

'It's a long story, son.'

'Who is the mother?'

'You don't want to know, Archie.'

'I do want to know, Dad!'

A stony silence follows.

'Did you stand by her, or did you run?' Archie interrogates.

'Hmmm . . .' Kane's brow furrows, and a stupefied look takes over his face. He's obviously caught in a corner.

'How about starting at the beginning, Dad?' Archie urges in a much stronger tone.

Thinking that Archie is like a dog with a bone, Kane stares straight ahead in silence as Archie drives the jeep. Sensing that Archie is exasperated with him, he finally decides to speak.

'Our mother died when we were quite young. We were still kids when she passed away, and for many years, we had a housekeeper who came to Marvell Street to look after us. She was a local Aboriginal woman whose name was Winnie. Rebecca and I loved her.'

Archie notices that Kane's face softens when he mentions her.

'Later on, when I was older, Winnie brought her daughter over to Marvell Street and one thing led to another. The long and the short of it is that I knocked her up in the sleep-out.'

'You've got a wonderful way with words, Dad.'

'Sorry, son. I made love to her daughter, and she became preggers. Is that better?'

'What was Winnie's daughter's name?'

There is another long pause while Kane thinks about her. 'Her name was Ronnie. I think it was short for Rhonda, but I only knew her as Ronnie.'

'Did you ever see your baby?'

'No,' Kane answers emphatically, shaking his head from side to side.

Archie steers the jeep, looking alarmed.

'After Winnie told my father about her daughter's pregnancy, Dad became unbelievably angry with me and he forbade me ever to visit her. He told me if it became public knowledge that I was the father of her child, I'd disgrace the Stenmark name. He said if I ever admitted to having a child with the Aboriginal girl, he'd strike me out of the will. I had to swear to him that I would never reveal it, and never to go near her again. My father said she was part of the curse that the elders had placed on his father.'

'Poor Ronnie . . . What happened to her?'

'I heard she came to the hotel one day when she was almost at the end of her pregnancy. With her belly out and proud, she wanted to find me, but when I wasn't there, my father slung her some petty cash from the till and sent her away, telling her she was never to set foot in the place again, or he'd have her hunted down. I heard she threw the money back at him and disappeared back to the bush.'

'I see.'

'When her daughter was old enough, Ronnie sent her off to boarding school, but I've heard on the grapevine that after sending her child away, Ronnie appeared lost. She'd go off on walkabouts on her own, and lots of people reported seeing her aimlessly roaming the streets of Byron Bay like a homeless person. It's common knowledge that she was the town's vagrant.'

'Dad, you abandoned the mother of your child!'

'In those days, intermarriage was looked on as a catastrophe, Archie. It was even against the law. Many thought mixed-race children should be drowned at birth because half-castes didn't belong on either side. Some said that God made black men and God made white men, but the devil created the half-caste.'

'For god's sake, Dad, you're a disgrace! How could you walk away like that? Didn't you feel any responsibility at all?'

Kane rubs his brow. Archie is making him feel so incredibly guilty.

'What are you going to do now? Are you going to face up to it? Are you going to try to find your daughter now that you're back in town?'

'It's too late now, Archie.'

'Is that why you never came back here?' Archie asks.

When Kane refuses to answer him, Archie figures that this could definitely be one of the major reasons why he has stayed away. The thought disgusts him.

'Well, I want you to find her, and what's more, I want you to introduce her to me. I want to meet her.'

'I can't, Archie.'

'Dad, it's time you took on some responsibility. It's time to accept that she is part of you . . . She's a part of us.'

'It all sounds so easy to you, Archie, but the Stenmarks are going to go ballistic if they find out there's an indigenous girl in the family tree.'

'To hell with anyone else, Dad! To hell with the Stenmarks! It's our life, and it's time we took it by the horns. It's time you owned up to the truth, because together, we may be able to help this girl.'

'It's all too hard, son.'

'Hey, why don't we call into the fruit and veg barn before we return to our guesthouse?'

'No, no, no! Archie, we can't go in there,' Kane protests, shaking his head vigorously.

'Why not? There's no time like the present. I'm turning in, and we're going to meet a member of our immediate family.'

After pulling up in the parking area at the side of the fruit and veg co-op, Archie manages to convince his father to enter the barnlike structure to find his daughter. The pair strides past some picnic tables out front where some families are consuming gelato under an awning, and they enter the huge barn. A heady mixture of coffee, spices, vegetables, and fresh fruit fills their nostrils as they search the wide aisles for Kane's daughter. Instead of examining the artfully displayed produce that has been placed in large wicker baskets along each aisle, the pair are searching for a member of their family.

The first girl they encounter has dark curly hair, but she doesn't look local enough. Thinking that she may have immigrated from the Middle East, the pair discount her as a possibility. The second girl they encounter is a bouncy blonde with a flawless complexion, but although she is an excellent example of what eating fresh produce can do for your skin, they quickly discount her as well. After unsuccessfully searching the entire barn for Kane's daughter, they give up their search, and after randomly selecting two mangoes and a bar of chocolate, they make their way up to the cashier. Behind the till, immediately in front of Kane, is a dark girl with jet-black hair scrunched up on top of her head. The girl appears to be about 24, and she possesses mesmerising eyes.

'Next, please!' she calls as she locks eyes with Kane, who immediately turns into a pillar of salt. She has to reach over and take the mangoes from his hands to ring them up. 'How are you today?' she asks chirpily.

Kane mumbles, 'Good, thanks' in response.

'These mangoes came in this morning,' she proffers. 'I love the smell of them.'

The girl sniffs each one before placing it into a brown paper bag. After she takes the bar of chocolate from Kane and begins to tabulate the total, he examines her face and finds it to be quite astounding.

Somehow her genetic make-up has caught the best of both races. She's an exotic queen, and what's more, he's positive that she is his daughter. If only he'd selected more items to prolong the encounter at the checkout!

Archie, who is standing behind his father, examines the girl's face too and he can discern a definite resemblance to Kane. He can also see that she is carrying some wonderful characteristics that she must have inherited from her mother ... her penetrating eyes for example.

Kane blushes when she looks up at him to give him his change, and when she hands over his bag of items he hears her say, 'Have a wonderful day now.'

The father and son stumble out of the store and around to their jeep.

'Wow, that was amazing! She's amazing!' Archie croons.

After settling back into their seats, the father and son remain motionless for some time, both contemplating what has just taken place. Archie notices that Kane appears embarrassed, and he wonders if his foster father is feeling guilty about how stupid he has been not to try to find his daughter before now.

'Do you know her name, Dad?' he asks.

Kane shakes his head.

'You don't even know her bloody name, do you? She's your daughter and she's nameless!'

'I never did know it,' Kane defends.

'Man, you sure did run a mile. You didn't even stay around long enough to find out your own child's name.'

'Quit the guilt, Archie. I admit I was an arsehole, but I regret it now, OK?'

'Sorry, Dad. I know times were different then, but you didn't face up to what you'd done. You didn't face it like a grown man . . . You just ran off like a bloody coward.'

Kane stares straight ahead, expressionless, but inside, he is full of regret. Even his son is balling him out for his pathetic behaviour.

'You owe that girl big time, you know, but I wonder if she'll even give you the time of day after you abandoned her like you did.'

'Can't you see it was difficult for me, Archie? I had no choice back then, and after all this time, I can't just bowl up to her and say, "Hi, I'm your long-lost father!"'

'Well, if you can't face her, Dad, I can.'

'No, Archie. Neither of us can confront her.'

'I disagree. I can ask her to meet up with me and I'll say that I have something to tell her about her father.'

'What?'

'I'll tell her you're a prize, arsehole! Yes, I'll tell her you're a pathetic loser and that we should join forces to hunt you down.'

'Archie, you are killing me.'

'You deserve it.'

Chapter 11

THE BAY CAFÉ

The following day, Archie revisits the fruit and veg co-op on his own, and he introduces himself to the beautiful Aboriginal girl, who tells him that her name is Alkira. In a quick conversation, he announces that he has information about her father that she should know about, and he invites her to meet him at the Bay Café after she finishes work.

Archie is the first to arrive at the café in the late afternoon and Roxanne Jarvis welcomes him warmly at the door.

'Hello, Archie. Nice to see you again. Are you on your own?'

'Hi, Roxanne. There'll be two of us,' he replies, and she leads him to a table with a view over the sea.

'Will your father be joining you, Archie?' she asks as she places two menus on the table.

'No, Roxanne. He's gone fishing,' he answers.

'I'd go fishing with him anytime,' she says with a wink.

After this remark, Archie raises his eyebrows, and they stay that way until the indigenous girl arrives at the Bay Café's entrance. Roxanne leads the girl to Archie's table.

'Hello, Archie.' She smiles, and Archie stands to greet her.

'Hello, Alkira,' he responds, helping her to draw in her chair.

'You're a gentleman,' she compliments.

'Thank you for agreeing to meet me, Alkira,' he begins. 'You must be wondering what the hell this is all about.'

'You have some knowledge about my father?' she asks, wasting no time.

'Yes, I do. I believe we are part of the same family.'

'Really? Are you sure about that?'

'Before we begin, would you like something to drink, Alkira?'

She nods, and after a short discussion, the pair order two freshly squeezed orange juices from Roxanne.

'Alkira, I haven't told you my surname yet. I'm Archie Stenmark.'

'Hi, Archie. My name is Alkira Merinda,' she offers immediately.

'I love your name,' Archie responds. 'I can't tell you how excited I am to hear you say it.'

'Why does it make you so excited, Archie?' Alkira asks, thinking that it's quite a strange statement.

'Because I think . . . I think we have the same father.'

'Are you having me on, Archie? You can't be at all serious. You are joking with me, right?'

'I'm deadly serious, Alkira.'

'Archie, we don't look remotely alike, so I doubt that we are related in any way.'

'I know we look different, Alkira, but that's because we have different mothers.'

'You're confusing me, Archie. I'm an Aboriginal girl, and in case you have poor eyesight I'm black. Look at my skin.' Akira rubs her fingers along her dark arm. 'How could you possibly figure that we could be from the same family? For heaven's sake, be serious!'

'It's a long story, Alkira. Have you got the time to hear it?'

'I'm here, aren't I? And I must say, Archie, I'm very curious to hear you out.'

The freshly squeezed orange juices arrive just as Archie asks, 'Is your mother's name Ronnie?'

'Yes, Archie. Her name is Ronnie . . . It's short for Rhonda, and she's in hospital at the moment.'

'I'm very sorry to hear that, Alkira.'

'She has a serious heart condition, but go on with your story.'

Archie sips on his orange juice, wondering how to start.

'You saw my father at the fruit and veg barn when we came in yesterday. Well, his name is Kane Stenmark.'

'Yes, I do believe I saw him briefly. I think he bought two mangoes and some chocolate.'

'Well, let me tell you what I think happened. For many years your grandmother was the housekeeper at the Stenmark home on Marvell Street. My father told me her name was Winnie, and that she used to look after him when he was a child. Later on, when my father was older, he got to know her daughter, Ronnie, and the long and short of it is, that my father got her pregnant.'

'You're joking with me, Archie.'

'It's true.'

'My grandmother's name was Winnie, and as I told you, my mother is called Ronnie,' Alkira concedes.

'There you go, Alkira. You were the baby that came from the union of Ronnie Merinda and Kane Stenmark.'

Alkira is incredulous at this information. Her jaw drops, and Archie can see that she is having a great deal of trouble taking it all in.

'Archie, I never knew who my father was. My mother brought me up on her own in the local clan, but she always refused to talk about my father. I thought he'd died or that something had happened to him. I suppose I haven't got jet-black skin like most of my tribe, and maybe I knew there was a white man in the mix somewhere along the line, but to think that my actual father is a Stenmark . . . That's very scary.'

'Why is it so scary?'

'Because I've been told to stay away from the Stenmarks, that's why.'

'Was there a reason you were told to stay away?' Archie enquires.

'Because they have a curse on them.'

'I'm a Stenmark,' Archie declares. 'Do you think there's a curse on me?'

'Yes, there could well be, Archie. Now by the sound of things, there could be one on me too. We could both be cursed.'

After a nervous giggle, there is a pause in the conversation, during which both of them sip on their orange juices while they consider the situation at hand.

Alkira looks squarely at Archie. 'How do you fit into the picture then?' she asks.

'Kane Stenmark met my mother in Nimbin and fell in love with her. She died of breast cancer when I was 2 and Dad brought me up on his own. I know it sounds crazy, Alkira, but somehow both of us are part of the same family.'

'Why have you come to Byron Bay, Archie? Have you come to visit your family?' Alkira asks.

'Well, to tell you the truth, Alkira, I've come here to do a little research.'

'Into what?'

'I'm a writer, and my editor has asked me to write about the curse that was placed on the Stenmark family. You don't happen to have any inside knowledge about it, do you?'

'Everyone around here knows about it, Archie. I've known about it since childhood. My mother told me that my mob pointed the bone at Joseph Stenmark when he fenced off sacred land on Broken Head back in 1880.'

'Tell me what pointing the bone means,' Archie asks, digging for first-hand information. Alkira immediately becomes pensive.

'We sometimes call it pourri-pourri,' she explains. 'It happens when a tribe member wants to seek vengeance on someone else.'

'Who pointed the bone at my great grandfather?'

'Our elders did. When Joseph Stenmark locked them out of their sacred meeting ground, where my tribe had congregated for over 65,000 years, they pointed the bone at him. That's what started off the curse.'

'He upset them?'

'That's an understatement Archie! He disrupted our song-lines … the songs that sang our world into existence. These songs revealed the creation of the land.'

'Oh?'

'We believe an unsung land is a dead land, and if we forget the songs we lose our way. Joseph Stenmark interrupted the footprints of our ancestors when he blocked the tracks that connected all the tribes of our nation.'

'Wow! No wonder the elders were angry.'

'They were furious.'

'Do you think the curse will ever stop?'

'In my opinion, if this problem of exclusion continues unresolved, the curse will always continue.'

'I understand that many tragedies have befallen the Stenmark family over the years,' Archie fields.

'That's right. I've heard there has been one tragedy after another.' Alkira sips on her orange juice again.

'Do you know why I've been working at the fruit and veg co-op each summer, Archie?' she asks.

'Why do you work there?' he asks.

'To earn money so that I can study land rights. You may not know it, but I've just finished my law degree in Sydney, and it's my great hope that one day I'll be able to assist my people to get their sacred meeting place back.'

'Alkira, have you thought that it might be an advantage to be a Stenmark? The name may open doors for you.'

'I'm sure that idea won't go down too well with my mob,' she cautions.

'If you look on the bright side, Alkira, it might be an advantage, as we're a rich and powerful family, you know.'

After this remark, Alkira suddenly rises from the table and disappears through the café's French doors to escape onto the veranda. Once outside she grasps tightly onto one of the veranda posts and begins to sob. Concerned that he has upset her, Archie follows Alkira, but when he catches up with her, he finds her crying into a napkin that she has inadvertently brought outside with her.

'Are you all right?' he asks, touching her lightly on the arm.

'I'm in shock, Archie. I can't believe I'm one of them.'

Tears cascade from Alkira's beautiful cheeks, and while she is dabbing at them with her napkin Archie's heart goes out to her.

'I know it's a lot to take in all at once, Alkira,' he sympathises as she buries her face deeper into the napkin. 'I only found out about it two days ago myself.'

'You didn't know either?' she asks, as she removes the napkin from her face.

'I had no idea until Jimmy let it out at the Aboriginal camp. I presume he must have known about it all along.'

'Jimmy told you, but he's kept it a secret from me all these years!'

'Kane may have sworn him to secrecy,' Archie ventures.

'They're bastards, both of them! How dare they play with my life like that!'

'I agree . . . It appears they have both been conspiring to keep it a secret, Alkira.'

'Why would your father keep it from you, Archie?'

'I guess he was too embarrassed to admit it,' Archie ventures.

'What a jerk!'

'Yes, I agree with you. He's been a despicable jerk. We should both gang up on him and give him a bloody hard time.'

Alkira's face takes on a serious demeanour. 'Archie, he abandoned my mother when she was pregnant. He discarded her like trash, leaving her to fend for herself. The poor woman had to raise me on her own.'

'In my opinion, he should be hauled over the coals for abandoning you, Alkira. He owes you big time.'

'He does,' she sobs.

'The only thing I can say in Dad's favour is that he looked after me when my mother died, and he brought me up on his own,' Archie defends.

Alkira wipes the tears from her face. Archie's news has obviously unsettled her, and she finds herself struggling to stay in control. In her wildest dreams, she could not have considered belonging to the dreaded Stenmark family, because up to this point the entire concept of being directly related to them had been quite inconceivable. They are her enemies, for god's sake!

After a long silence, Archie coaxes Alkira back inside, and when she has settled herself back at the table, the pair sip on the remainder of their orange juice. Although he knows that Alkira has been upset by his revelation, Archie has another important thing on his mind to ask her before they part.

'Alkira, I don't mean to spring this on you, but the Stenmarks are having a celebration next Sunday afternoon for Uncle Abel's fiftieth birthday. He's the one who runs the Sands Hotel. They plan to hold the private function in the hotel's beer garden, and I'd love it if you came along with me as my date. We both deserve to be there because we are part of the family, and I think it's important that we take our place with the other family members. I desperately need your support.'

'The Stenmarks will kick me out, Archie.'

'They'll have to kick both of us out, Alkira, because I promise you that I won't be leaving your side.'

'I'm sorry, but it's not a good idea, because if I attend, it will be like sleeping with the enemy. But give me time to think about it, Archie. I still have to get my head around being linked to this diabolical family in the first place.'

Archie is pleased that Alkira has not refused him outright.

When Roxanne Jarvis notices that Archie and Alkira are preparing to leave, she rushes to make out their bill, but when Archie is paying it, Roxanne utters, 'Say hello to that sexy father of yours, Archie.'

The pair depart from the café without responding to Roxanne's comment, both wishing to ignore her unwitting faux pas.

Chapter 12

WATEGOS BEACH

After a restless night reliving some of the horrendous massacres that Rebecca had described two evenings ago, Archie feels quite sluggish when he wakes up. Initially, he is tempted to stay in bed to catch up on some much-needed sleep, but when he checks the weather outside his window, it promises to be such a glorious summer's day that he decides to cycle out to Wategos Beach for a morning swim.

After riding his rented bicycle in a south-easterly direction for a couple of kilometres, he reaches the celebrated beach. He parks his cycle adjacent to one of the magnificent houses on Marine Parade, known locally as Millionaire's Row, and he steps down from the roadside to the sandy beach.

Wasting no time, Archie rushes towards the ocean, but as he enters the water, he notices that the waves are flowing from right to left across the beach. This unusual wave pattern puzzles him initially, but after thinking about it for a moment, he concludes that the beach must be facing due north rather than due east, which would account for the direction of the flow. With the conundrum settled in his mind, he swims out to the break to enjoy some exhilarating body surfing.

Feeling quite refreshed after his ocean swim, Archie returns to the back of the beach, where he stretches out on his towel and falls into a deep sleep. After many hours of lying on his stomach in the hot sun, he is awoken from his slumber by a curious seagull approaching too close to his head. When he sits up, Archie checks his watch and is surprised to find that he's been out like a light for close to four hours. Desperately needing a drink, he pulls on his T-shirt, gathers up his towel, and wanders off to find something to quench his thirst. At the west end of the beach, he finds an elegant restaurant called Raes, and after strolling onto its stylish terrace, he takes a seat under its pristine white sailcloth. From its pricey menu, he orders a serving of prawn-and-scallop dumplings, and to accompany it, he requests a bottle of sparkling mineral water.

While he waits in the corner of the terrace, Archie watches some brush turkeys scratching for food in the brush, but as he is observing their antics as they rustle about on the grass in front of him, his peripheral vision starts pixelating. Thinking he may have become too dehydrated after lying on the beach for so many hours, he gulps down some of his mineral water, but after swallowing it, he becomes nauseous. Thinking he may be suffering the effects of sunstroke, Archie decides to forego his dumplings. He quickly pays his bill and escapes down the restaurant's steps to retrieve his bike.

With flashes of light disrupting his vision, Archie mounts his bicycle and peddles resolutely towards his guesthouse. At one point on the way back, he becomes so unbalanced, however, that he swerves off the road and lands in some banksia bushes growing on the edge of the road. After vomiting into them, he wipes his face with his beach towel, and feeling quite wretched, he doggedly peddles the final kilometre towards his guesthouse.

At the Pacific House, Archie dumps his bicycle out front and scrambles into the room that he shares with his father. Once inside, he strips off his clothes to check himself in the full-length mirror, but he is alarmed by his reflection. His back is a blanket of scarlet-coloured sunburn and the there are scores of clear blisters on each shoulder. He knows he is in trouble because some of them are as big as ten-cent coins. When Archie checks behind his knees, he finds that the skin there is a particularly deep shade of crimson. After deciding to gulp down some aspirin in a bid to relieve his throbbing headache and aching legs, he stretches out on his stomach on the top of his single bed. Later, when Kane returns to the Pacific House, he finds Archie lying in the nude, shaking with a fever.

'You bloody idiot, Archie! Look at you. You look as if you've been roasted in an oven!'

'I'm sore, so sore, Dad . . . and I'm cold,' Archie whimpers.

'Did you apply any sunscreen?'

'No. I fell asleep on the beach at Wategos after my swim.'

'It looks dreadful, son.'

'I know.'

'Archie, I know about three sunburn remedies, so leave it to me,' Kane states confidently. He covers Archie in a light cotton sheet and leaves him on the bed, while he dashes out to buy some aloe vera gel, oatmeal, turmeric powder, potatoes and a bottle of vinegar. After returning to the guesthouse with his collection of disparate items, Kane announces, 'First, I'll gently apply the aloe vera gel to your back and legs, Archie, because it'll cool you down ... It's a natural remedy.'

He gently smooths the gel over his son, and Archie immediately feels its cooling effect.

'You're very burned behind your knees, you know,' Kane observes.

'I know, Dad. They're bloody sore and my legs are aching.'

'Now I'm going to run a cool oatmeal bath for you, son. I'll mix the oatmeal into a paste, and then I'll sprinkle some turmeric powder in with it. It should give you some relief.'

'How do you know all this, Dad?'

'Well, you can take the boy out of Byron, Archie, but you can't take Byron out of the boy.'

'That's for sure,' he answers.

When Kane announces that it's ready, Archie gently lowers himself into the oatmeal bath and remains there for about twenty minutes until the heat subsides from his body. In the bath, it is the first time that Archie has felt calm since he returned from the beach.

'We still have a few more remedies up our sleeve, Archie. We still have vinegar mixed with water and there's raw potato still to come.'

'You're a bloody quack, Dad,' he retorts. 'Hey, Dad, I haven't told you yet that I met up with your daughter the other day.'

Kane stops in his tracks, raises his eyebrows, and returns to the bathroom door.

'You didn't waste any time, did you?'

'I met her at the Bay Café, and I told her the history of how you came to be her father. She didn't believe me at first, so I told her about Winnie and Ronnie. When I finally convinced her, she was furious that you had deserted her mother.'

'Archie, stop throwing shade at me. It was different back then. Everyone wanted me to leave Ronnie well alone.'

'Everyone but Ronnie! You abandoned her, Dad, and you'll have to wear it. Aren't you going to approach her daughter to make an apology?'

'I've been thinking about it, but she may refuse to see me.'

'You won't know until you try.'

'Did you find out her name?'

'It's Alkira – Alkira Merinda.'

'That's pretty.'

'Times have changed, Dad. You've returned home after two and a half decades, and it's time you made amends.'

Kane remains silent.

'I've invited Alkira to come with me to the birthday luncheon at the beer garden, but I don't think she's too keen on the idea. She said she'd think about it, but she could easily refuse to have anything to do with us.'

'OK, Archie. You've convinced me. You're right. It is time I talked to her. I'll do the right thing for once and I'll go to the fruit and veg barn to introduce myself, OK?'

'Good for you, Dad!' Archie calls from the bath, delighted that his father is taking on some responsibility at last.

Chapter 13

THE FRUIT AND VEG CO-OP

When Kane arrives at the fruit and veg co-op, his timing is accidentally perfect because Alkira is about to go on a break.

'Hello, Alkira,' he greets cheerily. 'I'm Kane Stenmark, your long-lost father.'

Alkira's beautiful face freezes.

'I can understand it if you refuse to speak to me. You may even want to slap my face, Alkira, but I'm here to apologise to you, and I'd like a chance to talk if that's at all possible.'

Alkira does not answer him. With a deliberate movement, she locks her till and without looking at Kane, she hands the keys to a colleague and struts outside. After taking a seat at one of the picnic tables out front, she holds her head in her hands. Remaining in limbo for a second or two, Kane wonders if he should follow her out, and after deciding to throw caution to the wind, he meanders slowly out to the front, where he takes a seat opposite his daughter. He's pleased when Alkira doesn't move away from the picnic table.

'Can I buy you a juice?' he asks.

Alkira removes her hands from her face. 'A fresh orange juice would be nice,' she answers politely. Kane orders two juices from the bar nearby and returns.

'I have no right to expect you to give me the time of day after abandoning you and your mother as I did,' he begins as he hands the juice to her. 'The only thing I can say in my defence is that it wasn't complete abandonment.'

Alkira raises an eyebrow in disbelief at this remark.

'Someone had to pay your school and university fees, Alkira,' Kane informs her.

'You paid for me to go to college and university?' she asks incredulously.

Kane nods.

'That's very kind of you. Did it assuage your guilt at all?'

'Somewhat,' Kane answers.

Alkira looks down and sips on her juice.

'I have nothing to say to you because I think you are a despicable person. I've even heard that you were run out of town when you were younger, so I don't trust you and I never will. The only positive thing I can think of to say to you is that I like your son,' she declares.

'Thanks. I'm very proud of him. He's become a successful writer, you know.'

'Is that so?' Alkira replies, appearing disinterested.

'I know we are off to a rocky start, Alkira, but I'd like to make amends for my disgraceful actions in the past. I deeply regret what I've done, and the only thing I can say in my own favour is that I've given you a wonderful gift – the gift of an education. It's an important start in life, and I hope that in a tiny part of your heart, you can forgive me.'

'I'll never forgive you. You have no idea how desperate my mother and I were. We were destitute and hungry, while you were oblivious to our plight. How could you desert us like that? My poor mother has been poverty-stricken all her life, and she nearly died a couple of weeks ago – not that you'd care!'

'I'm so sorry to hear that, Alkira. I had no idea. You must appreciate that your mother and I were from vastly different backgrounds. In those days, it was forbidden to cross the line between the two . . . My family forbade it.'

'You've crossed the line today. Have you come here to claim me as a Stenmark?' Alkira challenges.

'Uhhh . . . Well, I *am* your father.'

'I want to make it clear to you that the Stenmarks are my enemies. My mob has cursed you all.'

'I'm not here to claim you, Alkira. I'm merely here to apologise. I'm keen to make amends, if that's at all possible. Archie and I would like to get to know you.'

Alkira looks away into the distance without answering.

'I hear Archie has invited you to the Sands Hotel this weekend for the birthday luncheon for my brother,' Kane continues.

'Yes, he has, but I'm not going.'

'Why don't you come? It will be an opportunity to bridge the gap.'

'Why would I want to do that?'

'Because you are in a unique position to be a catalyst for change, Alkira. That's why.'

'How so?'

'My generation has been very confrontational. We've excluded your people from any decision making and we've left you sidelined, but your generation has the opportunity to achieve an accord. Rather than remaining at loggerheads, don't you think it's time for us all to work towards reconciliation? You're in a unique position to be a champion for your people and I'm sure you could bring about change.'

'Yes, I suppose I am in a unique position now,' Alkira allows, thinking she is the only person she knows with a foot in both camps.

'You have an opportunity to heal the wounds,' Kane proffers.

This comment seems to strike a chord with Alkira, who answers, 'I do believe that reconciliation is the way forward for my people.' She nods slowly as if she's thinking it through.

'If we are serious about changing things, we should put all the groups with a common interest together so they can negotiate.'

'I agree wholeheartedly with that too,' Kane replies before standing up. 'I won't keep you from your work any longer, Alkira. I want to thank you for allowing me to apologise to you, and please think about joining Archie on Sunday, because it would mean a lot to both of us to have you there. If you come, it could even be the first step towards reconciliation. You'll find that most of the Stenmarks are decent people . . . well, everyone apart from my brother and his family, that is.'

Chapter 14

REBECCA STENMARK'S HOUSE

It takes three days and three nights before Archie Stenmark feels well enough to call his aunt again. He has spent these days and nights recovering from his painful sunstroke. When he wakes up on the fourth day, however, the pain has finally gone, and although his skin is peeling, he considers that he is well enough to hear the final episode of Rebecca's story.

It is seven o'clock in the evening when he arrives at her house for dinner, and he tells her he has commenced in earnest to write about the curse. Rebecca is delighted to hear that someone is finally putting pen to paper about it, but Archie cautions her that his progress has been quite slow because of his sunstroke ordeal. Rebecca is completely sympathetic.

'I know first-hand what it's like, Archie,' she tells him. 'I've been in agony too, just like you. I have the type of skin that burns to a crisp in the Byron Bay sun, and I've already had a couple of melanomas cut out.'

Keen to find out more about the line of tragedies that have befallen the Stenmark family, Archie tries to pick up the threads of their last conversation. 'I think the last time we spoke, we were up to the death of Joseph Stenmark, weren't we? I'm wondering what happened to his son, Jake.'

'Oh, when my father was old enough, he ran the hotel!' Rebecca exclaims. 'He married the local schoolteacher, whose name was Elizabeth, but unfortunately, our mother died of cancer quite young, leaving the three of us to grow up without her. Didn't your father ever tell you anything about us, Archie?'

'No, Dad never talked about the family ever. It's as if he blocked you all from his mind once he left Byron. He did tell me who looked after the three of you after your mother died though. It was an Aboriginal woman named Winnie, wasn't it?'

'Yes, it was Winnie. Kane and I thought she was wonderful, especially when she told us the legends of her people, but Abel thought her legends were risible.'

'This could have been what sparked the beginnings of his bigotry,' Archie advances.

'Possibly.'

'Jake must have given his sons the biblical names that his mother was going to use,' Archie suggests.

'Yes, that's right. Dad hadn't forgotten that his mother was going to call the twins Kane and Abel.'

'Did you work with Abel at the hotel when you were older, Rebecca?'

'Yes, I did once I got old enough, but in the end, Abel assumed complete control of it, especially when his father took ill. After he died of pneumonia, Abel enlarged the beer garden and renovated the interior, which made the Sands Hotel a popular destination for both locals and visitors.'

'It's a great drinking hole,' Archie agrees.

'Over the years, the townspeople have a tradition of frequenting the pub at sunset, because it's a great place to have a tipple late in the day when the sun casts a warm glow over Julian Rocks. Lately, the numbers have swelled at the Sands, with patrons arriving in their hordes. They pile into the hotel during the afternoon and many of them stay on until later in the evening when the pub becomes a dance hall.'

'So Abel became the publican. He must be regarded as the good seed of the family,' Archie proffers, a little tongue-in-cheek.

'Well, let's say he became the problem solver. He could fix most things. I think he must have inherited these skills from Joseph. Abel married an actress from Sydney named Stephanie Stewart. I think you met her when you first got here. She was a beauty in her day, but she's very highly strung. She's a very theatrical person by nature, always playing roles. She knows many people in Sydney's film world, and she regularly invites them to stay at the pub to play charades with her. She's turned the hotel into a chic destination for the artsy crowd, and she's become a kind of fixture at the pub on Sundays, surrounding herself with all sorts of actors, directors, and playwrights.'

'She creates drama in the beer garden then,' Archie quips.

Rebecca nods knowingly. When the main course is over and it's time for dessert, Rebecca heads for the kitchen to retrieve a small pavlova that she'd baked earlier that afternoon. As Archie spoons the delicious meringue, cream and fruit into his mouth, he appreciates Rebecca's excellent culinary skills.

'Corrie is lucky to have a chef on the premises,' he flatters.

'The poor boy needs a few perks,' she answers.

When Archie finishes his dessert, he's keen to shift the conversation onto his father. 'Was my dad always the bad seed of the family?' he asks.

Rebecca pauses mid-spoonful to reflect on this question. 'Kane and I have always had a special bond, Archie,' she discloses while holding a full spoonful of pavlova in the air. 'Although I'm much younger than he is, we've always got along really well. When he was a teenager, he was quite a worry though. He was always hanging out with the Aboriginal boys and supplying them with drinks.

'Why was he always chosing to be with them?'

'I suppose he liked their grit, tenacity and strong will to survive. When they wanted to party, he was the one they came to for all the alcohol they needed. Abel hated that.'

'Was Dad always rebellious?'

'Well, now let me see . . . He started acting up pretty early, often disrupting the classes at school. He was expelled at one stage for hoisting an Aboriginal flag up the school flagpole. He hated the way his indigenous mates were being denied fair treatment, and although he was quite young, he was always trying to make a point.'

'He told me about the flagpole incident. It sounds as if he had a social conscience at an early age.'

'Yes, Kane did. He would always tell the truth, but sometimes the truth hurt those around him.'

'That sounds like Dad. I've heard there was a fuss about a missing girl.'

'How on earth did you hear about that, Archie?'

'Your friend Roxanne Jarvis brought it up initially, but I also heard about it when the next-door neighbour at Marvell Street recognised Dad. Mrs Boyle accused him of murdering the girl.'

'That subject is off limits I'm afraid. It's a subject never to be spoken about in the Stenmark family.'

'Why not?'

'When an indigenous girl went missing after the bachelor and spinster ball in 1975, a lot of people blamed your father, and to get away from it all, he had to leave town. As a family, we have all decided to keep quiet about it.'

'Why did everyone blame him?'

'Because he'd had an altercation with the girl earlier that evening. He had scratches on his arms to prove it. Kane always swore he knew nothing about her disappearance, but no one in Byron Bay believed him.'

'When did he leave?'

'About a week after the B&S ball. Abel had had enough of his nonsense, and he kicked him out of the beer garden.'

'That's when he decided to run away,' Archie states.

'Yes, the search for the indigenous girl turned out to be a fruitless exercise, and to this day she remains a missing person in a cold case.'

'Dad has never spoken to me about the incident, but I suspect he found an accepting community over in Nimbin, where he could hide amongst the alternative crowd.'

'I believe that's what he did, Archie.'

'Did he ever come back here?' Archie enquires.

'No, he couldn't. With everyone in Byron Bay thinking he'd killed the girl, it was best he stayed well away. Even his friend Jimmy suspected him of abducting his sister. Have you met Jimmy yet? He's the one with the horrific scars on his face.'

'Yes, I have met him, Rebecca. Dad told me that a man glassed him in the beer garden.'

'Oh, it was dreadful, Archie. Those "tradies" should have been jailed. Abel has a cruel streak, you know. He had no sympathy for the indigenous boys on that occasion and it was clearly not their fault.'

'Abel seems to have little tolerance for integration,' Archie observes.

'None at all, whereas Kane has always been the opposite. When he was younger, he actually won the older tribesmen's confidence and he was able to witness some of the local tribe's most secret ceremonies. Kane told me that Jimmy took him to places where the men conducted their fertility rites under the cabbage tree palms. Not many white men can boast that.'

'That sounds like very secretive men's business to me,' Archie responds. 'Do you think he was kicked out of the pub because he was identifying with both cultures?'

'Yes, that's exactly what it was, Archie. Kane identified with the plight of his mates, but it wasn't an easy position for him to hold. He was constantly defending them from the local bigots who dismissed the indigenous boys as incompetent savages. Most of his local white peers were xenophobic, happy if the blackfellows stayed out of their way and remained invisible. Each time Kane defended them, his white mates would accuse him of siding against them.'

'My dad must have felt as if he was between a rock and a hard place in those days,' Archie surmises.

'Yes, I think he was. In time, the hotel scene became an anathema to him, because there seemed to be one law for the whites and another for the blacks.'

'What happened on that last day?' Archie asks, keen to confirm the story his father had told him.

Rebecca sighs before gathering her thoughts.

'After a day of fishing with his mates, Kane and the indigenous boys arrived to have a drink in the beer garden. They ended up in a horrific fist fight, during which Jimmy's face was slashed. Abel threw Kane and his mates out, telling them never to come back. He even told Kane to never set foot in the place again, or he'd kill him.'

'That was a hideous threat!'

'Your father had a quick reply though, Archie.'

'What did he say?'

'"You can't get rid of me forever, Abel, because one-third of this place will always be mine, and there's nothing you can do about it!" Kane always held this ace up his sleeve, and Abel knew it.'

'After the fight, Dad must have made the decision to separate himself from the family,' Archie concludes.

'That's right. After he was banished, he disappeared and stayed out of sight. He could have died for all we knew. He'd become an embarrassment to the family, and except for me, no one seemed to care what had happened to him.'

'So Dad was the black sheep then – the bad seed of the family,' Archie concludes.

'His name was never to be spoken. Some of us had even thought his disappearance was yet another example of the elders' curse. Archie, that's all I have to tell you tonight . . . It's getting late again.'

Archie looks at his watch and it shows that it's 11:30 p.m. already. Rebecca walks him to the door, and once again he thanks her for the detailed family history lesson. When Rebecca hugs him at the door, her arms press onto Archie's sunburn, but he doesn't complain.

'The curse continues,' Rebecca confirms as she opens her front door to let him out.

'Rebecca, thank you again. You've been so generous with your time,' he acknowledges.

'I just hope I've been able to give you some background for your story,' she replies.

'You certainly have. I've been completely unaware of the Stenmark family history until now and I thank you sincerely for filling me in.'

'Now get to it, Archie. It's worth writing about.'

Chapter 15

ALKIRA'S APARTMENT

Against her better judgement, Alkira has agreed to accompany Archie to the birthday luncheon at the Sands Hotel. She is well aware that Abel Stenmark had previously discouraged members of her tribe from entering the beer garden, often discouraging them to such a point that they regarded it as out of bounds for them. She even remembers her mother telling her that in the early days, a sign once hung at the gate saying Whites Only.

By attending this birthday luncheon, Alkira is concerned that she may be crossing a line, especially when she considers the racist attitudes of the publican, who is today's guest of honour. Aware that Abel has the reputation for throwing her dark-skinned brothers out of the hotel – and not always for their poor behaviour – Alkira is wary. She has only to think about the horrific scars on Jimmy's face that resulted from a brawl in the beer garden, to understand the long-standing, prevailing racist attitudes.

During her short life, Alkira has come to realise that racism can strike at any time. At university, she could be minding her own business and suddenly be confronted by it. At these times, she needed a buttress of spirit to stand up to the belittlement. Alkira refused to be frightened by these racial slurs however, as she regarded them as taunts of subordination that she was prepared to resist. She'd made up her mind to stand up to subversion and she vowed to always testify to her own truth. Alkira wasn't sure if there was a higher power, but she believed in her own power, which gave her a personal stature and confidence that she had no intention of relinquishing. Alkira often wondered if God saw the injustices her people faced – or was he blind? He was no doubt loving and kind, but blind.

After deliberating at great length, Alkira decides to put on a brave face. Instead of being intimidated by the Stenmarks, she decides to face up to them, especially now that she's found out that she's one of them. Despite her resolve, some voices in the wind continue to urge her not to join the party, but she tries to fend them off.

After getting dressed for the luncheon, Alkira returns to her bathroom one last time to add a finishing touch to her outfit. She places a frangipani bloom behind one ear, and once it has been secured in place, she waits for Archie in her front hall. While she waits, Alkira imagines how she will feel when she reaches the beer garden gate. The thought of crossing the threshold petrifies her and she castigates herself for accepting Archie's invitation.

When Archie finally knocks on her apartment door, she knows the moment of truth has arrived and, with her stomach in a tangle, she pulls the door open.

'Wow, you look absolutely gorgeous!' Archie exclaims, admiring Alkira's beautiful face set off by the delicate frangipani blossom.

'I'm having second thoughts about going, Archie,' she declares immediately.

'We both deserve to be there, Alkira. We belong, and to hell with what anyone else thinks!'

Chapter 16

THE PACIFIC HOUSE

After a refreshing morning swim, Kane returns in the late morning to the Pacific House. As he approaches the building on his return, he appreciates its traditional architectural style. Like the family house on Marvell Street, the building is also a Queenslander, possessing wide verandas, plantation shutters and delicate fretwork. When Kane opens the door to his room, the ceiling fans are gently turning, evoking the carefree subtropical days of his childhood. On his bed, he finds a note.

"I'll see you at the beer garden Dad. I've left to pick up Alkira, Love Archie"

Kane looks at his watch and immediately realises that he hasn't left himself much time to dress for the luncheon. He immediately drops his shirt and board shorts on the white floorboards and rushes into the shower to wash off the salt and sand. After drying himself off with one of the guesthouse's soft bath towels, he checks himself in the magnified bathroom mirror. In close-up he is bitterly disappointed with his aging reflection, as his craggy face shows the ravages of time. To counteract this unfortunate phenomenon, he decides to dress as youthfully as possible for the luncheon, and with this in mind he reaches deep into his suitcase for his favourite outfit – a body-hugging black chamois T-shirt, a pair of stovepipe leather trousers, and his favourite studded riding boots.

After all this time away, Kane is edgy about showing up in front of his entire family, so to steady himself he pours a generous scotch into a tumbler that he finds on the top of the minibar. After adding some ice, he takes a sizeable swig, and struts nervously around the room searching for a cigarette to go with it. Kane knows there is a full package of Marlboros somewhere in the room, but for the life of him, he cannot locate it. In desperation, he places his scotch on the coffee table and starts rustling through his battered suitcase, hoping he'll find an old pack somewhere inside. His searching fingers finally discover an almost empty packet, and after hastily removing the last crumpled cigarette, he smooths it out and lights it up. Relishing the distinctive tobacco taste and the strong odour of his final Marlboro, Kane sinks back onto his bed to luxuriate in the haze.

'Thank god Roxanne has agreed to accompany me today.' He sighs aloud, aware of how desperately he needs her moral support. After finishing the cigarette, he rises from his bed to recheck himself in the mirror. 'I wonder if anyone at the luncheon will confront me about Matilda's disappearance,' he asks his reflection, but his stupefied aging face refuses to answer him. It just stares back accusingly, with every wrinkle and freckle evident.

'I'm such an ugly mongrel,' he finally declares, as he turns away in disgust.

There is a knock on the door to his room and when Kane flings it open, he countenances Roxanne Jarvis, who is standing before him on dangerously high heels wearing an extremely short silvery dress. When Roxanne vogues for him in various modelling poses in the doorway, Kane is impressed by her long shapely legs recently enhanced by a fake tan. Holding a half-finished bottle of beer in one hand and a cigarette in the other, she glances down at Kane's studded riding boots.

'You look ready for a showdown?' she fields.

'Am I ever!' Kane replies, clicking his heels and beckoning for her to come in.

'Don't worry, Kane. Your family will welcome you back with open arms. It may be Abel's birthday, but you'll be the one in the limelight,' she postulates.

'Like hell, Roxanne! My family tree is like a cactus bush – everyone on it is a prick.'

Roxanne laughs uproariously at his joke and after taking a swig from her beer bottle, she slings her body onto Archie's bed. When she looks up, however, she notices that Kane's face appears somewhat glum.

'What's the matter?' she asks.

'It's time to run through the procedure of our entry,' Kane tells her.

'How should we bloody well enter?' she enquires.

'The minute we come through the gate, I'm going to guide you over to the main table, and that's where we'll take our place right at the bloody centre. That's when everyone present will know that I'm back where I belong. I'll be announcing by that gesture, that I'm ready to be part of the family again. I'm bloody-well not going to sit anywhere else.'

Chapter 17

THE SANDS BEER GARDEN

Fluttering about in the afternoon breeze, scores of white balloons with black fifties printed on them dangle from the branches of the massive tree in the centre of the beer garden. As promised, Stephanie has organised the hotel staff to cover the picnic tables with white tablecloths, and on each is a huge platter filled with ice. Oysters, prawns, lobsters, and crabs spill from the platters in great abundance, supplied, of course, by Freckle from the Bay Fish Market. Beside these sumptuous seafood platters are salads of varying types, and for those who prefer meat, a BBQ is sizzling in the corner of the beer garden, ready to supply tender Angus steaks grilled rare medium or well done by two fellows wearing chef's hats.

A string quartet plays songs such as 'Let's Do It, Let's Fall in Love' as the invited guests search for their place names at assigned tables. Waiters hover around the guests as they settle, offering French champagne, wine, beer, or spring water.

Corrie Stenmark limps into the beer garden on his crutches with his friend Andy at his side, but en route, he is required to answer scores of questions from the guests about the size of the shark that attacked him, and even more details about his recovery. When he finally finds the cousins' table, he slumps exhaustedly into a chair beside Brett, a fit young lad with a swimmer's body, who is one of the host's two sons. Brett's brother Jude is the next one to mooch over towards the cousins' table to join them. He is a sight to be seen with multiple piercings in his ears, a nose ring and a dramatic Mohawk haircut.

Usually, Rebecca would have been with her partner at the main table, but after his untimely and painful death a few months ago, she enters on her own. After taking her seat at the main table, she waves to Corrie over at the cousins' table and then listens intently to the quartet, who, by this time, is playing 'It's a Wonderful World'. Wondering if it really is a wonderful world, Rebecca sits alone, waiting for Abel and Stephanie to join her.

The hosts are nowhere near, however, as they are still at the entry gate, welcoming guests. Dressed in a cream-coloured summer suit, Abel looks a lot like Tennessee Williams, while Stephanie, who is wearing an outrageously oversized straw hat, looks more like Greta Garbo. The brim of her colossal hat has been turned up at the front, fastened by a large diamond brooch. As she air-kisses the notable screen and TV personalities, each kiss has to be a careful manoeuvre, with the guests trying vainly to dodge her large brim.

Every head turns when Kane appears at the gate with Roxanne Jarvis on his arm. Many people haven't seen Kane for over two and a half decades, and they are eager to see what he looks like after such a long absence. When he strides purposefully towards the main table in his black leather trousers, studded riding boots and aviator sunglasses, they stare at him. Roxanne, who is tottering unsteadily at his side is still smoking on a cigarette. Rebecca greets the couple warmly when they join her at the main table, and they take their seats in the first vacant chairs they can find.

Having finished their welcoming duties, Abel and Stephanie make their way back towards the main table, only to find that their seats are occupied.

'Well, if it's not my long-lost brother in my seat,' Abel greets.

'Fuck off, Abel. It may be your birthday, but I don't give a shit,' Kane rejoins, stubbing his cigarette out on a side plate.

'Move, brother,' Abel orders, and there is a momentary stand-off.

'We were here first,' Roxanne declares possessively.

'Look at the place tags, brother . . . You're definitely in the wrong seats.'

After viewing the tags, Kane prudently decides that it is too early to make a fuss, and he stands up. 'Look, bro, for old times' sake I'll move along, but it's the last concession you'll get from me today,' he warns.

Abel shakes his head, thinking that it *is* like old times.

'I'm back to claim what's rightfully mine. You can't keep me away forever,' Kane mutters, while he and Roxanne shuffle noisily into their correct seats, allowing Abel and Stephanie to be seated at the centre of the main table.

When the quartet stops playing, Stephanie stands in front of the microphone, ready to begin her welcome speech. She is just about to start when Archie appears at the door with Alkira on his arm. When everyone's head turns from Stephanie to the handsome couple, she is forced to pause.

Archie looks as if he has just walked off a yacht, wearing a lightweight pale-blue summer suit, an open-necked white linen shirt, sandals, and a straw hat. Beside him, Alkira appears like a youthful Billie Holiday, wearing a virginal white dress and a frangipani bloom in her hair. Many of those present wonder if they have flown in from some film set to join Abel on his landmark birthday, but when they join the family at the cousins' table, they ponder about what close connection they have with the Stenmarks. After locating the nametag Archie & Friend, the pair take their seats beside Brett, Jude, Corrie, and his mate Andy. As they settle, Corrie's face suddenly breaks into a huge smile. He has recognised Alkira as the girl who saved him from the shark.

Still dwarfed by her huge hat, Stephanie begins her speech. 'Welcome, everyone. Today is indeed an auspicious occasion. Abel has turned 50 and we are all here to celebrate him finally reaching maturity!'

There are a few hoots and some polite claps when Stephanie delivers this remark, and she blows a kiss towards Abel.

'We are fortunate to have the entire Stenmark family present here today, and I'd like to welcome our friends who have come from as far as Western Australia, Queensland, Victoria, and South Australia, not to mention all you locals from the Byron Bay coast and hinterland.'

'Don't forget Nimbin!' Kane calls out, and the comment causes a few of the young people to giggle.

'I am delighted that all of you have come here to share this important occasion with us,' Stephanie continues, ignoring Kane's remark. 'I want you to know that it's the first time our entire family has been together in twenty-five years.'

Some of the guests politely clap when Stephanie delivers this statement, but the comment prompts Kane to stand up and swipe the microphone from Stephanie's hand. She attempts to get it back, but after a brief scrap Kane convinces her to step aside

'Remain still for just a moment, Stephanie,' Kane's voice booms over the microphone. 'I have something important to say before you start your speech.'

Stephanie reluctantly retreats to her chair.

'Ladies and gentlemen, I am Kane Stenmark, Abel's estranged brother. This birthday bash is supposed to include the entire Stenmark family, but ladies and gentlemen, our hosts are unaware of some important family members who are present here today. Let me tell you the truth. Stephanie and Abel are totally unaware of some of the members in their immediate family tree, but it is my intention here and now to fill in these details for them, so they remain ignorant no longer.'

The crowd falls silent, not knowing what to expect.

'First of all, let's focus on the main table, because up here, ladies and gentlemen, in pride of place, are the three Stenmark siblings of my generation. There is my darling sister, Rebecca, on my left, my controlling brother, Abel, in the centre, and then, of course, there's me. Sadly, Rebecca has recently lost her husband to a serpent, but Abel and I are fortunate to be here with our partners. Now then, Rebecca has one son, and many of you know him because he's been in the news lately. Her son, Corrie, is the one who narrowly escaped being taken by a great white shark a few weeks ago. Corrie, you don't have to stand up, mate. Just wave your crutch so everyone knows you've survived.'

As Corrie waves one of his crutches back and forth, everyone in the beer garden claps enthusiastically.

'Now to the birthday boy. Yes, you all know Abel, because he's the one who runs this wonderful hotel. You all know too that he is married to the actress here.' Kane waves his finger from Abel to Stephanie. 'Most of you are aware that they produced two boys, Brett and Jude. Stand up, boys.'

Brett and Jude stand and receive loud applause.

'I hear on the grapevine that one of you is a swimming star and that one of you is gay. I'm not sure which is which, but that's by the by. Just get on with it, I say.'

There is a murmur in the beer garden at this disclosure, with Abel in particular finding Kane's comments about his sons to be in poor taste.

'Let Stephanie finish her welcome,' he protests. 'It's not your bloody party, Kane. Give the microphone back.'

'Wait a moment, brother. This is the important bit, so hold your horses for a little longer, because your family tree is not as you think.'

'What are you saying?'

'Until a few days ago, ladies and gentlemen, my brother, Abel, and his wife had no idea that I have a son, who at 24, is a successful author. He's their nephew, but they knew nothing about him. So today I'd like to introduce him to you all. Stand up, Archie Stenmark.'

Archie reluctantly gets to his feet in his pale blue suit and stands sheepishly while everyone tentatively claps.

'That will be a surprise for some of you, I'm sure, but, ladies and gentlemen, are you ready for an even bigger surprise?'

Archie retakes his seat.

'There's more?' Abel asks incredulously.

'Yes, there certainly is more, bro. Ladies and gentlemen, I also have a daughter.'

There is a gasp as everyone wonders who it is.

'Please welcome to the family my lovely daughter, Alkira Stenmark.'

The guests turn once again to the cousins' table as Alkira reticently comes to her feet. Underneath her shy expression, Alkira is furious that Kane has introduced her as a Stenmark, but fearful of being rejected, she beams at the guests, who are immediately captivated by her winning smile. The crowd responds by bursting into wild accepting applause.

'Some of you may not know that it was my brave girl who dragged Corrie Stenmark to safety after his vicious shark attack,' Kane states, to even more enthusiastic applause.

'I just wanted you all to meet the family in its entirety,' Kane adds before handing the microphone back to Stephanie.

'Well, goodness gracious me! Our family is growing in front of my eyes! What a brave girl!' Stephanie quips before launching into her prepared accolades about her husband.

When the speeches are over and the quartet strikes up again, the cousins eagerly introduce themselves to Archie and Alkira, who have become instant celebrities at the gathering. Some of the guests venture over to them, eager to know who their mothers are, but Archie and Alkira prudently inform them that they will have to wait until the next family gathering to find out those personal details. Alkira turns to Corrie to ask him how he is recovering and he tells her that his wound is healing well.

'I've spent the last few days trying to find out who you are,' he discloses. 'None of my mates knew your name, even though they'd seen you out surfing countless times.'

'I'm Alkira,' she responds, 'and I'm led to believe that I'm your cousin.'

Alkira extends her hand to Corrie, and he clasps it warmly with both of his.

'You saved my life, Alkira. I wouldn't be here today if it wasn't for you.'

'You were looking pretty pale when the ambulance took you off, Corrie. I was wondering if you'd make it.'

'I managed to pull through, but I'll be forever in your debt, Alkira. They told me I was in the ambulance with your mother. How is she?'

'Oh, luckily, she pulled through too, Corrie. She's in a fragile state these days though. She's recuperating in Lismore.'

'I hope she soon gets better, Alkira,' Corrie remarks, reflecting briefly on his smelly ordeal in the ambulance.

While Corrie and Alkira are conversing, Jude is having a private conversation with his brother, Brett.

'I didn't know she was allowed in here,' Jude mutters, nodding in Alkira's direction.

'Jude, she's part of the family. Of course, she can be here,' Brett points out.

'But Dad always insisted that it's a "whites only" beer garden,' Jude persists.

'Jude, don't go there. Please hold your tongue,' Brett warns.

'Why not, Brett? Rules are rules,' he retorts.

Overhearing the brothers' conversation, Archie immediately deduces that Jude is referring to Alkira's presence in the beer garden.

'Jude, you've turned out to be a bigger bigot than your father,' he interjects.

'I'm just saying that she's breaking the hotel rules, that's all,' he responds.

'What rules?'

'The rules of the beer garden.'

'You can no longer segregate people in this country, Jude. It's against the current laws to preclude someone by race,' Archie reminds him.

'If you allow one in, the floodgates will be open for the whole bloody tribe,' Jude responds in a raised voice.

Overhearing the racial slur, Alkira immediately stands up. 'Let's go, Archie. We're leaving right now. I don't have to put up with this.'

Alkira turns on her heel and strides briskly towards the exit gate, and remembering he'd promised not to leave her side, Archie runs at a fast clip behind her.

As the pair disappear through the gate, the string quartet is striking up with some up-tempo music, and hearing them try their hand at Elvis's 'Blue Suede Shoes', Roxanne Jarvis is keen to strut her stuff on the boards. Dragging Kane behind her, Roxanne charges onto the dance floor and begins gyrating in front of him in a coquettish fashion. In response, Kane kisses her on the neck, but these moves provoke a strong reaction from Abel, who watches in horror as Roxanne simulates an orgasm as part of her dance moves.

Abel strides onto the floor, demanding that she behaves, but when she ignores him, he insists that Kane removes Roxanne from the beer garden. When Kane refuses to obey his brother, a nasty scene ensues, with each of the brothers attempting to punch each other's lights out. Observing the fracas, Abel's sons decide to separate them, and they drag the feuding pair from the floor.

When Archie and Alkira reach Alkira's apartment building two blocks farther up Jonson Street, they stop at the foot of the stairs.

'Well, Alkira, you've now been officially introduced to the Stenmark clan,' Archie ventures bravely.

'It was so embarrassing, Archie. I wasn't ready to be introduced as a Stenmark. My name is Alkira Merinda.'

'Dad did that because he's proud of you, Alkira. He couldn't let the occasion go by without announcing that you are part of his family.'

Tears flood Akira's eyes. 'He's taken a long time to come around to accepting me, hasn't he?' she sobs. 'He's hidden his secret for decades, and now he's suddenly gone public with it all.'

'I'm afraid he has. In the past, he would have considered it a sin to have had a child out of wedlock, but now, for some reason, he couldn't be prouder.'

'Archie, what you mean is that he was ashamed to have fathered a piccaninny child.'

'That may have been true in the past, Alkira, but times have dramatically changed since then, and now he wants everyone to know about you.'

'I'm so mad at him, Archie! I wasn't ready to be labelled a Stenmark. He's such a jerk, announcing it in front of everyone.'

'I know,' Archie agrees.

'And what about that freak, Jude? If there was a Ku Klux Klan in Australia, he and his father would both be members. Archie, I should never have gone!'

Chapter 18

MARVELL STREET

When Abel wakes up the next morning at Marvell Street, he is in a very disgruntled mood. He looks disparagingly at his wife, who is lying flat on her back in bed beside him, wearing a sleeping mask.

'I told you not to invite Kane to my birthday bash, Stephanie,' he reprimands.

'What are you on about?' she groans sleepily.

'He ruined it, as usual . . . just like he's ruined every other birthday I've ever had.'

'Ugh.'

'He's a bloody flake. He was a flake as a kid and he's still a bloody flake as an adult.'

'Well, why don't you give him a wide berth, darling? Just keep out of your brother's way.'

'Why did he come back? Everything was going smoothly without him, but he's returned out of nowhere like a bad smell.'

Stephanie turns over to face Abel, and after removing her mask, she gently strokes his cheek to soothe him. 'Kane's just a fly in the ointment, darling. Don't let him upset you,' she placates.

'While he's been off gallivanting around Sydney, I've been keeping all the bloody balls in the air,' Abel boasts.

'I know, darling . . . You're the reliable one of the family.'

'If Kane thinks he can march back here unannounced and upset the apple cart, he's got another think coming. Why in god's name did he return?'

'Darling, I've heard on the grapevine that he's returned to clear his name. Apparently, he's on a mission to find out what happened on the night of the bachelor and spinster ball all those years ago.'

Immediately sensing trouble, Abel's face pales. 'My brother is a bloody millstone around my neck, Stephanie. When he was out of the picture, I could pursue my dreams, but now that he's back, I have to deal with the irrational bastard at every step.'

'What dreams are you talking about, darling?'

'My dream for Broken Head, of course.'

'Oh, that! You haven't mentioned much about it lately, Abel. How are your plans coming along? Have you heard anything from the architect?'

'Actually, I'm expecting the model to be delivered to my office tomorrow morning.'

'Really, darling? How very exciting! You've waited a long time for this moment, haven't you?' Stephanie kisses Abel on the forehead.

'If you want to know the truth, Stephanie, I just can't wait to see the bloody thing.'

Chapter 19

NIRVANA

Over the past few years Abel has been secretively working on his grand plan to develop the Stenmark family's vast tract of land at Broken Head. He has been careful to keep it a secret until now because he anticipates there will be some strong opposition to it, especially from the local indigenous community, who still regard the land as theirs.

After finishing the scale model, Abel's architect has been busy setting it up in Abel's office all morning, and when Abel sees it for the first time, a huge smile lights up his entire face. The model shows off his dream perfectly.

Now that it is finally in his office, the time has come for him to show off his dream to his siblings, because as directors of Stenmark Inc., they will be required to put their signatures on the upcoming development application.

Abel decides to call Rebecca first, and once she has accepted his invitation to view the model, he calls Kane. When Kane hears Abel's voice at the end of the line, he expects him to be reprimanding him for his poor behaviour at his birthday luncheon, but when Abel makes no mention of it, he assumes that his brother has put the incident behind him. He is correct, because all that Abel desires right now is his brother's and sister's approval of his plans.

At lunchtime, Abel's solicitor, Felix Barker, calls in to his office unannounced, and Abel takes the opportunity to haul him inside to see the model.

'Come in, Felix. The model is here at last,' he announces excitedly. 'I've had the architect here all morning setting the bloody thing up.'

Felix Barker has been aware of Abel's development plans for some time, and as Abel's legal advisor, he expects to benefit hugely from the conveyancing of all the luxury villas that will ultimately be on offer for sale. 'The architect took a long time creating it, Abel, so what's the bloody verdict?'

Abel takes Felix by the arm and marches him over to the shiny model.

'Wowee, Abel, it looks like an entire Balinese village! What are you going to call it?'

'Nirvana,' Abel replies.

'That's absolutely perfect, Abel.' Felix raises both of his thumbs in the air in agreement.

'I'm told by the architect that to create the buildings, he had to painstakingly cut them to size out of foam core, latex and rubber, before placing them on the topography of the land. They've all been cut to scale, Felix. Just look at these trees. Aren't they lifelike?'

Felix focuses on an avenue of Bangalow palms made from wire and coarse turf leaves.

'We plan to have hundreds of these palms throughout the development, Felix. They'll line all the streets and make it look like an exotic oasis.'

'It's superb, Abel. These villas look magnificent. How many will be right on the beach?'

'They tell me they're able to build 450 villas facing the beach and a further 650 set back a little facing Tallow Creek. Each of them will have triple garaging and a private infinity pool.'

'I'd imagine the villas on the oceanfront could fetch about four or five million each, wouldn't you think?' Felix fields.

'We'll be expecting a little more than that, Felix,' Abel counters. 'The market has improved so much recently that they are more likely to be in the region of six to seven million each, I should think.'

Felix quickly tabulates the likely windfall in his head and then nods appreciatively. 'What's this spectacular glass building in the middle?' he asks.

'That's the classy Broken Head Hotel, Felix. It will have three infinity pools, four restaurants, a wellness centre, and several state-of-the-art conference rooms. Those green areas are the tennis courts.'

'The only thing it seems to lack is a heliport,' Felix jests.

'Ha ha! A bad oversight, eh, Felix?' Abel responds.

'I hadn't realised how big the property is, Abel. It covers such a huge area, doesn't it?'

'Yes, we're dealing with an enormous tract of land here, Felix. We're only turning half of it into residential housing at this stage.'

Felix looks into a treed area on the perimeter. 'What's this thing way over here?' he enquires, pointing towards a separate fenced-off section where some excavation equipment is scattered around a strange-looking shaft. Felix bends his head closer to read the sign. 'Broken Head Gold Mine!' he exclaims.

'Yes, we're going to continue with the gold mine, Felix. It's been here since the 1880s, and it's still a productive asset.'

'I agree. If it doesn't intrude too much on the rest of the development, you should keep it going,' Felix concurs. 'What's this area over here?'

he asks, pointing to another forested section on the western side of the model.

'Oh, that area is being fenced off as there's the potential for us to extract natural gas from it later on. I had it tested recently, and I was told there are vast reserves of gas below the surface of our land. Down the track, I'll get Oz Gas to do some fracking, as it promises to become a very lucrative gas well.'

'That'll mean even more money into the coffers,' Felix enthuses, and both men spontaneously rub their hands together. 'What's the next step then?' Felix asks, dragging his eyes from the shiny model.

'Well, after I get approval from my siblings, I'll submit the project to council. I imagine Rebecca and Kane will agree to the development application, especially when they calculate the multimillions of dollars that will be deposited in their accounts without them having to lift a finger.'

'Do you foresee any problems with them, Abel?' Felix asks tentatively.

'They may need a bit of persuading, Felix, but money talks you know. I should be able to get both of them on side when they hear how much will be coming their way.'

'Do you think the council will agree to it?'

'I suppose I'll have to grease the mayor's palm to get it through,' Abel responds.

'I've heard he's a stickler about allowing developments along the coastline, so I imagine he'll need considerable encouragement. How do you plan to get him on board?'

'When I offer him one of these multimillion-dollar villas, I'm sure he'll quickly agree to it, Felix. He's a greedy bastard, you know!'

'Abel, I have to hand it to you. If you manage to pull this off, it will be a significant gift to the community. It will create the biggest boom Byron Bay has ever seen since the introduction of the railway.'

'I know, Felix. When all these wealthy consumers arrive en masse to Byron, I expect the local economy will take off like a rocket.'

Felix stops for a moment to consider the likely obstacles that could be in Abel's way, and deciding to act as a devil's advocate, he asks him the difficult question. 'What about a possible native title claim, Abel?'

Abel's face pales at the thought of it. It is as if Felix has dropped a heavy weight on his toe.

'Abel, if the local tribe mounts a court case against you,' he continues, 'I can foresee it prohibiting you from getting the development off the ground.'

Abel turns towards Felix, ready to dump that responsibility squarely on his shoulders. 'With your legal help, Felix, we'll knock any native title claim on the head quick smart, won't we?'

'The Abbos could very well put in a claim, Abel,' Felix answers.

'But whose name could they put it under, Felix? As far as I can work out, they don't have a bona fide claimant,' Abel responds.

'I've heard rumblings before now that they've thought about selecting one of the Merinda family. Apparently, that family have lived inside the Broken Head compound in a cottage,' Felix counters.

'They're a bunch of losers, the lot of them,' Abel sniggers. 'The only three members of that family who could possibly go on a claim are Scarface, his vagrant sister Ronnie, and that girl who went missing twenty-five years ago. What credibility do any of them have?'

Both men are quick to scoff at the Merinda family's potential ineptitude.

'If a claim does come in, Felix, you should be able to throw it out of court, shouldn't you?' Abel asks, staring his solicitor directly in the eye.

'Don't worry, mate. It'll be a walk in the park,' Felix answers, and the two men break into a conspiratorial grin. 'Do your siblings know anything about these development plans yet, Abel?' Felix asks.

'Not yet, Felix,' Abel responds. 'I've been waiting for the model to be ready before I surprise them.'

'Now that it's here in your office, when do you propose showing them?'

'They'll be here in a few minutes, Felix,' Abel replies, checking his Rolex watch.

'Abel, I suspect your siblings may need a little convincing. You'll have to use your silver tongue on them, mate. I'd better leave you to it.'

Felix picks up his hat and walks towards the door.

'Congratulations, Abel. The whole concept is nothing short of brilliant . . . It's of an international standard too.'

After placing his hat squarely on his head, Felix Barker quickly makes his getaway before Kane and Rebecca arrive.

Chapter 20

KANE AND REBECCA VISIT ABEL'S OFFICE

'Come into my parlour,' Abel beckons.

Like innocent flies soon to be caught up in Abel's tangled web, Kane and Rebecca step inside his office, and the moment they see Abel's enormous model sitting in pride of place on his conference table, they both are wide-eyed with surprise.

'What in hell's name is this?' Kane calls, as he strides over to it.

'It's my proposed new development for Broken Head, bro. It's called Nirvana,' Abel replies proudly.

'You've kept this a dark secret, haven't you, Abel?' Rebecca says pursing her lips.

'Yes, Rebecca. I've been working on it with the architect for some time, but I've kept it under wraps until now. The model only arrived here earlier today, so you're the first ones to see it, except for Felix.'

Abel runs through the various points of interest. 'It's an entire village. There are hundreds of multimillion-dollar villas here. It will be like a millionaire's oasis,' he expounds.

Blown away by the magnitude of the development, Kane exclaims, 'Just look at all these luxury villas under the palm trees!'

'Yes, Kane. We'll all become mega-wealthy when each of them sells.'

Kane and Rebecca approach the model for a close-up view of the various architectural designs of the villas.

'They look superb, Abel, but who on God's earth will be able to afford them?' Kane asks.

'Only the very rich,' Abel replies.

'What's this over here?' Rebecca asks, pointing to the splashy hotel.

'That "on trend" glass structure is the Broken Head Hotel, sis,' Abel replies. 'It will be a five-star luxury resort.' Abel points out the various features of the hotel, and when his siblings seem suitably impressed, he presses on to explain what constitutes the rest of the development.

'What do you think of it, Kane?' he asks at the end of his presentation.

'It's bloody amazing, bro,' Kane replies, super impressed by the quality and size of Abel's vision.

'How are you going to get it through council?' Rebecca prudently asks.

'Leave that to me, sis. I have a fair bit of influence there.'

'It looks as if it will be a mammoth windfall for the three of us,' Kane enthuses. 'If it all goes to plan, I'll finally be able to retire from the hospitality business in Sydney.' Kane throws his arms in the air after saying this, and Abel laughs.

'I don't know about you, Rebecca,' Kane continues, 'but I'm running on empty right now, and I like this plan a lot. In fact, it's the most sensational use of Broken Head I could ever imagine.'

'What opposition to it do you envisage, Abel?' Rebecca asks, fully aware that the local tribe will be up in arms about it.

'Rebecca, I'm confident that Felix Barker will be able to deal with any objections that may come our way. In the meantime, our family should stick together like glue to get this wonderful plan off the ground. I've created it in honour of Joseph Stenmark, because he's the man who acquired this land for us in the first place. As the three directors of Stenmark Inc., we'll all be following in his entrepreneurial footsteps,' he states grandly.

'What's the next step then?' Kane asks.

'As soon as you two have signed the development application, I'll lodge it to council.'

'What do you mean, Abel? What do we have to sign?' Rebecca asks warily.

'Stenmark Inc. is the developer of the project, sis, and as the three of us are its directors, we all must put our signatures on the DA.'

'What will you do about objections to it?' Rebecca asks.

'Well, I expect the Abbos will make a paltry objection to it, but Felix assures me that we'll be able to knock their objections on the head quick smart.'

'What if their claim is successful?' Rebecca asks unabashed.

'Don't be negative, Rebecca. Felix has promised me he'll take care of all that. Don't you worry your pretty little head about it. All that is required is your signature.'

Chapter 21

THE TEMPEST

Later that same afternoon, Kane decides to relax on the swing chair attached to the front veranda of his guesthouse. He places a glass of scotch on a table beside it, and he swings back and forth playing 'Forever Young' on his guitar. Kane hasn't felt so high-spirited in a long time.

After viewing Abel's model of the Nirvana development, a heavy load seems to have been taken off his shoulders. The development has the potential to set him up for retirement, and instead of struggling along in the hospitality industry in Sydney, he imagines that in the future he'll be on easy street, living off the enormous profits that Nirvana will deliver.

Confident that his life will finally be sorted, Kane swings back and forth without a care in the world, but as life is generally a series of swings and roundabouts, it is not long before a few deeper thoughts creep into the corners of his mind.

> *When Abel announces his plan, how will Jimmy react to it? After recently reviving my relationship with him, will I lose him for a second time? If Jimmy objects to the development, will he become my arch-enemy?*

Kane gulps down some of his scotch for consolation, but the alcohol provides him with little solace, because even more perturbing questions start bombarding his consciousness.

> *What will Archie and Alkira think of the plan? Will I be able to convince them that Abel's inspired vision is in their best interest?*

Kane is beginning to realise that Abel's dream is not all plain sailing, as it possibly has the potential to damage some of his most cherished relationships. Although it is undeniably attractive, the development may have to travel a rocky road before it ever sees the light of day.

While Kane is contemplating these seemingly insurmountable personal obstacles, he has been too preoccupied to notice that there have been some fleeting shadows passing over him, and that storm clouds have been gathering high overhead. He only realizes that a cool change is afoot, when the breeze that was earlier gently brushing against the stubble on his face, becomes more insistant. By the time he has slung his guitar over his shoulder, however, tiny drops of rain are already making dots on the veranda floor and he can smell the dust settling in the guesthouse grounds. As he scurries along the veranda towards the French doors in a bid to escape the oncoming storm, he hears the first burst of thunder rolling overhead, giving him fair warning of the wrath that is to come. Kane has left his run too late however, because by the time he reaches the doors, a bolt of lightning is splitting the heavens apart and it is frightening him out of his wits.

To escape the untamed elements, he feverishly presses on the door handles to his room, but a catch on the floor is preventing him from opening the French doors. Before he has figured out how to release the catch, another jagged streak of lightning pierces the air beside him. Hearing the resounding crack, he hollers in fright as he cowers in front of the doors. After desperately fiddling with the catch in the pelting rain, he finally releases it and after flinging the doors open, he is blown inside by a strong gust of wind.

Once inside, Kane bolts the doors behind him and watches in awe as the torrential downpour pelts against the window panes. Feeling secure behind the glass at last, he stands dripping on the room's white painted floors listening to the rain as it relentlessly pounds against the widows and the tin roof. His mind goes back to the frightening subtropical storms he'd experienced as a child, when he cowered under the blankets in abject terror while the thunderous storms boomed all around him.

Feeling protected at last inside the Pacific House, Kane swaps his saturated clothes for a comfortable tracksuit, and calms himself by pouring another scotch. As he sips on it, he listens to the rain overflowing the gutters and wonders if the storm has been sent to him as some kind of warning.

Perhaps the gods are trying to tell me something. Are the local tribe's ancestors warning me to make a prudent decision about their land?

Chapter 22

ARCHIE AT THE ABORIGINAL CAMP

The next day, when the storm has passed, Archie asks his stepfather if he'd take him out to meet up with his friend Jimmy. As background for his book, Archie is keen to find out more about the local tribe's customs and traditions. Even though Kane's prolonged absence had initially strained his relationship with his old mate Jimmy, after his recent friendly visits to the camp, he is now optimistic that he can convince his friend to provide Archie with some insights into his tribe's way of life.

'What was it about Jimmy that you liked when you were a kid?' Archie asks his father on the way out to the camp.

'Oh, Archie, I liked Jimmy's intense interest in nature,' Kane replies. 'When Jimmy finds himself in an uninhabited area, his face lights up and an enormous spiritual joy fills his heart. He delights in seeing pouched animals drag their languorous bodies across the land, or following the path of a native willie wagtail to find out what it eats and where it nests. He spends most of his life following the path of some animal, bird, reptile, or insect in its primitive state.'

'He's a home-grown naturalist by the sound of things,' Archie surmises.

'Yes, Archie. Natural things overwhelm him and dominate his feelings. It's hard for me to explain, but it is as if an uncontrollable force engulfs him, especially if he is in unexplored virgin territory.'

'His relationship with the land is a spiritual one then,' Archie concludes.

'That's exactly right. When we were kids, sometimes he'd involve me in his Dreamtime thoughts. One time I remember him telling me that his ancestors were all around him, hidden in the sky and the sea, even under the earth. These superhuman heroes shaped his world daily, creating order out of chaos and life out of lifelessness. I learned that some of them were part human, possessing emotions and intellect, while others were animals, birds, or reptiles. Even inanimate objects such as stars and rocks seemed to have a life of their own.'

'Wow!'

'Jimmy is a bit of a mentor too, you know. He helps his mates understand life, and he champions them to deal with the challenges of survival. It has been a hard fight for some of them, you know.'

'I know so little, Dad. Do you think some of his mates will join Jimmy today?'

'I hope so, son.'

When Kane explains to Jimmy that Archie is writing a book, to his immediate relief, Jimmy tells him he'd be delighted to be interviewed by him, and he instantly instructs three of his fellow tribesmen to join him inside the communal building. When all four men are sitting cross-legged on the dirt floor, he signals for Kane and Archie to join them.

'This is Dingo, Willy, and Mick,' he says, pointing to each in turn.

Archie recalls hearing the men's names in his father's story about the notorious fishing trip that preceded the pub brawl twenty-five years ago. Jimmy has obviously selected his old mates.

Dingo, who is possibly in his late forties, is a gaunt man with four parallel scars on his bare chest. He has a broad nose, bloodshot eyes, and a missing front tooth. Willy, who is Dingo's best mate, is another thin fellow whose hair is standing up on end as if he's just seen one of his least favoured ancestors. The third man sitting in the circle with them is Mick, who is a little younger than the others. He appears quite shy as he avoids eye contact with both Archie and Kane. Mick's most distinguishing features are his enormous cheeks. Archie sees an immediate likeness to Satchmo, and he imagines that Mick's cheeks have stretched after a lifetime of playing the didgeridoo.

'You wanna learn more about our mob?' Jimmy asks.

'Yes, Jimmy. I'm interested in finding out about your culture because at the moment, I'm pretty ignorant about it,' Archie replies with a degree of self-deprecation.

'What d'ya wanna know then, ya bloody ignoramus?' Jimmy jokes and all the men laugh out loud, obviously appreciating Jimmy's bawdy humour.

Archie has previously heard from his father that some topics are likely to be off limits, being deemed to be secret men's business, so he judiciously chooses a broad topic. 'Well, Jimmy, for a start, I've always wanted to know why your mob suddenly goes on a walkabout.'

The tribesmen all break into laughter at this statement, and Archie laughs self-consciously along with them, wondering if they are laughing about him calling them a 'mob' or if they are amazed that he doesn't know what a walkabout is all about. Archie has heard about Aboriginal people going on walkabouts, and he has always thought that they just picked up sticks and left for no good reason. He envisions young men and women vanishing into the blue or, more accurately, disappearing into the blinding light of the Australian sun, while the kookaburras laugh at them from the squiggly gum trees. He waits for a response from Jimmy to see if it is any different.

Jimmy has a serious expression on his scarred face as he formulates an answer. He looks Archie squarely in the eye. 'We have totemic ancestors, Archie. In the past, our ancestors travelled through country, scattering a trail of words and musical notes with their footprints,' he explains.

'Do these notes help you when you're on walkabout?' Archie asks.

'Yes, 'em help a lot,' Mick utters in response, nodding eagerly. 'Like you follow a map, we follow a song.'

'Is that how you fellas find your way across country then?' Archie asks, trying to encourage the men to contribute.

'Yeah, mate. Our songs are deadly. They're like a direction finder. If ya know the song, you'll find your way. An' if ya stay on the track, you'll find people who've shared your dreamin'.'

'I get it now. It's a ritual journey you're making where if you know the song, you can tread in the footsteps of your ancestors.'

'Yeah, mate. That's right.' The tribesmen all nod in unison, happy that he has comprehended what they've said.

'It's like a passport or a meal ticket,' Kane adds to clarify further.

'Do you sing while you're on walkabout?'

'Yeah, mate, we do. We sing up country. It makes country come up quicker,' Dingo explains.

'Everywhere we go, we pass on our song-lines because we're always tryin' to extend our song map,' Jimmy expounds.

'It sounds as if you are endlessly accumulating details. If you know the songs, you become connected with a labyrinth of corridors,' Archie paraphrases.

'Yeah, we learn about the stars, each waterhole, each tree, each cave for sleepin' for miles and miles,' Mick adds.

'It sounds as if your songs are memory banks for finding your way,' Archie concludes.

'You're right, Archie. That's what they are. Our challenge is to be always on the move, following the old trails' 'n' putting 'em to memory. It's a test to know country and the stories of the past,' Jimmy explains.

'What are the biggest obstacles to your walkabout these days?' Archie asks.

'Fences, mate. Bloody fences! They interrupt our song-lines. There weren't any here until you white fellas put 'em up all over the bloody place.'

'I know my great-grandfather fenced off a large tract of land on Broken Head a long time ago. Did that have any effect on your tribe?'

The backs of the indigenous men stiffen. Archie knows he has ventured into dangerous territory because the demeanour of the tribesmen has dramatically changed. Each man is now glowering at him with a look of angst. He's obviously struck a raw nerve.

'Oh hell yes,' Jimmy responds forcefully. 'Our elders were mad as hornets to have their conception site blocked off. It had always been a place for us to come back to. This part of country was a sacred meeting ground, not just for us but also for the whole nation . . . all the tribes who lived up an' down the coast.'

'Is that why the elders pointed the bone at my great-grandfather then?' Archie asks provocatively.

'Too right mate, and the bastard deserved it. He banned our mob from visiting Cavanbah.'

The tribesmen suddenly stand up, all nodding angrily.

'We want to get it back from you Stenmarks,' Willy utters, pointing his wrinkled finger directly at Kane and then at Archie.

'I hope one day you do,' Archie quickly sympathises.

'Have you seen the old grave on Broken Head, Archie?' Willy asks.

'No, I haven't,' Archie replies.

'It's a disturbin' sight, mate. I hate seein' it. Joseph Stenmark an' his wife and their two dead kids are all buried in that bloody grave. It causes me pain knowin' they're there.'

'Me too . . . It's not right,' Dingo agrees, nodding solemnly.

'Why?'

'It's like intruders on country . . . They're not welcome on that sacred land.'

'The bastards broke our song-lines, an' one day I'm gonna dig their bones up,' Willy asserts.

'No, Willy. Don't go to Broken Head. You'll be trespassin',' Jimmy cautions.

'It's our land, Jimmy . . . They're the ones who are trespassin'.'

'Archie, you're the next generation, mate. You should write about it an' maybe you can help us get it back,' Jimmy entreats.

'I'll try, Jimmy. I promise,' Archie answers.

The men appear to like Archie's positive response, and Willy even pats him on the back in appreciation.

As the men start to walk towards the door of the community building, Jimmy confides, 'We have a feeling of great unrest, Archie.'

'What do you mean, Jimmy?'

'Our fathers taught us that life is one long journey and that only the unfit are left behind. We go on walkabouts, but before we die, we must return to our conception site, because that is where we should smile at death in the face. As the black cockatoos screech overhead, we need to return to the earth, and Archie, we all want to do it at Cavanbah, free of the bloody Stenmarks.'

As Archie and Kane depart from the camp, they feel an uncomfortable sense of guilt. Their family has caused a horrific dislocation to the lives of these people, and it is abundantly clear to the both of them that the Stenmarks are still perceived to be their arch-enemy. Before they drive off, Kane and Archie thank the men sincerely for their time and for the valuable tribal knowledge they've imparted. By way of a thank-you, they remove a case of beer from the hatchback of the jeep and they present it to the group. The men receive the beer with much delight, smiling broadly with toothy grins in appreciation.

On the short journey back to Byron Bay, Archie turns to his father to ask, 'Have you ever witnessed any of their initiation ceremonies, Dad?'

Kane nods.

'Really?'

'Yes. I was invited to Jimmy's circumcision when he was 14.' Kane's face stiffens, wincing with the recall. 'At the initiation, the elders said he had to prove he was fit to be a man.'

'What did he have to do?'

'He wasn't to cry when he had the foreskin of his cock chopped off with a blunt knife. He told me the experience was like putting his cock inside the mouth of a dingo. He yelled out with the pain of it, but he didn't cry. They also tested him by digging wooden nails into his skull. They were sharp needles like thick toothpicks. These were to mark him for manhood.'

'How long did the initiation last?'

'It took them four bloody days to sing him from boy to man, and to heal the wounds, they made him crouch over a fire of smoking ti-tree so that his wounds wouldn't turn septic.'

'It sounds so cruel.'

'It was. Jimmy was in such a bad way after it was over that I secretly brought him a tube of antiseptic for his wounds. That's why we consider ourselves blood brothers now.'

Chapter 23

ALKIRA'S APARTMENT

While Kane has been pacing up and down, weighing up the pros and cons of his commitment to the Nirvana project, Archie has been working feverishly on his dented laptop. Following his lengthy conversation with Rebecca and his recent interview with the tribesmen, he has launched headlong into the origins of the conflict between the local clan and the Stenmark family.

His aunt Rebecca has been so forthcoming with the family history that he has been able to start his story from the time Joseph Stenmark fenced off the land, and after his recent chat with the men at the Aboriginal camp, he can now identify with their feelings of alienation, inertia and powerlessness, since being locked out from Broken Head. He is feeling confident that he has gained valuable insights from both sides of the fence.

Archie knows that a good writer should have remorseless energy and be committed to following the trail like some bloodhound from hell. His words should float like a vast draft, glimmering with the poetry that is lacking in real life. If he is going to write something that will last forever, his imagination must turn despair into light, and beauty should lie in the intensity of his words. As he struggles to attain a golden truth, he must drag his vision onto the page, and after giving shape to his imagination, he must excavate the human condition to find a place that a heart might survive.

Up to this point, he has spent his time lost in libraries reading obscure texts, but now that he's in the real world, his sentences must save him. Everything he has learned so far has brought him to this moment, and now that he is here, he must be ready to tell everything he knows.

It has been well over a week since the hotel luncheon, and Archie feels it is time that he faced Alkira again. On his way over to her apartment, he stops at a local shop in search of a bottle of wine and some specialty cheeses, and with these in hand he nervously climbs up the stairs to her apartment. After the debacle in the beer garden, he wonders what kind of reception he will receive, and his heart is beating like a piston engine by the time he knocks on her door. Archie's handsome face lights up like a Christmas tree when Alkira welcomes him inside with a smile.

'It's not as good as bush tucker, but I have an acceptable bottle of chardonnay, some crisp crackers, and some French brie here,' he entreats, holding out his offerings to Alkira.

'Your gifts are graciously accepted,' Alkira responds, signalling for him to come in. Archie follows her into her galley kitchen.

'Have you forgiven me for embarrassing you at the beer garden?' Archie asks.

'You didn't embarrass me, Archie . . . It was your father and that weird Jude fellow.'

'I'm so sorry, Alkira. They were both completely out of line.'

Alkira's face remains concerned. 'Kane started it all when he made me a laughing stock!' she exclaims.

'Hardly. In my opinion, everyone welcomed you as a heroine,' Archie quickly responds.

'Thank god it's over now, is all I can say. I'm trying not to give it any more thought. The moment Jude wanted me banned from the beer garden, I knew I should never have gone.' Alkira reaches up high into her kitchen cupboard. 'Here are the glasses, Archie. If you open the bottle of chardonnay, I'll unwrap the cheese and crackers. I think we'll sit out on the balcony today. It's nice sitting out there in the breeze under the shade of my single Bangalow palm.'

Alkira walks barefoot over the polished boards of her living room, carrying the cheese and crackers on a small wooden tray. Archie follows her, carefully holding the two glasses and the cold bottle of wine.

'I must say I'm surprised you're here,' Alkira voices as she settles herself into a wicker chair.

'Why are you surprised?'

'I thought your family would have had a word in your ear by now. I thought they would have told you to stay away from me.'

'Well, it's not the case, Alkira. So far, there's been absolutely no impediment to me seeing you at all.'

'Well, time will tell.'

'Alkira, like it or not, the Stenmarks must recognise that you are part of our family now – an exotic part, I'll admit, but a part nonetheless.'

Alkira pours the wine. 'Cheers to us,' she toasts as she raises her glass.

Archie is delighted to drink to that.

After taking a sip on the wine, Alkira gazes out past the palm tree without speaking. She is thinking about what Archie may be writing about in his novel.

'Now, Archie, tell me about your new book,' she ventures.

'Well, I think I told you that it's about the elders' curse, didn't I? It's about how it came about and what has caused it to perpetuate.'

Alkira appears concerned. 'I'm afraid I know the other side of the equation, Archie. I know our side of the saga. I have no sympathy for the Stenmarks I'm afraid. I instinctively understand why our elders pointed the bone at Joseph Stenmark and I've experienced first-hand how the lockout adversely affected us. So I can say nothing supportive about it.'

'I want to hear your view on it, Alkira,' Archie responds.

'Your family will kick me out if you tell them what I think.'

'Look, I am not writing a one-sided version. To hell with the Stenmark family's view of it . . . I want to hear how the lockout affected you as an indigenous woman.'

'Archie, I'm reticent to tell you, because I blame the Stenmarks entirely. I don't think they gave two hoots about how fencing off the land at Broken Head would desecrate our once-great nation.'

Archie cuts off a wedge of brie and offers it to Alkira on a cracker.

'Alkira, you are the best person to tell me about the destruction it has wrought,' he encourages.

Alkira takes a bite of her cheese, leans back in her wicker chair, and gazes out past the palm tree again. 'It's been such a sorry business, Archie. I find it hard to know where to begin.'

'Start at the beginning,' he advises.

Alkira takes in a deep breath. 'It was shocking. From the moment that settlement grant was awarded to Joseph Stenmark our traditional way of life was interrupted. Once he was in possession of his pastoral lease, our tribe was forced from our land and left on the margins of town unable to sustain ourselves economically. Even if we could find work, we were expected to perform the most menial of jobs. To make any money at all, most of us were forced to become itinerant workers, destined to be continually travelling about the countryside. Over time our world became full of prohibitions – we were banned from staying in hotels and banned from community facilities like swimming pools. Our people were endlessly hounded by the police, who would tell us constantly to move on.'

'That sounds so unfair, Alkira.'

'Settlement grants were awarded only to white people, Archie, and they were responsible for irreversibly interrupting our traditional Aboriginal culture. At the stroke of a pen, they caused generations of us to become impoverished, often relegated to a life of discrimination, bigotry and exclusion.'

'You personally?' Archie asks.

'If you want an example of how this affected me personally, you only have to think about my mother. She's now a derelict - an outcast of society. She was denied the right to her land, to her native language, and to her health. She was not even counted as part of the population until she was given the vote in 1962.'

Archie has an incredulous expression on his face.

'Archie, we were only counted in the census as Australians after the referendum in 1967 and those are recent times.'

Archie shakes his head slowly, sympathetically.

'Does that make me a New Australian?' Alkira asks. It is a challenging question, and she stares directly at Archie, waiting for him to answer.

'Your ancestors were here over sixty-five thousand years ago, Alkira. I could never call you a New Australian. You are an indigenous Australian, the oldest there is.'

Alkira looks down and remains silent, and seeing her beautiful face appearing forlorn, Archie feels her heavy heart.

'It was a bloody insult that the government did not count you as citizens of your own country,' he empathises, in an attempt to break the pregnant silence.

'We were not counted as human,' Alkira adds, shaking her head in total disgust. 'Archie, we have lost our civilisation, and at best, our culture is a lost relic from the past. The state has designed ways to scare us over the years. They've taken our children from their mothers, taken away the names that we inherited from our forefathers and they've forbidden us to speak our languages. In other words, they've made us ashamed of our heritage. As a consequence, we are losing our identity, and these days we are suffering from the tyranny of low expectations. Apart from the physical indignities that we've suffered, the mental ones are also vast.'

'That is incredibly sad, Alkira,' Archie responds. 'I had no idea how bad it was.'

'That's because white Australia wears a moral blindfold, Archie. The historians have ignored us. In your history books, we are faceless, nameless and lost to anonymity. Acquiescence and silence have gone hand in hand, I'm afraid.'

'We have been so cruel,' Archie admits.

'Everything was about feeding the white folks, Archie. It was all about their banks, their companies, their colleges and their homes, while we've been suffering unnoticed in the back blocks, out of sight. An Aboriginal woman goes particularly unnoticed.'

'How do you manage as an Aboriginal girl in a white society, Alkira?' Archie asks, trying to delve into Alkira's personal struggle in these modern times.

It is a big question for Alkira to answer, because it causes her to consider her own identity. 'I share a deep attachment and a definite kinship with my people and I share this bond with all Aboriginal communities throughout Australia, but I believe it's a trap for me to look at myself as being just one sole identity.'

'What do you mean?'

'Thanks to my mother's insistence and your father's financial help, I now have tertiary qualifications and they have allowed me the opportunity to look wider afield than most of my brothers and sisters. I'm no longer just a local girl now Archie. I'm not confined to working at the fruit and veg co-op all year, you know.'

'I know you aren't.'

'I'm indigenous, but I have other identities too. I like to think I have layered identities now. I've decided not to hitch myself to victimhood by saying that I'm from any particular community.'

'Whoo! You have thought this through, haven't you?'

'Well, Archie, I've been called a coconut – someone who is brown on the outside but white on the inside. This label is grossly unfair, however, because I'm merely choosing to take my place at the centre of Australia's social, political, and economic life. Rather than remaining local, I'm trying to live on a broader stage. I'm running my own race by breaking away from what others perceive I should do.'

Archie can see that Alkira is on a roll.

'Toleration is not the same as acceptance, you know. Acceptance is what is needed for the coexistence of diverse cultural identities, and acceptance grows from shared experiences. I cannot expect to be accepted unless I'm worthy of it, but when I'm worthy of it, I should be able to claim it as a right.'

'I love you, Alkira,' Archie suddenly blurts. 'I love your strength of purpose.' Archie can't help himself. His new sister has a robust fighting spirit, and he can only hope that she will appreciate him as much as he adores her.

Alkira spontaneously reaches over to Archie and she takes both of his hands in hers. 'We must stick together,' she confides.

Archie agrees with this sentiment wholeheartedly and he squeezes Alkira's hands back by way of reply. After hearing Alkira's devastating account of the demise of her people, he knows he should be feeling quite despondent, but somehow, as he departs from Alkira's apartment, he is unable to wipe the smile off his face. His lovely indigenous sister has become a true friend.

Chapter 24

IRONBARK

Under the guise of research for his novel, Archie asks Alkira if she would take him to the place where she was born. When she agrees to show him, they both don peaked caps to shield themselves from the fierce sun, and they head off on their bikes to Ironbark.

It is a two-kilometre ride to Iron Bark, but when they arrive there, Alkira is bitterly disappointed with what she sees. Only a few of the original buildings that she remembers still remain at her birthplace and her beloved Iron Bark bares scant resemblance to what she recalls as a child. Left with little with which to identify, she instantly decides to move on, and urges Archie to ditch his bike in the bushes alongside hers, so they can commence a hike on foot towards Tallow Creek.

Directly south of the Byron Bay lighthouse, Alkira leads Archie down a sandy path to a beautiful place where white wading birds stealthily stalk the sandy shallows of Tallow Creek for their food. Archie sees little water striders darting about on the surface of the water and scores of wriggling mosquito larvae just below the surface. Countless flitting dragonflies are eating the aforementioned creatures, as hundreds of minnows swim around the reeds. Archie imagines they are all feeling quite comfortable because there is safety in numbers. Alkira points out to him that it was here that the *jarjun* used to catch yabbies and tadpoles.

'What's *jarjun*?' he asks.

'Children, of course.'

'Right,' he responds.

'We used to paddle here in this pond for hours, looking for frogs. I can still remember two types, the wallum froglet and the wallum sedge frog, but I've heard there are very few of them left these days.'

The pair begin an immediate search for the endangered frogs in the reeds by the water's edge. Alkira's experience pays off as she is first to locate a small frog with white dots forming a line under its throat.

'Look. It doesn't have any webbing on its feet and has no toe pads either . . . It must be a wallum froglet,' she states excitedly.

Alkira holds the little endangered froglet on her palm for Archie to see and Archie is impressed. Later, Archie finds a much bigger green frog with a narrow head and a sharp snout.

'If it has a yellow underbelly, it's a sedge frog!' Alkira calls from a distance. 'The sedge frog attaches its eggs to the reeds,' she tells him as she approaches to examine the creature in Archie's hands. 'Yes, that's a rare sedge frog, Archie,' she confirms. 'You can tell by that beautiful blue colour on its groin. Be careful with it . . . They're endangered.' After they examine it together, Archie carefully places the frog back into the water.

After leaving the pond, the pair continue along the sandy track, with their wet shoes making squelching sounds on the sand beneath them as they walk.

'See this plant over here? We used to call it five corners, because it has five small leaves like a star. We used to eat its yellow berries when we were kids,' Alkira recalls. Archie picks a translucent yellow berry off the bush to taste it, and finds it to be similar to a salty kiwi fruit.

'See this morning glory vine? We'd make it into a skipping rope,' Alkira enthuses.

Archie smiles.

'There's lots of bracken fern here too. Do you know what it's good for?' she asks.

'It's good for nothing, Alkira . . . It's a bloody weed,' Archie scoffs.

'It's good for bull ant bites,' she reproaches him.

Archie is impressed with Alkira's familiarity with the bushland plants, but for some fun, he decides to test her knowledge by asking her about the many bushes they pass as they stroll along.

'What's this?' he asks, pointing to a geebung.

'They've got a hard seed, but around it is sweet flesh, like a mango. You should try one,' Alkira replies. Archie bites into the flesh around the seed and finds it to be sweet.

'Oh, here's a bush lolly . . . Taste one of these too,' Alkira urges. Archie takes a white-and-purple berry from Alkira's hand to chew on it. 'Mmmm, it's really sweet,' he declares.

The duo move further along the path until Alkira points to a Dubay plant.

'When I was young, I used to strip it with my thumbnails and weave it into baskets with the other women in our tribe.' It all sounds so quaint to Archie, who has spent most of his life in the city and he breaks into a grin.

'I know what this is,' he declares triumphantly, pointing to a plant that he recognises. 'It's a blackboy.' 'We call them Mudigan trees, Archie,' Alkira answers. 'They keep mosquitoes away.'

The pair continue to walk along the path towards the beach until Alkira points out some banksia bushes. 'We used to call these nobbies, Archie. If you shake the bushes early in the morning before the parakeets get to them, you get the sweet nectar.'

By the time the duo arrives at the end of the track, Archie has been suitably impressed with Alkira's local knowledge. She not only recognises the various plants, but also knows which ones are edible and which ones have medicinal properties. After this excursion into the bush, Archie now realises the deep spiritual connection that his sister has with her native land.

'We used to find middens in this area that dated back at least 1,500 years, but most of them have been disturbed now,' she tells Archie.

'I'm such an ignoramus, Alkira. What's a midden?' he asks naively.

'It's a place where you find shellfish remains and bones of fish. Sometimes there are bones of animals that have been eaten for food by previous inhabitants. There's an undisturbed one at the Pass, not far from the lighthouse - They've even found early rock tools there.'

When Alkira and Archie reach the long expanse of Tallow Beach, where the Pacific Ocean meets the most easterly coast of Australia, Alkira points up into the sky towards a white-bellied sea eagle flying high overhead. 'We call the eagle *mi-wing*, which means hunter,' she tells Archie, as the majestic bird soars in the air above them. Archie and Alkira decide to remove their wet shoes and sit side by side on the sand to watch the bird glide back and forth in the wind.

Feeling thrilled to be with Alkira on her home territory, Archie takes her hand in his and when she accepts the gesture, it confirms to him that he has formed a strong bond with her. When he clasps his fingers tightly between hers, his heart soars like the eagle above him. When he embarked on this trip to Byron Bay, he had no idea he'd find a girl who'd turn out to be his sister. As an only child with no family to speak of except for Kane, he is stoked to at last have a sibling, and as he sits with her holding her hand, his heart is full to bursting.

With the waves continuing to slam into one another beside them, hand in hand the pair hike barefoot along the edge of the ocean. When they arrive at the Broken Head beach a little bit farther south, they spot the Three Sisters' Rocks, which are a formation in the ocean that Archie recalls hearing about in his father's fishing story.

'Do you want to hear my Dreamtime story about them?' Alkira asks him.

'Shoot,' he answers.

'Three sisters were bathing off the headland when one became caught in a current. The others swam out to save her, but all were swept away. If you look, you can see them trapped in the swell. It's a warning for swimmers about how dangerous the ocean can be.'

'It certainly can be treacherous,' Archie acknowledges as he watches the waves crash onto the three outcropping rocks.

At the headland, the duo stop to look back towards the Byron Bay lighthouse, a beacon for seafarers strategically positioned on Cape Byron. This view to the north is a panoramic one, and from here, the pair take stock of the considerable distance they've trekked.

At the end of their journey, the siblings follow a stone path down to a small lonely beach that is flanked by pandanus palms. Small rocks cover a large part of this beach, and previous visitors have piled some of them into little towers.

'We used to pile them into towers like this when we were kids,' Alkira declares, delighted that the tradition has continued to the present day. 'Let's make an offering to my mother,' she suggests, and the duo set to work.

While Alkira is building her tower, she thinks of Ronnie languishing in a care home located next to the Lismore Hospital, and when she completes her tower, she makes a wish that her mother will make a full recovery. Archie, on the other hand, makes a wish that his relationship with his sister will become as solid as the rocks he is handling.

After they have finished their tower making, Archie is feeling quite exhausted after the long trek, and he suggests that the pair stroll back towards the Aboriginal camp in the hope that they will be able to hitch a ride back to Ironbark to collect their bikes.

After reaching the camp, the duo are delighted when Jimmy offers to drive them back to Ironbark in his ute, and although it is only a short journey, the pair happily squeeze into the cabin with him.

When the trio reach Ironbark however, they are alarmed to see a burly fellow erecting a gigantic real estate sign out front. At the top of it in large letters, is Nirvana, followed by the words Soon for Sale. The large sign includes a subdivision map displaying hundreds of numbered lots that are depicted in primary colours. Below this colourful map are three glossy pictures: one of a luxury villa, another of the proposed hotel, and the third of an avenue of palms that lead to a sandy ocean beach. On the very bottom of the sign is a telephone number to call. Initially, the trio are so gobsmacked that they remain silent, but soon, their attention turns to the man beside the sign who is hammering stakes into the ground.

Jimmy calls out to him. 'This sign is on our sacred land!'

The man ignores him and continues to hammer in the support stakes.

'Who instructed you to erect this?' Jimmy queries in a louder voice.

The burly man stops his hammering and stands assertively beside the sign with his legs astride. 'Abel Stenmark ordered it.'

Alkira turns towards Jimmy, her face showing immediate alarm.

'Jimmy, this is preposterous!' she declares, and he replies, 'It looks like the Stenmarks are plannin' to turn our Broken Head into a bloody suburb.'

Unperturbed by their comments, the burly man continues to hammer in more stakes.

'Isn't this where you used to live, Jimmy?' Archie asks.

'Yeah, I've lived here all my life, Archie,' he answers. 'My cottage is just a few hundred metres beyond this fence.'

'Really?'

'Yeah, it's the only house inside the compound. Didn't ya know it was built for my old man, Archie? He was the first caretaker at the Stenmark mine.'

'No, I didn't know that,' Archie responds.

'During the great gold rush, he had to guard the gold mine against intruders, an' when he died, that's when I took over his job.'

Seeing a golden opportunity going begging, Alkira asks, 'Seeing you lived inside the compound, Jimmy, would you consider being the claimant on my proposed native title bid?'

'No, no, Alkira! I'll never sign any white man's documents, girl. I can't read properly, an' you know how they can twist and turn what ya say. I can never understand the fine print, girl. No, no, I will never go on it because I can never trust the bastards.'

'Jimmy, I'm a lawyer. I can help you understand it,' Alkira encourages.

'No, Alkira! No, girl. It's a definite no. I can't trust 'em, so don't ask me.'

Determined to avoid any further urging, Jimmy jumps back into his ute, and after calling out, 'Hooroo' to Alkira and Archie, he drives off, leaving them at the sign. Bitterly disappointed that Jimmy has refused her, Alkira despondently turns away to search for her bicycle.

Chapter 25

ALKIRA'S APARTMENT

Realising that they must do something to block the impending development at Broken Head, Archie and Alkira begin a serious discussion.

'It's time we stopped the Stenmarks in their tracks, Archie. It appears they're planning to carve up Broken Head to make it into a rich man's club,' she states.

'That's what it looks like, Alkira. What they're planning is absolutely appalling. It will end up being an enclave for the wealthy on Aboriginal land,' Archie responds, shaking his head at the very thought of it.

'If we don't act immediately, I'm afraid that we'll lose it forever,' Alkira frets.

Archie strokes his chin, wondering what can be done to stop the development. That real estate sign was a definite wake-up call.

'The time has definitely come for me to prepare my native title claim,' Alkira declares. 'I'm just hoping that I'm not already too late.'

'Do you know the procedure?' Archie asks.

'Yes, Archie, I do. I've done some research on it already, so I know what's required.'

'What do you have to do?'

'Well, the first thing I have to do is form a group of like-minded people from my tribe to fight alongside me as a consultative committee.'

'What exactly do you want to achieve?'

'I want to negotiate an indigenous land use agreement.'

'You'll put yourself on the line if you do that, Alkira. The Stenmarks will fight you tooth and nail, you know, especially now that they have a plan for the land.'

'I'm aware of that, Archie, but there's no way around it. They're going to be my arch-enemies no matter what.'

'How do you propose to start the ball rolling?'

'I'll set up an interview with one of the TV stations to announce my intentions.'

'You'll become a political activist over night if you do that, Alkira.'

'I'll be doing it for my mum, Archie . . . It's what Ronnie always wanted.'

Chapter 26

RONNIE'S NURSING HOME

Archie asks Alkira if he can join her when she next visits her mother at the nursing home in Lismore.

'Why do you want to meet my mum?' she asks.

'I'm just curious, I guess. Do you mind if I join you when you visit her today?'

'It won't be a pretty sight, Archie. Ronnie is still recovering from an operation.'

'I'm very interested to meet her, Alkira. Please?'

'OK. But I'm warning you – you may not get a good reception.'

'Why not?'

'Because you're a Stenmark, you idiot.'

'I'm up for it, Alkira,' Archie responds.

As Archie and Alkira march along the nursing home's grey-and-pink floral carpet, they can smell a distinct odour of urine and bleach, and as they get closer to Ronnie's room they also get a whiff of fish. Before they even reach Ronnie's door, the pair can hear her wailing voice protesting loudly to a nurse.

'I can't eat this bloody stuff . . . It stinks to high heaven!'

'Hi, Mum!' Alkira calls out, keen to interrupt her mother's protests.

'The fish here stinks like dead possum's piss,' Ronnie raves on unabated.

When Alkira approaches her bed, Ronnie holds out her dinner plate for her to smell it. Alkira obligingly sniffs the plate, but after inhaling the strong odour, she palms the dish away towards the nurse, telling her to get rid of it.

'What's going on, Mum?' she asks.

'They're tryin' to poison me, Alkira,' Ronnie complains.

'Mum, I think you're looking better than I've seen you in a long time, so some of the food here must be OK,' she counters.

'It's whities' food, love . . . Give me bush tucker any day.'

'I thought you liked fish,' Alkira rebuffs.

'I'll only eat it if it comes from Freckle's fish shop or if I can catch it myself.'

'Mum, I'd like you to meet my . . . my friend, Archie.' Alkira takes Archie by the arm and escorts him towards her mother's bed.

'Hello, Ronnie,' Archie greets, immediately transfixed by her pure white hair, which is standing up on end. He stretches out his hand to greet her, but it hangs there when Ronnie makes no move to accept it.

'Have you given up on ya own mob these days, my girl?' she asks her daughter.

'Mum, Archie is an author, and he's writing about how our ancestors pointed the bone at the Stenmarks.'

'Are you tryin' to get secrets out of my daughter, white boy?' she challenges.

'I'm just trying to find out the truth behind it all,' Archie clarifies.

'Well, for a start, the opening line in your book should be that the Stenmarks are a pack of murdering bastards!' she exclaims.

'Mother, don't say that . . . Archie is a Stenmark.'

'Well, you should stay away from my daughter, young man. She's all I've got left,' she orders.

Keen to change the subject before it gets out of hand, Alkira asks, 'Mum, how are you feeling after your operation?'

'The bastards have given me a pacemaker, girl. Look at it – they've turned me into a bloody robot!'

Ronnie bares one of her sagging breasts so that her daughter can see the scar above it. Alkira inspects the slightly raised bulge where the doctors have implanted the device, and after a brief examination, she readjusts Ronnie's hospital gown to make her presentable again.

'You're as good as new now,' she placates, patting her mother on the shoulder, before adding 'It looks as if it's healing nicely.'

When the pacemaker inspection is well and truly over, Archie returns to the bed. 'Ronnie, I've brought you a book to read,' he says, handing over a brown paper bag.

Ronnie snatches it from him and drags the book out to read its title.

'Yes, yes, yes! *Plains of Promise*! I've been dying to get my hands on this book. It's all about the Waanyi mob in the Gulf of Carpentaria!' she exclaims.

Archie is intrigued that Ronnie already knows about the story. 'Are you familiar with Alexis Wright's books, Ronnie?'

'I've only read *Grog War* so far. Freckle gave it to me at the fish shop. She writes about how the demon grog has invaded our culture. Did you know there was so much abuse up in Tennant Creek that they banned grog from the whole town?'

'I think I did know that,' Archie answers.

Pleased with Ronnie's reaction to his gift, Archie immediately forgives her for her earlier gruffness, and feeling as if he's off to a good start, he hopes that sometime in the future, Ronnie will deliver some first-hand knowledge about the clash of Aboriginal spirituality with white colonisation. Indeed, on first glance Ronnie appears to have a timeless soul, coupled with a daring spirit, and if she opens up to him it's bound to be a uniquely rewarding experience.

Chapter 27

KANE, ALKIRA, AND ARCHIE

Unaware that Alkira and Archie have already seen the Nirvana sign at Iron Bark, Kane decides that it's time he told them about the proposed development. Under the ruse that he has a surprise for them, he asks them to meet him in front of the Sands Hotel, and as soon as they arrive out front, he quickly whisks them towards Abel's office door.

'Close your eyes,' he instructs before thrusting the office door wide open.

When Alkira and Archie open their eyes, Abel's model, in all its oversized glory looms in front of them. Alkira's eyes go wide at the sight of it, and she immediately thinks that the development is an indefensible statement of greed. She gulps in horror. It is worse than she ever could have envisaged.

'Is this travesty of urban planning destined for our sacred land at Broken Head, by any chance?' she enquires, already knowing the answer.

'Yes, it is,' Kane replies. 'Abel has been working on it for ages. Isn't it sensational? He tells me each of these villas will fetch about six to seven million each, and that we'll all be rolling in cash when they sell.'

Archie and Alkira are in shock at the sight of Abel's model, but they remain silent while Kane extols the virtues of the plan. As they stare at it with open mouths, he points out its salient features, describing the various styles of villas and the avenues of palm trees that will one day line all the streets.

Keen to locate Iron Bark where she was born, and Tallow Creek where she played as a little girl, Alkira walks up to the model to scrutinise the topography of the land. On close scrutiny, she's horrified to discover that both of these locations are now destined to be lined with luxury villas.

'I know your tribe used to live on this land in the past, Alkira, but in modern times, the land has belonged to our family. Ever since Joseph Stenmark was awarded it in the 1880s, it has remained in our hands,' Kane proselytises.

Alkira remains silent, waiting for him to finish.

'Abel told me that he wants to continue Joseph Stenmark's entrepreneurial spirit by creating the highest and best use of the land,' Kane regurgitates.

Archie is astonished at how Abel's grotesque land grab has so bedazzled his father.

'Did you see the hotel?' Kane asks them. 'It will be a "state of the art" design with three infinity pools and—'

'Stop!' Alkira shouts. 'It's disgusting! It's a travesty of our sacred land!'

'No, Alkira, it won't be,' Kane retorts. 'It will be an internationally important development . . . one that will greatly enhance our fortunes.'

'It's nonsense!' she replies.

'Alkira, I know you spent your first few years living at Iron Bark, but now it's time to look forwards, not backwards. It's time to move on.'

'Kane, I thought you had an understanding of our people. After spending time with Jimmy over the years, I imagined you'd have learnt to respect the rights and interests of the traditional owners of country, but for monetary gain, I can see you'd ditch all your principles.'

'You know, Alkira, it's a real shame,' Kane replies.

'What's a shame?' she asks.

'That your people still crave for their old life. Time has moved on, and everything has changed. These days, we must think of our own future, which will be assured if this project goes ahead.'

'It's urban sprawl on a grand scale and you know it,' Alkira responds sharply.

'What's this?' Alkira asks, pointing to the fenced-off area on the model.

'Abel said that he might try fracking for gas in that section. Apparently, there are reservoirs of gas below the surface.'

'I see,' Alkira sighs, turning her face away. 'Thank you for showing us Abel's plan, Kane, but I must tell you here and now, that I have other much more inclusive plans for Broken Head.'

'Have you now?' Kane scoffs.

'My dream is for it to return to our local tribe so they can fulfil their cultural aspirations there. It's time it was cleaned up after the damage that mining and sewage have created. It's also time to bring back the native frogs, birds, wallabies, and echidnas that once lived here. Our people need to reconnect themselves with their homeland, and in my plan, the local community will be invited to join us.'

'Have you thought about how lucrative Abel's plan will be for us as a family, Alkira?' Kane rejoins, not yet convinced with her ideas.

'Kane, it's time we joined with others, be they white or black, who are interested in making Broken Head a national park, run by our First Nation people.'

'That's a bloody pipe dream, Alkira,' Kane rebuffs sternly.

'Kane, you said that it is your turn to benefit. Well, in my plan, everyone will benefit, because we will welcome visitors to country so they can understand our culture and customary folklore.'

'As I said before, Alkira, that's just a pipe dream. This land has been fenced off since Joseph Stenmark was awarded it, and it will be mighty difficult for your mob to prove they have had a continuing relationship with it.'

'We'll see about that, Kane,' Alkira retorts.

Appalled by Kane's stance on the project, she and Archie march from the Sands Hotel, leaving Kane behind, scratching his head.

Chapter 28

PACIFIC HOUSE

After Alkira and Archie's strong rejection to the Nirvana plan, Kane retires to the Pacific House to rest and think. While he's lying on his bed, he projects himself into the future by imagining that he is living in one of Abel's new villas. On a stylish deck overlooking the ocean, he envisages relaxing with a scotch on the rocks in one hand and a cigarette in the other. He imagines a perfect scenario, where he is living a life of ease, sitting by the infinity pool at sunset playing his guitar, after a successful day out fishing. It will be a dream come true, not having to front up to work in the mad Sydney hospitality industry ever again.

Once he and his sister have signed off on the development, he anticipates that the conflict between him and his brother will dissipate. With their goals at last aligned, their relationship will no doubt become more hospitable. Although he has had a rocky start in introducing the plan to Alkira and Archie, he hopes that in time, he'll be able to convince them that it will be in their best interests to support his brother's wonderful development.

When Kane stretches out on his bed at the Pacific House, it is not long before he drifts off into a deep sleep, but in a dream, a group of angry men from the local tribe appear before him, wearing war paint.

Shaking their spears overhead, the men angrily advance towards him, shouting 'Traitor, traitor!' To escape them, Kane takes off like a frightened hare into the thick Broken Head scrub and with birds fluttering off in all directions, he runs until his heartbeat is all he can hear.

When Kane reaches the Wallum Heathland however, the sparse heath bushes provide him with little cover, and feeling exposed, he looks back to check if his pursuers are closing in on him. When he sees that they've made up a lot of ground, he decides to make a mad dash towards the Cibum Margil Wetland.

Still and dark in front of him, the stagnant low-lying wetland is a shady waste containing effluent that has been diverted from the town. The bog which swallows all the light, reeks of rotting matter and smells of death. Unfortunately for Kane, there is no way back from here, and the only way for him to escape the tribesmen appears to be for him to wade through the wetland's murky depths.

With his pursuers advancing ever closer, Kane steps gamely into the cold black swamp, but the further he advances into it, the more it swallows him up. With the mud sucking around his boots, Kane attempts to lift his leaden legs, but each step forward seems to be progressively more difficult. When he is completely immobile in the mire, he hears the caw of a crow that seems to be heralding his impending death. Imagining that a spear will lodge into his back at any moment, Kane waits impotently. Soon he hears the warlike warbling of his pursuers readying themselves for the kill.

Suddenly, above all the commotion, Kane discerns Jimmy Merinda's raspy voice and for a moment, he imagines that he might be saved. Unfortunately however, it is Jimmy who is giving the orders.

'Kill 'im! He's a traitor . . . Kill the bastard!' he hears him shout. Trapped in the putrid mud, Kane waits in terror for a sharp spear to take him out.

Kane suddenly jerks awake, and sweating with anxiety, he sits upright in bed peering towards the tangle of blankets that are trapping his feet. With his heart thumping like a tom-tom, he struggles to release each foot from the entanglement. He finally frees himself from them, but it takes him quite some time before his brain can switch back to reality.

After some minutes of confusion, he calms himself and begins to wonder if there is a lesson to be learned about deserting his indigenous mates. *Could it be something to do with fairness?*

After recovering from the shock of his nightmare, Kane retreats with his guitar out onto the veranda to strum a few tunes, but just as he is about to start, Archie arrives back at the Pacific House.

'Are you OK, Dad?' he asks, noticing Kane's pallid complexion.

'I'm fine, son,' he answers, not yet wishing to disclose the details of his disturbing nightmare.

After visiting Ronnie in her nursing home, Archie is keen to convince his father to meet up with her too, as he envisages that a visit to the mother of his child could be just the thing to bring him to his senses. Although Kane has tried to banish Ronnie from his thoughts for two and a half decades, Archie believes that now that he's here in Byron Bay, he has a pertinent responsibility to assist her and her people. He believes that the time has come for Kane to recognise Ronnie publicly, because, after all, she is the woman who gave birth to his first biological child

'Dad, I met Ronnie today,' he declares.

'What?'

'I went to Lismore with Alkira and I saw her. She's recovering from a heart operation in a nursing home.'

'Archie, why are you telling me this?'

'Because it's time you paid her a visit.'

'For fuck's sake, Archie! It's too late now to do an about-face. Why don't you leave my past alone?'

'C'mon, Dad. You've paid for Alkira's schooling all these years, so I imagine you must have stored up a few brownie points in your favour.'

'No way, son. I'm not going to dig up my past.'

'Dad, if you are going to change your life, you have to face up to the truth fairly and squarely.'

'Give me a fucking break, Archie!'

'In my opinion, you can't ignore her any longer. She's here, she's alive and it's time you gave her the respect she deserves. When you go, I'll come with you if you like, because I want to hear her side of the story.'

'Archie, no.'

'Stop being a bloody coward, Dad! Don't you see this is your chance at redemption? She's not well and this may be your last opportunity to apologise to her for abandoning her.'

Kane looks down. He knows in his heart that Archie is right, but he wonders if he is brave enough to survive Ronnie's bedside attack.

Chapter 29

ALKIRA PREPARING HER CLAIM

While Archie is trying to convince his foster father to meet up with Ronnie, Alkira is working feverishly at her dining room table, trying to familiarise herself with what is required to make her claim for a native title bid. She has read that the British government initially declared all lands in Australia to be terra nullius, which means they belonged to no one, but she has also read that this concept was nullified in 1993, when the Native Title Act of Australia was passed, decreeing that the concept of land belonging to no one was no longer applicable. The historic act was the first one to open up the possibility that indigenous people could reclaim their land under a native title.

Alkira has also found that to make a successful claim, she must show that her people have ongoing traditional rights and interests in the land in question. The problem she foresees in her particular case, however, is that her tribe has been denied access to Broken Head ever since Joseph Stenmark fenced it off.

As the application for a native title requires that Alkira be authorised by her group to represent them, it is imperative that she obtain their official consent before setting about procuring the required survey maps, technical descriptions, details of land tenure and the plethora of ancestral stories she'll need to bolster her case.

Chapter 30

THE SANDS BOTTLE SHOP

Archie and Alkira's newfound cousin Brett, who is a champion swimmer, trains in Brisbane during the week, but he returns to Byron Bay on the weekends to earn some cash by working at the bottle shop at the Sands Hotel.

Recently, at the Australian Swimming Championships in Brisbane, he entered himself into the four-hundred-metre butterfly event and easily qualified for the final. In his final swim, he timed his dive perfectly and stayed underwater for an extraordinary length of time before emerging well in front of the field. Employing his impressive double-dolphin kick, he moved his hips back and forth in time with a powerful stroke of his arms to propel himself like a fast-turning windmill towards the finishing line, where he impressed the judges with his record-breaking performance. A few days after the event, the local *Byron Shire News* posted a picture of him on its front page, lauding him as a potential Australian Olympic champion with sights set on competing in the Sydney Olympics.

After his triumphant win, Brett has returned to Byron Bay and has arrived at the bottle shop well before the time of his shift to check that the shelves are full.

His first customers are a group of drunken "tradies" who stagger in, demanding to be served. One of the men, who is wearing a dirty navy-blue singlet, has some bold tattoos on his neck and when he comes up to the counter, Brett is able to read the words 'I'll roam the world to take what's mine' tattooed onto his throat. Brett is disturbed by the tattoo, as he considers it to be a bold statement bordering on a threat.

'Hey, mate, we, um . . . We want a case of XXXX beer,' the tattooed man demands, but while he is making his order, one of his mates, who is looking much worse for wear, joins him in the bottle shop. 'Yeah, give us some fuckin' beer,' he endorses, but this second man appears quite unbalanced and has to grasp onto the counter for support. When he lets go of it however, he collapses onto the bottle shop floor.

'It looks as if you guys have had enough to drink already,' Brett cautions, as he watches the unsteady man struggle back up from the floor. While he observes him the man unzips his fly and begins to urinate.

'For Christ's sake, get your bloody mate out of here! He's pissing in my shop!' Brett orders, pointing towards the wet floor. The tattooed man merely stares at his incontinent mate with a bland face. 'Hand over the beer first . . . We demand service!' he retorts.

Brett Stenmark is at the end of his tolerance by this time, and he lifts the countertop up to emerge in front of the two men. Suffering no more insolence, he grabs the incontinent fellow by the scruff of his neck and hurls him out onto the footpath. After removing him, Brett returns inside, but as he re-enters, the tattooed man grabs him forcibly by the arms and slams him up against the bottle shop wall.

'You give us a two-dozen pack of XXXX beer, or you're a dead man,' he threatens. Brett feels the blade of a knife jabbing into his nose.

'It's against the law to serve you . . . You guys are intoxicated,' Brett insists bravely. The man removes the knife from below Brett's nose and plunges it deep into his stomach and Brett sinks slowly to the floor, clutching at his wound.

A younger man, who is the third in the group, quickly enters the bottle shop and scales the counter. He collects a twenty-four-pack of XXXX and after stepping over Brett on his way out, he departs with it on his shoulder. The others follow him towards the beach, leaving Brett unattended on the urine-soaked floor.

Jimmy, who plays an unofficial caring role in his tribe especially on the day the welfare cheques arrive, has been searching the streets to check on his indigenous mates. Aware that some of the younger men can get into trouble when they have money in their pockets, he swings by the bottle shop to see if the manager there has seen them.

When Jimmy enters the bottle shop, he immediately sees Brett Stenmark clutching at his stomach groaning in agony on the wet floor. He kneels beside him to ask him what has happened.

'I've been stabbed,' Brett moans. 'The bastards have taken off with a pack of XXXX and left me here to die.'

'I'll help you, mate . . . Where's your phone so I can call 000?'

Brett nods towards the phone on the counter and Jimmy immediately dials 000. A female telephonist answers.

'Hello, you've called triple O. How can I help?'

'There's been a stabbing. Jesus, a man has had his stomach ripped open with a knife!'

'Is he breathing?'

'Yes.'

'What's your name?'

'Jimmy.'

'Where are you, Jimmy?'

'The Sands Hotel bottle shop.'

'Is it in Byron Bay?'

'Yes.'

'What's the address?'

'Hey, mate, what's the address here?' Jimmy asks, but as Brett has passed out, he responds, 'I dunno the address . . . It's by the beach.'

'How can we send someone to help you if we don't know the address?'

'Hold on.' Jimmy says.

He dumps the phone onto the counter and runs out of the shop and into the hotel. 'What's the address 'ere, mate?' he asks a barman.

'It's the Sands, mate. Everyone knows where the Sands is . . . Next, please.'

With the barman too busy to answer him, Jimmy rushes out to the street to find a street sign and when he locates Jonson Street, he rushes back to the phone.

'It's Jonson Street,' he tells the woman, but all he hears is a dial tone.

Exasperated by this, Jimmy hangs up the phone and kneels beside Brett to check if he's still breathing. In the absence of any help, he decides to try CPR, and he is in the process of conducting it when Brett's father strides into the shop.

'What are you doing to my son?' Abel calls in alarm.

'Someone stabbed 'im, mister.'

'What the hell? Get out of the way!'

Abel rushes over to Brett, who, by this time, has blood leaking profusely through the front of his shirt. Abel unbuttons it to get a look at his son's stomach, but quickly finds out that it is not a pretty sight.

'Oh no, Brett! Brett, wake up, wake up!' he calls, but after receiving no response to his orders, he looks up at Jimmy. 'You ugly black bastard! Why did you stab my son?'

'I didn't stab 'im, mister. I found him like this, an' I was tryin' to help.'

'I'm going to call the ambulance and the police,' Abel declares, as he reaches for the phone.

When Jimmy hears the word "police" he turns on his heel and runs for his life, leaving Abel urgently dialling the number. As Abel makes the call, he looks back at his unconscious son.

'It's the bloody curse again, Brett. Damn it! It's the blackfellas' curse!'

Chapter 31

BYRON BAY POLICE

After Abel's call, the police arrive on Jonson Street, intent on capturing Jimmy. When they find him harbouring under a Casuarina tree on nearby Rawson Street they shout at him to climb into the police van.

Knowing that he is innocent, Jimmy is reluctant to step forward.

'Ya have the wrong man!' he calls to the officers, but when the police see him covered in blood, they decide to take no chances with him, and they demand that he move immediately towards the police vehicle.

When Jimmy refuses to comply with this directive, one of the officers aims his Taser gun at him and he zaps him repeatedly from close range. Weakened by the Taser, Jimmy drops to the ground under the Casuarina tree, unable to move. The officers then drag his limp body over to their vehicle and thrust him inside.

By the time Jimmy has been delivered to the local police station on Shirley Street, he is desperately in need of medical attention, but oblivious to his poor condition, the police officers perform a breath test on him and then throw him into an airless cell.

Feeling wretched, Jimmy remains on the cell floor for some time, shivering and vomiting. On several occasions he yells for help, but when he receives no response to his pleas, he scrambles up onto his bed and for most of the night, he sits crouching forward, holding his head in his hands with a high-pitched tinnitus scream resounding inside his head.

The next morning, Kane learns from Abel that the police have arrested Jimmy for the stabbing in the bottle shop, and alarmed at this news, he rushes around to the police precinct to see his friend.

'You don't look too good, mate,' he declares when he is confronted by Jimmy's sunken grey eyes. After scanning his cell, Kane notices a pile of vomit on the concrete floor beside him.

'I feel so sick, Kanee.'

'Did they let you call anyone, Jimmy?' he asks.

'No, Kanee . . . There's no phone in 'ere, mate, an' there are no windows either.'

'What in the hell happened to you?'

'I've been blamed for somethin' I didn't do, mate.'

'What was it? What in the hell happened?'

'I called into the bottle-o last night at the Sands to see if any of my mob had been there. I found your nephew lyin' on the floor, groanin'. You know the one. He's a champion swimmer. He was on the floor bleedin'. Someone had stabbed him in the guts.'

'Jesus!'

'I tried to revive him, Kanee . . . There was blood everywhere. I called 000, but I didn't know the address of the pub, an' the bloody sheila hung up on me.'

'Not helpful.'

'Then I started to do CPR on Stenmark, an' that's what I was doin' when your brother came in. Abel Stenmark accused me of stabbing his son, an' when he said he was going to call the cops, I bolted. They caught me down near the beach with the swimmer's blood on me hands.'

There is a knock on the door, and an officer enters. 'Jimmy, there's an Aboriginal woman here to see you. Do you want me to let her in?'

'Yeah, of course,' he answers.

The constable ushers Alkira into the smelly cell.

'Hi, Alkira. What are you doin' here, girl?' Jimmy asks.

'I came to see you, Jimmy,' she replies.

'I suppose you know, Kanee,' Jimmy says.

'Yes, I do. He's declared himself to be my father and announced it to the whole world.'

'I'm sorry, Alkira. It was insensitive of me to introduce you to the family as I did, but I just had to set the record straight.'

Alkira ignores him and turns to Jimmy. 'Jimmy, I understand that the police brutally tasered you. How are you faring?'

'I feel sick, Alkira.'

'I bet you do. You'll be pleased to hear that I have the whole thing on video, Jimmy.'

'Good for you, Alkira. How come?'

'A girl offered it to me on Lawson Street, not far from the beach. She said she witnessed your arrest and filmed it. She transferred it to my phone, and I now have it as evidence.'

'Good . . . Those cops nearly killed me, girl, and I'd done nothing.'

'Did you see who stabbed the Stenmark boy, Jimmy?'

'Nah. The bastard was well gone by the time I got there. It should be on the hotel's security tape though.'

'Jimmy, you need someone to represent you legally. This is an attempted murder investigation and you're in a lot of trouble. If you like, I can represent you. It'll be pro bono . . . That means free.'

'In that case, I accept,' Jimmy immediately answers. 'You know, Alkira, I haven't had a run-in with the cops since I stole a bike when I was twelve.'

'I remember that, Jimmy,' Kane quickly adds. 'Didn't they come into Broken Head looking for you at night with flashlights?'

'Yeah, that was scary – but not as scary as last night.'

'Don't worry too much, Jimmy. I'll call a doctor to look after you, and I'll have you out of here the moment the police lay their eyes on that security footage,' Alkira promises.

Chapter 32

THE BYRON SHIRE NEWS

When the next edition of the *Byron Shire News* comes out, it carries an arresting headline on the front page:

LOCAL SWIM CHAMP STABBED.

The headline catches Archie's attention when he sees it face up on a pile of newspapers in the foyer of the Pacific House. He quickly picks up the newspaper to view it, and sees a sizeable picture of Brett Stenmark taken after he had won the final of the four-hundred-metre butterfly championship in Brisbane. He then reads a quote underneath the photograph attributed to Abel Stenmark:

> "A black fellow stabbed my son when he refused to supply the drunken bastard with alcohol."

Archie shakes his head at Abel's racist remark and reads on.

> 'The local police have captured an Aboriginal male named Jimmy Merinda, who they claim had blood on his hands after a stabbing incident at the Sands Hotel bottle shop on Saturday night. The local man is now in custody after being found hiding under a Casuarina tree a short distance from the hotel.

Subsequent DNA tests of the blood have linked him directly to the victim, but after being breath-tested at the time of his capture, his test proved to be negative, showing he had not consumed any alcohol.

A woman named Alkira Merinda, who is a relative of the accused, is defending the man, but Miss Merinda suspects that police brutality occurred at the time of her client's arrest. She claims to have footage of the man being tasered by the police, even though he was showing no signs of resisting arrest.

Ms Merinda, who is a recent law graduate at Sydney University, has requested to see additional security footage from the Sands Hotel bottle shop because she believes there has been a wrongful arrest.'

"It is yet another incident where indigenous people have been considered guilty without substantial evidence to back it up," Miss Merinda has stated. "The blood found on my client was there because he was administering CPR to the bleeding victim on the bottle shop floor."

The article concludes by saying:

'After undergoing emergency surgery on his stomach, the local swimmer is recuperating in intensive care at the Lismore Hospital, with the hospital describing his condition as "critical." Was this yet another example of the curse that the indigenous elders placed on the Stenmark family many generations ago?' The writer asks.

When Archie closes the paper, his mobile phone rings. His editor has already read the same article on her computer in Sydney and she has become alarmed that there has been another tragic incident involving the Stenmark family.

'Hello, Archie.'

'Hello, Sue.'

'Archie, I've just read about the attack on the Stenmark boy. What's going on up there?'

'There was a brutal stabbing in the Sands Hotel bottle shop yesterday, Sue.'

'It sounds as if this story is hotting up, Archie. If you don't hurry up with your finished draft, you'll be beaten to the punch, my boy. It's already hitting the papers here, and soon, it will be out as a novel under the name of another author and another publisher.'

'The story is still unfolding, Sue,' Archie defends.

'Why haven't you sent me anything yet, Archie? Haven't you written anything that I can peruse?'

'I'm not finished yet, Sue.'

'Well, bloody well get to it, boy! Send me something, for god's sake!'

'I'm on to it,' Archie answers defensively.

Sue Barkham remains silent.

'I'm doing my best, Sue, but it's like continual breaking news. This story keeps unfolding right in front of me.'

'Get to work, young man. As I said, I want some bloody good copy on my desk by the end of this month.'

Archie puts down his phone feeling perplexed, but he has no time to dwell on his feelings, because another call is coming through from Alkira.

'Archie, can you do me a big favour?'

'Yes, what can I do?'

'Can you try to obtain a copy of the security footage from the bottle shop? It's vitally important that we get our hands on it. Perhaps your aunt can get it for you somehow. Please try to get a copy before the police subpoena it.'

'I'll ask Rebecca,' he promises.

'I'll make it worth your while,' Alkira responds.

'I'll definitely get it for you then,' he replies.

Chapter 33

ALKIRA ON TV

Alkira has been scheduled to appear on ABC Television to talk about land rights, and curious to hear what she has to say, Abel and Stephanie have invited Rebecca and Corrie over to Marvell Street so they can all watch it together as a family. The four of them are settling down in Stephanie's living room, to sip on gin and tonics with finger lime, when Stan Bowles appears on the screen.

'Good evening, viewers. I'm Stan Bowles,' the ABC announcer begins. 'You are watching *As it Happens* and tonight we have a young indigenous woman by the name of Alkira Merinda from Byron Bay with us. She will be speaking on behalf of her First Nation people. Welcome, Miss Merinda.'

'Hello, Stan.'

'There has been an incident in Byron Bay that has caused a lot of public interest this week. I'm referring to the stabbing of the champion swimmer Brett Stenmark. Tell me, how are you involved in that tragic event?'

'I am representing the accused, Stan.'

'Legally?'

'Yes. I've recently graduated in law from the University of Sydney, and this is the first case that I've taken on.'

'Good for you.'

'You don't need to patronise me, Stan.'

'Don't be oversensitive, my dear. I'm delighted that you are completing higher education and using your studies to defend your people.'

'That's enough about me,' Alkira retorts, and Stan waves his palm to allow Alkira to continue.

'The reason I'm here today is to announce that I plan to protect and conserve the cultural heritage of my people, whose land at Broken Head was taken away from them. Their connection to this land has been interrupted and it's time they got it back.'

'Before we get into the subject of land rights, Miss Merinda, I want to ask you about this man from your tribe who has been arrested for attacking the swimmer Brett Stenmark.'

'It is not what I came here to talk about today, Stan, but it is one of the sensitive issues that I'm dealing with at the moment.'

'I hear your client has blood on his hands.'

'One of our indigenous men has been arrested for this serious crime, but, Stan, he's an innocent man.'

When Abel Stenmark hears this declaration, he jumps to his feet and bellows in protest at his TV set. 'Like hell he's innocent! I found the ugly bastard in the bottle shop with blood all over him!'

'I understand his name is Jimmy Merinda and that he was caught shortly after the incident with the victim's blood on his hands. How can you possibly think he's innocent?' Bowles asks.

'Stan, I was going to withhold this information, but seeing that you want proof right here and now on television, I can tell you that I've managed to obtain security footage from the bottle shop.'

'What bloody proof can she have?' Abel questions, while Rebecca remains tight-lipped. 'She can't have obtained our hotel tape, can she?' Abel asks as he strides around his living room.

'It's common knowledge that our people are persecuted daily, well beyond what is reasonable. You just have to see the high percentages of us locked up in correctional facilities.'

'She's waffling,' Abel interjects.

'Be specific, Miss Merinda. Now is not the time for general statistics. What actual evidence do you have that shows that Jimmy Merinda is innocent?'

Alkira digs into her handbag and produces the copy of the security footage that Rebecca has had duplicated for Archie.

'Here is a copy of the tape from the bottle shop on the night of the stabbing,' Alkira declares as she hands the hotel security tape over to Stan Bowles, who immediately passes it on to his assistant.

'How the hell did she get that?' Abel exclaims.

'Archie asked me to get it for him, and I got Corrie and Andy to copy it for me,' Rebecca admits.

'Well, you're a bloody stupid fool, Rebecca!' Abel accuses, shaking his head at her in disgust.

'The truth is . . . the truth,' Rebecca rebuffs before taking a deliberately slow sip on her gin and tonic.

The four Stenmarks gaze intently at the TV screen with open mouths as the footage from the bottle shop unfolds.

On the tape, a rough Caucasian man with bad teeth enters the bottle shop with a drunken mate, who is so intoxicated that he collapses onto the floor beside the counter. When he scrambles back to his feet, they watch him urinate on the floor. The viewers then see Brett throw him out onto the street before returning inside. The footage then captures the toothless man pressing Brett against the wall while holding a knife to his face. The family gasps when he brutally stabs Brett in the stomach. The tape suddenly stops running.

'Owww, that was bloody gruesome! Poor Brett!' Corrie utters as the screen goes blank.

'The callous bastard!' Rebecca vents.

'He stabbed my son for just a case of beer!' Stephanie sobs, as she wipes away her tears with a handkerchief. After seeing the demise of her son, Stephanie is in shock, and her body begins to shake uncontrollably.

Seeing his wife so distressed, Abel joins her on the couch and he wraps her in his arms, but as he comforts her, he stares across at Rebecca with a sullen face. He's furious that she has organised the release of the tape without his permission.

In close-up, Stan Bowles speaks to his viewing audience.

'Viewers, we apologise for broadcasting this unedited footage. We had to stop it because the content could offend some of our viewers. It is obvious from what we did see, however, that the indigenous man is not the perpetrator of this heinous crime. Instead of incarcerating him, the police should be pursuing the thugs we witnessed on the security footage. In my view, Jimmy Merinda should be released immediately.'

Hopping mad that Rebecca has handed the video footage to Archie, Abel growls, 'Rebecca, you have a bloody hide giving that tape to Archie. You might have known he'd hand it over to Alkira.'

'I'm not to blame, Abel. You're the one who accused Jimmy Merinda without any evidence. The tape exonerates the poor man, whom you falsely accused. The police are likely to have a copy of it too, you know.'

The family's attention swings back to the television as Stan Bowles asks, 'Miss Merinda, have you anything further to add?'

'Yes, I do, Stan. I want to tell the viewers that there is further footage later in this same tape that shows Jimmy Merinda attempting to revive Brett Stenmark by giving him CPR. That was how he received blood on him. Rather than perpetrating a crime, my client was in fact trying to save Brett Stenmark's life.'

'Indeed. It appears that Jimmy was actually being a good Samaritan,' Stan Bowles concurs.

'This is a prime example of the persecution that our people face on a daily basis,' Alkira emphasises again, this time looking directly into the camera.

'Miss Merinda, I understand you also have in your possession some footage of Jimmy's arrest.'

'Yes, I do. Would you like to see that as well, Stan?'

'Yes, please.'

'It's a clip from a cell phone taken by a bystander who filmed Jimmy while the police were repeatedly tasering him,' Alkira explains.

ABC plays the footage, and at the end of it, Alkira comments,

'This footage is damning. My client was not resisting arrest. He was the unfortunate victim of aggressive policing.'

After watching the footage on TV, Rebecca is appalled at the rough treatment that Jimmy has received. 'You are as bad as the police, Abel. You condemned this poor man publicly with no evidence to back it up and look what they've done to him!'

'Shut up, Rebecca! You've turned into a bleeding-heart liberal!' Abel rebukes, then keen to catch Alkira's final statement, he turns away from Rebecca to watch the end of the programme.

'Stan, I originally came onto this programme to tell you about our sacred site at Broken Head, so before I go, I'd like to announce that I plan to make an application under the Native Title Act to recognise the land that is presently held by the Stenmark family, as rightfully belonging to its traditional owners. My application will be for the land to be returned to our local First Nation people of Byron Bay.'

'Whee-ha! That's a lofty goal, Miss Merinda!' Stan Bowles comments. 'Good luck with that one!'

'Stan, the time has come for my people to negotiate a land use agreement between the NSW government, the local council and the Stenmarks, and it should include a representative from every stakeholder that has been involved with the land in the past. If we are successful, our First Nation people will have a chance to develop new opportunities to care for country.'

'For fuck's sake! Now she wants to take our land from us!' Abel shouts at the TV. 'That will never happen!'

'Maybe it's time they got it back,' Rebecca rejoins, but Abel glares back at his sister in disbelief, and he shakes his head in a disparaging fashion.

'Do you want the land back for old times' sake, Miss Merinda?' Stan Bowles asks provocatively.

Alkira finds the question to be extremely contentious, and she snaps back, 'Stan, we do not want the land returned to us for nostalgic reasons. We want to set up a joint management program to make it into a national park so we can share our culture with the wider community.'

'Miss Merinda, you're a brave woman to take on the Stenmarks, because I understand they have other plans for that land.'

'Maybe so, Stan, but you may not know that I have an ace up my sleeve.'

'And what would that be?'

'I'm a Stenmark. My father is Abel Stenmark's brother, Kane.'

'That bitch is saying she's one of us, while at the same time, she's threatening to take Broken Head from our family so she can give it back to her tribal mates. That will be over my dead fucking body!' Abel rants.

'Well, Abel, it was theirs in the first place, wasn't it?' Rebecca reminds him.

'Look at it this way, Rebecca. If they take this land back, the next thing they'll be after will be the Sands Hotel. We just can't let that happen. You're a co-owner. You must support me in this. We must block this push at every step, or Nirvana will have to be scrapped.'

'Abel, the truth is that our grandfather seized their land when he took out a settlement grant. Initially, that grant gave him a pastoral lease, but now it continues year by year. Under the Mabo Legislation, the First Nation people may be entitled to the land, especially if they can prove they've had a continuing connection to it. Their case could have some merit, seeing as they've used Broken Head as a sacred meeting place for centuries.'

'I've heard enough of this bleeding-heart claptrap, Rebecca! The bloody natives have no claim to it. We locked them out the moment we were awarded the pastoral lease.'

'I'm not so sure about our tenure now, Abel.'

'For fuck's sake, Rebecca, we must stand together. I need you to be beside me on this or our development will be in jeopardy. We must fight tooth and nail together. I've protected you over the years, so now it's your turn to return the favour. I'm going to set up a meeting with Felix Barker, because it's high time we engaged his legal help. You are going to support me in this, sis, come hell or high water!'

Chapter 34

SOLICITOR'S OFFICE

Seeking to clarify the family's position should a native title claim be lodged on Broken Head, Abel makes an appointment with his lawyer. Rebecca is the first to arrive at Felix Barker's plush wood-panelled office and while she waits for Abel to arrive, Felix offers her some coffee in a bone china cup. As he hands it to her, Rebecca envisages the snout of a wombat in the legal eagle's face.

'What's this meeting all about?' she asks the wombat.

'Abel has called the meeting. I believe he fears there's going to be a threat to your estate,' he answers in a serious tone.

'Has Kane been invited?' Rebecca asks.

'Yes, we invited him, but the idiot is refusing to attend.'

Rebecca raises one eyebrow.

When Abel arrives, he takes a seat beside Rebecca in front of the wombat's large polished cedar desk, and he wastes no time getting down to business. 'Felix, what legal action can we take to stop this indigenous woman from challenging us?' he asks.

'This woman has a name,' Rebecca interjects.

'What is it?' Felix asks.

'She's Kane's child and her name is Alkira Merinda.'

'Is that so? I never knew Kane had a piccaninny child,' Felix quips.

'That's a derogatory term, Felix. I demand you retract it immediately,' Rebecca reprimands.

Felix quickly shrugs the reprimand off. 'Yes, well, this is an interesting situation. We have the illegitimate daughter of one of the co-owners of this estate threatening to claim a determination to release the Stenmark land to its previous indigenous inhabitants,' he paraphrases.

'Yes, that's the unfortunate situation,' Abel states, nodding. He obviously agrees with Felix's summary.

'Are you agreeing with this proposal too, Rebecca?' Felix asks.

Rebecca looks across at Abel, who glares back at her with a fixed stare. She knows he is challenging her to agree with him.

'Well, in the beginning it was their land, but a lot of water has passed under the bridge since then,' she proffers diplomatically.

'Felix, there is already an industry on our land. Our gold mine has brought in a handsome profit every year since the gold rush and in addition, there are vast reserves of natural gas under the surface that is yet to be tapped. But in my opinion, one of the most valuable assets of all is the undeveloped beachfront land.'

'Yes, Abel, I agree. Broken Head represents an extremely lucrative asset.'

'You've already seen my plan, Felix. You must agree that it's a developer's dream. The family should be fighting tooth and nail to keep the land. Who knows what its value will be into the future?'

'What about you, Rebecca? What are your thoughts?' Felix asks.

'Well, I'm not sure if Kane's daughter has lodged a native title claim yet, but if she does, she's a very courageous girl.'

'Rebecca, I warn you . . . If you go against me, you'll be very sorry. You know an outrageous claim like this cannot go ahead.'

'Are you threatening me, Abel?'

'Put it this way, Rebecca. If you support Alkira, your life as you know it will never be the same. When I reveal your dirty little secret to the world, you'll suffer such a whirlwind of scorn, you'll never recover.'

Unable to muster the strength to rebuff her brother any further, Rebecca retracts into her shell.

'If you support a native title claim for our land, Rebecca, you'll undermine everything I've done to build up our family fortune,' Abel continues. After this statement, Rebecca feels a tide of resentment building inside her and she retorts,

'I'm getting sick to death of your stand-over tactics, Abel. You're a bloody bully and if you don't go easy on me, I won't sign your DA.'

'You'll sign the bloody thing, Rebecca, because if you refuse, your life won't be worth living in this town.'

After hearing this threat, Rebecca stands up and defiantly strides towards the legal eagle's door.

'I don't know how you two sleep at night,' she scolds, before strutting from Felix Barker's office. The door slams loudly behind her leaving the two men looking at each other in silence.

'I don't think Rebecca has grasped the real value of Broken Head, Felix,' Abel comments.

'She doesn't appear to,' the lawyer concurs.

'Seriously, Felix. If a native title claim comes in, we have to knock the bloody thing on the head straight away.'

'Don't worry, Abel. I'll be objecting to it. We'll have thirty days to lodge a rejection claim from the time it's published.' Abel nods slowly.

'How about Kane? Is he on side with your development?' Felix asks.

'I think he likes it, Felix. In the past, Kane and I have never agreed on very much, so I can't be too sure about him. He's a bit flaky, you know.'

'If he refuses to sign it, Abel, have you thought of buying him out?'

'Buying him out of Stenmark Inc.?'

'Yes. Why don't you make him an offer he can't refuse?'

'What do you mean?'

'Why don't you make him an offer that is so attractive that it will convince him to leave town again, and once he is out of the picture, you and Rebecca can go ahead without him?'

'But that would involve a huge payout, Felix.'

'In my business, it happens all the time, Abel.'

'It's a great idea, Felix,' Abel tentatively agrees, and his fingers tap on his chin as he seriously countenances it.

'I'm serious, Abel. Get rid of the bastard . . . or even better, go it alone.'

'What are you saying?'

'I mean, if your siblings are out of the picture entirely, you could single-handedly run Stenmark Inc. In my opinion, your siblings are holding you back.'

'Do you mean that I should eliminate Rebecca too?'

'Yes.'

'You are a clever-clogs, Felix. I wonder what would make Rebecca release her grip on Stenmark Inc.'

'Get your family to help you, Abel. I understand there's no love lost between Stephanie and Rebecca. Why don't you get your wife in on the act? Involve your sons too if you can, because, after all, it would be in their best interests for you to hold all the cards.'

Abel rubs his hands together. He has never thought seriously about a complete coup, but the thought of supreme control does excite him enormously. He continues to rub his hands together until Felix interrupts him.

'Look, I tell you what I'll do for you, Abel.'

'Are you being creative, Felix?'

'To besmirch Kane's reputation even further, I'll make a statement that I saw him driving the red car on the night of the B&S ball all those years ago. That will ignite more anger in the town, and no one will want to have anything to do with him. Hopefully, he'll want to leave again, especially if you offer him an incentive.'

'You'd do that for me, Felix?'

'Yes mate.'

'You're a true friend.'

'It's business, Abel ... It's just good business. Remember, Abel, you three are joint tenants. If anything happens to the others, you will inherit the lot . . . That's if the local tribe doesn't get it first.'

Chapter 35

MARVELL STREET

All the way home from Felix Barker's office, Abel ponders how he can get his family to help him gain control of Stenmark Inc. Felix's proposition preoccupies him until he storms through his front door at Marvell Street.

'How did it go, darling?' Stephanie calls from the kitchen.

'My sister is bloody insane!' he calls back.

'What do you mean?' Stephanie asks, turning from the sink.

'She doesn't realise that we could lose the bloody lot if Alkira and her mob win a native title claim. The blacks could end up getting Broken Head, and potentially, they could even inherit the Sands Hotel too.'

'What in the blazes are you saying, Abel?' Stephanie asks, drying her hands on a tea towel.

'Stephanie, this beautiful house belongs to the company, and we could lose it.'

'How do you figure that, darling?' Stephanie flings the towel over her shoulder. Her husband has her undivided attention.

'If I die, you could end up penniless, because all my estate will go to my siblings. You'll get absolutely nothing.'

'What? How come?' Stephanie stares at her husband in disbelief.

'Stenmark Inc. is a joint tenancy.'

'That's preposterous, Abel!'

'Darling, the only way we can inherit the entire estate is if my siblings die first or they sell their shares of the estate to us.'

Stephanie's mouth remains open.

'Look at this scenario, Stephanie. If Rebecca dies, then the inheritance is a fifty-fifty split between Kane and me. Then if I die, Kane gets the lot. And potentially, when he dies, bloody Alkira and Archie will get it all.'

'Abel, I've never heard of joint tenancy, but it sounds like a can of worms.'

'Darling, the only way we can stop the rot is to make sure that we are the last ones left standing. We must be the ones holding the deeds to the estate. Do you get my drift?'

'I do get your drift, darling. We must definitely do something about it.'

'What do you suggest?' Abel rejoins.

'Well, I'm not an actress for nothing. I could take Rebecca out on a boat trip and try to reason with her, or better still, something could happen.'

'What do you mean something could happen?'

'I've never liked your sister, Abel. I'll take her out in the boat and try to convince her to support us.'

'What if she doesn't agree?'

'I'm creative, darling. If Rebecca doesn't agree, I can organise a boating mishap or something.'

'Stephanie, you're joking with me, aren't you?'

'You'll see.'

Chapter 36

BOAT TRIP

With Abel's fishing boat behind her Range Rover, Stephanie picks up Rebecca and drives over to the Pass boat ramp which is located between Clarkes beach and Wategos beach. She reverses down the slope, and when her trailer is sufficiently submerged, she jumps out to float the boat. After asking Rebecca to hold the mooring rope, Stephanie drives off to park the Range Rover and trailer.

As Rebecca stands knee-deep in the brine, holding onto the mooring rope, she wonders why Stephanie has invited her to go out for a spin. Suspecting that she will try to talk her into supporting Abel's development at Broken Head, she steels herself for a barrage of arguments on the boat trip ahead. When Stephanie returns, the two women load Rebecca's picnic basket onto the boat and then jump on board themselves.

As the pair motor out from Fisherman's Lookout, Rebecca peers towards the north-west to see if she can see Mt Warning, the highest peak in the shire. The local indigenous people have always called the peak *Wollumbin,* 'the cloud catcher'. It was Captain Cook who had changed its name to Mt Warning to alert mariners of the dangerous offshore reefs that he'd encountered on his voyage in 1770. After locating the distinctive peak in the distance, Rebecca notices that Stephanie is turning the boat towards the iconic Byron Bay lighthouse, which is perched majestically on Australia's most easterly point. Rebecca is aware that the lighthouse was built by Charles Harding in 1901 and that the iconic structure was converted over to mains electricity as late as 1956.

Stephanie expertly steers the boat past the impressive structure and motors around the spectacular headland to a sheltered beach called Cosy Corner. From there, the pair take in the beautiful expanse of Tallow Beach, with its white sand stretching for kilometres to the south, fringed by Bangalow palms.

'Do you know why it's called Tallow Beach, Stephanie?' Rebecca asks.

'No, but I'm sure you'll be reminding me,' Stephanie replies.

'In the old days, when Byron Bay was a whaling station, the good ship *Volunteer* capsized along this coast. It dropped 120 casks of tallow, which was washed ashore.'

'Oh, an early spill,' Stephanie retorts, and Rebecca nods.

'Rebecca, look . . . From here, you can see Broken Head clearly,' Stephanie points out. Rebecca looks off to the south, where Stephanie is pointing, and in the distance she takes in the magnificent headland.

'We may lose our beloved land to the Aborigines if this Alkira person wins her battle,' Stephanie warns.

Rebecca braces herself for the debate to come. 'Don't you think it's time we gave it back anyway?' she responds.

'No, Rebecca, I really don't. Once you give that mob an inch, they'll take a mile.'

'Why have we come out here, Stephanie? Is it because you want to convince me to oppose Alkira?'

'I thought it would be a good place for us to talk with our own land right here in front of us,' Stephanie replies.

'You're worried we'll lose it, aren't you?'

'Yes, I am, and you should be too, Rebecca. You should be joining Abel and me, because it looks as if it may become the fight of our lives.'

'I can't join you, Stephanie. In my opinion, Abel is as belligerent as our grandfather was, and he was the one who put the first owners offside in the first place. He's the reason the local tribe cursed our family.'

'Rebecca, listen to me. The only way forward is to stop them in their tracks. We must join forces and oppose any land rights claim they may lodge.'

'I don't agree, Stephanie. We took Broken Head from them and now it's time we gave it back.'

'Never, Rebecca! It's ours, and that's how it will stay.'

'Stephanie, I don't want to argue with you, but you must understand that we took away their sovereignty when we expropriated their sacred land.'

'For heaven's sake, Rebecca, you sound as if you're one of them!'

'I am on their side, Stephanie.'

'Well, I'm not! The land is ours, and it always will be ours.'

Stephanie decides that the time has come for her to have it out with Rebecca once and for all and she switches off the motor so that she can drop anchor.

'Can't you see where this push for Broken Head is leading, you fool?' she challenges her sister in law. 'The blacks are on a march for our land, and once they get their hands on it, they'll try to seize our hotel too. If we aren't careful, we could lose the goose that lays the golden egg.'

'That's pure supposition, Stephanie.'

'By supporting them, you're causing us grief, Rebecca. You are forming a roadblock that stands in the way of progress. In my opinion, you should support us or bow out.'

'What do you mean by bow out?'

'Abel has spent his whole life building up the Sands Hotel, and he has prepared a wonderful plan to improve Broken Head, but you are eroding it from underneath him. By siding with Alkira, you're sleeping with the devil, Rebecca. You should be fighting tooth and nail to keep our land and our livelihood. In fact, I think you should leave the company.'

'The problem with you, Stephanie, is that you are unable to empathise with the plight of others, because you can only think of yourself. I don't think you have the capacity to understand why the local tribe needs to be back on its land.'

'To hell with them . . . Their reign finished once the first fleet sailed in!'

'That's such an offensive comment. I find it hard to believe how narrow you are.'

'You've never liked me, have you, Rebecca?'

'Well, Stephanie, you are a mean-spirited bitch from time to time.'

'You've always been jealous of me, haven't you?'

'Poppycock! I've never been jealous of you.'

'You've always wanted to be in the centre of things, but you were sidelined when I married your brother.'

'You're deluded, Stephanie. If you want to know what I think, you're scared that you won't inherit Marvell Street. You're aware that if something happens to Abel, the survivorship of Stenmark Inc. will go to the other joint tenants, and that's Kane and me.'

Knowing this is true, Stephanie remains silent.

'If that scenario occurs, Kane and I will end up with everything.'

'You're right, Rebecca. I am concerned about that.'

'You're worried that you could be left out in the cold, aren't you?' Rebecca challenges.

'Yes, I am, and that's what could happen unless we are the ones still left standing.'

Rebecca finds her sister-in-law's argument to be unnerving and she decides to divert her attention onto food. 'I brought a picnic. Let's have something to eat,' she suggests.

'OK, let's eat,' Stephanie agrees.

In her mind's eye, Stephanie has already imagined Rebecca's death. She envisages she'll be like a drowning Ophelia from *Hamlet*, floating off with her sundress billowing above the surface of the water as she cries out, 'Save me! Save me! I can't swim!'

When Rebecca bends down to open her picnic basket, Stephanie is poised to push her overboard. She knows that all she needs to do is to give her a little shove, and Rebecca would topple over the back of the boat.

'I've made some turkey sandwiches with cranberries and Swiss cheese. Would you like one?' Rebecca asks, oblivious to her sister-in-law's plan. Rebecca retrieves a fresh sandwich from her picnic basket and holds it out.

'Thank you,' Stephanie answers sweetly.

As Rebecca is holding the sandwich out to her, Stephanie pretends to lose her footing and she bumps into Rebecca. Losing her balance, Rebecca flounders towards the back of the boat. As she grasps desperately for the boat's rear railing, Stephanie has the opportunity to give Rebecca an extra shove which would tip her into the brine. At the last minute however, she pushes the murderous thought from her mind, and instead she extends her hand to Rebecca so that she can regain her balance.

On the return journey, Stephanie steers the boat back to the Pass in silence, furious with herself for baulking at the last moment. Her prime mission for the boat trip was to eliminate Rebecca from Stenmark Inc. but she'd failed miserably. She castigates herself for allowing her better side to triumph.

Feeling seasick, Rebecca retreats into the boat's cabin and wrapped in a blanket, she attempts to quell her nausea. Convinced that Stephanie had intended to kill her, she feels extremely fortunate to have survived the outing.

As the boat pulls into the ramp, Rebecca is relieved to escape from the confined space of the cabin, and quickly disembarks over the side with her picnic basket, with a face as pallid as potato skin.

'What's wrong with her?' a man at the ramp asks after noticing Rebecca's pasty face.

'Oh, she's depressed about a snake killing her partner and a shark attacking her son,' Stephanie answers flippantly.

Chapter 37

FISHERMAN'S LOOKOUT

Stephanie admits to Abel that on the boat trip, she'd failed to convince Rebecca to leave Stenmark Inc. and that she'd also been unsuccessful in convincing her sister in law to oppose Alkira's push for native title for Broken Head.

'Don't worry, darling. I'm sure you did your best,' Abel placates her, but deep down, he's bitterly disappointed at the poor outcome. 'Tomorrow I'll call Kane and with any luck, I'll have more success with him,' he responds in an effort to console her.

Knowing that Kane sleeps in, Abel waits until midday before he calls his brother. Even though it is twelve noon, Kane is still half asleep when his mobile phone rings.

'Hi, bro. I have a wonderful proposition for you. I think we should meet up and talk,' Abel proposes.

'Sure, dear brother. When would you like to meet up?' he answers, still in a daze.

'How about meeting at Fisherman's Lookout straight away?'

'It's too bloody early, Abel. I'm hardly awake. I was just thinking as I lie here that it's the end of summer and that's the only time of the year that laziness has some sort of respectability.'

'There's no rest for the wicked, Kane. It's a beautiful day, and I have a super deal for you. The early bird catches the worm, bro. After our chat, you can go for a swim to clear your head.'

'OK, I'll meet you there in half an hour,' he reluctantly agrees.

After struggling out of bed, Kane dresses in a pair of board shorts, a short-sleeved shirt, and a pair of Jesus sandals before strolling from his guesthouse over to Clarkes Beach. As he walks along the water's edge, he fills his lungs with fresh salty air, and watches the seabirds as they plummet from a great height into the water beside him. He marvels at their rate of success in coming up with a fish.

As Kane approaches Fisherman's Lookout, he wonders what sort of proposition his brother has in mind for him. He sees Abel sitting on a rock, beckoning for him to come over and join him.

'Hi, brother. How's it going?' Abel asks him in an upbeat tone.

'Look, Abel, before you say anything, I've been thinking about your development, and I've come to the conclusion that it's unfair on the First Nation people.'

'Not you too, brother! Kane, you must be a complete idiot if you can't see that Nirvana is our pathway to becoming mega-wealthy. If you don't sign up to it, you'll be giving up on an absolute fortune.'

'Believe me, I've thought about it, Abel, but it doesn't sit well,' he responds.

'You know, Kane, you're a bloody flake. Can't you see that this is our future? Where's your backbone?'

'I'm out, Abel. I loved your plan initially, but after I thought about it carefully, I've decided it's unfair. Anyway, I need to support Alkira, who wants Broken Head to be a national park, as does my mate Jimmy and his mob.'

'You're a fucking idiot, Kane!'

'I didn't come here to be abused, Abel. What do you want to talk to me about?' he asks.

'I have a deal for you.'

'If it's another one of your crooked schemes, I'm not interested.'

'You won't get a deal like this anywhere else but from me, I can assure you, bro.'

'Out with it.'

'I'm prepared to offer you a huge amount of money so you'll walk away from the family business. You know we can't work together, so this is the best deal you are ever going to get.'

'What dumb deal are you proposing?'

'I'm proposing to buy you out.'

'What's the extent of the bribe?'

'Twenty million dollars.'

'Fuck that, Abel! Do you think I was born yesterday? My share is worth way more than that now.'

'I want an end to it, Kane. I can't have you hovering around, threatening to give our property away.'

'That's Alkira's plan. It's got nothing to do with me.'

'But you agree with her, don't you?'

'Yeah, I do, because it's fair, but you don't know the meaning of the word, Abel.'

'Fuck you, brother! You've done nothing all these years, while I've spent my whole adult life building up our company's wealth.'

'You're doing it for yourself, Abel. You've given me nothing.'

'Look, Kane, I'll raise the payout to twenty-two million dollars. It's all the bank will lend me. I'm offering it all to you, and you can walk away from Byron Bay with it all in your pocket. You'll be a rich man, and we can call it quits.'

'You're a bloody skinflint, Abel. Anyway, I don't need the money, so there's no way,' Kane lies.

'Twenty-five million then.'

'No, you can keep your twenty-five pieces of silver, Abel. I'm not interested.'

'Fuck you, Kane! I'm done! You're impossible to deal with!'

Suddenly, Abel sees red and leaps at Kane, and after grasping him in a tight headlock, he drags him into the water. Kane struggles desperately to be released, but Abel tightens his grip around his neck and continues to march him forward deeper and deeper into the sea. When the water is up to his waist, Abel dips Kane's head into the brine and holds it down. Unable to breathe, Kane struggles to raise his head back up to the surface, but Abel's grip on him is as firm as a vice.

Realising that he must make one last concerted effort to release himself before it's too late, Kane musters all his strength and flings himself into a somersault. Fortunately for him, the sudden movement causes Abel to release his grip, which allows him to escape towards the shore. With water splashing wildly around him, he scrambles away from his brother, but Abel follows him like a hungry crocodile. When Abel catches Kane's shirt, he pulls him back into the water where they wrestle in the shallows in a fight to the death.

At one point, Kane manages to push Abel backwards, which causes him to flounder in the water. As it is his big chance to give him a dose of his own medicine, Kane pounces on top of his brother and holds him beneath him. For some time, he watches him splutter, but Kane cannot go through with it, and he allows Abel to emerge from the water, gasping madly for air.

'You deserve to die, Abel, but I can't do it,' he declares, as he leaves his brother gasping in the shallows.

Wondering why his brother hates him so much, Kane saunters off up the beach alone, his wet clothes dripping onto the hard sand with each step. He is sure that if the tables had been reversed today, he'd have been drowned at Fisherman's Lookout, but even though he's been the victor, he takes no joy from his triumph.

Chapter 38

ALKIRA'S APARTMENT

Unaware of the peril that his father has been through at Fisherman's Lookout, a barefoot Archie sits on Alkira's balcony, wearing just a pair of board shorts. Alkira has invited him to work on his novel at her apartment while she is at work at the fruit and veg co-op, and Archie has chosen to sit out on the balcony, not only because it is cooler out there, but because her dining table is presently out of bounds for him. It is strewn with native title documents awaiting her further research.

Archie is oblivious to the fact that he has a visitor on the balcony. A huge spider, the size of a lumberjack's fist, has managed to squeeze under the balustrade to join him. Unaware of its presence, he continues to type at his dented keyboard, but when he finally spots the huge furry ball, his eyes widen with fright. Having never seen a spider of this alarming size before, he is spooked by it. When the hairy creature advances towards him, Archie deftly lifts his bare feet onto the seat of his chair, and balancing up there in a froglike position, he hopes he'll be out of harm's way. Archie finds the spider's furry body to be extremely repulsive, but almost as abhorrent as the ugly fur, he hates the way the spider's eight legs seem to all move in tandem.

Having never been in this precarious position before, Archie goes through his options. *Should I remain frozen on this chair until the spider moves away, or should I yell for help? Can a spider of this enormous size climb up the leg of a chair?*

After making several jumps towards him, the creature finally stops at the foot of his chair and raises its front legs as if it is ready to climb. Convinced that it is coming for him, Archie panics, and in a desperate attempt to escape, he hurtles his body towards the living room. After landing awkwardly between the double doors that lead into Alkira's apartment, he quickly scrambles for safety, but Archie's spider ordeal is not yet over.

He can feel a nasty clawing sensation on his leg, and when he looks down, he's alarmed to see the huntsman gripping onto his skin just below his shorts. Archie swipes wildly at the hairy creature, but unfortunately for him, the arachnid manages to survive his desperate attempts to flick it off. Tenaciously gripping onto his leg, it raises its head defiantly. Repulsed by the look of its beady eyes, Archie swipes wildly at it again, and this time, he manages to flick it across the room, where it scurries for refuge under Alkira's living room sofa.

With his heart pounding, Archie scours the area around the couch, but the huntsman remains annoyingly out of sight. After ten long minutes however, the spider creeps into view. It crawls stealthily towards Alkira's bedroom, but as Archie is not about to follow it in, he observes from a distance as it makes its purposeful journey. Once the spider has disappeared inside her bedroom, Archie closes the door, locking it inside.

When Alkira returns, Archie immediately relates his scary ordeal to her and informs her that his last vision of it was when it was crawling into her bedroom.

'Don't worry about it, Archie,' Alkira replies nonchalantly. 'Huntsmen are harmless creatures. I actually like having them around because they catch flies and other creepy-crawlies.'

'Don't you want to find it and get rid of it?' he asks.

'No, not particularly. Spiders don't worry me at all,' she responds.

Amazed at her composure, he asks, 'Are you sure?'

'There's nothing to be afraid of, Archie,' she replies, as she disappears into her bedroom to change out of her work clothes.

Archie retreats to the kitchen at this point to heat up some green curry that he'd purchased earlier, and once it is ready, he invites Alkira to join him for a casual meal in front of the television. It proves to be an uneasy dinner for Archie, however, because he is continually on the alert, watching for the hairy huntsman to reappear from underneath Alkira's bedroom door. Alkira, who is more interested in what is happening on TV, asks Archie to turn up the volume, because there seems to be an arrest taking place on the evening news.

'Look, Archie, they've caught the bottle shop gang!' she exclaims. 'There's the guy with the ugly tattoos and the bad teeth. I hope they nail the bastard.'

'Me too.'

Exhausted after her busy day at work, Alkira decides not to work on her native title documents until the morning when she will be fresher, and despite the presence of the spider in her room, she is able to enjoy a restful night's sleep. Archie however, tosses and turns on her living room couch dreaming of being trapped in a spider's web.

When Alkira wakes the following morning, the huntsman is clinging to the ceiling directly above her bed. She gives it a cursory glance before following the aroma of coffee which is emanating from the kitchen. She finds Archie at the percolator.

'Perfect timing. You're just in time for a serious caffeine hit,' he says when Alkira appears at the door.

'I'm ready for one, Archie. I need a jolt before I launch into my research,' she replies, staring at the daunting stack of papers on her dining room table.

Deciding to waste no time, Alkira pulls up a chair and scrutinises one of the documents she finds on the top of the pile. The paper she picks up happens to be hugely relevant to her application, as it shows a historical timeline of everyone who has ever occupied Broken Head since colonisation.

'Broken Head has had no freehold claims on it!' she exclaims excitedly after examining the paper.

'What did you say?' Archie calls.

'There was a pastoral lease conferred on Broken Head in 1880, but as it wasn't exclusive, it didn't extinguish the native title.'

'Is that good news?' Archie calls back.

'It sure is!'

'Why?'

'Joseph Stenmark was granted a one-hundred-year lease which did not continue into perpetuity. The Stenmark lease is now from year to year, and that clears the way for us to apply for a determination.'

'What do you mean by a determination, Alkira?' Archie asks, as he presents her with a steaming hot mug of coffee.

'It means we can apply for a native title, but we need to identify which native title right, interest, traditional law, or custom we want conferred.'

'Right,' Archie replies, looking somewhat confused.

'What actually is a native title determination?'

Archie realises that this is a very fundamental question, but it is an excellent place for him to start understanding the process.

'It recognises the traditional rights and interests of Aboriginal people to land and waters,' Alkira replies with the assurance of an experienced legal eagle.

Archie sits beside her.

'A native title will confer on my people a right to live, camp, conduct ceremonies, hunt, fish, collect food, build shelters, and visit places of cultural importance on Broken Head,' she reads aloud.

'Sounds bloody good to me, but how do you go about obtaining the wretched thing?' Archie asks.

'We have to prove that we've had a continuing association with the land . . . That's how.'

'I don't want to sound negative, Alkira, but I reckon proving that may prove to be mighty difficult.'

'Why?'

'Well, didn't Joseph Stenmark completely fence off Broken Head to keep your tribe out?'

'Yes, he did.'

'Won't that be a big problem, darling heart?'

'Do you remember Jimmy telling you at the Nirvana sign that his father was the original caretaker of the gold mine?'

'Yes.'

'He also told you that when old Bobby died, the role of caretaker went to him.'

'Yes, I knew that.'

'Jimmy, Ronnie, and Matilda were all Bobby's children. Archie, they all lived inside the compound.'

'Does that mean that they could all qualify as applicants?'

'Technically, yes, but I wish it was that straightforward.'

'What's the hitch?'

'I'd like to put Jimmy on the claim, but he doesn't want to have anything to do with signing any white man's papers, and his sister Matilda has gone missing for more than two and a half decades. The only one left in the family who has lived there continuously is Ronnie, but you must appreciate that she's hardly the most reliable applicant.'

'You can say that again.'

'Be kind, Archie.'

'Sorry, but your mother is not what you'd call a strong claimant.'

'It says here that we have to provide historical documentation about how our tribe continued its customs and traditions as far back as European settlement. That'll be no easy task,' Alkira admits.

'What documents do the federal court require?' he asks.

'It's very daunting, Archie. They want to know if there were any previous agreements or payments made by the tribe up to the time the Stenmarks obtained their pastoral lease.'

'Really? Why?'

'They want to be sure that we haven't given away our rights to the land. We have to prove that our common law continued to exist unencumbered. If there are no such agreements, our customs will be deemed to have existed alongside the pastoral lease. That's if an act of government hasn't extinguished them. I'll have to do more digging into that.'

'Do you think the Stenmark lease could affect your claim then?' Archie asks.

'It says here that these pastoral leases did not confer rights of exclusive possession, so I'm hoping the National Native Title Tribunal will look favourably at our evidence. To prove this strong connection, we'll have to show that we've continually engaged with the land for centuries.'

'It sounds like a mountain of work, Alkira,' Archie sighs.

'Yes, it will be,' she agrees. 'We'll need survey maps, technical topographical descriptions of the land, details of any previous tenure, plus information from our elders about our habitation,' she replies.

'Are you ready for all this?' he asks, reeling under the mammoth task ahead.

'Historically speaking, we are talking about recent times. This land has been the basis of our relationships for thousands of years, and if we can prove that we've had a continued connection with it through our storytelling, ceremonies, and political activism, I think we'll have a chance of getting our claim through.'

'What's the first thing you have to do then?' Archie asks, already enlisted in the fight.

'The first form required by the federal court is evidence that I'm authorised by my group to make the application.'

'Do you have it?'

'I'm about to get it.'

Chapter 39

MEETING WITH THE TRIBE

When Alkira calls a meeting at the Aboriginal camp, a large crowd rallies, and during the meeting, she is elected president of a committee that authorises her to pursue a native title for Broken Head. Two of her Dubay dancing friends take up positions on the committee too, one as secretary and the other as treasurer. Jimmy also sits with them, having been co-opted by Alkira to represent the elders of the tribe.

At the meeting, Alkira explains that in the future, she will be setting up an umbrella joint management committee, which will represent the relevant stakeholders that have been historically involved with the land. Along with the local tribe, this committee will also include the Byron Shire Council, the NSW Parks & Wildlife Service, and the Stenmark family. To settle everyone down, she points out that under any new land use agreement, this joint management committee will appoint local indigenous people to manage the proposed new national park.

She explains to the indigenous group that the way forward is for the tribe to prove that it has had an ongoing relationship with Broken Head, and to do this, she'll need their help. She explains that after the passing of the historic Mabo Legislation, the term "terra nullius", which means the land belongs to no one, no longer applies in Australian law.

'What does this mean?' Daisy calls out, a little bewildered by the terminology.

'It means we can now apply for a title to the land, Daisy,' Alkira is quick to reply.

'About bloody time! We've waited long enough!' she rejoins.

'How will it end up?' an old man asks from the back of the hall.

'If we are successful, sir, we will have access to country again,' Alkira answers confidently.

'Are you sayin' we'll be free to conduct our rituals an' customs on our land again?' he enquires.

'Yes. And we'll be able to invite others to come and respect it with us too. We'll be able to welcome the larger community to country while promoting our own culture at the same time. It will even create meaningful jobs for many of us,' Alkira answers.

During the meeting, most of the assembled crowd seem pleased with what Alkira is proposing, and they encourage her to pursue the first steps towards obtaining indigenous land rights on their behalf.

One old lady even calls out, 'Alkira, you've given us hope, girl! I'd given up. I thought we had no chance of ever gettin' back on country again.'

Another man with a more cautious view, however, raises his stick at her. 'You're a Stenmark, aren't you, girl?' he challenges. 'How can we trust you? How can we be sure you're not on the side of our persecutors? How do we know you don't want to grab our land for them?'

'I'm just like you, sir,' Alkira rebuffs proudly. 'My goal is clear. I want the land at Broken Head returned to our people.'

'But you live outside, girl. I hear you've left us to live in Sydney,' he rejoins, lifting his stick into the air again. 'I also hear you hang out with the Stenmarks. You could be forsaking us. If you want us to put our trust in you, my advice is to stay within your tribe.'

Alkira is taken aback by the man's remark. 'I'm a modern woman, sir,' she rebuffs. 'I won't let any one place or any one group confine me. I am a woman of the world, and I want everyone to enjoy Broken Head.'

'But we are the traditional custodians. Don't forget that,' the man retorts.

'And we will be again, but this time, we'll have the government and our local council to help us effectively manage the land so we all can enjoy it.'

'Don't be sleeping with the devil, girl,' the old man warns, raising his stick at her for the third time.

As Alkira makes her way back into town after the meeting, she reflects on what the old man had said. She must not be seen siding with the Stenmarks or she may be perceived as sleeping with the devil, and it may appear that she is betraying her people. Alkira considers keeping Archie at arm's length.

Chapter 40

ALKIRA'S CALL

It takes many months for Alkira to collate the information required for her native title claim, but when she has assembled a comprehensive historical account of her tribe's association with Broken Head, she transcribes it onto the required Form 1. In her submission, she attaches her detailed research, which includes historical and modern maps of the land to show exactly where her tribe had conducted corroborees and important cultural gatherings in the past.

To demonstrate the continuance of the tribe's rituals and traditions over time, Alkira includes videoed interviews with the elders, who have provided her with a valuable oral history. Part of her claim catalogues the daily activities and diet of her people over the years, detailing the digging for yams and the collecting of seasonal fruits and nuts for their staple food. Lilly-pillies and wild cherries are some of those she mentions, along with macadamias and pine nuts. Alkira includes information about the traditional medicines that her tribe has used over the years such as painkillers and antiseptics, and also includes details of the various animal skins the tribe wore as clothing. In her submission, she includes many of the elders' descriptions of shelters made from grass and palm fronds, and she includes details of fish traps and spears. Some of the tribesmen speak about how they hunted wallabies and kangaroos using spears launched by a catapult called a *woomera*.

To explain how the entire nation used the land, Alkira documents how the local people would invite the neighbouring tribes to be part of activities. She describes the annual 'mullet run', which was an event shared with neighbouring tribes so they could share in the abundance.

In addition, Alkira provides information about shells and bones that were collected from the local midden at the Pass. After being carbon-dated from the midden's basal layers, these specimens offer compelling evidence that her people have been on the land for at least the last one thousand years. Confident that her submission includes enough historical evidence of her tribe's continuing laws and customs dating back to and predating European settlement, Alkira submits her claim, designating her mother, Rhonda Merinda, as her claimant.

When Alkira returns from delivering her submission to the Native Title Tribunal, she sinks back onto her living room sofa, sighing with relief after all her hard work. She is not able to rest for long, however, because her telephone rings. Stan Bowles is on the line with a request.

'Hello, Alkira,' he greets.

'Hello, Stan. What a surprise to hear from you.'

'Alkira, I'm ringing to tell you about what happened after our last television interview on the ABC. Did you know that our ratings skyrocketed? Lots of people were applauding you for saving that Stenmark boy and you also received accolades for providing pro bono legal support to your Aboriginal mates. There appears to be some momentum building about supporting your rights to Broken Head too. Tell me, do you intend to apply for a native title determination?'

'Yes, Stan. That is precisely what I'm doing.'

'Tell me more.'

'Well, just this morning, I lodged our application claiming that we have had a continuing relationship with the land at Broken Head and that we have a legitimate right to have the land returned to us.'

'Under whose name did you claim these rights, Alkira?'

'I lodged the claim under my mother's name, Rhonda Merinda.'

'Your mother!' Stan repeats, incredulous that the applicant is the town vagrant. He laughs haughtily.

'What's so amusing about my mother lodging the claim? She's always lived on Broken Head, you know. She was born there,' Alkira adds.

'I thought the land had been fenced off. Didn't Joseph Stenmark block your clan from entering?'

'You're right, Stan, he did. But you may not know that my grandfather Bobby Merinda was the Stenmarks' caretaker, and that he and his family were the only ones allowed to live inside the compound. He lived in a cottage inside the gate so that he could check on the gold mine day and night.'

'Is that so? Is Bobby still alive, Alkira?'

'No.'

'What happened when he passed on?'

'His son, Jimmy, took over from him, and Jimmy has continued to live there ever since. His two sisters lived with him until one went missing.'

'This is very interesting, Alkira. It sounds as if your family has continuously lived inside the Stenmark compound.'

'Yes, that is what I am pursuing in the claim, Stan.'

'For confirmation, I'd like to interview the applicant on your submission. Would that be at all possible?'

'Well, I suppose I can arrange for you to visit my mother in her nursing home if you're interested to meet her. I'm sure she will confirm our family's connection to the land.'

'I'll take you up on that, Alkira. I'm dead keen to follow this claim, as it appears to be a David-and-Goliath struggle!'

Chapter 41

KANE VISITS RONNIE'S NURSING HOME

About half an hour before Stan Bowles is scheduled to interview Ronnie, Alkira, Archie, and Kane arrive at the nursing home attached to Lismore Hospital. Alkira enters carrying a branch of bright yellow native wattle for Ronnie and after presenting it to her, tries to organise with the nurse on duty to find a vase large enough to hold it.

Kane barely recognises Ronnie when he sees her. It has been over twenty-five years since he last laid eyes on her, and when he examines her worn, torn face, it is obvious to him that she is world-weary from the hardships she has suffered over many years.

'Hello, Ronnie,' he calls.

'Who's this?' Ronnie asks Alkira.

'It's Kane Stenmark,' Alkira replies.

'What didja bring that bastard here for? Get him out of my sight, girl!' she scolds, but Kane steps towards her, his face flushed.

'I want to tell you how sorry I am for abandoning you, Ronnie,' he entreats.

'You bolted like a brumby escapin' from a lasso, Kane Stenmark,' Ronnie replies.

'I know I did. At the time, my family forbade me to come anywhere near you, and I was never allowed to admit that I was the father of your baby. My father threatened to throw me out of the family if I stayed in contact.'

'You bastard! You bolted the minute you found out I was pregnant!' Ronnie blasts.

Kane nods, admitting that she is correct.

'You Stenmarks are a pack of bastards, every last one of you!' Ronnie shrieks.

'Ronnie, I'm truly sorry. I've been hoping that after all these years, you might forgive me. I never missed a payment for Alkira's college fees, you know.'

'Well, that was your only saving grace, Kane Stenmark. Somewhere inside you – very deep down, I might add – you've proven you've got a heart.'

Kane remains silent as Ronnie's eyes lock with his.

'What I've always wanted to know is whether you killed my sister. Did you murder Matilda, you mongrel?'

'No, Ronnie. Everyone has blamed me over the years for her disappearance, but I can assure you it wasn't me,' Kane defends.

'Who the hell was it then? I've always thought it was one of you bastards.'

'I'm still trying to get to the bottom of it, Ronnie. Lately, I've been like Sherlock Holmes trying to find out.'

'I loved Matilda,' Ronnie blurts. 'She had a foul mouth on 'er, but she was so kind. She helped me a lot when Alkira went away to school.

Then one night she was gone, an' no one knew where she went. I blamed you Stenmarks – you bet I did!'

'All I can say is that it wasn't me, Ronnie,' Kane repeats before turning away.

'Before you go, daddio, what's this I hear about you lot turnin' Broken Head into a housing development?'

'It's my brother's plan, Ronnie. Abel has grand ideas for Broken Head.'

'If that ever happens, Kane, I promise you that the curse on you lot will never end. For your own good, you should stop the bastard in his tracks right now. Hear me, Kane – stop 'im now!'

The film crew announce their arrival at the nursing home, and one of the nurses starts straightening up the blankets on Ronnie's bed. She plumps up her pillows, hands her a fresh glass of water, and starts to comb her unruly hair. Ronnie waves the nurse away.

'They can take me as I am!' she bellows.

Chapter 42

RONNIE'S INTERVIEW

'Ladies and gentlemen, today we are at the nursing home attached to the Lismore Hospital. I am here to interview Rhonda Merinda, an indigenous woman who has been listed as the applicant on a native title claim to return a vast tract of land at Broken Head near Byron Bay to her tribe. Many of you may have seen Rhonda out and about on the town's streets. Welcome to our show, Rhonda!' Stan Bowles announces in an upbeat tone.

'For Christ's sake, call me Ronnie. Everyone else does!'

Prepared to take no nonsense, Ronnie sits up in her bed, surrounded by soft white pillows, her white hair reaching skywards in the usual disarray. Behind her bed is a large vase containing the branch of wattle that Alkira brought in. Its bright yellow blossoms have been placed strategically behind Ronnie's head so that in a close-up, she looks as if she's in the bush. When Stan Bowles approaches closer with a microphone, Ronnie clutches tightly to her daughter's hand.

'Jingi walla jugan!' Ronnie announces in a loud guttural voice.

'For those of you who don't know,' Stan Bowles explains to his viewers, "Jingi walla jugan" is a welcome to country. We must always remember that we are on land that once belonged to the local

Aboriginal people, and we should always honour the elders past, present, and emerging.'

'It always will be our land too,' Ronnie replies curtly.

'Yes, well, that is a moot point at the moment, Ronnie,' Stan corrects.

After this comment, Ronnie takes an immediate dislike to Stan Bowles and she curls up her lip as if she is about to spit at him.

'Ronnie, let's talk specifically about Broken Head, shall we?' he asks, trying for firmer ground. Ronnie stares at him warily, thinking he's got off on the wrong foot.

'Were you born on Broken Head?' he enquires.

'Uh-huh.'

'What can you tell us about your birth?'

'Winnie gave birth to me on her own in the bush at Iron Bark. There was a birthing tree there and that's where I was born.'

'I presume that's on Broken Head.'

'Yep.'

'What do you remember about your childhood there?' Stan asks.

'We ate yams and lilly-pillies, wild cherries and black apples,' Ronnie replies.

'Did you have any siblings to play with?'

'What are they?' Ronnie asks, turning to Alkira.

'Any brothers and sisters?' Alkira advises her mother.

'Yep. I had two . . . a sister and a brother.'

'And you all lived on Broken Head?'

'Uh-huh,' she affirms.

'Can I ask what your siblings' names are?'

'My brother is Jimmy, and my sister was Matilda.'

'That name rings a bell. Wasn't she the young woman who went missing about twenty-five years ago?'

'Yep.'

When Ronnie looks down, Alkira squeezes her hand, and a little tear appears in one of Ronnie's eyes when she thinks about her sister.

'Before we get to that, Ronnie, can I ask more about your childhood?'

'Uh-huh.'

'Did all of you grow up in the Stenmark compound?'

'Yeah. No one else from our tribe was ever allowed in except my dad. He was the caretaker for the Stenmarks, an' his family was the only ones allowed inside.'

'What was your mother's name again?'

'Mum's name was Winnie, an' Dad's name was Bobby. Mum looked after us while our dad went to the mine. She taught us lots of songlines at Broken Head when we was kids.'

'Can you describe exactly what your father did?'

'My dad's job was to keep everyone out of the compound. The Stenmarks were mining for gold, and his job was to look after all the gold-mining equipment. He also did a little forestry work.'

'What happened to Bobby, Ronnie?'

'Bobby got sick. Luckily, over the last few years of his life, he taught my brother the ropes, an' when he died, Jimmy was able to take over from him.'

'Was your sister born in Broken Head too?'

'Yep.'

Ronnie stares straight ahead for a moment, trying not to cry, but finally loses the battle and bursts into loud sobs. Alkira quickly grasps a tissue box from a nearby cabinet and gently wipes away her mother's tears.

'I'm sorry to ask you about your sister, Ronnie. I know her disappearance has been an unfortunate affair,' Stan apologises.

Ronnie splutters and wipes her eyes with the backs of her gnarled fingers.

'What can you tell me about her?' Stan asks, fishing for information about the abduction. Ronnie takes a deep breath.

'One day, when I was five years old,' she begins, 'one of the miners came up to our house an' grabbed hold of my mother. He was a big man, and the bastard forced Mum into the kitchen and raped her in front of me. Mum was screaming the house down the whole time, but I was only a kid, and all I could do was hide behind the door until it was all over.'

Ronnie's eyes fill up with tears, and her body begins to shake. Everyone in the room can see that it is a painful memory for her.

'That would have been so traumatic for you as a young child,' Stan empathises. 'For both you and your mother,' he quickly adds.

Ronnie remains silent, with her hands pulsing into fists and then releasing.

'What a cruel son of a bitch!' Stan utters spontaneously, shaking his head in sympathy as Ronnie tries to compose herself.

'Nine months later, my sister Matilda was born with skin much lighter than mine,' Ronnie adds, touching her arm.

'I understand why,' Stan comments. Ronnie stares at him as if he is an imbecile.

'For years after that, Mum kept clear of the mine, because she was scared of the men who worked there. She warned us never to go anywhere near it, so we kept away.'

'I've always wanted to know what happened to your sister, Ronnie,' Stan states, expecting Ronnie to explain how she disappeared. Ronnie ignores him.

'When I was 5 and Matilda was almost 2, a big black car arrived at Broken Head. I don't know who had let them in through the gate, but the car pulled up outside our house like a hearse. Dad was at the mine at the time, but Mum was in the house with the three of us. When some men in suits knocked on the door, my mother wouldn't open it.

"We want to speak to Matilda Merinda!" they called out loudly.'

'My mum had heard from her friends about these white officials from the government who would suddenly arrive out of nowhere, sayin' something about an intervention. Her friends had warned her that they took children from their parents, and they seemed to prefer the kids who had a lighter skin.'

'The NSW government agencies deemed them to be more easily assimilated into white society, I suppose,' Stan adds to enhance Ronnie's story, showing he knows at least a few details about the Stolen Generation.

"Quick! Jimmy, take the girls into the bush and hide! Go now and stay until night-time!" my mum ordered as she bundled us out the back door. I hid in the woodshed, while Jimmy dragged Matilda farther out into the scrub. Mum finally returned to the front door.'

"Are you Mrs Merinda?" the officials asked.

"Yes."

"We want to speak with your daughter, Matilda Merinda," they announced again, reading her name from a notebook.

"She's not here."

"Where is she?"

"With her father," my mother answered, thinking on her feet.

"Where are they now?"

"At the mine."

"The gold mine?"

"Yes."

'After hearing this, the men abruptly left the front door, but before they got back into their car, they made a quick search around our cottage. That's when they found me shaking like a leaf in the woodshed behind a pile of firewood.'

"What's your name?" they bellowed.

'I decided on the spot that I'd give my sister's name to protect her. "M-M-Matilda," I answered meekly'.

'They bawled "Come with us, Matilda," and they dragged me over to their black car and slung me into the back seat.'

'As they drove off towards the compound gate, they were sayin', "She looks full-blooded … It says in this notebook that she was younger and that she was going to be half-caste."'

'When I looked out the back window, I saw my mother standing in front of our cottage. I'll never forget it. Her hands were coverin' 'er cheeks, and she seemed to be calling, "Bring back my child! Bring back my child!"'

'That was the moment you became part of the Stolen Generation, Ronnie,' Stan gasps.

'Yeah. The bastards drove for miles, and in the back of their car, I cried for hours on end. I didn't have a clue where I was when they pulled up at a large brick building late at night. When I got out of the car, they placed me in the hands of a nurse, who put me down in the register as 849. Next to this number, she put down my name as Matilda Merinda and that my age was 5 and that I was full-blooded.'

'Did the place have a name?'

'Yeah, it was called the Cootamundra Home for Orphans and Neglected Aboriginal Children. They said that I was from a child race an' that I needed to be protected for my own good.'

'Did they tell you why they were separating you from your family?'

'Yeah, they said they were dealing with our inferiority by removing us from our families. They said we'd only become proper members of society if we were removed to learn white ways.'

'That sounds shocking!' Stan exclaims.

'They threw me into a cold dark dormitory with girls from other tribes. Most of them were of lighter skin than me, but I couldn't understand any of them. It was really tough because they forbade us to speak our native language, insistin' that we speak only English, but many of the girls had only a few words. Each morning, we saluted the Australian flag, and even though we were just kids, we were made to do hard domestic labour all day long, like doing the washin', endless ironin', cleanin', and gardenin'. At night, we were under strict control too. We were all so miserable because we weren't free, but if you kept cryin', the hidings got harder and harder. In time, I learned to stifle my cry.'

'It sounds like a juvenile prison,' Stan comments.

'Uh-huh. During my time there, they were runnin' out of funds, and as their money shrank, our diet was reduced. Every morning we had dry porridge for breakfast, a soup of boiled bones with no vegetables for lunch, and dinner was often just bread and jam with a cup of tea. They didn't regard us as equals in that place and they dished out harsh punishments for disobedience. Some of the girls had their heads shaven because they had nits, and if you wet the bed, they chained you to it for the day without giving you any food. They dealt with runaways even more harshly. They were flogged with a hosepipe and left for days, often in the rain, standin' on a concrete slab. It was meant to deter them from ever tryin' it again.'

'Did you feel homesick?' Stan Bowles asks.

'What a dumb question! We were all so desperately lonely there, because we had no love . . . We'd all left our hearts behind.'

Stan nods sheepishly.

'I felt lucky that I knew where I came from, because some of the other girls were totally lost. Some didn't know where they had been taken from or what their mother's name was.'

'You must have suffered extremely harsh psychological and physical abuse in this place, Ronnie,' Stan fields, trying to sound sympathetic.

'You're dead right, mate! I was either abused or neglected, and I was always made to feel ashamed of my heritage. They stripped me of my dignity in that place. I was in bondage, like a slave,' Ronnie answers forthrightly.

'The only good thing about it was that one of the nurses taught me how to read.' Ronnie allows a smile. 'As a lot of you know, these days, I'm a bloody bookworm.'

'How did you finally get away from that dastardly place?' Stan asks.

'When I was 7, they threatened to adopt me into a family of white people and it was then that I knew I had to plan my escape. I pretended to be desperately ill, an' they placed me in the "fever hut". It was like a quarantine station on the edge of the grounds, separate from the main building. When the nurse turned her back, I ran for my life through the gate, an' I managed to survive for three weeks on the roads, tryin' to find my way back to Broken Head.'

'What was it like when you got back?'

'Oh, I remember being so happy. I hugged everyone, especially Mum, Jimmy, and Matilda. Not Dad because he was sick with TB and they'd taken him away somewhere. He died a few years later. I told everyone how terrible it was in the institution, an' they couldn't believe how cruelly they'd treated me.'

'You endured it all on behalf of your little sister,' Stan states.

'Yep. That's what sisterly love is all about, ya know,' Ronnie answers.

'You're a very extraordinary person, Ronnie Merinda, so utterly courageous and selfless.'

'When I got home to Broken Head, my mum couldn't stop hugging me, but her news to me was that she was about to leave Broken

Head for good. She'd experienced another encounter with one of the miners, an' she couldn't risk staying there any longer. That's when she took me to a camp in downtown Byron Bay. Yeah, Mum and I moved to Lawson Street after I got back home. Matilda and Jimmy stayed on at Broken Head because Jimmy had his caretaking job to do, an' Matilda decided to stay with him to keep him company.'

'You left Broken Head then?' Stan Bowles asks.

'Yes, I did. Mum and I left. I remember it well, because on the day we left Broken Head, Jimmy had presents for Matilda and me. He had made two bangles out of some gold that he'd collected from near the mine, an' he had one engraved with my name on it and the other with Matilda's. I remember him giving them to us on the day Mum an' I moved off to Lawson Street.'

Ronnie twirls her gold bangle around on her left wrist as she sits up on the hospital bed.

'So, Ronnie, to be absolutely clear, Winnie and you left Broken Head after you returned home, and both of you went to live at the Lawson Street camp?'

'Uh-huh.'

'So you didn't live continuously on your sacred land at Broken Head then?'

'That's right, mister.'

Alkira raises her eyebrows in complete surprise. She had always believed that her mother had lived her entire life on Broken Head. This whole sad story of her removal is entirely new to her.

'Mum, I thought you'd always lived at Broken Head.'

'Alkira, I lived there until those white bastards dragged me off to Cootamundra. I was forced to spend two bloody years of my life in that hellhole, but when I returned home, Mum took me off with her to the Lawson Street camp.'

Alkira is in shock. Her mother has deliberately kept this critical information from her, no doubt wanting to free her from any association with her past.

'Were you happy at Lawson Street?' Stan Bowles asks, deciding to move right along.

'Yes, I loved living close to Clarkes Beach. It was there that I felt free again, but in time, the council thought the camp was too unsightly, an' they tore the bloody thing down.'

Chapter 43

ALKIRA'S CLAIM IS ASSESSED

After hearing Ronnie's story on television, Felix Barker is elated. He is now armed with enough information to stop Alkira's native title claim dead in its tracks. Under instruction from Abel, he makes a non-claimant application to the Native Title Tribunal, making his objection on the required Form 2. He submits it before the three-month notification period has lapsed, and in his submission, Felix states that the Stenmark family was awarded a hundred-year lease in 1880 and that it is still in continuance. He points out that Rhonda Merinda, the claimant, didn't always live at Broken Head and as evidence of this, he cites her admission on television that she had long breaks in her domicile there.

He cites her first break when she was institutionalised in Cootamundra and the next when she lived in a camp on Lawson Street, Byron Bay. Felix Barker requests that the Native Title Tribunal deny the claim because Rhonda Merinda is obviously an unqualified claimant.

After making its preliminary assessment, the National Native Title Tribunal duly notifies Alkira by letter that they have denied her claim outright. On reading this, Alkira bursts into tears. Her mountain of work has come to naught. The tribunal had accepted that her people had indeed continued their customs and traditions on the land, both before and during the hundred-year lease, but the actual claimant on the form was found to have lived away from the land for considerable periods. As the claimant had gaps in her domicile at Broken Head, they had no option but to refuse the application. The tribunal ended the letter by inviting Alkira to try again if she could find a claimant who could show no such break in their connection with the land.

Alkira knew her claim was in jeopardy the moment her mother had declared on television that she'd been forcibly removed from the property as part of the Stolen Generation. Even so, after her countless hours of hard work, she couldn't help but be bitterly disappointed by their decision.

'I'm so gutted, Archie,' she sobs loudly. 'After that mammoth amount of research, I was vainly hoping that they'd entertain my submission – if only to reward me for my efforts.'

Archie gives Alkira a tight hug to comfort her, but Alkira remains inconsolable, and she continues to sob in his arms.

'You did your best, Alkira, but unfortunately, your mother snookered you,' he voices. This comment only serves to upset Alkira even further, and her sobs increase in volume.

'It's a long race, Alkira. You've just failed to jump the initial hurdle. Don't give up yet, because it appears that the door is left open for you to try again.'

Archie tries to give Alkira hope, but no matter how much he tries to comfort her, she remains disconsolate. Deep down, she is embarrassed that they've wiped the floor with her claim. She'd given her First Nation people hope that their land would be returned to them, but it was a false hope based on incorrect information. She had been unforgivably naive.

How could I not have known the crucial details about my own mother's life? How could I not have known she was part of the Stolen Generation, so tragically reefed away from her parents?

Because of her gross ignorance about the facts, Alkira knows that she has misled her people and in the process, has quashed their aspirations.

Later that day, Alkira musters the courage to return to the Aboriginal camp to admit to her people that she takes full responsibility for the failure of the claim. When she arrives at the camp, still feeling embarrassed and wretched, she finds many of her friends and relatives are weeping about the adverse decision. Through their sobs, many of them openly criticise her for her ignorance of the facts. She offers up to them the lame excuse that her mother had held back the details of her past to protect her from being shackled to her life of despair, but this excuse does little to placate their overwhelming disappointment. Alkira asks some of the older women if they were aware of her mother's past, but they tell Alkira that her mother always refused to speak to them about her hardships and tragedies.

Chapter 44

KANE'S SEARCH FOR THE TRUTH

In his quest to personally investigate what went on at Marvell Street on the night of the B&S ball all those years ago, Kane decides to face his brother again. In the past, Abel had always denied any knowledge about the Aboriginal girl's disappearance, but Kane believes his denial bears further scrutiny. He arrives at Marvell Street, hoping to find his brother at home alone so he can interrogate him about it.

When Abel sees him at the door, he barks, 'What are you doing here, Kane? Have you decided to accept my twenty-five-million-dollar offer?'

'I'll never accept your offer, brother. It was a bloody insult!'

'Well then, why are you here?'

'I want to know what happened on the night of the B&S ball.'

'For fuck's sake, Kane, it was over twenty-five years ago, and I've already told you everything I know.'

'Tell me again, bro, because ever since that night, I've been blamed for that girl's disappearance.'

'I told you before that I went home because I'd had enough of the loud music. I think it was around one o'clock by the time I'd walked back to Marvell Street. When I got there, the house was dark, and I went straight to bed. I slept like a baby, if you really want to know.'

'Go on.'

'That's it, bro. The next day, I heard the girl had gone missing.'

'Why did you leave the B&S ball on your own?'

'I told you, I'd had enough. Everyone was getting drunk, and it was way too rowdy for me. I left on my own because no one wanted to leave with me at the time. Actually, when I left, you seemed to be having a good time chatting up some bird from Mudgee.'

'Yeah, I was with her for quite a while, but she ended up ditching me for some other bloke. I think it was that guy who was tearing around on the motorised lawnmower.'

'Oh, him!'

They both laugh.

'Mrs Boyle told me she heard a shot go off from here around midnight,' Kane presses.

'It was probably just one of those pickup trucks backfiring,' Abel suggests.

'Are you sure nothing happened here, Abel?'

'I heard absolutely nothing, bro. As I told you, I slept like a baby.'

'Did you drive my car that night?'

'No, Kane. Why would I drive your car?'

'Some people said they saw it on Bangalow Road. I wasn't driving it, that's for sure.'

'As far as I know, it was parked out front all night. It was certainly there when I arrived home, and it was there again in the morning too.'

'You have no clue about what happened to the girl?'

'Not a clue.'

Kane leaves Marvell Street after gleaning very little from his brother, but he has a strong suspicion that Abel is hiding something from him.

Chapter 45

KANE GRILLS REBECCA

Wondering if Rebecca will corroborate Abel's account, Kane leaves his brother's house and heads over to Rebecca's place to find out her version of events.

'Hi, sis. I've come to interrogate you,' he announces at her door.

'What's wrong, Kane?' she asks as she welcomes him in with a kiss on each cheek.

'I'm trying to get to the bottom of what happened to Matilda again. Lots of people are still blaming me for her disappearance. Apparently, after all this time, I'm still the prime suspect.'

Rebecca's face falls.

'You slipped out of the house that night, didn't you, sis?' Kane challenges.

'Who told you that?'

'Some partygoers on a pickup truck told the police that they saw you running home.'

Feeling cornered by this report, Rebecca decides to agree.

'Yes, it's true, Kane,' she admits. 'I did escape from the house, and I did stroll down Bangalow Road that night. When it was all a bit too scary however, I ran back home.'

'What scared you, Rebecca?'

'Oh, pickup trucks were backfiring, and there was a lot of yahooing going on.'

'Did you meet anyone?'

'No,' Rebecca lies, shaking her head, with her eyes lowered.

'Later in the night, when you were home at Marvell Street, did you hear a shot?'

'No, Kane. Everyone keeps asking me that.'

'Who has asked?'

'The police, for one.'

'Did you see my car out front?'

'Yes, it was there all night. The last time I saw it was when I got back from Bangalow Road.'

'Rebecca, I know there's something you're not telling me,' Kane presses.

'What do you mean?'

'Well, two indigenous boys told the police that they followed you home to Marvell Street. Don't you think you should tell me what happened? After all these years, it's bloody well time you told your brother what the fuck went on.'

Rebecca starts to shake.

'You *do* know what happened, so out with it, sis. I deserve to know.'

Rebecca bursts into tears, and Kane patiently waits for her to compose herself, his eyes remaining firmly directed towards her tear-stained face.

'Tell me exactly what went on at Marvell Street that night,' he orders firmly.

'I can't, Kane. I've been sworn to secrecy.' Rebecca wipes her tears on her sleeve.

'By whom?'

There is a short silence before the both of them chorus, 'Abel!'

'I knew the bastard was in it up to his neck!' Kane exclaims.

'Don't grill me anymore, please Kane. Please stop. I can't say anything further. I'm a closed book on the subject.'

Deciding that the conversation is over, Rebecca stands and walks towards her front door and feeling utterly guilty, she ushers her brother out.

Chapter 46

ARCHIE AND KANE

Later that day at the Pacific House, Kane tells Archie about his conversations with his siblings.

'You know, Archie,' he begins, 'I think my sister knows a lot more about Matilda's disappearance than she's letting on.'

'Does she now?'

'She won't tell me about it though, because she's been sworn to secrecy.'

'Sworn to secrecy by whom?'

'By bloody Abel.'

'What's he got to do with it?'

'I reckon he has a lot to do with it, Archie. When I went around to Marvell Street to talk to him, I came away thinking he knows more than he's saying.'

'Do you think both of them are hiding something?'

'Yes, I do.'

After all the hours he has spent listening to Rebecca's stories about the Stenmark family, Archie wonders if he might be the one to get Rebecca to spill the beans.

'Maybe I should go over and try to get it out of her, Dad. As she's told me a lot about the Stenmarks already, maybe I can convince her to tell me the full story as part of the family history. You never know – she might open up to me just for historical accuracy.'

'Go for it, Archie,' Kane urges. 'I couldn't get it out of her, but maybe you can.'

Chapter 47

ARCHIE AND REBECCA

Archie arrives at Rebecca Stenmark's house on a mission to obtain the truth, and after being invited inside, he wastes no time broaching the subject.

'What goes on at a bachelor and spinster ball, Rebecca?' he asks.

'Is this for your book?' Rebecca asks.

'Yes.'

'You've never had the chance to attend one, have you?'

'No, I haven't.'

'That's because you've always lived in the city, Archie. The B&S ball is a popular event for country people. It's held in many towns throughout Australia and serves as a get-together for young people who live in remote areas.'

'I hear people dress up for it.'

'Class and elegance are rare features at these booze-fuelled parties, Archie.'

Archie raises his eyebrows.

'Drunkenness and fist fighting are more the order of the day at these events, I'm afraid,' she adds.

'I see,' Archie replies, thinking that the event could easily get out of hand.

Rebecca wonders if Archie is wanting details of country life for his novel or if he is searching for information about the disappearance of Matilda. She decides that he needs to know about events like the B&S ball.

'When it was Byron Bay's turn to host it in 1975, the local Young Farmers Association wisely decided to hold the event in a paddock, located a safe distance from town. They announced that the dress code was to be "fine attire," and many of the young people made various attempts to comply with this directive, donning their version of formal wear, before they flocked out to the paddock to congregate in huge marquees.'

'Did the young people come from far away?'

'Yes, they did. Some of the partygoers arrived from hundreds of kilometres away and some of them were even hoping to find love.'

'It sounds like a place for the desperate and dateless,' Archie quips.

'That's true. While some were angling for a wedding proposal, others just came to binge-drink until they passed out.'

Archie notes that "Fine attire" sounds a bit formal for an event in a paddock.

'Yes you're right Archie, "fine attire" received a broad interpretation at this B&S ball. Cowboy boots and Akubra hats were worn with formal jackets and party dresses.'

'What reaction did these young revellers get from the townsfolk?' Archie asks.

'Oh, many of the locals fled from Byron Bay early, knowing the event would shatter the peaceful atmosphere of their seaside town.'

'The smart locals left town then,' Archie deduces and Rebecca nods.

'How did the young people get out to the paddock?' he asks.

'They crowded into pickup trucks. I can tell you there was plenty of "key banging" going on as they journeyed out from town.'

'What is "key banging?"' he asks.

'It's a tradition at events like these, Archie. The drivers deliberately make their trucks backfire. On the night of the ball, deafening pops shattered the coastal air when their trucks drove out of town, and sometimes flames would shoot out from the back of their vehicles.'

'It sounds pretty spectacular,' Archie comments. 'I guess Abel and Kane both attended.'

'Yes, they both joined the crowd of revellers that night. Abel told me later that a band was playing loud music to an already animated crowd by the time their truck pulled up at the gate. I think he said the song that greeted them was "Stand By Your Man".'

'Were they dressed up?'

'Yes. The boys left home wearing cowboy hats and R. M. Williams boots. Kane wore a red bow tie and a matching red cummerbund, while I think Abel sported a tartan bow tie and tartan suspenders.'

'Whee-ha!' Archie responds.

'Abel told me that they got into a scrap at the entry to the paddock. Apparently an indigenous girl who was about 15 years old was waiting at the gate trying to get in. I hear she was a big girl with bare feet, scruffy hair and a dirty floral dress. The only thing of value that Abel could see on her person was a gold bangle that she constantly twirled as she begged to get in. Kane apparently recognised her immediately as Jimmy Merinda's younger sister from Broken Head. The girl asked Kane to bring out some beer to her, but Kane told her he couldn't do that, explaining to her that if she wanted to be part of the festivities, she had to have purchased a ticket beforehand. Abel, who couldn't countenance her joining them under any circumstances continued inside, leaving his brother to deal with her on his own.'

'Abel deserted Kane?' Archie asks.

'Yes.'

'Did Kane speak to her?'

'Yes, he told her she was underage.'

'"Bring me some beer… I'm fuckin' thirsty, ya know" was her reply to him. Kane said the girl had a colourful turn of phrase.'

'A rough diamond,' Archie rejoins and Rebecca nods.

'The story goes that Kane was about to turn on his heel and disappear into the crowd when the girl bypassed the security guards and rushed towards him. She apparently grasped Kane by his arms, and in the ensuing scuffle, her sharp nails left several deep scratches on his forearms. Kane said she shrieked about how the paddock once belonged to her mob and that she couldn't understand why she was being told to fuck off. One of the security guards reported that during the incident she slapped Kane around the head quite a few times, while she kicked at him with her bare feet.'

'What an ugly incident . . . She sounds like a banshee woman,' Archie comments.

'Kane explained to me the next day that he understood her intense feelings of dispossession.'

Archie nods encouragingly.

'By the time Kane had arrived at the first marquee, one of his badly scratched arms was bleeding so profusely that he had to wrap it in a handkerchief. When he finally entered the tent, Abel was waiting inside at the bar for him with a bottle of cold beer opened at the ready.'

'Was his arm OK?' Archie enquires.

'He apparently kept it wrapped in his handkerchief all night. I hear it didn't stop him from enjoying himself.'

'It's hard to stop him from enjoying a party,' Archie acknowledges from first-hand experience.

'I've heard that at one point, there was loud cheering outside the marquee and when everyone peered out beyond the flaps to see what was causing the commotion, they saw a bare-chested young fellow in Speedos, wearing a bow tie at his throat, adding to the merriment by driving a ride-on lawnmower around the paddock. When the crowd hooted at him, he made smoke billow from two tall exhaust pipes while he made circles in the grass. Kane said that Abel was raising his eyebrows at this behaviour, as it seemed a little bizarre so early in the evening.'

'The B&S ball was already starting to become a little too surreal for him,' Archie chimes.

'This incident was just the beginning of the merriment, Archie. The crowd was just starting to let its hair down.'

'Fun, fun, fun for everyone! What a pity you were too young to attend, Rebecca. Being only 12, you would have missed out on all the revelry,' Archie sympathises.

'Would you like to know what happened to me, Archie?'

'Shoot.'

'During the day preceding the event, Abel had helped set up the marquees in the paddock, and he'd left me at home, warning me that I could be in physical danger if I ventured out onto the streets. He said Byron Bay had turned into a zoo and that under no circumstances was I to leave the house. He left me wondering what the hell was going on.'

'You didn't disobey him, did you, Rebecca?' Archie baits.

'Well, Archie, it was an understatement to say that the event had piqued my interest. I was desperate to find out first-hand what had drawn these hordes of beautiful young people to Byron Bay. At first, I waited patiently at home as instructed, but by about 10:30 p. m. after hearing all the loud "key banging", my curiosity got the better of me.'

'Rebecca, what did you do?'

'I dashed up to my bedroom, put on my best white cotton party dress and applied some lipstick to my innocent lips.'

'Rebecca, you didn't defy your brother's orders, did you?'

'Yes, I did, Archie, but I must say that I was looking a little older than my twelve years by the time I had left the house.'

'Where did you go?'

'I strolled along Bangalow Road to find out what the hoopla was all about.'

'You were a little naive to venture out, don't you think?' Archie asks and Rebecca nods.

'I walked south for about a kilometre and at one stage, I passed a group of indigenous teenagers who were loitering on the other side of the road. One of them was a dark girl with hair like a bird's nest. She called out to me, but I ignored her. The girl called out to me again and this time she told me that she'd seen my brother putting up the beer tent earlier in the day. I was surprised that she knew who I was, but she continued to converse, saying that there was plenty of beer flowing inside the tents. She was complaining that the bastards at the gate wouldn't let her in and she wondered if I'd go in and get some grog for her.'

'What did you do?' Archie asks.

'I told the girl I wasn't attending the B&S ball and that I was just observing the crowd. She urged me again to ask my brother for some booze, telling me that if I did, she'd leave me alone.'

'She wanted you to be a courier,' Archie states.

'Yes. At the time, I remember feeling that it was a veiled threat that she was making.'

'It was.'

'The girl became angry when I told her that I wouldn't do it. When I told her I was going back home, she said that if I didn't get her some booze, my life in this town wouldn't be worth living.'

'That's quite a strong threat, Rebecca.'

'Yes, it was. To substantiate it, she signalled for two of her male friends to join her and when two boys stood on each side of her like sentinels, I knew that I was totally out of my depth. When the girl said she knew where I lived, I realised that it had been a huge mistake to come onto Bangalow Road. It was time I bolted from the scene.'

'That was possibly your best option under the circumstances,' Archie agrees.

'On my way back home, a truckload of partygoers saw me sprinting wildly back towards the township. They hooted at me from the back of their pickup truck and when a loud "key bang" went off, it frightened me so much that I burst into tears. With my legs ratcheting like pistons under my white party dress, I fled from the scene in terror, to the safety of Marvell Street.'

'I'm sure you would have left them for dead,' Archie remarks.

'Well, I was quite a fast runner in my day, Archie. At one point in my flight for safety, I glanced behind me, only to find that the Aboriginal trio were following me in hot pursuit. Panic-stricken, I burst into our garden and raced through to the front door of our house. I switched on the lights and grasped Abel's rifle from the gun cabinet. After switching the lights back off again, I waited in the dark for my pursuers.'

'You didn't intend to shoot them, did you, Rebecca?' Archie enquires, his eyes remaining intently on his aunt's.

'Just scare them,' she replies.

'What happened?'

Rebecca wonders if she should stop recounting the details of what transpired that evening, knowing that if she continues, she will be breaking her promise of silence. She is on a roll however, and feels a strong compunction to finish her story.

'Please go on, Rebecca,' Archie urges.

'As I sat on the porch floor pointing the rifle towards the garden, my heart was pumping like a jackhammer. The girl must have been the fastest runner of the group, because she was the first one to arrive at our picket fence. I can still remember her unruly hair being silhouetted against the night sky, as she brazenly flung the gate open and entered our front yard.'

'How frightening.'

'She advanced across our lawn and when she reached our Poinciana tree, she signalled for her mates to join her, and once they were all together, she called out to me to tell me that she knew I was at home. After explaining that she'd seen the light on, she ordered me to go into my kitchen and get some grog out of the fridge. She warned me that if I didn't get it for her, she'd come in and help herself.'

'What did you do?'

'Shaking with fear, I raised the rifle up and aimed it directly at her.

'Her final words were "Bring out the fucking grog you bitch or you'll regret it!"

Hearing this, I gauged that she was losing patience with me, and my finger trembled on the trigger. Suddenly, an ear-splitting shot filled the air as Abel's rifle went off unexpectedly.'

Riveted by Rebecca's story, Archie leans forward to hear what she did next.

'Hearing the deafening sound, the girl's friends screamed in terror and ran for their lives, leaving the big girl to fend for herself.'

Archie's mouth remains open in disbelief.

'I was on the porch floor shaking in shock, looking out into the front garden.'

'Did you see anything?'

'When I couldn't detect any movement on the grass, I ventured outside, and in the dim light I saw a dark shape under our Poinciana tree. It was the girl's body splayed on the ground.'

'It was you who shot her then, Rebecca!' Archie exclaims.

After this outburst, Archie's aunt bursts into loud sobs in front of him.

'Yes Archie. I'd accidentally pulled the trigger!'

With her face streaming with tears, Rebecca continues with more details.

'When I bent down to observe the girl's face, there was a bullet hole beside her eye. Archie, I'd shot her in the temple!'

Archie covers his mouth with his hands at this declaration, genuinely shocked by his aunt's admission.

'I stood there in a catatonic state looking at the girl for some time, and I was still peering down at the girl's dead body when Abel appeared at the gate demanding to know why I was outside the house in the middle of the night. I screamed back at him hysterically that I had shot the girl, and after telling me to keep my voice down, he asked me to quietly recount what had happened. I explained that I had been curious about the B&S ball, and that I'd sneaked out to find out what was going on, and that three indigenous teenagers had followed me home.'

'What was Abel's reaction when you told him that?'

'Oh, he was angry. After ordering me to wipe off my lipstick because "I looked like a tart", he started to question me about the body on the grass.'

'"Did this lubra lips follow you home?" he asked, pointing down at the indigenous girl's face. I repeated that there were actually three of them who had followed me home, and that they had asked me to bring out some grog to them.'

'"What happened to the others?" he asked and I told him that the two boys had run off after hearing the shot.'

Telling Archie about the shooting causes Rebecca considerable anguish and she covers her face with her hands and begins to sob.

'What did Abel advise you to do, Rebecca?' Archie asks.

'Abel said we had to get rid of the girl's body.'

"Really?"

"I was surprised that he would consider this option, and I suggested instead that we call the police. Abel rejected this idea however, stating that calling the cops was a crazy idea because I'd be up for murder."

'What did he suggest instead?'

'He ordered me to run off and get Kane's car keys from the sleep-out, and while I was searching for them, he lugged the girl's body over to the back of Kane's car. I was ordered to grasp the girl's dirty feet, while he took the end with the head and shoulders, and together, we struggled with the girl's heavy body until we'd managed to roll it into the boot of Kane's Ford Falcon. Once the body was inside, I quickly slammed the boot of the car down, and asked him where he was going to take her.

'He answered, "Don't worry, I'll think of somewhere".'

'I was astounded that he had no plan, but an idea must have suddenly come to him, because he told me he'd thought of the perfect place to bury her. When he asked me to get the old key to the Stenmark compound from the hook in the kitchen, I knew the girl's body was destined for Broken Head.'

'You suspected he was planning to bury her in the Stenmark compound?' Archie questions.

'Yes, Archie. The minute he asked me to get the key, I knew that was his plan. He grabbed a shovel and a flashlight from the garden shed, and after throwing them into the back seat of Kane's car, he squeezed himself in behind the car's thin steering wheel and he started it up. Before he drove off, I asked him if we were doing the right thing, but he ignored my question, instructing me instead to to clean his rifle and return it to the cabinet. He also asked me to clean up the mess under the Poinciana tree.'

'You were instructed to remove any evidence of foul play from the crime scene.'

'Yes.'

Archie is truly shocked by Rebecca's account of the shooting, but as she was such a young girl at the time, he has some sympathy for her. The best part of her story however, is that his father is cleared of any wrongdoing.

'What did you do when Abel drove off, Rebecca?' he asks.

'After cleaning up the blood on the grass, I stood by the picket fence with tears streaming down my face. I'd lost my childhood innocence and would have to deal with a devious cover-up.

'I suppose Kane was still at the B&S ball while all this was going on,' Archie asks.

'Yes, Archie. Kane had stayed on at the paddock.'

Archie nods as if that is to be expected.

'The next morning Abel told me that he'd driven along Bangalow Road with his lights on low beam, because he didn't know how to work the light switch on Kane's car. After entering the Stenmark compound, he said he took the track to the right and drove up until he reached the family grave. With the car's headlights causing long shadows on the grass, he carried his shovel across to the grave, and leveraged the slab on the tomb until it was wide enough to up end Matilda into it. After tipping her in, however, he was unable to manoeuvre the slab entirely back into its original position, and had to leave it slightly askew.'

'Rebecca, you have kept this a secret for twenty-five years,' Archie chastises.

'Please let me finish, Archie,' she hushes, keen get the entire story out at last.

'When Abel returned to Marvell Street, he parked the car in precisely the same position, and after replacing the shovel and flashlight in the shed, he entered the house to collect some cleaning equipment. In the middle of the night, he cleaned the blood from the boot of Kane's car, and after he had removed every trace of evidence, he slunk back into the house, unnoticed by anyone except me.'

'A true cover-up,' Archie confirms.

Rebecca nods.

'As Abel climbed up the stairs to his room, I was hiding under the covers in my bedroom shaking with fear and regret. I tried to sleep, but I was still wide awake when Kane returned home two hours later. Ignorant of the fatal incident that had transpired before his arrival, he staggered into his sleep-out and passed out.'

'I'm interested to hear what Abel said the following morning,' Archie voices, wondering if he had any signs of remorse. 'Did he say anything to you, Rebecca?'

'After telling me the details of how he had buried the body in the old grave, he said I would have been up for murder if he hadn't acted so decisively.

I thanked him for being "my saviour", but he found this comment to be flippant, and enflamed with rage, he grasped me by both of my arms and commanded me to always keep the incident a secret, even from Kane. He demanded that the details of the incident were never to leave the walls of Marvell Street, explaining that if it ever got out, it would ruin our family forever.

I promised him that I'd always keep it a well-guarded secret and that it would always be just between him and me. He shook my hand formally and the deal was sealed. As he left the kitchen he cautioned me to tell no one.'

'You made a contract with the devil, Rebecca,' Archie states.

'Yes, I did, and until today I've stuck to it.'

'Didn't the police grill you on the girl's disappearance?' Archie asks.

'Yes, they did. Later that same morning the local constabulary visited Marvell Street to ask some pointed questions. They informed us at the time that two indigenous boys had reported being at Marvell Street last night with their friend Matilda, but that they'd bolted when they heard a shot. Abel managed to put the police off by saying that it must have been the "key banging". Abel also said that none of us had heard any gunshots, and his assurances seemed to appease them at the time.'

'You never felt the need to set the record straight?'

'Oh yes, many times, Archie. I continually felt guilty about it, but Abel kept reminding me of our pact.'

'He blackmailed you into secrecy,' Archie confirms.

'Yes, he did. I was upset when people in the town blamed Kane for the indigenous girl's disappearance, but after the scrap he'd had with the girl at the gate to the B&S ball, the scratches on his arms seemed to be enough proof that he was the culprit. Some thought it gave him a motive for revenge'

'Rebecca, Kane had to leave town when everyone turned against him. In my opinion, it was an unforgivably cruel thing for you to do to your brother.'

'Yes, I know it was. It's true that many of the locals gave him a hard time, and even his friend Jimmy from the Aboriginal camp told the police that he wondered if Kane was involved with his sister's disappearance. The whole thing was unfair and it ruined my relationship with Kane.'

'Rebecca, this has been an outrageous cover-up. You have maligned your brother and made his life a living hell.'

'You're right Archie. I've been feeling guilty about it for over two and a half decades and I'm glad to finally get it off my chest.'

'I realise that you were young at the time, and that it was difficult for you to come out with the truth, but as an adult, didn't you want to set the record straight? Now that you have admitted it to me, isn't it time you owned up to Kane about what happened that fateful night?'

Rebecca bows her head racked with guilt, unable to speak.

'And isn't it time you reported the whole thing to the police?' Archie adds.

Rebecca doesn't look up. She merely nods in agreement.

Chapter 48

KANE CHALLENGES ABEL

When Archie returns to the Pacific House with the news of what happened at Rebecca's place, his father is on the veranda strumming on his guitar. Kane stops playing the moment he sees Archie.

'How did it go, son?' he asks.

'Your little sister was responsible for Matilda's death,' he answers.

'What?'

'Rebecca is the one who shot Matilda.'

'I thought you'd be telling me that Abel killed her, Archie.'

'No, Dad. It was Rebecca. Did you know she was out on Bangalow Road earlier that fateful night?'

'No.'

'Well, she was. She said three indigenous kids followed her home and that one of them was Matilda. When Rebecca saw them enter the front garden at Marvell Street, she aimed Abel's rifle at them to scare them away, but the rifle went off accidentally.'

'Fuck! No wonder she's a closed book! What did she do?'

'When the boys heard the loud shot, they took off, leaving Matilda dead on the grass.'

'What did Rebecca do?'

'She panicked.'

Kane waits with his mouth open, ready to hear the gruesome details.

'When Abel came home, he took over and ordered Rebecca to help him load the body into the boot of a car.'

'It was my car they loaded her into, wasn't it?'

'Yes.'

'Where did he bury her?'

'Rebecca wasn't with him, but Abel told her the next morning that he'd buried Matilda in the Stenmark compound.'

'Bloody hell! And the two of them have kept this from me all this time?'

'Yes Dad. They made a pact to keep it a secret . . . Your siblings have duped you!'

'Fuck!'

Chapter 49

KANE

To confirm the story, Kane makes an immediate beeline for Marvell Street to confront his brother.

'What in the hell do you want this time?' Abel bellows when he sees Kane at his front door again.

'You were the one driving my Falcon on the night of the B&S ball, you bastard!' Kane challenges as he pushes his way inside.

'What makes you think that, brother?' Abel asks.

'Rebecca has owned up to shooting Matilda and she's saying you took the girl's body away.'

'You're crazy, Kane. Rebecca would never say that.'

'What did you do with her body, Abel? Rebecca said she helped you load it into the boot of my car before you drove off.'

'She's lying. I was at the B&S ball until very late.'

'Like hell you were! I didn't see you. You came home early and found Rebecca had shot the girl, and instead of reporting it to the police, you hid the bloody body, didn't you?'

'If she said that, she's making it up.'

'No, Abel. My red car was seen heading down Bangalow Road and you were driving it. Where did you hide her body?'

'It wasn't me, bro. It wasn't me in your car,' Abel defends.

'Yes, it was you, Abel, and you were heading for the Stenmark compound, weren't you?'

'Kane, you're in a bloody flight of fantasy!'

'No, I'm not! I've taken the blame for her abduction all these years, but it was you who committed the crime, brother!'

'You're a crazy bastard,' Abel retorts.

'Abel, all these years, you've accused me of something that you did.'

Defiant to the end, Abel shakes his head.

'Come to think of it, I remember something else, brother.'

'What's that?'

'The morning after the B&S ball, I remember looking for my keys, and you had them. Now, Abel, you can't deny that.'

'Piss off, Kane! You're a bloody troublemaker!' Abel points towards the door. 'Get out!'

Chapter 50

ENLISTING JUDE

After Kane's visit to Marvell Street, Abel is spooked by the news that Rebecca has spilled the beans about the shooting of Matilda. Thinking that Kane will soon be demanding that searches be conducted inside the Stenmark compound, he becomes concerned that the police will want to dig up the family grave. If they do open it up, they'll no doubt find traces of Matilda's bones lying on top of whatever is left of his grandparents' remains.

Over the years, Abel had convinced himself that he'd committed a selfless act by burying Matilda. As his acts protected his sister from prosecution, he finds it difficult to understand why she would suddenly break her pact of silence, as the disclosure would place them both in major jeopardy. If she has abandoned ship, however, the time has definitely arrived for him to start protecting himself.

Remembering his solicitor's advice to use his family's assistance when the going gets tough, Abel considers engaging his son Jude to assist him in removing traces of Matilda from the grave. After all, the boy owes him a favour since he helped him rent a house in the pretty little town of Bangalow.

The following morning, Abel calls Jude to ask him if he'd meet him at the Lismore Hospital. He explains to Jude that they will not only be able to visit Brett, who is recovering from the stab wound inflicted at the Sands Hotel bottle shop, but also talk about something vitally important.

After agreeing to meet him, Jude struggles out of bed, takes a shower, and dresses in his usual black leather. After combing some stiffening gel into his Mohawk, Abel's second son mounts his trusty Harley Davidson and speeds off towards Lismore, looking as if he has just escaped from a *Mad Max* movie set.

On arrival, Jude pulls up at the hospital's emergency entry and parks his motorcycle illegally in the ambulance section. With his boots clicking like a Gestapo secret service agent, he passes through the emergency area and down the hospital's highly polished linoleum floors to his brother's ward.

Jude's defiant attitude deflates the moment he sees his elder brother's yellow face peering at him from behind a white sheet. Brett has tubes entering his body via his nose, while above his bed, there is an ominous sign saying "Nil by Mouth". Jude sees a mound above Brett's stomach that is covered by a sheet, where more tubes seem to be carrying fluids in and out. When he approaches his brother's bed, a strong mix of gastro-intestinal gases fills his nostrils.

'Are you going to pull through, Brett?' he asks, as he locks eyes with him.

Brett tries to be brave with his response. 'You bet, mate,' he answers, but Jude is not at all sure.

'I hear they caught the bastards,' Jude comforts.

'They may have, bro, but look how they've left me. What about my ideas of representing Australia at the Sydney Olympics?'

'You'll be back, Brett. You've always been a winner in the past,' Jude replies, giving his brother a reassuring pat on the arm.

'Jude, can you come in closer? I've got something to say to you,' Brett requests in a weak voice.

Jude bends to hear what his brother has to say.

'I'm fucked, mate. I'm gonna die. Don't let the medicos fool you. I'm a goner.'

After hearing this, Jude slowly raises his head and thinks about how to answer his brother.

'It looks bad now, Brett,' he responds, 'but you'll get back to health soon. Mark my words.'

After Jude issues these words of encouragement, Brett moves his head from side to side, appearing already resigned to either death or the life of the severely disabled.

Abel arrives at the hospital with Stephanie, who is carrying a huge bunch of white freesias from her garden at Marvell Street.

'How's my boy today?' his mother trumpets, attempting to be upbeat.

'No good, Mum. The doc says I've developed jaundice.'

'They'll give you a shot of penicillin, and you'll be as good as gold, son,' she placates.

The bravado is strong, but everyone present knows the situation is gravely serious.

After Stephanie has found a suitable vase for the freesias, she places them on the side table beside Brett, and kisses him on his yellow cheek before settling in beside him to hold his hand. The freesias give off a strong perfume, however, and when the scent mixes with the other hospital smells, Jude detects a strange metallic taste in his mouth.

'Now that we are all together as a family, I have something to tell you all,' Abel announces in an earnest tone. 'I want to advise you that our family has to stick together like glue, because we are under siege and we must close ranks against the enemy.'

'Who exactly is the enemy?' Jude asks.

'The enemy is Kane and his daughter. That Alkira girl is threatening us, and if we're not careful the blacks will take over everything we own.'

'What are you worried about, Dad?' Jude asks.

'Well, Jude, I've asked you to come here today because I have something important to tell you about your inheritance.'

'Shoot. I'm all ears,' Jude encourages.

'The first thing I want to talk about is Stenmark Inc. and what is likely to happen to it into the future. Our partnership agreement decrees that my siblings and I are operating under a joint tenancy, and this affects how our assets are assigned after we die. For example, if Rebecca dies, Kane and I will be 50 per cent owners, but if Kane dies first, Rebecca and I will be fifty-fifty. You should be aware that if I die, the other two will own all of our assets. I've asked you to come here today to make sure that you boys understand that should Rebecca and I die, Kane will get the lot. He'll inherit the Sands Hotel, the land at Broken Head, our house on Marvell Street, and all the shares we own. He'll get all of it, and you'll miss out on your inheritance entirely.'

'Fuck! Is that true?'

'I'm deadly serious, boys. When I die the whole lot goes to my siblings, who are the joint tenants.'

'Dad, that's totally unfair! We can't let this happen!'

'I'm particularly worried about Broken Head, boys. You know it's been my dream to develop it so that it becomes a windfall for us all. But let me tell you here and now – it's under threat. Bloody Alkira is campaigning against us. She wants to return it to her people, and it's time someone shut the bitch up.'

Jude's face shows immediate concern and his mind starts spinning into motion, as he desperately tries to think of ways to prevent Kane and Alkira from making a march on his inheritance.

'I can't help you do anything,' Brett weakly voices from his bed. 'I'm as useless as tits on a bull.' When the family turns to look at him, each of them realises that he is actually uttering the truth.

'Leave the girl to me, Dad,' Jude finally states, deciding to take up the cudgels against Alkira. 'I'll shut the bitch up. By the time I finish with her she'll wish she'd never been born.'

'Jude, if you take care of the girl, I'll deal with Kane. Is that a deal?'

'Deal.'

The father and son shake hands earnestly, each knowing they are shaking hands with the devil.

At the end of the visiting hour, when the able-bodied members of the family are leaving the hospital, Abel turns to Jude. 'If you're free later this afternoon, son, can you accompany me on an urgent mission to the Stenmark compound?'

'I suppose I can, Dad. What's so urgent?'

'I've got something I need help with at the family grave.'

'Really? I've always wanted to see our great-grandparents' grave,' Jude responds. 'I'll join you for sure . . . It's time I paid my respects to them.'

Chapter 51

JUDE AT THE GRAVE

Jude Stenmark is carrying a backpack containing a six-pack of XXXX beer and his trusty pistol when he rides from his house in Bangalow to Marvell Street. En route he stops at a store in Byron Bay called Crystal Destiny located on Lawson Street, because he's keen to buy a few items that he'll need for a vigil that he plans to conduct at the family grave. After selecting a box of votive candles, some matches, and a bottle of Golden Light oil, he pays the lady at the counter and places the newly purchased items into his backpack.

Jude pulls up outside the family home on Marvell Street and parks his motorcycle beside the shed.

'I've wanted to check out the wrinklies' grave for years,' he tells his father as he opens the kickstand on his motorbike. 'Do you think I'll be able to make a dedication to my great-grandparents while I'm at the grave, Dad?'

'I'm sure you can,' Abel answers, wondering what his son has in mind.

'As Joseph and Bella have set our family up, I want to respect them for that while I'm at the grave,' he explains.

'Good for you, Jude. I'm proud you are intending to respect our ancestors. It's true that we wouldn't own Broken Head or the Sands Hotel if it weren't for them,' his father responds.

'What are we going to do at the grave that is so urgent, Dad?' Jude enquires.

'The last time I was there, I noticed that the slab on their grave was a little crooked, so I've thrown in some rope and a shovel in the hope that we might straighten it,' Abel advises, keeping the real reason for his visit a secret at this stage.

'I'm pleased to be of help,' his son replies.

Abel drives his Range Rover along Bangalow Road until they reach the Stenmark compound. After pulling up at the gate, he hands the key over to Jude so he can jump out and open it. Jude turns the key in the lock, removes the rusty chain, and pushes the gate wide open. After his father has driven through, he closes it again, but he has great difficulty locking it.

'The lock's fucked, Dad! We'll have to leave it ajar until we return!' he calls.

Abel is uneasy about leaving the gate unlocked, but as he has a pressing agenda, he decides to drive on through.

About ten minutes after the father and son have passed through the gate, Jimmy's friends Willy and Dingo are hiking past the entry to the Stenmark compound, and they are about to continue on past the gate, when Willy notices that it has been left unlocked.

'Look Dingo, the gate's been left open! Maybe we can get inside!' Willy calls.

Dingo strides over to check the lock. 'You're dead right Willy!' he exclaims, and he pushes at the gate. It opens wide.

'Do you think we should go in?' Willy asks.

'You bet,' Dingo urges. 'This is our big chance to dig up the bloody Stenmarks once and for all. Those bastards have brought nothin' but bad karma to Cavanbah all these years. I reckon we should do it while we have the chance.'

Knowing it's a rare opportunity to get rid of their oppressors' bodies, the indigenous men rush back to the Aboriginal camp to find a shovel.

When Abel and Jude arrive at a clearing high up on Broken Head, there is a breathtaking view in front of them. They have arrived just as the sun is setting, and a rosy glow has lit up the low-level clouds on the horizon. The father and son decide to disembark, and for a moment or two they take in the sublime scene from a rocky outcrop. As they sit there appreciating the impressive vista, they both feel incredibly proud that the Stenmark family owns this exceptional property.

'We'll never give this place up to the Abbos, Jude,' Abel confides, as he places a fatherly arm around his son's shoulders.

'Never,' Jude replies.

For some time the duo gaze proudly over their domain at sunset, before resuming their journey to the top of the rise. After parking his vehicle by a thicket of trees, Abel strides with his son over to the low wrought-iron fence enclosing the family grave. Overgrown by wild grasses, the lonely grave has an unkempt appearance and Jude moves in closer to read the inscription on the tombstone.

In loving memory

Bella Stenmark 1868–1898
who died in childbirth.
Mother of Jake & babies Kane and Abel.

Joined forever by husband and father
JOSEPH STENMARK 1840–1920,
who died in an automobile accident.

Jude is overjoyed to read the inscription on the stone as it confirms the story that he'd heard countless times as a child – that his father and his uncle were named after the two children who had died during childbirth. To celebrate being here at last, Jude dives into his backpack for two cans of beer and after twisting one open for his father, he opens a second can for himself.

'Here's to my great-grandparents,' he toasts proudly.

While Abel gently sips on his can, Jude drains the entire contents of his in one go. He pitches his empty can into the scrub and opens another. After wolfing the second one down, he marches towards the grave with the empty can in his hand. To his father's genuine surprise, Jude begins to quote from Frank Hudson's classic Australian poem 'The Pioneers'.

Here's to you olde worlde people.
Yours were the hearts that dared.
But your youth is spent and your backs are bent,
And the snow is in your hair.
Your axes rang in the woodlands,
Where eucalypts grew in the sand.
You fought the blacks and blazed the tracks.
So we might inherit the land.

'Good for you for remembering that, Jude,' Abel applauds.

'It's about the only thing I can remember from boarding school,' Jude replies.

'I think you got some of the words wrong towards the end, son, but that's generally how it goes,' Abel chides.

After discarding his second can into the bushes, Jude stares intently at the inscription on the gravestone and begins praising his ancestors.

'Joseph and Bella, today I acknowledge your legacy to our family and I salute you for what you achieved while you were here at Broken Head. Right now, I'm getting a strong message from you both that you want me to protect this land from invasion.'

As Abel leans on his shovel with his rope slung over his shoulder at the ready, he finds Jude's words to be somewhat ominous, but he decides to wait patiently until his son has completed his observance.

Jude delves into his backpack and retrieves the box of votive candles that he'd purchased from Crystal Destiny. He places them carefully into a small circle on the grave's crooked slab.

Abel hopes his son's vigil will be a short one, because he is eager to get on with opening up the grave. He watches somewhat impatiently as Jude takes the lid off a small bottle of oil and pours the contents of the bottle onto the crooked slab. Jude sprinkles the liquid between each of the candles and then strikes a match, before dropping it onto the slab. The Golden Light oil flares up in front of him, showering his face in a brilliant glow.

'Let me be the one to banish those who threaten to invade us,' he chants.

Nightfall is approaching by the time Willy and Dingo have made their way up to the Stenmark gravesite, but on arrival there, the indigenous men are quite startled to see Jude Stenmark's face lit up in the strong glow of candlelight. Immediately fearful, the duo retreat into the nearby bushes to watch in silence while the flames from the slab flare up in the shape of a circle. The men suddenly hear Abel Stenmark's loud voice calling out to his son.

'That's enough of that, Jude. Put the fire out, son and come and help me with this bloody rope.'

Startled to hear Abel's authoritative voice so close to where they are hiding, Willy inadvertently lets go of his shovel. When the implement crashes noisily into the scrub, it alerts both Abel and Jude that they have company. With eyes peeled, the father and son peer into the bushes in search of the source of the noise, and after scrutinising the bushes for a short time, Jude detects a pair of eyes peering back at him from between the leaves.

'Who's there? Come out, whoever you are!' he bellows loudly.

When there is no answer, he digs into his backpack for his pistol and after cocking it at the ready, he aims it directly at the eyes in the bushes.

'Come out, or I'll shoot!' he calls.

When there is no response to his order, he squeezes the trigger and an ear-splitting shot rings out over Broken Head. Following the shooting, there is a wild scream as a thin indigenous man emerges from the bushes, jumping up and down in obvious distress.

'You shot my mate! You shot Willy!' he howls, as he continues to jump up and down.

'Stand still, for fuck's sake, or you'll be next!' Jude orders.

Alarmed at what has just transpired, Abel yells at his son, 'Jesus Christ, Jude! Why did you shoot him?'

Ignoring his father's question, Jude advances into the thicket, with Dingo following close behind. Deep into the bushes, he discovers the black man's friend who is lying lifeless by his shovel with a bullet hole in his forehead

'Awww . . . You bastard!' Dingo calls.

'You've killed Willy!' The indigenous man rushes past Jude and kneels beside his friend's dead body. 'Willy was a good bloke. He was me best mate,' the man laments with tears streaming from his eyes, as he places his face against the dead man's cheek.

'Enough of that! Get over by the grave,' Jude orders, forcing Dingo out of the scrub by grabbing him by the scruff of the neck.

Abel, who is in shock at what has just unfolded in front of him, scolds Jude. 'Son, you've just shot a man in cold blood!'

Jude ignores his father's protestations, however, preferring instead to interrogate the indigenous man. 'What are you doing on these grounds?' he bellows at him. 'Answer me, you black bastard!'

'We . . . We found the gate open,' Dingo responds.

'It's private property. Didn't you idiots read the "Strictly No Admittance" sign?'

'That sign means nothing to us, mister. This is our sacred land . . . This is Cavanbah,' he declares proudly.

'You blacks never listen! You hanker after your bloody ancestors, but they're long gone ... It's our ancestors who are here now.'

'You wrong! You white men are the devil,' the man retorts.

Jude, who has a short fuse, has had quite enough of the fellow's insults, and he levels his pistol at him. 'You come with me. What's your name, darkie?'

'D-D-D-Dingo,' the scared man replies.

Jude grabs Dingo by the scruff of the neck again and drags him towards a substantial camphor laurel tree.

Abel watches in trepidation. Alarmed at the level of his son's aggression he calls, 'What in the hell are you going to do with him, Jude?'

'You'll see.'

'You've murdered one man. Isn't that enough for one day? Stop right now Jude, you're out of control!'

'Stand against this tree, Dingo.'

'I done nothin' to you,' the man protests.

'What were you going to do with that shovel then?'

'We was gonna shift you bloody Stenmarks from our sacred land. That's what we was gonna do,' Dingo replies bravely.

'You Abbos have no respect. Our ancestors are buried on this land now, and their bones are here to stay.'

'No, it's our land! You bastards took it from us. You Stenmarks are bloody murderers. That's what you are, pure an' simple!'

Jude lifts his pistol and aims it at Dingo's heart. 'You fucking Abbos. You're a blight on the face of Australia,' he spits, and he pulls the trigger.

When Dingo slumps to the ground, Abel's hands fly up to his face in horror.

'These Abbos have no respect, Dad,' Jude defends.

Abel remains in shock. He has witnessed his son commit two cold-blooded murders within a matter of minutes and alarm bells are ringing inside his head. 'Jude! Are you out of your bloody mind? Why did you kill him?'

'The darkies have to know that this is now our land and it always will be ours,' he retorts.

Freaked out by what he has witnessed, Abel wonders what he should do. He had come here to remove Matilda's remains from the grave, but now he has two more indigenous bodies to get rid of.

'You've put me in an awkward position, son. I've been a witness to the murder of these men, and if anyone finds out, you'll hang for killing them. As I see it, you have only two options. We can call the police and tell them what has happened, or we can bury the bodies in the family grave.'

'Dad, we can't throw them in with Joseph, Bella, and the kids!'

'We don't have many options left, Jude, unless you want to own up,' Abel cautions.

'Are you kidding me? I'm certainly not going to the fuckin' cops!'

'Matilda is already in this grave, son . . . They'll just be joining her,' Abel informs him.

'What? Did you bury her here, Dad?'

'It's a long story, son, but yes.'

Jude deliberates for a few moments about what he should do, and after reviewing his meagre options, he agrees with his father.

'I don't like the idea of burying the bastards in our family grave, but under the circumstances, I suppose it's the quickest and easiest solution, isn't it?'

'I'm afraid it is, Jude.'

'Let's do it then,' he urges.

As the light dims around them, the father and son use Abel's rope to drag the slab away from the grave. When the opening is wide enough to take the bodies, Jude kneels at the edge of the grave and squints into the dark abyss.

'There's something shiny down at the bottom, Dad. It looks like gold!' he exclaims.

'Forget it, Jude. Let's get these bodies into the grave. It's getting late,' Abel replies, keen to get the new burial over and done with.

The father and son drag each of the indigenous bodies across the grass to the grave, and after lifting each one over the low iron fence, they drop them unceremoniously into the Stenmark family plot.

Once the slab is securely back in place, the men dust their hands on their trouser legs. 'Job well done,' Jude says as he replaces his pistol into his backpack. Abel tosses the shovel and rope back into his vehicle and with their mission accomplished, the partners in crime retreat from the gravesite. At the compound gate, Jude tries his hand at turning the key in the lock once again, but when it refuses to turn the father and son are forced to leave it ajar.

After their monumental misadventure, the duo arrive back at Marvell Street in the dark. Abel removes his rope and shovel and takes them to the shed, while Jude climbs back onto his trusty motorcycle. After turning on his headlights, Jude is about to roar off into the night, but before he departs, he delivers a disturbing directive to his father.

'Dad, you say one word about this to anyone, and you're a dead man walking.'

Chapter 52

DUBAY DANCERS

At breakfast the next day Archie asks Alkira if she is going to dance rehearsals.

'Yes, Archie. I'm riding out to the Aboriginal camp at ten,' she answers him.

'What time does the dance session end, Alkira?'

'About eleven thirty. Why?'

'After you've finished the rehearsals, I was wondering if we could walk through to the Stenmark compound. I'm intrigued to see our great-grandparents' grave.'

'We've always been shut out of the compound, Archie. How do you propose we'll get through the gate?'

'Dad told me he has an old key and if it works, we'll be OK.'

'Do you think we'll be safe in there?'

'Yes. Why do you ask?'

'That "Strictly No Admittance" sign on the fence is so forbidding,' Alkira responds.

'The land belongs to our family, Alkira. As the son and daughter of one of the owners, we have a right to visit. We are officially Stenmarks, you know.'

'OK then. Why don't you meet me out in front of the camp at eleven thirty? I'll be right there where we stash our bikes,' she advises.

Whenever she returns to Byron Bay, Alkira joins the Dubay dancers. In her local language, Dubay means 'woman', and that is why the group is exclusively female. As an infant, she used to watch her mother dance with the group, and later when she became old enough, she insisted on joining in too. Since she has been away at school and university however, she has had fewer opportunities to join the group, except for her study breaks. There is a wide disparity among the ages of the Dubay dancers, but all the women in the group have a common abiding urge to express their traditional way of life through movement.

Each session usually begins by honouring country. The women warm the land by sweeping out all the evil spirits with branches so they can bring in the good.

One of Alkira's favourite dances is the welcome dance, where they thank Mother Dugong before honouring their female elders by evoking the tasks they regularly perform. To the sound of rhythmic hand clapping and the sound of clap sticks, the women simulate the gathering of pippis from the beach, the collecting of berries from local bushes, and the weaving of straw baskets from the reeds of a pond. During the dancing session, Alkira re-establishes a strong bond with the local women and at the end of the session, she invariably feels quite revitalised and grounded. Today at the end of the session, Alkira hugs each one of the troupe members in turn before rushing out onto the road for her rendezvous with Archie.

As she waits by the side of the road, Alkira feels a strong sense of belonging, but her satisfied expression soon changes when she sees a motorcycle approaching a little too quickly towards her. When she observes the rider's unmistakable Mohawk haircut, Alkira immediately recognises him as her newly found cousin, Jude Stenmark, the bigot who caused her to leave Abel Stenmark's birthday luncheon in tears. Alkira is about to flee when Jude Stenmark aggressively skids towards her on his Harley Davidson.

'Get on the back,' he orders.

'I've got my bike here, Jude. I don't need a ride. Thanks,' Alkira replies, wanting nothing to do with him.

'I said get on the back behind me. I'm not telling you again,' he orders, this time producing his pistol from his belt. 'You have a choice, bitch – you can ride with me or be left dead in the ditch.'

Alkira is shocked at Jude's menacing tone.

'What's it to be?' he asks, pointing his pistol directly at her.

After assessing her bleak options, Alkira reluctantly climbs onto the seat behind Jude Stenmark, who roars the accelerator on his motorcycle before speeding off with her feeling terrified on the pillion behind him.

After a ride along several curved roads, Jude and his passenger arrive in the verdant hinterland above Byron Bay. When they reach the quaint village of Bangalow, Jude burbles past the pricy boutiques and trendy cafés until he reaches the local hotel, where he turns right onto a gravel lane. After stopping at the end of it, he orders Alkira to alight.

'Why are you doing this? Why are you abducting me?' she asks.

'Shut the fuck up and get in here,' Jude orders, bundling Alkira towards a corrugated iron barn. He turns the key in the lock of a giant door, and after sliding it open, he shoves Alkira inside.

'Why are you putting me in here?' she queries.

'Quit the questions, bitch, or I'll blow your head off,' Jude replies.

Once inside, Alkira's eyes search around the barn, clocking the plethora of bric-a-brac and vintage memorabilia that hang from every wall. In front of her are farm tools from days gone by, stored on wooden shelving. Retro kitchen appliances have been piled up beside some antique crockery and some old advertising signs are lying about in the dirt. There is even an old Vegemite sign with a girl sporting rosy cheeks leaning up against an old Shell petrol pump.

Jude leads Alkira to a rusty iron bed in the centre of the barn that has an old stained mattress slung across it. 'Stay here and don't move,' he directs.

Although Alkira is shaking with fear, she attempts to stay as still as she can while Jude fossicks around in a crate beside the bed. Finally, he drags out an old chain with a padlock attached to it and he locks Alkira to the railings of the iron bed.

When Jude is confident that his captive is secured, with just enough chain to conduct her bodily functions, he announces,

'Now I'll find a pot for you to piss in.'

After announcing this, Jude searches through some piles of junk and finally returns with a potty that has a retro design of pink roses on the side.

'This is your toilet, sweetheart . . . It's the prettiest one I could find. I hope you enjoy your stay.'

'How long do you intend keeping me here?' Alkira enquires.

'Oh, this will be your final place of residence, sweetheart,' he answers glibly.

While Jude rubs his knuckles against his leather jacket, Alkira takes in the enormity of his comment. Jude is proud that he has completed stage one of his plan; he has successfully abducted his victim and detained her in the barn.

'I want to know why are you are doing this to me?' Alkira implores.

Jude steps forward, and with his face just millimetres from hers, he answers her question with another question.

'You didn't think you could take away my inheritance without a fight, did you?'

'If this is about the land at Broken Head, Jude, I'm merely trying to return it to its original custodians.'

'It's not going to happen, bitch!' he taunts, and he throws a roll of toilet paper at her feet.

Leaving Alkira shackled to the bed, Jude strides off towards the massive wooden doors, and after sliding them open to let himself out, he slides them back into place. Alkira's heart sinks when she hears his key turning in the lock, and the last thing she hears are her abductor's jackboots crunching on the gravel as he strides towards his rented house next door.

Chapter 53

ARCHIE AT BROKEN HEAD

Immersed in his novel, Archie has let time slip away. Hopelessly late for his rendezvous with Alkira, he clambers down the stairs from her apartment two at a time, and after mounting his rented bicycle, he rides like a madman towards the Aboriginal camp. As expected, he finds Alkira's bike in the designated spot out front, but there is no sign of her. Wondering why she is not waiting for him, he decides to search further inside the camp to find her. The first person he encounters is Maisy, who is the woman he met when he had first visited the Aboriginal camp with his father a few weeks back. When she tells him that Alkira had rushed out immediately after the class was over, Archie decides to return to the roadside again to search for her. After some time shuffling from one foot to the other, he wonders if Alkira might have confused their meeting place and has already started walking towards the Stenmark compound.

He mounts his bicycle again and peddles towards the compound gate, and discovers on arrival that the gate has been left unlatched. Wondering if Alkira has ventured in ahead of him, he decides to ride up the steep trail to the right that leads to a thicket of trees at the top. Panting with the effort of peddling uphill, he dumps his bike at the thicket and strides over to the family grave.

For a brief moment, Archie stands in front of the headstone, reading the inscription, and after reading it, he reflects on his father's grandparents whose bodies lie in the ground beneath the slab. He tries to imagine Bella's final agony as she strove to deliver the twins, but shudders when he thinks of the suffering she must have endured.

Before he turns away, Archie notices that there is a residue of candle wax and some droplets of oil leaving the shape of a circle on the slab. He quickly deduces that someone has been here quite recently performing some kind of ritual. These thoughts are confirmed when he also sees that the grass around the grave has been flattened. After peering briefly into the bushes, he calls out for Alkira, but when he hears no reply, he abandons his search.

With a heightened concerned for her safety, Archie returns to the Aboriginal camp to ask the Dubay dancers if they have seen anything in the interim, and he is about to leave without gleaning any further information, when Maisy remembers hearing the roar of a motorbike at the end of the class. Archie thanks her profusely for this clue before riding off like a madman towards Byron Bay. Archie hopes to find Alkira at home, but when she is not at her apartment, he becomes frantic.

Chapter 54

JIMMY AT BROKEN HEAD

As Jimmy Merinda has lived inside the Stenmark compound all of his life, he has always had easy access to the Stenmark gravesite. Lately however, Abel Stenmark is concerned that he could start searching for his mates around the grave, and that he might find clues that could ultimately lead to his conviction. After some serious thought, Abel decides to remove Jimmy from the compound, and he wastes no time instructing his lawyer, Felix Barker, to deliver the cruel ultimatum.

In his black Mercedes, Barker reaches the compound gate and drives up to Jimmy's cottage to deliver the blunt termination notice.

'Although we have appreciated your loyalty over the years, Jimmy, we wish to advise you that effective immediately, we are dispensing with your services,' Barker states bluntly.

'Are you firin' me?' Jimmy challenges.

'Yes, Jimmy, I am,' Barker confirms. 'My instructions are from Abel Stenmark, who has informed me that your services are no longer required inside this compound.'

'What have I done?' Jimmy asks.

Felix places his palms upwards, signalling that he is just the messenger and that he hasn't the slightest idea why he has been asked to sack him. Jimmy is dumbfounded. As his identity has always been inextricably tied up with Broken Head, Barker's ultimatum has a brutal impact on him.

'What a bitch of an act!' he retorts.

Jimmy is mortified to be dismissed from a job that he has performed with so much pride over the years. 'Why the hell am I being given the chop?' he asks. He is trying to fathom a reason, but Felix is unforthcoming in delivering any plausible answer. He merely shakes his head in silence.

Hearing no explanation for his dismissal, Jimmy's next reaction is anger.

'The Stenmarks are bastards!' he barks. 'I've been a loyal worker all my adult life for them and now they're letting me go with no good reason.'

Displaying no discernable compassion, Barker advises Jimmy to start packing up his belongings.

'Better start packing up your goods and chattels, Jimmy boy,' he urges as he turns towards his vehicle.

Jimmy slumps to his knees in front of him, his hands clutching at the soil beneath him. With the sacred dirt slipping through his fingers he sobs loudly, but unperturbed by Jimmy's emotional groans, Barker opens his car door, locks himself in, and speeds off, leaving Jimmy in the dirt.

The day following his dismissal, Jimmy is astounded to see a removal van arrive unannounced in front of his cottage. After alighting from the van, the driver and his companion explain to him that they have been instructed by Abel Stenmark to transfer all of his belongings over to the Aboriginal camp. Shocked at the military precision of his eviction, Jimmy watches as the men load up all his possessions. At this moment, he realises just how ruthless the Stenmarks really are. When they have completely emptied the cottage, the men in the removal van pull away, leaving Jimmy and his sons to follow on foot.

After farewelling their life on beloved Broken Head, Jimmy and his sons arrive heartbroken at the Aboriginal camp. When they tell their mates how heartlessly the Stenmarks have treated him, the tribesmen still are visibly shocked, but showing immediate compassion, the elders welcome him and his sons into the camp, even inviting Jimmy to take on the official role of mentor for the males in the tribe. Keen to play an active role, Jimmy gratefully accepts the position they offer him.

The morning following his eviction from Broken Head, Jimmy responsibly checks if all the men and boys under his supervision are safe. He soon discovers however, that Willy and Dingo have not spent the night at the camp, and this gives him grave concern. With his senses heightened like a black tracker, he begins a search for them on the accessible paths around the camp. After finding no sign of them in the immediate area, he decides to search a little further afield. After combing Tallow Creek and the Cibum Margil Swamp area, he ventures up to Cosy Corner, just below the lighthouse, but unable to discern any recent activity, Jimmy reluctantly returns empty-handed along the vast expanse of Tallow Beach towards the camp.

It is midday by the time Jimmy is passing the entrance gate to the Stenmark compound, but as he walks purposefully by, his keen eyes detect that the gate has been left slightly ajar. It occurs to him that his mates may have ventured inside.

Jimmy reflects on the time when Archie and Kane visited the Aboriginal camp to interview him about his cultural traditions, and he recalls Willy and Dingo telling Archie that the Stenmark grave had brought bad karma to country, and that they wanted to remove the Stenmarks from it.

Jimmy stands at the compound gate in a quandary. He dearly wants to check if his mates are inside, but as he has been fired from being the compound caretaker, he no longer has the permission to investigate past the fence. Although it disturbs him to trespass, Jimmy finds it imperative that he continues his search.

While most life forms have already cowered from the midday heat by this time, the local cicadas are out in force, squealing loudly against the mean sun. Jimmy knows that their ratcheting monotone is caused when the males vibrate their abdomens, but he also wonders if the overpowering hum of the insect is, in fact, a warning from his ancestors not to proceed.

After some deliberation, he makes the decision to enter the compound, and he quickly ventures up the rise to the right. Once at the top, he glances hastily at the magnificent view, but he has no time to enjoy it, as he's on a critical mission to find his mates.

As he approaches the grave, Jimmy hears the voices of his ancestors screaming at him,

'*This is sacred ground. Get it back, Jimmy . . . Get our land back.*'

Inspired by the voices in his head, Jimmy bursts into an old song that his father had taught him when he was a boy. Jimmy chants the entire song-line in his native tongue and his gravelly voice rings out over Broken Head.

After completing the chant, Jimmy resumes his examination of the area around the gravesite and when he observes some flattened grass beside the grave, he enters the scrub. It is not long before he discovers Willy and Dingo's shovel.

After recognising it as a tool from the Aboriginal camp, Jimmy becomes concerned that the two men could have entered the gravesite with the intention of digging up the grave. He anxiously turns his attention to hunting for more clues and soon comes up with a collection of used matches and two bullet shells. Concerned that his mates may have been caught red-handed, he places the evidence in his pocket before carrying the shovel back towards the camp.

On his way to the exit, Jimmy becomes worried about what will happen to him when he presents his findings to the police. When they see him holding the evidence, they could easily victimise him again, as they did when they suspected him of stabbing Brett Stenmark in the bottle shop. Jimmy becomes concerned that they could throw him into a windowless cell again, as the police may regard him as a trespasser, now that he doesn't officially live inside the compound. Perhaps the safest strategy might be for him to stay out of sight?

After some serious deliberation, Jimmy rationalises that because he is merely a first responder and not the perpetrator of a crime, it may be safer for him to report his findings by telephone, rather than in person. After deciding on this as being the best strategy, he picks up the telephone at the Aboriginal camp and tentatively dials the number of the local police station.

'Byron Bay Police Station. Constable Parker speaking,' an authoritative voice answers.

Jimmy is unable to speak.

'Hello? Is anyone there?' Parker enquires.

Jimmy quickly replaces the phone. He can't risk it with the cops. Instead, he'll announce his findings via the media.

Chapter 55

BREAKFAST AT MARVELL STREET

Abel spends a sleepless night worrying about the shootings that his son has committed on Broken Head, and desperate to avert any eye contact with his wife at breakfast, he peers down into his coffee mug, when Stephanie makes a routine enquiry.

'Abel, I meant to ask you how everything went with Jude out at the grave. You haven't said a word about it.' Stephanie guards the toaster while she waits for an answer.

'Not so good,' Abel replies.

'Why not?' Abel deliberates whether he should keep the whole murderous incident from her.

'Go on, darling. Tell me, please,' she begs, while rescuing some burning toast.

Against his better judgement, Abel decides to confide in his wife.

'Jude started lighting some candles at the grave to honour our grandparents. He was making a kind of vigil.'

'That's a nice thought, darling, but don't you think it's a little strange?' Stephanie fields.

Abel places his hands over his face.

'Did something happen at the grave?' Stephanie asks.

When Abel removes his hands, he has such an anguished expression on his face that Stephanie senses his high level of anxiety. Holding both of Abel's hands in hers, she coaxes her husband to tell her what is concerning him.

'Two Aboriginal men arrived at the gravesite and interrupted Jude's vigil.'

Stephanie is riveted.

'How did they get in there, darling? Isn't the compound gate always locked?'

'When we were at the gate, the key wouldn't work in the lock.'

'Oh, so you left it open?'

'Ajar.'

'Oh.'

'I think the Abbos intended to dig up the grave, because they were carrying a shovel. The minute Jude saw them he was incensed. He dragged a pistol out of his bag and shot both of them.'

'What?'

'He shot them dead in cold blood, Stephanie.'

'No, Abel! No!' she shrieks, her hands flying up to her face. 'No wonder you've been so quiet! Did you report the incident when you returned?' she asks. Her hands remain on her flushed cheeks.

'Jude swore me to secrecy . . . He said I'd be a "dead man walking" if I ratted on him.'

Stephanie gasps in horror.

Behind them on the kitchen radio, Stephanie can hear a morning news bulletin in the background. Recognising Stan Bowles's voice, she reaches over to the radio to turn up the volume.

'I understand you wish to report that two of your clansmen have gone missing, Jimmy Merinda?' Stan Bowles states.

'Yes'm.'

'Where do you think they could be?'

'I reckon they're in the Stenmark compound.'

'Did you go inside the fence?'

'Yes'm.'

'Were you trespassing on private property, Jimmy?' Stan Bowles asks.

'I was the caretaker at the mine until they sacked me a few days ago, an' I've always had a clearance to get inside. I went in because I thought me mates might be in there. They didn't come home last night.'

'What made you think they'd gone inside the compound?'

'The gate was open.'

'Did you have anything to do with their disappearance?' Stan asks boldly.

'No, not on ya nelly, mate! How could ya think that? I was just lookin' for them in there, that's all,' Jimmy defends, taken aback by Stan Bowles's question.

'You found it unusual to find the gate open?' Stan asks.

'Yeah, it's always locked, mate.'

'Who do you think is responsible for the disappearance of your kinsmen then?' Stan Bowles questions.

'It's bleedin' obvious, isn't it? The bloody Stenmarks are ta blame.'

'Did you see anything past the fence that would lead you to suspect them?'

'Well, there was candle wax and oil on the grave slab, an' some matches on the grass. I also found two bullet shells and a shovel there. So someone must have been at the grave.'

Stephanie turns to Abel, ashen-faced.

'Abel, are you going to report Jude?' she asks.

'I can't, darling . . . I'll be a marked man if I do,' he responds.

'What is happening to our family?' Stephanie sobs. 'One of our sons is dying in the Lismore Hospital, and the other one's a murderer! And you, my darling . . . You're an accessory to murder!'

'It's the curse, Stephanie. Damn it, it's the bloody curse!'

Following the radio interview, the police haul Jimmy into the Byron Bay Police Station for further questioning, and not long afterwards, the ominous blue lights of the police vehicles are flashing vigorously as they make their way to the Stenmark compound in search of the missing men.

Chapter 56

ARCHIE SLEUTHING IN BYRON BAY

After hearing Jimmy's interview on the radio at the Pacific House, Archie decides to conduct some sleuthing to see if he can find out where the candles and oil were purchased. After setting to work as an amateur detective, he checks out Crystal Destiny, a New Age store on Lawson Street. He is aware that the store sells alternative products like incense, potions and figurines of dragons, but wonders if it may also sell candles and essential oils.

It is not a usual venue for him to be frequenting, as this type of store is more suited to those who are into spirituality and healing. At the entry he follows a waft of lavender scent and soon discovers that it is emanating from a large candle burning in an open jar on the store's glass counter. Behind it, dressed in a colourful kaftan is a lady with flame-red hair and a ring in her nose.

'Hello, I'm Moonbeam. Welcome to Crystal Destiny,' the woman greets, as she places her hands in a prayer position. Scores of bangles jingle down her wrists.

'I'm Archie,' he replies. 'I wonder if you recall anyone in the last couple of days making a purchase of votive candles and oil.'

'Let me think about that, Archie,' she answers, as her eyes float skywards. 'I actually do remember one young fellow coming in for candles and oil just a day or so ago.'

'You do?'

'How could I forget him? He was a spectacular fellow with a fabulous Mohawk haircut. He looked like a red Indian.'

'Really? Did he purchase anything from you, Moonbeam?'

'Yes, he did, darling. He bought a small box of votive candles and some matches. He took a long time sniffing my precious oils too.'

'What sort of oil did he buy?' Archie asks.

'Now let me see. Oh yes, it was Golden Light, darling.'

'Golden Light?'

'It's one of our special oils, one that awakens, inspires, and empowers. Would you like some?'

'May I buy just one small bottle, Moonbeam?' Archie asks.

'Yes, of course, you can, darling . . . Here. Sniff it, and it will awaken your inner being.'

When Moonbeam hands the oil over to Archie, he sniffs it as directed and he waits for edification.

'The Mohawk bought a large bottle of Golden Light for $45.95, but a small bottle will only cost you $25.95. I warn everyone who buys the oil that it's highly flammable, so be sure to keep it away from a naked flame, won't you?'

'I'll be careful,' Archie promises.

Archie pays Moonbeam for three items – a small bottle of the oil, a box of matches, and a single votive candle.

'I'm glad to be of assistance to you on your path to enlightenment, Archie,' Moonbeam parrots.

Archie hardly hears her final words because now that he's armed with all the evidence he needs, the time has come for him to stride over to Shirley Street to the Byron Bay Police Station.

After entering the station, Archie announces to the constable at reception,

'I'd like to meet the detectives who are dealing with the case of the missing indigenous men at Broken Head.'

'What is it you wish to tell them?' the constable asks.

'I have vital evidence regarding a possible killer,' Archie replies.

This statement gains the immediate attention of the constable on duty, who leads him into a consulting room where he waits until two interviewing officers arrive. The men who greet him announce their names as Chief Inspector James Gallagher and Constable Clive Parker.

'Please state your name before we begin,' Gallagher orders.

'I'm Archie Stenmark.'

'I hear you have some vital evidence for us, Archie.'

'Yes. I believe Jude Stenmark has been at the gravesite on Broken Head.'

'Jude Stenmark? Isn't he the son of the publican of the Sands Hotel?'

'Yes.'

'Why do you suspect him?' Gallagher asks.

Archie takes a deep breath before presenting his reasons.

'I had arranged to meet my sister at the Aboriginal camp after her dance practice was finished. We planned to cycle over to the Stenmark compound to visit our ancestors' grave, but I was running late for the appointment and by the time I got to the camp, I found my sister's bike there, but she was not.'

'She'd probably gone on walkabout,' Gallagher's sidekick interjects.

Archie ignores him. 'I made some enquiries at the camp, but her fellow dancers told me she'd left promptly at the end of the practice. I waited for a further fifteen minutes out front, but when she didn't appear, I decided to continue my search at the Stenmark compound.'

'Wait a minute. Let's back up, Archie. You were able to enter the Stenmark compound?'

'Yes. I'm Kane Stenmark's son and I got the key from my father, but when I arrived there, I was quite surprised to find that the gate to the compound was open.'

'Is that so? Let's start at the beginning then, Archie. When you were searching for your sister, did you go all the way to the grave?'

'Yes.'

'Tell us what you saw when you got there.'

'I saw a simple grave with a headstone. It was enclosed by a wrought-iron fence. The grave had a crooked slab that had a residue of candle wax on it. There was oil on it too. It looked as if a ceremony had taken place. I also saw drag marks on the grass beside it, but I kick myself for not exploring further into the bushes nearby. If I had, I might have found the missing indigenous men or, at the very least, picked up more evidence.'

'Aha! You knew something had gone on?'

'Yes, I thought someone had been there previously because of all the melted candle wax, but as I said, I should have searched deeper into the scrub.'

'Tell us what you did see, Archie, not what you didn't. It sounds as if you were the first one on the scene.'

'I may have been, Chief Inspector Gallagher.'

'Seeing you were the first one there, we must advise you that you are automatically under suspicion for the disappearance of the two men. Now tell us what you saw.'

'As I said, I saw candle wax on the grave. Candles had been placed in a circle, and it looked as if a ceremony had taken place. They'd burned down by the time I saw them, but between each one there were still patches of oil.'

'Go on.'

'Well, I wondered who had been at the grave, and I even thought that it might have been my sister, Alkira. I called out many times for her, but when she didn't answer, I left.'

'Where did you go?'

'I went straight back to the Aboriginal camp to ask the dancers if they had any idea where Alkira may have gone. I found it strange that her bike was still there in the bushes but there was no sign of her.'

'It is puzzling,' Chief Inspector Gallagher agrees.

'The only clue that I gleaned from one of the dancers was that she'd heard the sound of a motorbike at the end of the session. That's the first time I thought that it might be Jude Stenmark who had been involved in her abduction.'

'The publican's son?'

'Yes, Inspector. I know there are lots of people who own motorbikes in Byron Bay, but he's the only person I know who owns one.'

'You said you suspect him. Why?'

'As I said, I've done some investigating on my own since coming back into town and I've found out where the oil and the candles came from.'

'Really? You are quite the sleuth, aren't you?'

'I'm used to following clues, Inspector. I'm a writer.'

'Is that so, Sherlock?' Gallagher's sidekick retorts.

Archie ignores the sarcasm. 'I went into Crystal Destiny,' he continues.

'Crystal Destiny on Lawson Street?'

'Yes.'

'Did they tell your fortune?' More sarcasm.

'The lady behind the counter confirmed that a young man had bought some candles, a box of matches, and some oil from her store a day or two ago. She distinctly remembered the fellow as he had a Mohawk haircut and a nose ring. It sounded like a good description of my racist cousin, Jude.'

'Is that so?'

'While I was in the store, I bought a candle, a box of matches, and some oil from the lady to verify that they are the same as the ones Jimmy Merinda found at the grave.'

Archie pulls out the samples from his bag. 'You'll have to do the tests, Chief Inspector, but I know who bought them. If they match up, you'll have your suspect. I'd be looking in that grave if I were you. You may find the indigenous men inside.'

'Thank you, Archie. We'll look into it.'

'You're welcome, Chief Detective.'

'One more thing, Archie. Were you wearing these shoes when you were at the grave?'

'Yes.'

'We'll get a print of the sole of your shoe while you are here, if you don't mind.'

'It's not my shoe print you need, Chief Inspector Gallagher. It's that of Jude Stenmark. I'm worried that he has not only killed the indigenous men at the gravesite but also abducted my sister.'

Archie undoes his laces, takes off his shoes, and hands them to the detective, who paints the soles with ink. He makes a print of them on some A3 paper and holds the paper up to a screen to see if they match up against pictures of footprints they'd already taken at the gravesite. They match.

After his interview at the police station, Archie has a heightened sense of concern that Alkira is in jeopardy, and he is convinced that his cousin Jude has had something to do with it. He has heard that Jude has been in a juvenile detention centre after committing armed robbery, but he hasn't yet worked out why he would want to abduct Alkira. Although Archie knows that Jude has recently rented a house in Bangalow, he is unaware of his actual address, so at the end of his interview, he rushes from the police station over to Stephanie and Abel's house on Marvell Street to find out.

At Marvell Street, Stephanie responds to his query by retrieving her address book. After transcribing Jude's new address onto a little yellow pad, she tears off the relevant page and hands it over to Archie. The moment she does this, she has second thoughts, and she wishes that hadn't given it out. It is too late, however, because when Archie has Jude's address tight in his hands, he wastes no time making his getaway. After leaving Stephanie's front gate, he suspects that she is already dialling Jude on her mobile phone.

'What is it, Mum?' Jude responds after picking up.

'Archie is heading to Bangalow, darling. Is Alkira with you?'

Jude slams down the phone.

Chapter 57

THE BARN IN BANGALOW

At four in the morning, Alkira lies wide awake on the stained mattress in the centre of the Bangalow barn. After contemplating her fate in the pitch black for hours on end, she can only sense impending doom. As she listens to the possums scurrying around on the roof and the birds fluttering endlessly in the rafters, Alkira comes to the conclusion that Jude is trying to tear apart her lofty plans of returning the land at Broken Head to her people. She is beginning to realise that the Stenmarks are much more ruthless than she could ever have imagined.

With the endless night stretching before her, Alkira despairs that her situation is hopeless, because no one, except for Jude, knows where she is. By the time the morning chorus of birds announce the break of day, she is feeling so traumatised, that she breaks into desperate sobs, but although her sobs reverberate around the huge barn, nobody can hear them.

Next door, in his rented house, Jude wakes feeling quite refreshed after enjoying a vastly different overnight experience. Having slept soundly in the crisp white sheets that he'd recently removed from the Sands Hotel, he takes a shower, and enters his kitchen to start preparing Alkira's final breakfast.

First, he inserts two boiled eggs into silver eggcups, and then he lines up four slices of brown toast in a rack. Along with a smart set of salt and pepper shakers, a small dish of butter, some apricot jam, and two glasses of freshly squeezed orange juice, he places a sharp knife onto an antique silver tray. Jude carefully picks up the tray and walks over to the barn.

'Look what I've brought you,' he announces cheerily as he advances towards Alkira.

Having not consumed anything since her breakfast the previous morning, Alkira is desperate for some food, but in a show of defiance, she shows no interest in what is on his tray.

Appearing deliberately calm, Jude places the breakfast tray in the centre of the bed. 'I've taken time to prepare you a feast, Alkira, and as it will be your last supper, we are going to share it. It's a tradition to eat well before an execution.'

'I'm not hungry,' Alkira responds, alarmed at his pronouncement.

'Yes, you are.'

'But I'm not.'

Not pleased with Alkira's defiant attitude, Jude removes his pistol from his bag and levels it at her menacingly. 'Listen, lubra lips, if I say eat, you'll eat!'

Alkira finds Jude's racist comment despicable and as she desperately needs a diversion, she asks, 'These chains are hurting me . . . Can you please unlock them?'

'If I wanted you out of chains, I'd have unlocked them already,' Jude responds curtly, before returning his attention to the breakfast tray.

After expertly cutting the first egg with the sharp knife, he dusts a spoonful of it with salt and pepper and then extends it towards

Alkira's mouth. When Alkira turns her head away from him, Jude considers her action to be insolent.

In slow motion, he deliberately returns the spoon to the tray and then he picks up his pistol again. 'Do as I say, Alkira, or you'll have a bullet in your pretty little head.'

This threat affects Alkira and she begins to shake.

'Now I will offer it to you one more time, but this time, you will accept it,' he directs.

Jude raises the spoon to Alkira's lips once more, but this time, Alkira takes the egg into her mouth.

'Now swallow it,' he orders.

Alkira swallows the egg, and Jude repeats the operation.

'Good girl . . . That's the ticket,' he commends.

'Now for some toast.'

Jude butters a slice of toast very purposefully, and then cuts it precisely into two bite-sized pieces. After spreading some apricot jam onto one of them, he lifts it up for Alkira to eat. When Alkira turns away, Jude slowly returns the toast to the tray and in one smooth motion, he picks up his pistol and fires it into the mattress. The sound of the blast is deafening, and when it reverberates around the barn, it causes the birds to flutter madly, and the possums to scurry across the roof. Alkira is so startled by it that she bursts into loud sobs.

'Listen, you bitch, I'm not telling you this again . . . One more refusal, and you'll be dead meat!'

Chapter 58

INDIGENOUS PROTEST

After hearing Jimmy's account on the radio about the items he found in the Stenmark compound, the tribesmen at the Aboriginal camp become justifiably outraged. Having survived continual persecution from European colonists in the past, they feel as if they are once again under siege. Poor Matilda disappeared twenty-five years ago and now two more of their kin have gone missing under similar circumstances. What's more, it appears likely that all three of them have met their fate inside that cyclone fence.

Alerted about the unrest at the Aboriginal camp, Stan Bowles and his crew drive out along Bangalow Road hoping to capture the mood at the camp for the evening news. When their vehicle pulls up in front, they find a rowdy group of tribesmen yelling in protest. When a woman's shrill voice pierces the air in front of Stan Bowles, he holds his microphone in front of her to catch what she has to say.

'The bastards are rounding up our kinsmen!' she shrieks.

'Who is rounding them up, madam?' Stan enquires.

'It's happened before . . . The Stenmarks are after us. It's genocide – that's what it is!'

Eager to film more of the protest, Stan and his crew pass the screaming woman and enter the community hall. After pushing past some angry protestors, the crew can hear the plaintive sound of a didgeridoo above all the hubbub. Holding his decorated hollowed-out pole in front of him, Mick is squatting cross-legged on the dirt floor in the centre of the vast circular room. As he breathes in and out in a circular fashion, tears are streaming down his ballooning face. Mick is obviously lamenting the disappearance of his two closest mates, and it is such a poignant moment that Stan Bowles insists that his crew records his grief.

An older man with a white beard sits beside Mick on a wooden crate, waving an oversized Aboriginal flag. His weathered face peers out from under a black brimmed hat with a brush turkey feather in its band. Seeing his timeworn sadness, Stan Bowles holds his microphone in front of him to ask him a question.

'Tell us about your grievance, sir,' he says.

'You've already driven us to the brink of extinction, an' here we are, in the year 2000, still being massacred on our own sacred ground. When will you white ghosts stop?'

After hearing this, Stan wonders how the old man knows that the men have been massacred by a white person. He is about to ask him further questions about this assumption, when he hears loud shouting from the far side of the community hall. With his crew charging further into the melee, Stan is obliged to follow them until they stop in front of an indigenous man who is barking into a megaphone.

'We want revenge! The Stenmarks are killing us off one by one!' the man shouts.

Stan Bowles immediately recognises the gravelly voice and scarred face of Jimmy Merinda who is holding forth, dressed in a kangaroo-skin cape.

'We stand in solidarity!' Jimmy bellows. 'We reckon the Stenmarks have slaughtered our mates inside their compound, and it is bloody likely they've dumped 'em into their grave on Broken Head. I reckon it's time they opened up the bloody Stenmark grave!'

The mob around him all hoot in agreement. 'Open the grave! Open the grave!' they yell in unison. At that moment, two young men unfurl a banner with 'Open the Grave' recently painted on it.

'Fall in behind the banner, everyone!' Jimmy calls. 'Today we're marchin' for justice!'

After his call, Jimmy's two sons rush towards him, eager to accompany their father on the proposed protest march. Jimmy takes each of them by the hand, and the trio stand defiantly at the front of the procession. Jimmy's family is soon joined by the old man with the black hat, who is still waving his oversized flag back and forth. Maisy and her friends from the Dubay dancers also edge in beside him, and scores of other indigenous protestors follow suit.

When a large man thumps out a marching rhythm on a tribal drum, the procession begins and an army of indigenous protestors start shuffling off along Bangalow Road. On their way to the Byron Bay township, many other people who are sympathetic to their cause join them, and with each kilometre, the chant gets stronger.

'Open the grave! Open the grave!'

When the marchers reach the front entrance to the Sands Hotel, still calling, 'Open the grave! Open the grave!' Jimmy grasps the megaphone. 'You Stenmarks are murderin' our kin, an' we demand justice!'

The mob behind him echo his words. 'We demand justice! We demand justice!'

Chief Inspector Gallagher arrives on the scene with a unit of police officers who are overdressed in riot gear. He immediately orders his men to confiscate the 'Open the Grave' banner and to seize the oversized Aboriginal flag.

'Arrest the ring leader in the kangaroo cape! He's the one with the scars on his face!' he shouts.

Responding to his command, two bullish police officers shove Jimmy to the ground and after placing their uniformed knees into his back, they roughly handcuff him.

'Our march is a peaceful protest. Why are you handcuffing me?' he queries, his face jammed into the bitumen.

'Because you're inciting a riot, you ugly mongrel,' one of Gallagher's henchmen responds, before hauling Jimmy over to an awaiting police van.

Unaccustomed to hearing their respected father being called 'an ugly mongrel' or seeing him treated as if he's a vicious criminal, Jimmy's sons burst into tears. Through their tears, they observe the police vehicle moving off through the crowd to a tirade of abuse.

When the vehicle has departed, Chief Inspector Gallagher turns his attention to the difficult task of dispersing the angry crowd. He seizes Jimmy's megaphone and begins to yell, 'All protestors must leave the area immediately! I repeat – leave the area now! If you don't disperse, we'll be forced to use tear gas!'

Initially, the group refuses to disband, but when the police fire off a couple of tear gas canisters at them, they quickly disperse, many with weeping eyes.

Chapter 59

FORENSICS

Outraged by the overzealous policing at the indigenous march, the Byron Bay community calls for the release of Jimmy Merinda, whom they claim was leading a peaceful protest. The editor of the local paper reminds its readers that the police were guilty of tasering Jimmy Merinda on a previous occasion for a crime he did not commit, and the editor challenges Chief Inspector Gallagher to find out what happened to the two indigenous men whom the protestors are claiming came to grief inside the Stenmark compound.

Acting expediently, Gallagher instructs his legal team to examine all the evidence they've found at the gravesite so far, and it is not long before his team come up with four initial findings.

First, they find that the candle wax on the slab matches the wax from the votive candle that was purportedly bought by Jude Stenmark from Crystal Destiny. Second, the oil on the slab also matches the Golden Light that he possibly purchased from the same store. Third, the used matches that Jimmy Merinda collected in front of the grave have been found to be on sale at the same store. The fourth discovery involves three beer cans found in the thicket near the grave. Two of those that were tested have Jude Stenmark's fingerprints all over them, while the third has fingerprints that belong to his father. Still under examination are the bullet shells which were found at the gravesite by Jimmy Merinda.

With many of the locals believing that the indigenous men have been interred in the Stenmark grave, Chief Inspector Gallagher is under mounting pressure to open the grave up for inspection. Before he can ask the local magistrate to request a license from the governor general, however, he must wait until his team finds out which firearm matches the bullet shells. He doesn't have to wait long, because a report soon arrives on his desk confirming that the bullet shells found at the site match a Beretta pistol.

Convinced that he now has something concrete to go on, Gallagher asks Abel Stenmark to sign a request to exhume the bodies from the Stenmark grave. When Abel refuses to sign it, however, he is forced to turn to Rebecca for authorisation. When Abel threatens that he will expose her, Rebecca also refuses to sign the exhumation request. Gallagher is left with no other option than to obtain the authority from Kane Stenmark, who signs his authorisation without hesitation.

On receipt of the license, Gallagher organises a removal unit to transfer the remains inside the grave into body bags, each with a separate case number attached. Forensic anthropologists then begin to take copious photographs of each cadaver, carefully recording all the bones, teeth, hair, and personal belongings that they find. Gallagher insists that the operation be conducted with basic dignity, but some of his team find the vision of several bodies in one mass grave to be an assault on their sensibilities.

They are not the only ones whose sensibilities are likely to be assaulted. If Willy's and Dingo's bodies are found inside the Stenmark grave, the local tribe will be seriously troubled. The men are members of the oldest living culture in the world and if they have not been given safe passage into their afterlife, they'll remain in limbo. If they are denied the symbolic chants and songs that are typically conducted by their loved ones, the dead men will be unable to evoke their Dreamtime creation ancestors, and as a result, they will not have been given the elaborate ritualistic rites that typically would connect them.

Willy and Dingo each had a particular totem animal spirit assigned to them at birth, and each of them was required to act as a steward for that animal's sustainability during their life. Each of these spirits should be recognised at a burial so that they will be passed on to those who follow. In addition, each of the men had been assigned a section of land to care for during their lifetime, and as their particular jurisdiction joined another group of clansmen's land, the whole area was energised. The tribe fears that spiritual forces could act against them if these boundaries are not acknowledged at a burial.

Chapter 60

EXHUMED BODIES

In front of the Byron Bay Police Station, Stan Bowles holds an ABC microphone in front of Chief Inspector Gallagher, who has signalled that he is ready to make a press release about the results of the exhumations in the Stenmark compound. Chief Inspector Gallagher needs to be aware that his imminent disclosure should be handled with the correct protocols, especially if he is releasing indigenous names.

'Ladies and gentlemen, I can announce today that our team of forensic anthropologists have finished examining the contents of the Stenmark grave on Broken Head.'

The large crowd becomes hushed, except for one heckler, who decries, 'About time!'

'I wish to announce that we have the disinterred bodies of two local tribesmen who recently went missing on Broken Head. The bodies of Willy Wampandi and Dingo Yukambal have now been officially identified by our team.'

Loud mourning sounds erupt from a group of emotionally wrought indigenous people at the back of the crowd. They are disturbed to hear Gallagher naming their mates, believing it will impede their spiritual journey.

'The protestors were right, Chief Inspector. There has been foul play,' Stan Bowles interjects.

'Yes, Stan. We are treating the grave as a crime scene.'

'How many bodies in total were found in the grave Chief Inspector?' Stan persists.

'I can confirm today that the remains of seven bodies in total were found in the Stenmark grave.'

There is a loud gasp of surprise from the assembled crowd at this disclosure and even more wailing from the indigenous group.

'Seven, Inspector?'

'Yes, there were seven bodies in total.'

'Please explain.'

'There was little to go on after all these years, but our first task was to identify the four original Stenmark family members who were buried there in the late 1800s. Luckily for us, the Broken Head soil has a neutral acidity, which allowed some of the ancient bones to be left intact. We are now confident that they are the bones of Joseph Stenmark, his wife, Bella Stenmark, and their two tiny babies, Abel and Kane.'

'That's the four original Stenmarks accounted for, Chief Inspector. What about the others?'

'As I said previously, in addition to the four Stenmarks who were buried in the late 1800s, there are the bodies of Willy Wampandi and Dingo Yukambal, who were buried there much more recently. We can confirm that these two men were killed by bullet wounds. Willy Wampandi was found to have a wound to his head, while Dingo Yukambal had a wound that entered near his sternum.'

There are murmurings among the assembled crowd, who are now wondering who was responsible for murdering the men and interring them in the Stenmark family grave.

'Who is responsible for murdering these men?' Stan Bowles asks.

'We are presently following up leads, Stan, and we are quite confident that we'll find the perpetrator or perpetrators of these serious crimes.'

'So far, you have identified six bodies, Chief Inspector. Who is the seventh?'

'I don't wish to name the seventh skeleton at this time, Stan.'

'Do you have any idea who it might be?' he presses.

'As I said, I am not speculating yet, but I can declare that the seventh body is female and that she was wearing a gold bangle on her wrist. We are still waiting for the results of DNA testing to confirm the woman's identity and that's all I can say about it at the moment.'

'Thank you for your time, Chief Inspector.'

'You're welcome, Stan. Thank you, everybody.'

As Gallagher strides off back into the police station, Stan Bowles turns to the camera to give his summary.

'Viewers, the saga from the Stenmark grave continues. Not only has the legal team unearthed the two missing indigenous men, who appear to have been murdered before being buried in the Stenmark family plot, but also, the disinterred bones of a mystery body has been discovered.

'Like all of you, I'm left wondering who it was who killed these indigenous men, but I'm also wondering if the skeletal remains of the seventh body found in the grave with a gold bangle around her wrist, belonged to Matilda Merinda, who went missing twenty-five years ago.

'Viewers, there are many unanswered questions here. For example, many people are asking if the Stenmark family is seeking revenge on the local tribe for opposing their development on Broken Head. But the big question that troubles me is . . . Does all this carnage have anything to do with the curse that was placed on the Stenmark family all those years ago when their ancestors took over sacred land?'

Chapter 61

THE PACIFIC HOUSE

After Stan Bowles's interview with Gallagher, the local community is understandably outraged. Many of the locals are deeply disturbed that the Stenmarks appear to be using their compound at Broken Head as a repository to hide murdered indigenous bodies.

Having learned that the likely perpetrator of these crimes is presently staying at a guesthouse called the Pacific House, a group of angry vigilantes are keen to demonstrate to Kane Stenmark their extreme disapproval. As the angry mob begin a march towards the guesthouse, Kane is quietly reading a magazine in his room. Suddenly, he hears loud protests outside his window.

'Come out and face us, you murdering bastard!' one of the older vigilantes yells.

'Come out of hiding, Kane Stenmark! You murdered Matilda Merinda twenty-five years ago, and now you've returned to kill two more!' another shouts.

Mortified by their offensive chants, Kane hides behind the white cotton curtains that hang on each side of the French doors of his room.

'You should be strung up and flogged! You're the one who should be buried six feet under, you murderer!' a shrill woman's voice calls. Kane recognises the voice. It belongs to old Mrs Boyle, his previous next-door neighbour.

'See how you'd like that, you cruel bastard!' she yells, her anger fuelled by many decades of conjecture. Some of the group start mounting the steps of the Pacific House and they pound on the front door.

'Let us in!' they call, as they thump loudly.

Concerned that the mob may break the door down, Kane briefly considers opening it to face them, but as it's highly likely they'll seize him and string him up on the spot, he quickly tosses this option from his mind.

Fearing for his life, Kane decides to make a quick getaway, and after grabbing his car keys, he dashes out through the rear exit of the guesthouse to the back lane, where he scrambles into the driver's side of his jeep. With his life in jeopardy once again, he roars off down the lane like a Formula One driver.

The present situation seems a little déjà vu, as once again Kane finds himself considering a return to Nimbin for refuge. The last time he was forced to leave town he left without saying goodbye to his mate Jimmy however, and he'd always regretted that decision. Rather than repeating the same mistake again, Kane decides instead to swing into the Aboriginal camp to pay Jimmy the courtesy of a visit.

Rationalising that this final visit will give him a chance to tell his friend that it wasn't him who had killed Matilda, Kane speeds towards the Aboriginal camp expecting that he will have the opportunity to tell Jimmy that it was his 12-year-old sister who had accidentally shot his sister Matilda, and that it was his brother who was guilty of burying her in the family grave.

Chapter 62

KANE AT THE ABORIGINAL CAMP

Chief Inspector Gallagher's news that three indigenous bodies were disinterred from the Stenmark grave has stirred up deep anger and unrest in the Aboriginal camp. Ever since Joseph Stenmark took their land from them 120 years ago, the tribe has been wary of the Stenmarks, and over the years, intense feelings of discontent have been simmering just beneath the surface. Having endured displacement, abuse, incarceration, racism, poverty, and marginalisation at the hands of these invading white men, the Aboriginal tribesmen have little patience for anyone who is summarily executing their kin. After hearing Gallagher's latest news about the exhumation, these festering feelings of unease have dramatically resurfaced.

A large group of tribesmen have gathered at the side of the community hall expressing their grievances, and all of them are indignant that the Stenmarks appear to be murdering their kinsmen, before unceremoniously dumping them into their family grave. As there has not been so much as a single arrest by the police so far, they consider it an appalling travesty of justice.

Keen to separate himself from the actions of his siblings, Kane steers his jeep into a parking space in front of the Aboriginal camp and strides purposefully towards the community hall. When he is almost there, he sees the group of angry men who have gathered around a roaring campfire.

'Our mates are being murdered, and no one is doing anything about it,' a man with a vexed face is complaining.

'Let our skin be our coat of armour!' another man calls.

Kane's body stiffens when he hears this, as he knows from experience that this comment is a black man's call to arms against white oppression. On hearing it, he realises that he may have arrived at a critical time in the proceedings, when the tribe are demanding retribution for the murder of its kinsmen. When he was a boy, Kane knew most of the tribesmen by name, but today, twenty-five years later, he doesn't recognise any of the faces around the campfire. Conversely, he imagines that none of them will know him. He is quite wrong.

'There's Kane Stenmark! He's the murderer!' a huge indigenous man shouts, pointing his long dark finger directly at him.

Kane instantly feels as if he has jumped from the frying pan into the fire. He has managed to escape the lynch mob in town only to become the target for the local tribe's anger. If he's not careful, he could become the victim of an Aboriginal lynching.

Initially, Kane doesn't know whether to run or hold his ground, but in no time at all, his moment of indecision is vanquished. The big man's accusation has galvanised a group of his followers into accosting him, and about five men rush towards him, intent on bringing him to the ground. After being pinned to the dirt against his will, Kane finds himself looking up into a sea of angry black faces, all glaring vengefully down at him, as they accuse him of murdering their kinsmen. Kane protests loudly that they are blaming the wrong brother, but his pleas fall on deaf ears, as the men appear intent on dealing with him according to their own tribal customs.

As they drag Kane towards the fire, he shouts at the top of his voice,

'I want to speak to Jimmy! I came here to tell him what happened to Willy and Dingo!'

'Jimmy has gone into town,' one of the men responds. 'He's not here to save you.'

Kane's heart sinks. Why is Jimmy not at the camp when he so desperately needs him?

'You Stenmarks are killing our people,' the huge man chides.

'It wasn't me,' Kane defends.

'You're a Stenmark, and you Stenmarks are all murderers!' he retorts. Kane now realises that he is guilty by family association.

'Please, please get Jimmy. Go and get Jimmy, I beg you. I want to tell him who killed your kinsmen,' Kane pleads, but his pleas are lost in the angry commotion.

When it is time for native justice to be delivered, the mob forces Kane to his knees, and two men tie his hands behind his back with a thin white rope. While some men tweak at his beard to shame him, others prod him in the ribs with sticks they've been holding over the fire. As Kane kneels in agony with burn marks on his skin, he dreads to hear what extreme punishment they will select as payback for the crimes they think he's committed.

Jimmy had told him about some of the traditional punishments that the tribe had deployed in the past. For instance, he'd heard that some of the men had their hair burned to shame them, while others had been speared in the thigh so that the scar would forever remind the culprit of the crime he'd committed.

'It's time for payback!' the big man calls ominously.

Hearing the word "payback" Kane becomes petrified that they'll form a kangaroo court and take it upon themselves to invoke their customary law.

'Blood should be shed to clean the slate!' the big man calls.

'No, please stop. I'm innocent. I'm not to blame for the killings,' Kane defends.

'It's time that our tribal law shamed the bastard!' the big man announces loudly, and the other tribesmen appear to be waiting on his decision.

'Burn the hairs from his body,' a thin man suggests.

'Yeah! Let's drag 'im through the fire and singe 'im front and back,' another agrees. Intent on dragging him closer to the fire, two strong men seize Kane by his arms and legs, and when he is dragged closer to the crackling fire, he becomes petrified that he will be offered up as a sacrificial lamb. At this moment, he literally feels the heat of two cultures colliding.

'Leave him!' a loud guttural voice suddenly calls out, as Jimmy rushes towards him in his kangaroo cape. 'What's going on here?'

'We've caught the murderer,' the big man informs him.

'Let him speak up,' Jimmy orders.

Kane has never been so happy to see his old friend's scarred face in his entire life.

'Kane Stenmark, why are ya here?' Jimmy asks.

'I came here to tell you what happened to Matilda and who is responsible for Willy's and Dingo's deaths,' Kane answers.

There is a lot of jeering and disapproval when Kane mentions the names of the dead. The angry men find it disrespectful that he is speaking their names.

'Let the man defend himself,' Jimmy demands over the strong dissent.

'I've taken the blame for it all these years, Jimmy, but I now know who killed Matilda. It was my little sister who shot her. She was only 12 years old at the time. She told me the gun went off accidentally.'

'Rebecca Stenmark shot my sister?' Jimmy queries.

'Yes.'

'How did Matilda end up in the Stenmark grave then?' Jimmy asks sternly.

'It was Abel who drove the body to the grave, Jimmy. He drove her to Broken Head in my car. He was the one who buried her.'

There is a lot of nodding and murmuring among the men following this revelation. It is as if they all knew that a Stenmark would be to blame.

'Abel swore Rebecca to secrecy all these years,' Kane adds.

'I knew it was one of you bloody Stenmarks!' Jimmy declares, and his kinsmen nod and grunt in agreement. 'Go on with ya story, Kanee. Tell us who killed our mates.'

'The police are investigating it right now, Jimmy,' Kane explains, 'but I'm sure they'll find out that it was Jude Stenmark who actually killed them.'

'The one with the Mohawk?'

'Yes.'

'I hate that bastard!' the big man calls.

'Kanee, we need our mates back 'ere so we can give 'em a proper burial, an' we want Matilda back 'ere too.'

'That can happen, Jimmy. I'm sure it can. The police will return Willy, Dingo, and Matilda to you as soon as they finish the identification process.'

Kane thinks he is saying the right thing, but there is a lot of loud murmuring among the tribesmen. The men don't like their dead kinsmen's names being spoken out loud as it could affect their journey into the afterlife.

'We want 'em returned to their conception site here in Broken Head,' Jimmy states, ignoring his peers' protests.

Familiar with the local tribe's burial rituals, Kane fully understands the tribesmen's need for this. 'I promise you that I'll get them back here,' he states in an attempt to placate them.

After this promise, Jimmy turns towards his kinsmen.

'Kane is an innocent man. We must set the bastard free. White man's law will deal with his sister for killing Matilda, and white man's law will deal with his brother for burying her. We must also leave it to the police to find out who is guilty of killin' our mates.'

'I'll make sure the police lock up the murderer,' Kane rejoins, rubber-stamping this process.

When Kane makes further assurances that the perpetrators will be made to go to trial, the tribesmen reluctantly untie him, and once free of their ropes, Kane breathes a massive sigh of relief, knowing that Jimmy has saved him from a heinously painful fate.

'You arrived in the nick of time, Jimmy,' he confides to his old mate, with relief evident on his face.

Jimmy smiles knowingly.

'They were going to throw me into the bloody fire, Jimmy.'

'You know, Kanee, you're a very lucky man. I nearly stayed on in town.'

Kane raises one eyebrow at this revelation, realising just how close he'd come to a fate that would have been almost worse than death itself. He pats Jimmy affectionately on the shoulder, knowing that he owes him big time.

Chapter 63

KANE'S TRIP HOME

Realising that freedom is often the distance between the hunter and his prey, Kane bolts towards his jeep before the tribesmen have a change of heart. With his heart still thumping wildly, he scrambles into the driver's seat and switches his headlights on. He reverses from the parking bay, but instead of going on to Nimbin as originally planned, he heads off back towards Byron Bay.

With his headlights confining his vision to the centre of the road, Kane tries to calm himself by meditating on the white lines, but he is so desperate for a cigarette by the time he reaches the Iron Bark turn-off, that he pulls his jeep over to the side of the road to search in his bag for a Marlboro.

After inhaling the warm smoke of the cigarette, he peers out from the open driver-side window and exhales into the night air. Dominating the corner position diagonally opposite him, he sees a giant real estate sign, and he impulsively swings his car over towards it to illuminate it in the full beam of his headlights.

The word "Nirvana" shines in all its glory in front of him at the top of the sign, and below it are three glossy pictures: one of a luxury villa, another of a palm-lined street leading to a spectacular beach, and the third a design drawing of a proposed luxury hotel. On a colourful map located beneath these pictures are the hundreds of lots that are on sale, some of them fronting onto the pristine ocean beach, while others face Tallow Creek. In Kane's view, the only people who will be able to afford the proposed luxury villas will be white people with deep pockets.

While Kane stares at Abel's glitzy dream, he knows that the development will completely destroy the surrounding habitat. As a schoolkid, he'd spent countless hours with his indigenous mates in this virgin land. It was their playground – a place where they followed bush trails and learned about the native animals that crossed their path. Tonight, as he stares at the mammoth sign in his headlights, Kane is sure that if this development goes ahead, all this virgin land will become a vast housing estate that will forever exclude the original inhabitants from their ancestral home.

As Kane contemplates this travesty, a sleek black Mercedes pulls up beside him, and the driver winds down his window.

'What are you doing here at this time of night, Stenmark?' the driver calls.

Kane recognises the driver as Felix Barker. 'I'm just thinking how monstrous this development really is,' Kane answers.

'Monstrous? It's the most magnificent solution anyone could imagine for Broken Head,' Felix Barker refutes.

'I'm going to vote against it, Barker. You can tell Abel that I think it should be a national park.'

'Your brother said you were a flake, Kane. Now I understand why he has that view. This development will make us all rich, you fool. It represents a unique windfall that we'll never see again. If you vote it down, Kane, Abel and I will see to it that your life won't be worth living in this town.'

After hearing Felix's threat, Kane makes a decision that he won't be bulldozed into agreeing with them. Both men obviously have no respect for local traditions. They can only see the dollar value of the land.

'If you can't support your brother, Kane, you should get out of town,' Felix advises.

'Fuck off, Barker!' Kane yells back to the solicitor.

Having heard enough of Barker's opinions, Kane jams his jeep into gear and reverses away. He speeds off along Bangalow Road, leaving Felix Barker at the sign. Kane's mind is now clear. In the future, he will act with honour and fairness, and he will disassociate himself from Abel's greedy plan. To rub salt into Abel's wound, he'll actively support the local tribe's claim for a native title for Broken Head.

When Kane looks in his rear vision mirror, he notices that someone is speeding up very fast behind him. Wondering if it is Felix Barker, he increases his speed in an attempt to outrun him. Kane's jeep is no match for Felix Barker's prestige car, however, and in no time at all the Mercedes is alongside him, with the wombat's face grimacing menacingly.

Barker edges Kane onto the shoulder of the road at high speed. When Kane hears his tyres ripping noisily into the gravel, he applies his brakes, but it is not the wisest of moves. His jeep immediately spins out of control, and after careening into an embankment, it flips onto its hood and skids in a whirlwind fashion along the bitumen road. Deafened by the sound of his jeep's metal roof screeching on the bitumen, Kane finds himself in an array of sparks until his vehicle comes to a complete halt in the middle of Bangalow Road.

Strung upside down by his seat belt, with his forehead bleeding profusely, Kane is astounded that he has survived the ordeal. With great difficulty, he extricates himself from his wrecked jeep and looks around for Felix Barker's Mercedes, but it is nowhere to be seen.

After his lucky escape, Kane leaves the smell of burned rubber and petrol behind him and begins limping off along Bangalow Road towards town. After he has walked about a hundred metres, however, he hears an explosion go off behind him, and when he looks back, he sees his rented jeep in an inferno of flames.

Chapter 64

THE SANDS HOTEL

Overcome with anger at Felix Barker's aggressive behaviour, and determined to confront his brother about the incident, Kane limps towards the Sands Hotel on foot. He finds it hard to believe that everyone in Byron Bay still thinks Abel is an innocent man, when in fact, he deserves everybody's wrath. He is tired of being the scapegoat for Abel's misdemeanours, and he is determined to let everyone know the truth while he is still alive to tell it.

With his forehead still dripping with blood, he limps into the front bar of the Sands Hotel. On entry, he can smell stale beer wafting up from the carpet, and he can hear balls ricocheting around the pool table. A few lads with their caps on backwards are staring at him as he comes through the door, each wondering what kind of hell he has just been through.

On a mission to find his brother, Kane edges past the young guns until he gets to the end of the bar, where he recognises an old fellow who is gazing haplessly into his schooner of beer.

'G'day, Cyril. Have you seen my brother around, mate?' he asks.

'You look like you've been in the bloody war, Kane,' Cyril responds, as he peers blearily at Kane's bloody face.

'You should have seen the other guy,' Kane quips, and the old man bursts into a grin. 'I'm lookin' for Abel. Have you seen him anywhere?' Kane repeats.

Cyril looks down at his watch. 'It's almost time for the chook raffle, mate. Abel is probably in the beer garden by now. Have you got a ticket?'

Kane looks at the old-timer with a wry expression, before edging further towards the door to the beer garden. In the doorway, Kane encounters some "tradies" who are waving their tickets in the air, obviously ready to win tonight's draw. After squeezing past their sweaty bodies, Kane emerges into the familiar outdoor beer garden space, where he hears the high-pitched *tickety-tick* of the giant wheel of fortune. Kane's brother is about to make an announcement on the screechy hotel microphone to alert the crowd of the impending draw.

'Ladies and gentlemen, the winner of tonight's raffle spin will receive a huge chook, dressed, ready to slide into the oven. Tonight there will be a second draw in which you can win a complimentary meat tray of snags, chops, and steak.'

As Abel approaches the giant wheel, the crowd hoots with approval.

'Here we go, folks. Have you got your tickets ready?' he asks, before setting the wheel of fortune in motion.

When the crowd hears the familiar *tickety-tick*, *tickety-tick* of the revolving wheel, it fills the beer garden with optimism. Intent on stopping it in mid-spin before it lands on a winning number, Kane lurches towards the wheel, to stop it prematurely. The crowd boos loudly when the spin is interrupted.

Unperturbed by their reaction, Kane snatches the microphone from his brother and announces, 'Before you take home the chook or the sausages, ladies and gentlemen, I want you all to know that this man here was guilty of burying the missing indigenous girl in our family grave!'

Kane points accusingly towards his brother. 'You should all know that he's as guilty as sin, and that the bastard has been blaming me!'

After hearing Kane's accusation Abel strides purposefully towards him, and with his face twisted in hatred, he throws a knockout punch. His tightly clenched fist connects with his brother's already injured face, and Kane collapses like a smashed pumpkin against the wheel of fortune, which tilts precariously, before crashing spectacularly onto the concrete floor. Kane lands on top of the wheel, with blood gushing profusely from his nose.

'Throw the bastard out!' Abel yells authoritatively to the security guards, who promptly seize Kane, and after dragging him out onto Jonson Street, they abandon him on the footpath.

Kane remains still for some time, too dazed and injured to move, but finally with the help of some strangers, he gets back to his feet. After thanking these good Samaritans for their assistance, he staggers off in the direction of Rebecca's house.

It is quite late by the time he reaches Rebecca's door.

'Rebecca, please let me in! Please!' he shouts, but he has to repeat it over and over before she finally appears at the door in her nightdress.

'Hell, Kane, what the blazes have you been up to?' she exclaims, seeing his bloody face in front of her.

After helping Kane inside, she watches him stumble over to her pristine cream sofa where he collapses. After inspecting his injuries, Rebecca orders her priorities. She cleans up his face, and then places his sore wrist in some ice. Kane surrenders to the amateur medico, who after disinfecting his cuts, places some plaster bandages on his forehead and flattened nose.

'You should have been a doctor, Rebecca,' he flatters.

'I know, Kane. I should have been a lot of things. Now tell me what in the blazes happened to you.'

So much has happened to Kane in the last twenty-four hours that he hardly knows where to begin.

'After escaping a lynch mob at the Pacific House, I escaped to the Aboriginal camp in my jeep, but the mob almost burned me alive.'

'What?'

'It's a bloody long story, sis.'

Rebecca is stunned by what Kane has uttered so far, but he shortens his account of what happened to him to the trip home from the camp.

'On my way back from the camp, I pulled in to inspect the new Nirvana sign at Iron Bark, but as I was looking at it, Felix Barker pulled up next to me in his Mercedes.

When I told him I wasn't going to support Abel's Nirvana development the bastard threatened me.'

'He's a nasty piece of work, that man,' Rebecca endorses.

'Barker told me my life wouldn't be worth living in this town if I went against Abel, and I ended up swearing at him before driving off in my jeep. The bloody wombat followed me in his Mercedes and the bastard cut me off on Bangalow Road.'

'What a prick!'

'He forced me into an embankment, and my jeep flipped onto its hood. I went spinning along the road, upside down, with sparks flying everywhere.'

'How dangerous! Did he stop?'

'No.'

'The bastard!'

'I'm lucky to be alive.'

'It sounds like it, Kane. Don't you think it's time we stopped Abel and Felix in their tracks?' Rebecca asks.

'Too right, sis. I'm sure they're targeting us. I reckon they're out to kill us.'

'I do too, Kane and I'm sick of Abel controlling me. He's been blackmailing me for over twenty-five years, and all that time, I've been feeling hideously guilty that you've had to wear the blame for that girl's disappearance.'

'I'm over it too, sis. I've decided that I'm not going to wear it any longer.'

'I want to apologise to you, Kane. Up until now, I haven't felt strong enough to go against Abel, but I've been totally wrong to keep Matilda's death a secret. I've been a bloody coward. I've allowed you take the wrap for something that I did twenty-five years ago.'

'I'm aware that you've been under Abel's thumb, sis. We all have in our own way, but it's time we teamed up against him. I'm reckoning that if we joined together we could outsmart the bastard. If we really wanted to we could stop him, you know. Why don't you and I take control of Stenmark Inc.?'

'Really? Would you go that far, Kane?'

'Yes, I would. But we can only wrestle control of it if we join forces.'

'Then let's do it,' Rebecca agrees excitedly.

'We can't do anything though until you clear the air Rebecca. I'm afraid you'll have to confess to shooting Matilda.'

'Ugh! If I confess to that, they'll lock me up, Kane.'

'You were so young then, Rebecca. I'm sure they'll give you leniency. You could argue that you didn't know how to operate the rifle properly.'

'But I've hidden a crime,' Rebecca frets.

'Yes, you have . . . and what's more, you've hidden it for two and a half bloody decades. They'll want to punish you for that, but you can argue that Abel blackmailed you.'

'God, Kane, if I own up to the killing, I'm going to need some bloody good legal help, and there's no way I'll be engaging Felix Barker.'

The siblings remain silent, both considering whom they might rope in to help them.

'Hey, I've thought of someone who could help you. How about engaging Alkira? She's a solicitor, you know,' Kane blurts.

'Yes. Yes, Kane! She's the perfect one to defend me. In addition, she may also be the one to help us wrestle back control over Stenmark Inc.'

Kane and Rebecca feel as if they are on a roll and their faces light up with optimism. It is the first time in a long time that the siblings have a united plan.

'How do you think she'll fare against the wily old Felix Barker?' Kane fields, playing the devil's advocate.

'She's a smart cookie, Kane. Don't you underestimate her. I'm sure she'll be able to challenge the old wombat.'

Kane laughs at Rebecca's description of Felix.

'I really hope she'll take us on,' she enthuses, as she crosses her fingers. 'What about Nirvana?' Rebecca asks as an afterthought.

'I can't support it now, sis. Initially, I was stupid enough to go along with it, but in good conscience, we can't develop Broken Head for ourselves. It's Abel's dream, but it's wrong.'

'Yes, I agree. The time has come for us to relinquish our control of it.'

'I realise now how important the land is to the local tribe. We have to give it back to them so they can manage it as a national park,' Kane declares.

'Good for you, Kane,' Rebecca applauds. She pats him on the shoulder to congratulate him on his change of heart, stating, 'At last, we're on the same bloody page, Kane.'

The brother and sister both hope that their relationship will continue to strengthen. In the past they have endured two and a half decades of separation, but now at last, they have a common goal.

Kane looks over at Rebecca whose face appears fraught.

'What's wrong, sis?' he asks.

Rebecca has been recalling her recent boat trip with Stephanie.

'Kane, I've been threatened too, you know.'

'By whom?'

'By Stephanie – The bitch nearly pushed me overboard when we were out on a boat trip.'

'Did she now? She must have known you can't swim.'

'She tried to convince me to support the Nirvana project, but when I told her it was a greedy land grab, she pretended to overbalance into me, and I almost went into the drink.'

'Sounds as if you had a narrow escape, sis.'

'I did. I think Abel and Stephanie are really out to get us, Kane. I'm serious.'

'That's another thing we agree on, Rebecca.'

'Well, what are we going to do about it?' she asks.

'Well, the first thing for you to do is to confess to the police that you shot Matilda. Then after your confession, Abel will be implicated in her burial.'

Rebecca remains rigid at this directive. She has considered confessing her crime many times over the years, but she could never quite pluck up enough courage.

'Go tomorrow . . . The earlier, the better,' Kane directs.

Chapter 65

REBECCA'S ADMISSION

After her serious talk with Kane, Rebecca mulls over what she will say to the police. Tired of Abel blackmailing her over her dirty little secret, she hopes her admission will put a stop to the endless accusations that Kane has had to endure over the years. In one fell swoop, she will be able to clear his name. She owes it to him, but she also owes it to the entire Aboriginal clan who have never known why one of their teenage girls had mysteriously disappeared.

Determined to get the whole sordid ordeal off her chest, Rebecca anxiously climbs the three steps leading into the Byron Bay Police Station, dressed in a tight-fitting green cotton suit and a matching perky hat. She has deliberately dressed up for the occasion knowing that it might be the last time she can. If she is arrested on the spot, she knows she could easily be thrown into a dark cell and may very well be wearing prison garb for quite some time.

After taking a deep breath she announces, 'I want to report a crime.'

The female officer to whom she is speaking leads her straight into an interview room, and she advises her to sit at a cold iron table. Rebecca feels like a felon whose liberty is about to be taken away from her at any moment. After a nervous wait, Chief Inspector James Gallagher comes through the door, with his handcuffs dangling ominously from his belt. The Inspector is accompanied by Constable Parker, who leans forward and switches on a recorder. Gallagher calls out the date, time, and place of the interview before looking up at Rebecca to ask,

'Please state your name, madam.'

'My name is Rebecca Stenmark,' Rebecca replies, trying to keep a stiff upper lip.

Gallagher observes that her manicured hands are shaking. 'Go ahead, Ms Stenmark. What is it you wish to report?'

'I want to own up to a crime I committed twenty-five years ago.'

'That's a long time ago, madam.'

'Yes, it is. I've been covering it up for two and a half decades.'

'Tell us more.'

'I was only 12 years old in 1975 when the bachelor and spinster ball was held in Byron Bay. My brothers attended the ball, but I was left at home alone because I was too young to go.' Rebecca states.

'Go on, Ms Stenmark,' Gallagher urges.

'At about 11:30 p.m., three indigenous youths entered our garden at Marvell Street. There was a girl and two boys, and they yelled out to me to bring them out some grog.'

Rebecca pauses again, and Gallagher watches the corners of her mouth twitch with anxiety.

'Please go on, Ms Stenmark,' the inspector encourages.

'I was so petrified at the time that I went over to my brother's gun cabinet to take out his rifle. I intended to scare them off, Inspector, but the gun went off unexpectedly. I wasn't aware that it had been left loaded. There was a thunderous shot, and the girl dropped to the ground, but the boys bolted off into the night.' Rebecca's whole body begins to shake.

'What did you do then, Ms Stenmark?' Gallagher presses.

'I was so terrified, I didn't know what to do.'

'Did you check on the girl?'

'Yes. I went out into the garden and saw that she'd been shot in the temple.'

'Was she dead?'

'Yes, she was dead.'

'Are you admitting to the killing of Matilda Merinda, Ms Stenmark?'

'Yes.'

'Why haven't you owned up to this before, madam?'

'I was sworn to secrecy.'

'By whom?'

'By my brother Abel.'

'I thought Abel Stenmark was at the ball, Ms Stenmark.'

'Please, Inspector, call me Rebecca.'

'OK, Rebecca. Wasn't your brother at the B&S ball that night?'

'Yes, he was, but he came home a little earlier than expected and he found me crying hysterically.' Rebecca pulls out a lace-edged handkerchief from her handbag and wipes her eyes.

'Go on with your story, Rebecca.'

'He asked me what had gone on, and I pointed to the dead girl on the grass. After I had told him that I'd shot her, he went over to the body to check if she was dead. Then he ordered me to get the keys to my other brother's car, which was parked out in front of our house.'

'Hold on a minute. Which brother came home?'

'Abel.'

'Whose car did you find the keys for?'

'It was Kane's car. After we had loaded the girl's body into the boot, Abel told me to stay at home while he drove off with her. About an hour and a half later, he returned to Marvell Street and parked the car in the same spot as before. Then he made sure the boot of the car was clean.'

'Where do you think Abel took the body, madam?'

'At the time, I wasn't completely sure, but the next morning, Abel told me he had buried her in our family grave.'

Gallagher and Parker exchange glances.

'Inspector, I am aware that your team has discovered the remains of an indigenous female on Broken Head.'

'That's correct, Rebecca. We have found Matilda Merinda's remains in your family grave.'

'Well, Chief Inspector, now that you have her killer, you should lock me up.'

'Rebecca Stenmark, you have covered up a manslaughter for over two and a half decades. It's a serious crime that you are admitting to. I am going to place you under immediate arrest.'

As Constable Parker switches off the recorder, Gallagher unclasps the handcuffs that are hanging from his belt. He locks them around Rebecca's wrists, and escorts her to a cell, where he reads her rights to her. He asks her if she wants to call anyone, but when Rebecca declines, Gallagher advises her that she must wait in the cell until bail proceedings are determined.

In the bleak jail cell, Rebecca sits alone on the hard bed, sobbing quietly. She has always known that someday she'd end up right here, confessing her crime and waiting to be punished for it.

Chapter 66

THE BARN IN BANGALOW

'Well then, Alkira, the time has come for me to take you out of the picture entirely.'

'What do you mean, Jude?'

'Do you know how they treated witches in the olden days?' he asks.

'I'm not a witch, Jude. I'm your cousin.'

'You're not a Stenmark, Alkira Merinda, and don't insult me by telling me you are. You're the half-caste illegitimate daughter of Ronnie, the town's mad woman . . . another witch.'

'Ronnie is my mother. She's not a witch,' she corrects.

Alkira realises that it is in her best interests to emphasise her connection to the Stenmark family.

'Kane Stenmark is my father, and he's your uncle. Believe it or not, Jude, I'm actually your cousin. I'm definitely a Stenmark.'

'In the olden days, they'd burn witches like you at the stake,' he continues, unaffected by Alkira's statements of family truth.

Jude picks up some rope from the floor, and after looping it in his hands, he throws the loose end behind his back. In a sharp movement, he jerks the rope forward like a whip and when the end of it strikes

Alkira on the face, she screams in acute pain. Jude withdraws the rope for another go, but this time he whips it forward with so much force that it makes a gash on Alkira's cheek drawing blood.

'You're a sadist!' she screams at him. 'What have I ever done to you?'

Jude refuses to answer Alkira's question because he is concentrating on rewinding the rope to prepare for a third strike. 'It's what you intend to do to me that worries me,' he finally utters. 'Give you lot an inch and you take a fuckin' mile.'

He whips the rope for a third time, but this time, it strikes Alkira's right breast.

'Owwww! Stop it, Jude!' she screams. 'You've gone way too far!'

Jude drops the cord to his booted feet and takes out the bottle of Golden Light oil from his backpack. As he withdraws it, he thinks about Moonbeam cautioning him that it will ignite if introduced to a naked flame. He had already proven how well it ignited when it flared up so majestically on the slab of his great-grandparents' grave.

'Don't even think about it, Jude. Let me go. You've gone way too far already!' Alkira implores.

Ignoring her protests, Jude advances with the opened bottle and he upends the contents onto Alkira's hair. She tosses her head right and left in protest, but the oil dribbles from her head onto her shoulders and it finally oozes down onto the mattress beneath her.

'You think you are red hot, don't you, Alkira? Well, now you're going to know the literal meaning of the words.'

'Stop, Jude, before it's too late!' she pleads.

'Your mob started the whole thing when they cursed our family, but now I'm going to turn the curse back onto you, my sweet.'

'Stop, Jude. We can work out something together . . . I'm sure we can solve it,' Alkira pleads.

Like a maniacal choir boy, Jude holds the lighted votive candle in front of him and slowly advances towards Alkira.

'Please don't put it near me . . . Please!' Alkira begs.

As Jude moves the candle towards Alkira's oily hair, he begins to chant, 'Let me be the one whose hand will banish those who invade our land.'

Feeling precisely like Joan of Arc about to be burned at the stake, Alkira lets out an ear-piercing, high-pitched, desperate scream.

Chapter 67

BYRON BAY

After Moonbeam has confirmed that a young man fitting the description of Jude Stenmark had purchased all the incriminating articles, Gallagher is now convinced that Jude Stenmark is his prime person of interest. Now that his team has linked the bullet shells found at the grave to a Beretta 22LR pistol, he is confident that when he finds the gun, he'll find the murderer.

He turns to Archie. 'We need to find Jude Stenmark urgently. Do you know where he lives?'

'He lives in Bangalow,' Archie replies.

'Do you know his address?'

'Yes, I do.'

'It's time we nailed the bastard. The psychopath must be stopped in his tracks before he murders someone else. Get in the vehicle with Constable Parker, Archie, and give him the directions to Jude Stenmark's house in Bangalow.'

Gallagher grabs his cap from the hook and hustles Archie into Parker's vehicle. At high speed, the two police cars speed out of Byron Bay towards Bangalow, and after a hair-raising fifteen-minute drive, Archie directs Constable Parker to turn right at the Bangalow Hotel. In moments, the police cars are skidding to an abrupt halt on the gravel outside Jude Stenmark's rented cottage.

Chief Detective Gallagher is first to alight from his vehicle, and he knocks loudly on Jude Stenmark's front door. When there is no answer to his sharp rapping, he directs his subordinates to force the door open, and once inside, the officers systematically search the cottage from room to room with guns drawn. In the bedroom, they see Jude's unmade bed and some gay pornographic magazines on the floor, while in the kitchen, they find evidence of food preparation. As there is no sign of the tenant, Gallagher is bitterly disappointed, and he instructs his men to retreat to the front door of Jude's cottage. They all spring to alert however, when a piercing scream comes from the adjacent barn.

Recognising Alkira's voice, Archie is the first to react. He sprints to the barn door and slides it open just in time to see Jude Stenmark, setting Alkira's hair alight with the votive candle. Alarmed to see his beautiful sister suddenly engulfed in flames, he dashes towards her. With her desperate screams ringing in his ears, he collects one of the army blankets from a pile on the counter and thrusts it over Alkira's burning hair. He holds the blanket tightly around her body desperately trying to block the air from fuelling the flames.

Seeing Archie subverting his plot, Jude reaches for his Beretta, and after cocking it at the ready, he aims it directly at Archie. 'Take off the blanket, or you're a dead man,' he orders.

Archie remains motionless, stoically hugging the blanket around Alkira and refusing to obey his command.

'Take it off, or I'll shoot,' Jude repeats.

A loud shot rings out, and Jude Stenmark drops to the dirt floor, screaming in pain. While his left hand clutches at the bullet wound in his leg, his right hand waves his pistol wildly in the air. Chief Detective Gallagher stands resolutely behind his own pistol, shouting,

'Drop the gun, Jude Stenmark!'

After considering firing it, Jude prudently decides to drop his Beretta to the ground. Then still screaming in pain, he grabs at his injured leg, while Constable Parker rushes over to overpower him. Another officer rushes towards Alkira with a fire extinguisher and showers her in a mountain of white foam.

'Alkira, how are you under there?' Archie calls, trying to decipher her shape beneath the foamy blanket.

'Archie, can you please take it all off me now?' her weak voice calls from underneath the mountain of foam. When Archie removes the army blanket, he is shocked to see Alkira's bedraggled face, her badly scorched hair and her bleeding cheek.

'Did he do that to you?' he asks, pointing over to Jude. When Alkira nods, Archie shakes his head slowly in disgust.

'You're a cruel bastard!' he accuses, as Jude Stenmark moans in pain on the dirt floor.

Archie turns back to examine the cuts that Jude's rope has inflicted on Alkira's face, but when he lowers his gaze, he also sees a nasty patch of blood on her breast. When Alkira bursts into loud sobs, Archie's heart goes out to her and he holds her badly injured body in his arms.

'Tell me where you are hurting,' he asks.

'I'm hurting everywhere, Archie . . . my wrists, my face, my arms, my breast, even my hair! Can you smell it? The mongrel set me alight.'

Archie sniffs in the distinctive odour of Alkira's singed hair. 'You poor thing,' he commiserates, his emotions fluctuating wildly between anger and love.

'Archie, I thought I was a goner. Thank god you rescued me.'

'It was a mighty close call, Alkira,' Archie discloses, as he lifts her locked hand up to kiss it.

'I'm sorry I wasn't there to meet you at the camp, Archie,' she apologises.

'I just couldn't work out where you'd gone or what had happened to you. Your disappearance was such a mystery to me. How in god's name did you end up in this barn?' he asks.

'That bastard kidnapped me after my dance session and he brought me here on his motorbike to kill me,' Alkira sobs, while pointing over towards Jude Stenmark who is still clutching at the bullet hole in his leg.

'How on earth did you find me, Archie?' she asks.

'You can call me Sherlock,' Archie jokes. 'I'll tell you about it later.'

'Archie, I wonder if you could get them to unlock me?' she requests, as she peers down at the chains that are shackling her.

Archie asks one of the officers to unlock her, and he finds the key in one of Jude Stenmark's pockets. He is just about to unlock her when Gallagher orders him to stop.

'We must take photographs of the victim in chains first,' he directs and Alkira is required to endure a little more time under padlock, while the officer takes copious photographs of her in shackles.

'You are very fortunate girl to be still alive, my girl,' Chief Inspector Gallagher declares between the flashes of the camera. 'If Archie hadn't led us to you, we would have been way too late.'

Alkira looks adoringly at her brother and she cuddles up to him.

'I really thought I was going to die in here, Inspector. Thank god you all made it in time.'

'All in the line of duty,' the chief inspector parrots. 'Alkira, I've called an ambulance to deliver you to Lismore Hospital, because you'll need some medical treatment for those burns and cuts. I imagine you'd like to accompany Alkira in the ambulance, Archie?' When Archie nods, Gallagher says,

'I'll contact you both tomorrow.'

By the time Alkira and Archie are ready to make their way out to the ambulance, a crowd of curious onlookers has gathered beside the barn. They gasp when they see Alkira's singed hair and her bloodied cheek. They wonder who was responsible for inflicting these injuries, but when Gallagher appears with the Mohawked felon limping beside him, the crowd quickly deduces that he is the culprit.

Before Gallagher departs in the vehicle with Jude Stenmark, he fires a few final orders at Constable Parker.

'Parker, under no circumstances are you to leave here until you've taken photographs of the bed, the mattress, the chains, the rope, the breakfast tray, Stenmark's mobile phone and his Beretta pistol, OK?'

Parker nods and raises his thumbs.

'Also, before you leave, you must go next door to Stenmark's cottage to take photographs of the kitchen and bedroom, because we'll need all of it for evidence in court.'

After delivering these orders, Gallagher settles into the back seat with the villain, and with the police vehicle's siren blasting through the hinterland air, he departs towards Byron Bay.

Chapter 68

JUDE

With hands cuffed and ankles shackled, Jude Stenmark sits alone at a table in the airless interrogation room at the Byron Bay Police Station. Shuffling constantly, Jude sometimes grimaces towards a dark window on one of the walls of the room. He knows from experience that officers are likely to be viewing him from an adjacent room.

After some time, Chief Inspector Gallagher enters the interrogation room and authoritatively slaps his file on the table, before taking a seat opposite his suspect. 'Jude Stenmark, you are being charged with two counts of murder and one count of abduction with an attempt to murder, occasioning grievous bodily harm,' he declares.

Jude looks away from him without reacting. Gallagher interprets his non-reaction as insolence.

'Your murder charges involve the shooting deaths of two indigenous men named Willy Wampandi and Dingo Yukambal at the Stenmark compound on Broken Head.' Jude does not react.

'Your abduction charge involves an indigenous woman by the name of Alkira Merinda, who was taken against her will to be tortured in a barn in Bangalow.'

Jude continues to remain sullen and unresponsive.

'You have the right to remain silent, Jude Stenmark, but it may harm your defence if you do not mention when questioned, something you may later rely on in court,' the chief inspector parrots.

'I don't wish to remain silent,' Jude rejoins.

'Do you have something to say then?' Gallagher asks.

'The darkies were trespassing on our land. I have the right to defend our private property from intruders.'

'You do not have the right to take the law into your own hands,' Gallagher corrects him.

'They were going to dig up my ancestors.'

'So you shot them?'

'I was there, but I didn't pull the trigger.'

'Who pulled the trigger then?'

'It was my father who shot them.'

'Are you saying that Abel Stenmark was with you at the gravesite at the time of the murders?'

'Yes, Gallagher, he's your man.'

Gallagher raises one eyebrow. He's perfectly aware that Jude Stenmark is clutching at straws, and he is aghast that Jude could turn on his father just to get himself off the hook. Gallagher expects that once there is a match between the Beretta bullet shells that were found at the grave and Jude's pistol, he'll have a watertight case. Jude's fingerprints will no doubt convict him on these first two charges.

Chief Inspector Gallagher opens the file on the table to read further details about the second charge.

'You seized an indigenous girl and transported her against her will to a barn in Bangalow, where you detained her and tortured her, occasioning serious bodily harm when you whipped her with a rope and set her hair alight.'

After hearing the details of the charge, Jude stands upright, and with his shackles clanking with every step, he shuffles across to the wall to peer up at the dark glass window above him.

'Fuck the lot of you! The bitch deserved everything she got! She's been plotting to take our land away from us!' he hollers.

'Calm down, Stenmark. Calm down,' Gallagher cautions.

'I can't calm down . . . The Abbos have to be taught a fucking lesson!'

'I said sit down, Stenmark!' Gallagher orders again. This time he grasps Jude by the shoulders and forces him back into his seat. 'Jude Stenmark, you have committed multiple indictable offences and you will be tried for each of them by a jury in the NSW Supreme Court.'

Jude protests with some choice expletives, but Gallagher is finished with him. He signals for his officers to remove him from the interrogation room and place him in his cell.

Chapter 69

LISMORE TO BYRON BAY

Alkira is quite a sight when she appears from the burns unit at Lismore Hospital. She has bandages around her head and arms, plus smaller plasters covering the welts on her cheek. She is pleased when the doctor explains to her that her burns are first degree, because this diagnosis allows her to return home. Before releasing her, however, the doctor hands her a packet of strong painkillers and directs the ambulance driver to return her to her apartment in Byron Bay.

Eager to attend to her every need, Archie helps Alkira into her favourite silk pyjamas, and he tucks his exhausted patient into bed. He gives her a careful yet tender kiss on her forehead, before leaving her to sink into a deep sleep.

At two o'clock in the morning, however, he hears a blood-curdling shriek. When he rushes into her bedroom from the living room couch, he finds Alkira sitting up in bed, sobbing inconsolably. Archie holds her gently in his arms and soothes her with words that tell her that she is now safe. Finally he coaxes her back into sleep.

The next day, when Alkira wakes, her burns are throbbing so badly that she struggles with her injured body into the bathroom to down some of the painkillers that the doctor at the Lismore Hospital had dispensed to her. She is in the middle of swallowing a couple of them when her phone rings. Archie takes the call for her and finds Gallagher on the line.

'Good morning, Archie. It's Chief Inspector Gallagher here. How's the patient today?'

'Actually, she's a little sore this morning, Inspector.'

'I don't doubt it,' he replies. 'She's been through a horrendous ordeal, the poor girl.'

Archie passes the phone to Alkira.

'I hear the burns are a little painful today, Alkira.'

'They are, Inspector, but I'm just so thankful that I'm alive.'

'Yes, it was definitely a close call. Do you think you'll be able to come into the police station tomorrow? We'll need to conduct a formal interview with you about your abduction.'

After she acquiesces to Gallagher's request, Archie asks Alkira if she would like to soak in a bath for a while.

'I'd love to have a bath, Archie,' she responds, but she has to think about the logistics of taking a bath whilst wearing bandages. 'I imagine I can keep my head and arms out of the water,' she says as Archie runs the water for her. He adds her favourite bath salts.

As Alkira luxuriates in the warm water, she revisits the horrific events that have transpired over the past few days, and she feels extremely fortunate that her brother has somehow managed to save her life. Realising that he has also become her personal carer as well, she allows a smile to creep over her face, thinking that he has become her knight in shining armour.

'I thank the universe that you have come into my life,' she says.

Chapter 70

BYRON BAY POLICE STATION

The next day at the police station, Alkira finds it extremely harrowing to relive the details of her ordeal with Jude Stenmark, but she is reassured when Gallagher announces to her, 'You'll be pleased to know that in your case, we've charged Jude Stenmark with attempted murder causing grievous bodily harm. After he's convicted and sentenced in court, I am sure it will be a very long time before the cruel psychopath will see the light of day.'

Alkira finds this statement reassuring. When the interview is over, Alkira asks Chief Inspector Gallagher if he is still detaining Jimmy Merinda at the station.

'No, Alkira. We've had to listen to public pressure, and we've released him with no charges laid,' he answers.

'That's excellent news, Inspector.'

'Are you related to him, Alkira?'

'Yes. He's my uncle, sir.'

'Oh.'

'In my opinion, Chief Inspector Gallagher, in the future, you should go easy on Jimmy Merinda. He's not a troublemaker, you know. On the contrary, everyone in our tribe regards him as an extremely moral person.'

'I'm sure you're right, Alkira. We did get it wrong. I'm sorry,' he apologises.

Alkira has not finished admonishing him.

'He was leading a peaceful protest, Inspector, and you and your men victimised him.'

'Yes, I'm afraid we did. I'm very sorry, Alkira. We overreacted at the time,' Gallagher admits.

'Not for the first time,' Alkira rebukes.

After this reminder, Alkira tells the police chief that she is delighted that Jimmy has been released, but before she descends the steps, she decides to call Jimmy on her mobile phone.

'Jimmy, I just want to let you know how delighted I am that you're free,' she tells him.

'Thanks for ya concern for me, Alkira, but I wanna know what happened to you, girl.'

Alkira tells him about her own horrific ordeal in Bangalow, explaining how lucky she is to be alive. 'Jimmy, that Jude Stenmark is one mean son of a bitch,' she tells him.

'He's straight out of a horror movie, Alkira. I reckon the boy needs some serious counselling.'

'Counselling? He's such a danger to society that I hope they'll lock him up and throw away the key.'

'You can say that again, girl.'

Alkira is about to end the call to Jimmy when Jimmy says, 'Oh, Alkira, I nearly forgot to tell you somethin'. When Willy's and Dingo's bodies have been returned to us, I'm gonna organise a memorial service in our community hall for them. I wanna make sure they can pass into the next world so they can connect properly with our ancestors. I'm hopin' you'll be well enough by then to be part of it.'

'Jimmy, I may be covered in bandages, but I'll be there, I promise you. I wouldn't miss it for quids.'

'Oh, another thing, Alkira. If you're gonna submit another native title claim, ya can put my name on it because I've decided to get brave at last.'

'That's the best news I've heard all day!' Alkira exclaims, aware that having Jimmy's name on her next submission will make all the difference.

After hearing Jimmy's change of heart, Alkira's spirits soar. She is so uplifted by this news that she decides to drop into her hairdresser's salon on the way home. Wondering if Darren can do anything to tidy up her charred hair, she enters his salon.

'What in god's name have you been up to, Alkira?' he screams, seeing the bandages. 'Come inside so I can have a good look at you,' he orders as he pats his hand on a vacant salon chair.

After taking a seat, Alkira tells Darren all about what happened in Bangalow, and it brings tears to his eyes.

'Don't you worry, honey child. I'll tidy you up as best I can,' he comforts, dabbing at his tears with a small towel.

While Darren is carefully snipping around Alkira's burns, she refuses to watch him, but in the end, when she looks at herself in the salon mirror, she sees an almost bald person reflected back at her.

Feeling self-conscious as she escapes from the hair salon, she wonders what Archie will think of her new closely cropped look. She is about to climb the stairs of her apartment to find out, when her mobile phone rings. As it is a call from Canberra, she stops to answer it before making the long climb to the top.

Keen to meet the deadline imposed by his editor in Sydney, Archie is making a decided effort to finish the first draft of his novel, and while Alkira has been out, he has been on her balcony, busily typing away on his laptop. When Alkira enters, however, he does a double take when he sees her extremely short hair. He leans back in his chair to fully assess her new image, and immediately decides that the new closely cropped style is actually quite adorable.

'You look gorgeous,' he flatters. 'Your burns are yet to heal, but the new short style looks great.'

'Do you really like it?' she asks tentatively.

'I love it, Alkira. It'll look even better when everything heals,' he replies.

Alkira comes out on the balcony to the table where Archie is working, and she wraps her bandaged arms around him. She places her cheek gently against his and says, 'Archie Stenmark, you saved my life.'

'You owe me big time now,' he jokes.

'Oh, there's something I haven't told you yet, Archie,' she ventures.

'Tell me all.'

'On my way back from the hairdresser, I received a call from Canberra, and guess what?'

'What?'

'I've been chosen to speak on Australia Day to represent indigenous Australians. It's called the people's address.'

'What?'

'I'll be on national television!'

'Alkira, that's so special!'

'Apparently, they saw my interview with Stan Bowles, and they were impressed. I'm scared stiff though.'

'What on earth are you going to say?'

'I have a few things already in my mind that I want to say,' she affirms.

After hearing this, Archie stands up and turns towards Alkira to give her a careful hug. 'Alkira, I'm so very proud of you,' he says warmly.

'I'll be doing it for Ronnie,' Alkira answers as tears spring into her eyes.

Archie hugs her a little more tightly. 'Now tell me how the interview with Gallagher went at the police station,' he enquires.

'Oh yes, he informed me that they've formally arrested Jude Stenmark for abducting me.'

'That's great news, Alkira. The cruel bastard belongs behind bars for the rest of his life.'

'Archie, the best thing that came out of this morning's meeting was that they're no longer detaining Jimmy. Chief Inspector Gallagher said they've released him from jail with no charges laid.'

'That's also great news, Alkira. Jimmy was leading a peaceful demonstration, for god's sake!'

'And guess what?'

'Tell me.'

'Jimmy told me he's going to be the claimant on my second try for a native title.'

'That's just fantastic! What a morning you've had!'

'Once I send in the second submission with Jimmy as my claimant, I'm hoping that everything will be back on track,' Alkira assures him.

Chapter 71

GALLAGHER VISITS MARVELL STREET

Eager to confirm Rebecca's account of what happened on the night of the B&S ball twenty-five years ago, Chief Inspector James Gallagher arrives at Marvell Street to speak directly to Abel Stenmark. On arrival, he finds Abel in the vegetable garden beside his house, wearing an old floppy hat. Before approaching him, he observes him for a few minutes as he digs up potatoes with his trusty shovel.

'Why do potatoes make good detectives, Abel?' he asks.

Abel shrugs, hardly interested to hear the answer.

'Because they keep their eyes peeled.'

'Ha ha!' Abel responds. 'What can I do for you, Jim?'

'Abel, you're no doubt aware that we have exhumed seven bodies from your family grave on Broken Head.'

Abel's body stiffens, wondering what Gallagher will say next.

'Yes, Jim. I've been following it on the news,' he answers casually. 'Our family plot was getting close to full.'

'You're right there, Abel. Someone has been mighty busy using the grave as a depository.'

Abel has a wary look on his face, and Gallagher detects a nervous twitch around his jaw.

'My team has completed their analysis of all the remains, and as you probably already know, they've found three indigenous bodies inside your family's grave. A female skeleton has been in there for decades, but the other two males were buried much more recently. Can you explain this, Abel?'

'I haven't got a clue, mate. Anybody could have put them there.'

'We can explain it, Abel,' Gallagher retorts.

'Well then, who do you think put them there, Jim?' Abel challenges, with his foot resting on the shovel in a demonstrative pose.

'As only the Stenmarks have a key to the compound gate, we are pinning the murder of the two most recent bodies on one of your family members.'

'Who, Jim?'

'One of your sons.'

'It couldn't have been Brett, so you must be thinking that Jude had a hand in it,' Abel deduces.

'Yes, Abel. We've arrested your son Jude for the double murder of Willy Wampandi and Dingo Yukambal. You weren't with him at the time, by any chance, were you, Abel?'

'No, Jim. I haven't been up there. Why are you asking me that?'

'Because one of the beer cans found up at the grave had your fingerprints on it, mate. That's why.'

Abel shakes his head. 'You're clutching at straws, Jim,' he rebuffs, but Abel is edgy. Things are hotting up.

'I want to leave that thought for now, Abel, because I want to move on to the skeleton of the female we found at the bottom of the grave. My team has identified these remains as belonging to the late Matilda Merinda.'

'The missing indigenous girl?' Abel asks, pretending complete innocence.

'Yes, Abel. Matilda Merinda.'

'I wonder if Kane put her in there, Jim,' Abel asks provocatively.

'It wasn't Kane who interred her in there, Abel. It was you. You were the one who buried her in the family grave twenty-five years ago.'

'Don't be crazy, Jim,' Abel scoffs, shaking his head.

'Your sister has admitted to shooting the girl and she's signed a statement admitting that the rifle she was holding went off accidentally. She said it was your rifle and that it was you who took the dead girl's body away in the boot of your brother's car.'

'If she said that, Rebecca's lying.'

'It makes sense to me, Abel. You buried her in the family plot on Broken Head, didn't you? C'mon, you were trying to protect your little sister from the law, weren't you, mate?' Gallagher presses.

'If she told you that, she's gone stark raving mad.'

'Well, she's admitted to killing the girl and she reported that she had to keep quiet about it all these years, because you swore her to secrecy. It's time you owned up to it, Abel. You buried the girl and told Rebecca to shut up.'

'Bullshit!'

'Abel Stenmark, I officially charge you with acting as an accessory to the manslaughter of Matilda Merinda in 1975.'

Gallagher removes the handcuffs from his belt and orders Abel to put his hands in front of him to be cuffed.

'For fuck's sake, Jim! Rebecca is just trying to get even. You're not going to believe her story over mine, are you?'

'Abel, that shovel you are using . . . Was that the one you used to open up the grave?'

'You've got the wrong brother, Jim Gallagher!' Abel retorts.

Chapter 72

TAKING CONTROL

Once he has convinced his bank to put up the five thousand dollars required to release his sister on bail, Kane delivers Rebecca's passport to the authorities and collects her from the local lock-up. Rebecca has suffered five long days and nights in a claustrophobic cell, and she is extremely relieved to be set free until her court case. As she leaves the jail holding tightly onto Kane's arm, she enjoys feeling the late summer sun on her cheeks, and breathing in the fresh coastal air.

'Freedom is so underrated,' she opines as they walk towards her home.

Over a cup of Earl Grey tea, Kane wastes no time informing Rebecca that he has been working at restructuring the Stenmark Inc. business partnership agreement. As he is of the opinion that it's time for them to start the ball rolling legally, he asks her if she would be up for a visit to Alkira the very next day.

'I am unable to contact her because she refuses to speak to me,' he, admits, explaining to Rebecca that he hasn't been able to establish a cordial relationship with his daughter since announcing that he liked Abel's development plans.

'We'll just have to make a surprise visit then,' Rebecca declares.

The following morning, when the duo have climbed up Alkira's many stairs, Kane is feeling quite anxious when he knocks on her door, a feeling that intensifies when it takes a long while for Alkira to appear.

'Oh, hello, Kane and . . . and Rebecca,' she greets, wrapped only in a towel. 'What brings you two up here?' she enquires, surprised to see their uninvited faces at her door.

'We're sorry to catch you unawares, Alkira, but we urgently need your help.'

'Please excuse my appearance. I'm just out of the shower. I'm still in a state of undress, but please come on in.'

After ushering her father and aunt into her living room, Alkira disappears to replace the bathroom towel with some clothing. When she returns, her hair is still wet, but she is now wearing a light cotton summer dress. She is carrying three glasses of iced water on a tray, and after placing two of them on the coffee table in front of each of her visitors, she retains one for herself.

'Now how can I help?' she asks.

'Alkira, we want to set up a new partnership agreement at Stenmark Inc. We feel it's time we modernised the family company structure to make it more efficient.'

'Doesn't the company already have a lawyer?' Alkira asks.

'Up till now, Abel has always dealt with Felix Barker, but we'd like to engage you to represent us rather than him,' Kane responds.

'What exactly do you want to achieve?' she asks.

'We want to reword the partnership agreement so that the directors become tenants in common rather than joint tenants. It will allow each of us to bequeath our one-third share to our offspring rather than to the other directors.'

Alkira nods, fully understanding the terms.

'In other words,' Rebecca adds, 'if Abel wants to, he can bequeath his share to his wife and sons, Kane can bequeath his share to you and Archie, while I can bequeath my inheritance to Corrie.'

'Is there more to it than that?' Alkira prudently asks.

Rebecca and Kane look at each other.

'Yes, there is,' Rebecca replies. 'We think that Abel has controlled the company for far too long. For decades, he has assumed absolute control of the Sands Hotel and the land at Broken Head, but we want to wrest it back.'

'How do you plan to do that?'

'We plan to use our majority vote to take over the management of the hotel and the land,' Kane informs her.

'Really?'

'We want to change the ambience of the Sands too so that it becomes more inclusive. To do that, we'll have to remove Abel from the management.'

'In my view, that will be a step in the right direction,' Alkira responds. 'Will your new plans make it more inclusive for my First Nation people?'

'Yes, Alkira, it will,' Rebecca replies instantly.

'That will be a big change for the Sands then,' Alkira rejoins.

'Under a new partnership agreement, we might even be able to stop Abel from developing Broken Head,' Rebecca quickly adds, and with this statement she has Alkira's complete attention.

'How will you do that?'

'We'll vote against the lodging of the DA.'

'What would your alternative plan for the land be?' Alkira asks pertinently.

'Well, Alkira, you'll be pleased to hear that after discussing it at great length, we've concluded that Abel's luxury development is grossly unfair. Instead of supporting it, we will both support your claim for Broken Head so that the land becomes a national park,' Kane declares.

A wide smile breaks out over Alkira's naturally beautiful face. 'I always held out the hope that you would change your mind, Kane, but I must say that for a while there, I thought you'd become a victim to the almighty dollar.'

Kane is embarrassed that his daughter is calling him out. 'Selling off all those luxury villas would have been such a lucrative proposition,' she continues.

'Yes, it would have meant multi-millions of dollars in our pockets, Alkira, but in the end, I came to the conclusion that the development just isn't fair.'

Alkira stands up from her lounge chair and walks over to where her father is sitting. She extends her hand out to him to formally shake his. 'Thank you for changing your mind, Kane,' she says.

'You're welcome,' her father replies.

'I will agree to represent you both, but first, you must sign a letter of engagement.'

'Great!' Kane replies, extremely relieved that his daughter is accepting the brief. He and Rebecca exchange a smile.

'Using time as the essence, I will set up a new legally binding partnership agreement for you, with decisions to be made by a majority vote. And when you have obtained all three signatures on the document, you'll be able to launch Stenmark Inc. Mark 2,' she states.

'Thank you, Alkira,' Kane replies.

'It's been a very productive meeting,' Rebecca states, quite delighted with how things have gone.

'Do you think you'll be able to get all three signatures?' Alkira asks pointedly.

'We're hopeful,' Kane replies, crossing his fingers that they will be able to convince Abel to sign.

Alkira ushers the pair to her door. 'Who would have thought that I would be legally representing the Stenmarks?' she remarks as she farewells them.

Chapter 73

ALKIRA VISITS FELIX BARKER

After signing the new partnership agreement, Kane and Rebecca request Alkira to present it to Felix Barker on their behalf, and as requested, she fronts up to the legal eagle's office looking extremely professional in a burgundy dress with matching high heels. Clutching the new agreement, she waits in Barker's reception area for over half an hour before Barker's aging secretary ushers her into his plush office.

'Good morning, Mr Barker. My name is Alkira Merinda and I represent Kane and Rebecca Stenmark,' she states confidently.

'No, you don't, Ms Merinda. They are my clients,' Felix Barker rebuffs.

'Your clients no longer,' Alkira retorts. 'I have their letter of engagement here.' Alkira passes the signed letter over to the legal eagle.

'Bloody hell!' Felix barks as Alkira holds out her hand for him to return the letter. 'What's this all about then?'

'My clients have requested that I draw up a new partnership agreement for Stenmark Inc., and as a matter of courtesy, I'm delivering it to you personally so you can advise your client, Abel Stenmark, to sign it.'

Alkira passes over the new document that Kane and Rebecca have signed, and Barker reads the first few paragraphs before exclaiming, 'This is preposterous! Abel will never sign this!'

'Mr Barker, you will note that in the old partnership agreement, the three Stenmark siblings were joint tenants, but my clients have requested that in this new agreement, they become tenants in common so they can bequeath their shares to their—'

'Yes, yes, yes, I know the difference, miss!

The original document has always worked in the past. Why not keep it?'

'It makes the company unstable, sir. None of the siblings want the others to inherit their shares in the company.'

'I will recommend to Abel that he never signs this,' Felix states emphatically, slapping the agreement closed.

Alkira feels that the time has come for her to explain the inducement that Kane and Rebecca have proposed to entice Abel to sign.

'To encourage your client to sign this agreement, my clients have generously offered to transfer the deeds of Marvell Street across to Abel, because he may need the house when his son is released from hospital. We can arrange for the settlement to occur immediately after his signature appears on the new document.'

'You think that that will entice him, do you, Ms Merinda?'

'It would be a multi-million-dollar windfall, Mr Barker.'

'My dear little girl, why should Abel Stenmark let go of the Sands Hotel when it's the goose that keeps laying the golden egg? And why should he give up his dream of developing Broken Head either, as that project promises to be an enormous windfall down the track?'

'In this new agreement – if you'd bothered to read on, Mr Barker – Abel retains his third share in the company, but all major decisions will now require a majority vote.'

'May I ask – if my client is foolish enough to accept this deal, would he continue to manage the Sands Hotel and the land at Broken Head?'

'I think not, sir. The Sands Hotel will likely be under new management, and I understand that his siblings are opposed to the Nirvana development at Broken Head.'

'By any chance, are they planning to support your native title claim instead, Ms Merinda?' Barker prudently asks, looking over his spectacles at Alkira with suspicion.

'I believe so, Mr Barker,' Alkira discloses.

Her words immediately ignite Barker's anger, however, and he stands upright behind his giant desk.

'Get out of my office, you traitor! Do you hear me? Get the fuck out!' he bellows.

As Barker points towards his door, with his face ballooning up like a crazed wombat, Alkira quickly gathers her belongings and with Barker continuing to howl at her, she retreats towards the door.

'You're a bloody charlatan!' he decries as Alkira escapes from his office.

Chapter 74

SIBLINGS VISIT THE JAIL

A short time after Alkira has fled from Felix Barker's office, Kane and Rebecca pay a visit to the local lock-up to play their part in convincing Abel to accept the new partnership agreement. Rebecca is not comfortable about returning to the place of her previous incarceration, especially when she hears the hollow clang of metal against metal when the guard opens and closes the security gates to let them inside. The guard's heavy footsteps echo throughout the building when he leads them along the clinical corridor leading to the visitors' room.

From the door to the visitors' area, the siblings can observe Abel in an orange suit, slumped forward over a small table. They approach him, and Rebecca touches him on the shoulder to let him know they are here.

'Hello, Abel,' she greets heartily.

When Abel looks up at her, his face is a picture of depression. Without answering her, he merely raises one eyebrow, as if to say, 'What do you want with me?'

'Are you OK, Abel?' she asks.

'This is what happens when you try to help your sister,' Abel replies sarcastically. 'I did it all for you, Rebecca, but this is what I get for all my efforts.'

'You might have thought you were protecting Rebecca, bro, but for decades, you let me take the blame for abducting Matilda Merinda, when it was you who buried her.'

'Fuck off, Kane! Why are you here?'

'It's my turn to give you a deal you can't refuse, bro. That's why I'm here,' Kane responds.

'We're making a family visit to see if you're OK,' Rebecca quickly asserts, vainly trying to soften the nature of the visit.

'You're so very kind, both of you,' Abel replies with more sarcasm.

'Let's not beat around the bush, Abel. We are here because you're in deep shit.' Kane states bluntly. 'You've been arrested for burying Matilda in our family grave and for blackmailing Rebecca into silence for over twenty-five years. Let's not forget that during all this time, I've had to take all the heat.'

'Poor little victim!' Abel scoffs.

'And I haven't forgotten that you tried to drown me at Fisherman's Lookout either, you bastard.'

Abel remains starchily sombre.

'Your wife almost tipped me overboard on a boat trip too,' Rebecca adds, making sure Stephanie hasn't escaped blame.

After this personal barrage, Abel remains expressionless.

'Chief Inspector Gallagher calls you "a serial burier", and he has proof you were with Jude when he shot Willy and Dingo too. He maintains you helped him bury their bodies in our family grave.'

'Give me a fucking break, Kane!'

'You don't deserve a break. And while I remember it, your friend Felix nearly killed me. He ran me off the road after I told him I wouldn't support your bloody dream development.'

Having heard enough criticism from his siblings, Abel holds his shackled hands up to his face in an attempt to block his ears.

'By the way, Abel, while you've been in here, I've been running the hotel, and as it's quite likely you won't be getting out of here anytime soon, Rebecca and I have had to make a few important decisions.'

'What are you saying?'

'We've decided that from now on, Stenmark Inc. is going to be run by us.'

'Like hell!'

'If you sign this new partnership agreement, however, we'll be very generous to you.' Kane produces the folder containing the new document, and places it in front of Abel.

'The minute you sign on the dotted line, we'll transfer the deeds of the family house at Marvell Street to you, so that you'll become the sole owner. But if you don't sign, bro, we'll vote to kick you and your family out of Marvell Street forever.'

'You wouldn't pitch us out on the street!'

'Yes, we will. When Brett is released from hospital, the poor boy won't have a home to come back to.'

'I've got news for you both. I'm not going to sign anything,' Abel informs them.

'If you don't sign, Abel, you'll be homeless by the time you get out of here.'

'I'm the one who has maintained that beautiful house, and I'm the one who built the Sands up to what it is today. I might add that I did it without your help. I've also created wonderful plans to develop Broken Head, so why would I sign your bloody agreement?'

'Because you'll lose the family house, that's why,' Kane retorts. 'If you don't sign the agreement, we will vote to evict you and your family, and as Rebecca and I will have the majority vote, we will no longer want you managing the hotel either. Your time is up, mate.'

'What about Nirvana?' Abel asks.

'Nirvana is finished too. When the time is right, we'll relinquish our tenure on the land at Broken Head and we'll sign it over to its traditional owners as a national park.'

'You'll give away a fortune if you do that, you bloody idiots!' Abel retorts.

'You have forty-eight hours to make up your mind, Abel,' Kane states as he raises his hand to signal for the guard to let them out.

After delivering their ultimatum to Abel, Rebecca and Kane make their way from the lock-up, but as they are about to part ways, they see Stephanie striding purposefully towards the entrance to the prison. Both Kane and Rebecca imagine she is on her way to visit either her husband or her son. Without acknowledging them, Stephanie struts past them with her chin held high.

'Hello, Mrs Stenmark. Which one are you visiting today?' the warden asks.

'My husband,' Stephanie replies, and the warden leads her to Abel.

'Have you had some visitors today Abel?' Stephanie asks, after kissing her husband on the cheek.

'Yeah. Rebecca and Kane came to see me . . . the bloody traitors,' he answers.

'I saw them out front. Why were they here, darling?'

'They say they want to kick me out of the Sands so they can manage it on their own. What's more, they intend to give away Broken Head.'

'Can they do that, Abel?' Stephanie asks.

'They can if they vote against me as a block.'

'Shit!'

'They want me to sign a new partnership agreement too.' Abel points to the folder in front of him.

'Really?'

'If I sign it, I'll still be a third owner of Stenmark Inc., but they'll vote me out of managing the Sands and Broken Head.'

'Don't sign it then.'

'The only good thing about it, Stephanie, is that in my will, I'll be able to pass all of my shares onto you and the boys rather than it all going to my siblings.'

'That's a move in the right direction, Abel. I like that part, but there must be a catch.'

'There is. If I sign, they'll take over the hotel and take charge of the land at Broken Head.'

'But what about Nirvana then, darling?'

'They plan to turn Broken Head into a national park run by the darkies.'

'They'll ruin your dream, Abel. Don't sign it.'

'As an inducement for me to sign, they'll transfer the deeds on Marvell Street to us, but if I don't sign it, they'll toss us out of the house.'

'What? Seriously? Abel, they've got us by the short and curlies, darling! You'll have to sign it . . . We can't give up our home.'

Stephanie grasps the partnership agreement folder from the small table, scrutinises it carefully and then opens it to the last page. Purposefully producing a pen from her handbag, she states, 'Sign the bloody thing, Abel! We can't lose Marvell Street. You must think of your family first!'

Abel appears confused.

‘Here. Sign here,’ she directs with some urgency, pointing the pen towards the signature page. ‘Once you sign it, Abel, I’ll take it straight over to Felix.’

Abel reluctantly signs.

Chapter 75

THE ANNOUNCEMENT

It is six weeks since Alkira changed the claimant's name from Rhonda Merinda to Jimmy Merinda on her revised submission to the National Native Title Tribunal. When she spots an official-looking government document in her letterbox, she wonders if it's a reply from the tribunal, and she nervously opens the envelope to read her fate. The letter advises her that the tribunal's determination will be delivered by a private telephone call in one week's time. The call is intended to give her the heads-up before an official announcement is made to the public.

When Alkira tells Jimmy about this arrangement, he thinks that it sounds positive, and he invites her to the Aboriginal camp to be with the clan when she receives the all-important call. Eager to be by her side when she hears the result, Kane and Archie also join her, and as the trio enters the community hall, some of the men approach Kane to apologise to him for the cruel treatment handed out to him on his last visit. Kane immediately forgives them, telling them that he understands their frustration.

Knowing that Felix Barker had already made an objection to her second claim, Alkira is understandably anxious about the forthcoming determination. In his objection to her second claim, he'd advised the tribunal that in his opinion, Jimmy Merinda was also an unworthy claimant. He based his objections on Jimmy's previous encounters with the law, citing his several incarcerations in the Byron Bay jail and his involvement with indigenous protests. He also pointed out that there are no records in Alkira's submission affirming Jimmy's ongoing employment at the Stenmark gold mine. Alkira is fully aware that the reason for the paucity of employment documentation was because Felix Barker had refused to supply them on behalf of the Stenmarks.

As the First Nation people assemble for the historic announcement, the distinctively haunting sound of a didgeridoo can be heard reverberating around the interior of the community hall. Once again, it is Mick who is blowing into his didgeridoo, and as usual, Archie listens for the familiar animal sounds in his music. At first, he hears only a resonant rhythmic humming sound, but in time, he recognises the howl of a dingo, the distinctive laugh of a kookaburra, and also a kangaroo bouncing.

Suddenly, Alkira's mobile phone rings, It is the cue for Mick to immediately stop playing his didgeridoo.

'I wish to speak with Alkira Merinda,' the voice on the other end of the phone requests.

'Yes, this is Alkira Merinda speaking,' Alkira answers excitedly, switching her phone onto speaker.

'This call is from the National Native Title Tribunal, madam. We wish to advise you of our determination to your native title claim.'

'Yes,' Alkira replies nervously.

'The tribunal hereby acknowledges the existence of your group's rights and interests in the land at Broken Head. You have provided us with sufficient evidence to satisfy us that your tribe's customs have been observed on this land, both before and since European settlement. We are also satisfied that the applicant on your submission has maintained a continuing connection to the said land and its surrounding water.'

Alkira's face beams with wondrous joy.

'We also wish to advise you that from the date of the official announcement, in one week's time, that your rights and interests will be recognised by the common law of Australia.'

'So are you saying that you will return our land to us?' Alkira asks, making sure she has heard the determination correctly.

'Yes, Miss Merinda. Your people will be able to form an indigenous land use agreement to control the land, so they can fulfil their cultural aspirations into the future.'

Alkira is in shock. She wants to thank the caller, but there is so much jubilation around her that she can't hear his last words. The tribe has burst into loud cheers and many of them are hugging Alkira, with tears of joy in their eyes. Archie takes over the call from the tribunal and thanks the judge on the end of the line, explaining to him that Alkira is unable to continue.

Feeling an enormous release from anxiety, the entire clan continues to whoop, clap, and hug one another. When Jimmy sees Alkira in tears of joy, he rushes towards her to offer his congratulations. Alkira clasps him by the arms to thank him for agreeing to be her claimant, explaining to him that he was pivotal in them obtaining the positive outcome.

'It's like the end of a football match when your side wins,' he voices and Alkira smiles in total agreement. Kane is next to congratulate Alkira on her triumph, and the father and daughter hug warmly, both feeling a decidedly stronger connection at last.

Archie's chest is bursting with pride too, and when he hugs Alkira, to applaud her accomplishment, he lauds,

'This is such a significant moment, Alkira. You've jumped the highest hurdle for your people and you've created history.'

As Archie hugs her, however, all Alkira can think about is her mother. 'I did it all for Ronnie, you know,' she sobs. 'After all is said and done, I did it for her.'

'She'll be so proud of you,' Archie responds, causing Alkira's tears to drop like rain onto Archie's shoulder.

While the siblings are having this moment together, Kane takes the opportunity to sidle up to his old mate Jimmy. 'You've triumphed against great odds today, Jimmy,' he applauds. The statement causes Jimmy's scarred face to light up with a proud smile.

'I can't believe it, Kanee! After being shut out for 120 years, our tribe now has its bloody sacred land back.'

'Thank god for Jimmy Mabo,' Kane replies, making a timely reminder of the man whose landmark claim was awarded the first native title determination.

'He should be a saint,' Jimmy responds.

After an hour of marvellous jubilation, Jimmy finally escorts Kane, Archie, and Alkira from the Aboriginal camp.

'I hope ya can come back 'ere on Friday, you lot,' he announces. 'We're havin' a grieving ceremony 'ere for Willy an' Dingo at two o'clock.'

Chapter 76

JIMMY'S CEREMONY

At precisely two o'clock on the following Friday, Archie, Alkira, and Kane arrive back at the community hall. This time, they are here for the grieving ceremony that Jimmy has arranged for Willy and Dingo. Jimmy is keen to have his mates sent off to their afterlife according to traditional Aboriginal protocol, but the women of the tribe have pressured him to include Matilda in his ceremony. Despite the fact that these grieving ceremonies are usually separate, he makes an exception on this particular occasion. Breaking with tradition, he allows the women to be included so they can farewell Matilda.

Dressed traditionally with garlands of leaves in their hair and more around their waists, the Dubay dancers line up at the entry to greet the attendees to the ceremony. Scores of Aboriginal flags are hanging vertically from the ceiling of the community hall for the occasion. They provide a strident red, black, and yellow effect as the visitors enter the circular room.

When he sees scores of black faces surrounding him, Archie soon realises that he is in the minority at this gathering, and feeling a little uneasy, he confides to Alkira, 'Now I know how you feel when you're outnumbered.'

In the centre of the room, a small fire with bluish smoke emanating from it smoulders on a large corrugated iron sheet. The smoke creates a hazy atmosphere in the room, and Archie can smell a pleasant woodland odour.

To start the ceremony, eight of the Dubay group rush in, waving branches of Ti- tree from side to side as part of their welcome dance. The women crouch and then jump in unison, imitating *Wajung* dolphins, which leap from the water. During the dance, Alkira whispers to Archie that Matilda's totem sign was a dolphin and that the dancers are honouring it.

The women then swish their branches over the smouldering fire and with each wave of the Ti-tree branches, they produce more and more smoke. As Archie watches the women dance around in the smoke, it appears to him as if they are willing away the evil spirits so that at last, Matilda's soul can merge with her ancestral creative beings.

Alkira has previously told Archie that life for the Aboriginal people is a never-ending cycle, and that death is just a transition to another entity. Aware that these ancient customs have endured over many centuries, Archie cannot help contrasting them with his own, more recent agnosticism, but the comparison only serves to make him feel shallow.

Just before the final routine, keen to engage Alkira in the last dance, Maisy strides over towards her to draw her into the centre of the hall. Being familiar with the routine, Alkira moves effortlessly with the women as they walk like crabs, swim like fish, and fly like birds. At the end of their dance, the Dubay dancers form a single line on the dirt floor, and surprisingly, they slither on their stomachs, forming a long *kabul*, a carpet snake. Finally, the women disappear from the room in a long wavy motion.

When Alkira resumes her place with Archie and Kane, she appears somewhat dirtier than she was before, but unperturbed about her appearance she settles herself down so that she is ready for the next part of the ceremony, which involves the men of the tribe. After a prolonged silence, the invited guests hear the plaintive sound of Mick's didgeridoo, which acts as a cue for Jimmy to arrive in the room in his kangaroo skin cape. Jimmy is ready to announce the sorry business.

'Jingi wahlu widtha,' he announces in his gravelly voice, welcoming everyone to country. 'Today we wish to pay our respects to our nation's ancestors – past, present, and emerging – before we honour those who have been taken from us. So that you all know, we are observin' our naming protocols today. We won't be naming our dead, because we don't wanna disturb their spiritual journey. We just wanna safeguard their passage so they can at last return to their spiritual birthplace.'

Walking with their legs apart to the beat of click sticks, twenty men approach the centre of the hall, their bodies covered from head to toe with white paint. Etched onto their skin are delicate marks made of dots and lines, with each man appearing to have his own particular design. The dancers all wear red headbands and red wristbands made of cloth, but on their ankles are fluffy white goose feathers. More feathers sprout from the tops of highly decorated burial poles that they thrust up and down while stomping around the room. When the men come close to Archie, he notices that some of them have fresh cuts on their bodies that are bleeding.

'Why have they cut themselves?' he asks Alkira.

'To show remorse,' she whispers.

Archie is mesmerised by the jerky movements of the men, who line up in various formations, strutting back and forth to the constant rhythm of their click sticks. At times, they brandish their decorated burial poles into the air in unison, while at other times, they rush towards those seated at the perimeter of the hall. It is as if the onlookers are their prey in a hunting ritual. When they come up close to Archie, he notices the skilfully applied designs that have been painted on their bodies and faces. He can imagine the hours of artistry that must have preceded the ceremony.

In their 'sorry dance', the men make small jumps forward with their legs apart, and after making many turns to the left and right, they end the dance on the final beat of the click stick. On that final beat, the men remain completely motionless, all standing on one leg. In the silence that follows, each of them stretches out his right arm, holding his burial pole in the air. It is such a precise movement that Archie has the urge to applaud.

In the dances that follow, the men continue to enact many of their ancestors' myths and legends, but in their final dance, Archie realises that they're honouring their two dead mates by re-enacting their individual life journeys. In this dance, the men interpret the skills that the dead men learned while they were here on earth. By celebrating the spiritual path they took during their lives, the dancers appear to be singing their mates off on their journey to their ancestors, so they can join a bloodline that stretches back an eternity.

At the end of the dancing, Jimmy, who is looking authoritative in his kangaroo skin cape, returns to the centre of the hall to deliver the benediction.

'The souls of our mates now go to the sky world to join the dreaming of our ancestors,' he declares.

After declaring this, he strides across to each dancer to touch him on his outstretched arm. This gesture signifies to the dancer that his part in the grieving ceremony is over, and once released the dancer runs from the hall. When the final man leaves, Jimmy strides out behind him.

'That was such a moving observance,' Archie expresses to Alkira, but his comment goes unanswered. Alkira has been brought to tears by the stories of the two male kinsmen who were being honoured in the ceremony. Feeling a deep affection for Alkira, Archie clasps her hand in his. His understanding of her world has increased dramatically of late, and he is content to sit quietly beside her after being overawed by her tribe's traditions.

Alkira suddenly looks down at her watch. 'Archie, we must leave straight away,' she states. 'I have a plane to catch.'

'Oh yes, I'd forgotten that you're off to Canberra tonight,' Archie replies. 'Let's go.'

Chapter 77

THE SANDS HOTEL BEER GARDEN

It is Australia Day 2000, and a large group is assembling in the beer garden at the Sands Hotel to watch Alkira deliver the people's address from the nation's capital. To capture the historical event, Kane has installed large screens throughout the hotel tuned to the national broadcaster. He has personally invited the local First Nation people to the pub for the occasion, advising them that his daughter will be making a historic speech about their land at Broken Head. To make sure a sizeable crowd attends, Kane offers free beer, wine, and food for the occasion.

Jimmy is the first to arrive at the hotel, accompanied by scores of his mates. Kane offers them jugs of free beer as promised and after a few toasts, he and Jimmy quietly recall the glassing incident that occurred in the beer garden more than twenty-five years ago. After remembering how Abel threw them out on the street, both of them are delighted that he won't be attending today, as he is locked up in prison, awaiting his court case.

A large contingent of indigenous women stream into the Sands Hotel to join the men, and keen to keep them all happy Kane hands out free wine. When Abel ran the Sands Hotel, the ratio between blacks and whites in the beer garden was usually 0 per cent blacks to 100 per cent whites, but today the tables have turned, and it's almost the reverse.

The local First Nation people have taken up Kane's invitation to hear Alkira speak from Canberra and they are arriving in droves. Although it was once a prohibited area for them, they flood into beer garden en masse. Some have walked, some have ridden bicycles, and some have crowded into the back of utes to arrive for the gala event. Alkira is the first Aboriginal person ever to be selected to give the people's address on Australia Day and the local indigenous community are extremely proud that one of their own tribe has been selected to represent them.

With beer and wine flowing freely, a party atmosphere soon develops especially when Jimmy's friend Mick arrives with his didgeridoo. The plaintive sound strikes a chord with the assembled group, who listen for the familiar animal and bird calls in their compatriot's rhythmic rendition. Their faces beam with delight when they recognise creatures such as frogs, dogs, and cicadas.

Soon, the unmistakable sounds of click sticks are heard from outside the walls, and there is a lot of love in the air when the Dubay dancers enter to perform their well-rehearsed routines in front of their admiring home crowd. Confidently moving to the beat they are creating, the women carefully make their way around the picnic tables until they reach the dance floor that Kane has set up in front of one of the huge screens. Some men join them on the boards and it's not long before everyone in the beer garden is up, grooving to the rhythms of the click sticks and Mick's didgeridoo.

When there is a break in festivities, Kane appears in front of the crowd to make an announcement. 'Ladies and gentlemen, in ten minutes, I'll be turning the screens on for my daughter's Australia Day address.'

'Bring it on!' someone shouts, and the entire beer garden cheers exuberantly.

Stephanie Stenmark peers into the beer garden, but when she sees the plethora of black faces singing and dancing, she decides to retreat to the hotel's front lounge for refuge. After ordering a stiff gin and tonic, she takes a seat near a potted palm. Stephanie has been in hiding since the arrests of her son and her husband and as this is her first foray into the public domain, she is justifiably nervous.

Archie, who is keen not to miss a word of Alkira's speech, selects a seat next to his father, who has positioned himself close to the big screen.

'What a turnout, Dad!' he enthuses. 'It's a colossal crowd . . . standing room only, I'd say.'

'I've never seen so many happy faces,' his father replies, before standing up in front of the screen to hush the crowd.

'I wish to take this opportunity to welcome you all to the Sands Hotel,' he begins, 'and today I want to particularly welcome the local indigenous community. I know Alkira Merinda's speech will have particular significance for you.' After receiving enthusiastic applause, Kane throws the switch on all screens and turns up the volume.

The governor general immediately appears in close-up.

'Ladies and gentlemen, this is Australia Day 2000, and we are broadcasting from Canberra in Australia's capital territory. Let me begin by acknowledging the Ngunnawal people whose ancestors walked on this land. I pay my respects to their elders past and present and extend that respect to all other Aboriginal people,' His Excellency begins.

There is a long pause while dignitaries file in behind the governor general to take their seats.

'Now, ladies and gentlemen, I have great pleasure in introducing Alkira Merinda, an indigenous woman from Byron Bay who will speak on behalf of all indigenous Australians in this year's inaugural people's address.'

To gentle applause, Alkira walks to the microphone, wearing a brooch of an Aboriginal flag. She nervously places her speech in front of her on the dais and takes a deep breath.

'What does it mean to be an indigenous Australian on Australia Day?' she asks, looking directly into the lens of the camera.

There is silence both in Canberra and in the Byron Bay beer garden.

'Today is January 26, the date chosen by our government to be a day of national unity. It was selected because it was the historic date the first fleet of British ships sailed into Sydney Cove to start a new colony in 1788. But let me tell you right here and now that on this particular date, everything changed for my people.

'As you are all aware, this new penal colony set up in Sydney was the first permanent European settlement in Australia, but it would prove to have a profound impact on our indigenous traditions and culture – a culture, I might add, that had previously remained undisturbed for possibly sixty-five thousand years.

'It is true that the original indigenous groups that lived on this land at the time of the arrival of this first fleet were disparate tribes, but even though they spoke different languages, they were bound by strong kinship rules and highly ordered social relationships. Our historians have been guilty of a "great Australian silence" on Aboriginal historical accounts because they have omitted the details of these kinship rules, which have mostly gone unrecorded. Ladies and gentlemen, we are talking here about some of the longest surviving traditions in human history!

'The arrival of Europeans on our land had a devastating impact on us. The invaders were fierce, confronting us with brute force. Those of us who stood up to protest against them were shot and large groups were massacred, while others fell prey to alien diseases such as smallpox. The indigenous groups who were lucky enough to survive these atrocities, soon found themselves marginalised in settlements on the outskirts of towns and were often refused entry to the downtown centre. After being effectively locked out of country by these pale spirits, our people felt demoralised, as they had no economic base and little opportunity to build wealth. Our ancestors were brutally rejected by mainstream Australia, who forced them to become the most impoverished and most imprisoned groups in our nation.

'One of the early colonial governors who was revered by our historians as having an enlightened vision, was Lachlan Macquarie. He was able to take the steps needed to transform the straggling, rum-soaked penal colony of Sydney into a prosperous settlement – a settlement that could attract free settlers to this country. In his diaries, however, we read that he planned harsh punishments for any hostile natives. In simultaneous punitive expeditions, he ordered his troops to fire on us and to hang offenders from trees so that he would, and I quote, "strike greater terror into the survivors".

'This, it must be said, was a standard practice occurring over time throughout the length and breadth of Australia. The Tasmanian governor George Arthur, for instance, wrote that John Batman, who was widely known as being the founder of Melbourne, "had much slaughter to account for".

'These are not comfortable thoughts for most of us to digest on Australia Day, while we are coming together to celebrate at our BBQs to toast modern Australia's successes, but for some of us it is, in fact, a day of mourning, and the best we can do on this day is to celebrate our survival.

'I am making the call today that the time has come for all of us to join together with one positive aspiration. We are all Australians now, and I believe the time has come for us to leave our complex and troublesome colonial legacy behind us, so we can embrace a new and independent future. White Australia indeed has had a black history, but despite this, we are ready to stand with you and be counted as a core part of Australia's identity. It is not so much about reconciliation as reckoning with our past.

'On that day into the future when we choose to stand together as one, the date of Australia's national day will have to change. It will no longer be appropriate to celebrate unity on the day some of us were invaded. My vision is that Australia should throw off its shackles of empire and become a republic. On the day that happens, we will be able to celebrate our true national independence.'

'Here, here!' shouts Kane, who has stood to his feet.

Many others in the beer garden stand up to join him. 'Here, here!' they chorus in support.

'Locally in Byron Bay, many of the locals are aware that I have made a claim for our sacred land at Broken Head to be returned to my people. Yes, I have had a dream for some time that this land will be released from private ownership to become a national park, to be jointly managed by my people and the NSW government. Today, ladies and gentlemen, I'm delighted to be able to announce that our claim has been successful.'

There is clapping in Canberra and loud cheers in Byron Bay.

'This is just the beginning, however, as my people must join the wider Byron Bay community to make this happen, and I am proposing that the first ranger of our new park be awarded to my uncle, a special man from our tribe whose name is Jimmy Merinda, one of the most knowledgeable environmentalists I know. Jimmy's primary goal will be to organise the rehabilitation of these disturbed lands, and where there is habitat destruction, it will be his responsibility to instigate regeneration plans to rectify them.'

'Here's to Jimmy!' a man shouts from the back of the beer garden, and in response everyone choruses, 'To Jimmy!' Jimmy's shy scarred face beams, and he raises his beer glass.

'I expect that in the not-too-distant future, with careful management, we will see the return of our totem animals to country,' Alkira continues. 'We will be able to explore Broken Head to see the wallum froglet, the beautiful fairy wren and the eastern whipbird, not to mention the short-beaked echidna, which is almost extinct. Our heathlands will return to us as they once were and mining on the land will stop. It is also my hope that the grave of the oppressive Joseph Stenmark and his family will be removed to the Byron Bay Cemetery to allow peace to return to country.'

'At bloody last!' Mick yells and everyone in the beer garden cheers in agreement.

'I have great hope that the new national park can be operational sometime in the year 2001. In the past, ladies and gentlemen, one white family excluded my people from our sacred land, but this new plan will enable us to return to country and share our traditions with the community at large and other visitors to Byron Bay.'

There is polite clapping in Canberra.

'I wish to conclude by wishing you all a wonderful Australia Day, a day that includes us all.'

There is vigorous applause in Canberra as Alkira elegantly walks from the podium with her speech in a folder. By the end of the speech, the entire beer garden is standing with raised glasses, all of them toasting their activist sister.

'Alkira! Alkira! Alkira!' they cheer.

Tears fill the eyes of many. They are tears born of hope. Many of the local indigenous people who have felt excluded for so long are now hugging one another, because at last, something momentous is happening in their lives. For many it's the first time that someone has articulated their sentiments so accurately. Alkira has empowered them and has triggered a communal joy.

Archie, with his chest bursting with pride, leans over to hug his father. Not only has his sister triumphed, but also, his father has gone along with the return of Broken Head to his indigenous mates. Aware that Alkira's speech has ignited a spark, Archie vows to his father that on her return, he will assist her so she will be able to capitalise on the considerable momentum. They will do it for Ronnie.

After watching the speech alone in the front lounge, Stephanie Stenmark has heard enough about native title rights for one day. She stands, and after defiantly pouring the remains of her third gin and tonic into the pot plant beside her, she struts towards the exit.

Chapter 78

THE PICNIC TABLE

The day after the Australia Day speech, Archie ventures towards Clarkes Beach with his satchel containing his trusty dented laptop. He has deliberately returned to this picnic table because it was where Ronnie had collapsed, and it is here that he intends to compile the final chapter of his story about the curse on the Stenmarks.

After setting up his laptop on the picnic table, he peers out towards Julian Rocks to examine the two large stones that majestically jut from the sea. Noticing that one is slightly bigger than the other, he recalls a tribal legend that Alkira had told him.

'A jealous husband threw a spear at a canoe that contained his wife and her lover. The canoe broke and sank, leaving only the prow and stern sticking out of the water, creating the shape of Julian Rocks. One of the lovers was from Cavanbah, and the other was from up the coast, but it was a doomed union.'

As Archie looks out at the two rocks today, he envisages the two lovers maintaining their individuality on the surface, while below the water, they hold hands to provide support for each other at the base. He sees a parallel here with himself and Alkira. While Alkira has been busy pursuing her lofty goals to obtain a native title for her people, he has been creating his novel about the curse. Although they've both been pursuing separate tasks, they've been a rock for each other along the way.

In his childhood, Archie had never known the love for a sibling, but now that he's experiencing it with Alkira, he finds it so sublime that he can't wait for her to return from Canberra. He makes a few more attempts to finish his novel at the picnic table, but as he is missing Alkira so much, he finds it difficult to concentrate. After producing little of any significance, he decides to wait until she returns before continuing with it. Admitting defeat, Archie packs up his belongings and retreats to the family hotel for a strong drink.

The moment Archie enters the Sands Hotel, he notices that Kane is sitting at a table in the corner of the front bar. As he seems to be concentrating on completing some hotel accountancy, he decides not to disturb him and takes a stool at the bar. He orders a scotch on the rocks from the barman on duty and then rests his head in his hands.

'What's the matter, son?' Kane calls out to him from the corner.

Archie raises his head. 'Oh, hi, Dad.'

'You look a bit depressed, Archie. What's up?'

'I'm just waiting for Alkira to return. I've missed her.'

'We've all been waiting for her to return, Archie. She's changed things around here. I think her speech has ignited a flame in this town.'

'She's a bit of a heroine these days, isn't she?' Archie fields.

'She sure is,' Kane agrees.

'Dad, I hear you've hired Corrie Stenmark as hotel manager,' Archie fields.

'Yes, Archie. He's terrific. Now that he has mastered his prosthesis and ditched his crutches, he's taken to the position like a duck to water.'

'So you're keeping the running of the hotel in the family, are you?'

'Not entirely, son. You'll never guess whom Corrie has hired to assist him.'

'Who?'

'Roxanne Jarvis.'

'She's a bit of a loose cannon, isn't she, Dad?'

'I was initially a little apprehensive about this appointment, Archie, but she's turned out to be exceptionally good with the clientele. She welcomes the indigenous clan just as enthusiastically as the regulars and she keeps a tight lid on any disputes that arise. She's like an experienced bouncer. Any nonsense from the "tradies", and she kicks them out.'

'Good for her. Are you two still an item these days?' Archie enquires.

'Keep it under your hat, but yes. I like her a lot, because she always calls a spade a spade.'

'Go for it, Dad. It's definitely time you stopped playing the field. You're not getting any younger, you know.'

Kane takes the comment on the chin, while Archie orders another scotch. Archie sits at the bar for another half hour or so, mostly thinking about what Alkira will need to do when she returns, as he's aware of an important upcoming event that she'll be expected to organise on her return. The local council are planning to commemorate her momentous native title win by having a historic handing-over ceremony up on Broken Head.

As he finishes off his third scotch, Archie wonders if his father intends to attend this historic event, and he calls out, 'Are you going to Broken Head for the big ceremony at the end of the month, Dad?'

'I wouldn't miss it for quids, Archie. I'll be there for sure. The signing of the land use agreement will be such an amazing historic moment for Alkira and her mob. What's more, I intend to bring along someone very special with me,' Kane discloses.

'Who will you bring?'

'You'll see.'

By the time Archie leaves the bar he is feeling slightly tipsy, and as he sways towards the exit, Kane calls, 'Take care on your way home, son! You look a little unbalanced.'

Archie stumbles towards the door.

'You go straight home, you handsome bugger!' Roxanne Jarvis calls to him as she enters the pub to start her shift.

Chapter 79

HISTORIC BROKEN HEAD CEREMONY

On her return from Canberra, Alkira has a great deal of work to do. The pressure is on for her to finalise the formulation of the indigenous land use agreement before the handover ceremony. In a short space of time, however, she is able to obtain a consensus among the interested groups involving a power-sharing arrangement, among the local council, the state government, and the local clan, with the agreement empowering her people to manage the newly formed national park.

The local council invites a plethora of dignitaries to the all-important ceremony, including all of the surrounding tribes. The response to the handover is overwhelming and on the designated day, interested groups arrive in droves to Broken Head, excited to be witnessing the historic signing.

Some of the indigenous tribesmen and women walk great distances to be present, and they are delighted to see Jimmy there at the gate to welcome them to Broken Head. Decked out in his tribal kangaroo skin cape, Jimmy stands with other elders from his tribe, who are each side of him draped in Aboriginal flags. The neighbouring tribesmen tell Jimmy they've been waiting for this special day for a lifetime and that they're hoping it will herald a return to the days when their tribes used to be invited to this headland to conduct corroborees with the generous local tribe.

Some of the visitors arrive in traditional dress carrying spears, boomerangs, and woven baskets, while others front up in modern dress, but all of them express the same delight, that the local tribe has finally been reinstated as the custodians of the sacred headland. They proudly march up to the top of the hill, eager to imbue the land with their cultural values once more.

At the top of the rise, many of them expect to see the old grave containing Joseph and Bella Stenmark, but they are relieved when they see in its place a substantial boulder to commemorate the occasion.

Kane has recently overseen the removal of the Stenmark grave from Broken Head, and has supervised the internment of the Stenmark family's remains into the local Byron Bay Cemetery. There is a palpable feeling of relief on the faces of the indigenous visitors when they read the inscription on the gigantic stone that has replaced the grave.

This stone commemorates the return of country
to the native people of Byron Bay
by the establishment of
the Broken Head National Park.
26 April 2001

Alkira and her committee are the final group to arrive at the thicket, accompanied by many distinguished dignitaries. At the commemorative boulder, Jimmy welcomes everyone to country and in his welcoming speech, he mentions by name the premier of NSW, the representatives from NSW Parks and Wildlife and the local lord mayor. As he looks out at the gathering, Jimmy sees a swathe of photographers recording his welcome, but the only media person he recognises in the melee is Stan Bowles, whose crew seem to be filming every detail from close range.

At the ceremony, the premier speaks grandly about the significance of the occasion, and after the historic signing, all the dignitaries shake hands cordially. When Alkira finally holds up the freshly signed document into the air, the indigenous groups cheer loudly.

Tears run down Jimmy's scarred face and he grasps onto Mick's arm to give it a heartfelt squeeze. 'We did it, Mick!' he exclaims proudly and in response, his mate pats him several times on the back.

Seeing the broad smiles on the men's faces, Archie comes over to congratulate them too. 'It's a great day for your mob,' he declares, and they look back at him bursting with joy. 'You'll be the boss of this place now Jimmy. I hear you're the new ranger,' he fields.

'S'pose so,' Jimmy replies, knowing it will be his responsibility to organise the rehabilitation of the land so that it reverts back to the pristine condition it once was in.

'Broken Head will be a gift to everyone now.'

Alkira moves among the dignitaries, thanking each of them for playing their part in the formation of the indigenous land use agreement.

'You are a wonderful advocate for your people,' the premier praises her.

'Did you know, sir, that I did it all for my mother?' Alkira responds.

'You may think you did it for your mother, Miss Merinda, but you did it for all Aboriginal people everywhere,' he corrects.

Archie bides his time before congratulating Alkira, knowing she must first speak with all the notable guests. He waits patiently on the sidelines, but when she becomes free, he rapidly approaches.

'Congratulations, babe!' he ventures. 'What a monumental achievement!'

He holds his arms outstretched, and Alkira enters them for her congratulatory hug. The moment Alkira is enclosed in her brother's arms, however, she breaks into tears, and her whole body starts to shake with emotion.

'Archie, I'm thinking of Ronnie,' she sobs. 'She's missed this wonderful moment. What a crying shame she couldn't make it.'

'You've given your mother a wonderful gift, Alkira. It's a tragedy that she couldn't be here to see it, but you've returned Cavanbah to her. You must celebrate your colossal achievement. It is a moment in history,' he replies.

At that moment, Kane Stenmark appears from behind the thicket, pushing Alkira's mother in a wheelchair. From a distance, Alkira can see Ronnie's unruly hair blowing in the wind. An Aboriginal flag on a long pole has been attached to her wheelchair and it blows proudly in the wind as she approaches. Alkira can't believe her eyes . . . *Ronnie is actually here!* As Kane pushes Ronnie over the uneven ground towards her, Alkira starts running towards the chair. The mother and daughter finally unite beside the commemorative boulder.

'You didn't think I'd miss out on this moment, did ya, Alkira?' Ronnie shrieks.

'Kane sprung me out of that bloody nursin' home before they poisoned me!'

Alkira crouches down in front of her mother and buries her head deep into her lap. In response, Ronnie proudly clasps Alkira's head in her gnarled hands and bends towards her daughter to kiss her on the top of her head.

'You inspired me, Mummy. You always wanted to get Broken Head back. I did it all for you.'

Ronnie lifts her daughter's head up and holds both of her cheeks in her hands. 'Ya did it for all of us, girl,' she corrects. 'I'm so proud of you that my heart is bloody jumpin' out of me body!'

Alkira kisses her mother's hands warmly, but as she kisses them, she notices that Ronnie has not one, but two gold bangles on her right wrist. She raises her eyebrows. 'You have two now?' she enquires.

'Yeah.' Ronnie nods. 'Chief Inspector Gallagher visited me at the nursing home. He said they'd recorded all the evidence they needed about Matilda, an' seein' that the investigations are now over, he wondered if I'd like to have Matilda's bangle.'

'That's so special, Mummy,' Alkira whispers.

'She'll be with me always now,' her mother replies, twisting the second gold bangle on her wrist. Ronnie looks up at Kane, who is holding steadfastly to the handles of her wheelchair. 'Now push me over to those VIPs, Kane,' she orders. 'I wanna welcome them to our land.'

Kane obliges her and even though it is a tough mission in the rough terrain, he manages to join the dignitaries.

'This is the best day of my life,' Ronnie tells the premier. 'I was born 'ere on Broken Head. It's my spiritual home, you know. It's the place that holds all my stories. Did ya know I was dragged off from 'ere to the "Cootamundra Home for Orphans and Neglected Aboriginal Children", Premier? I was part o' the bloody Stolen Generation!'

'No, I didn't know that, Ms Merinda.'

'Well, I was. The government took me away from my family when I was 5, an' I've been locked out of 'ere ever since. But today, at last, I'm able to come home to my conception site.'

'Well, welcome home, Ronnie,' the premier responds, shaking her wiry hand.

Ronnie moves on to meet the other VIPs and the many indigenous visitors who are representing the neighbouring tribes. Many of them praise her for her gritty tenacity in attending the celebration.

The moment Ronnie embraces her brother however, the full realisation of the event strikes her. The siblings hold each other by the arms and then quite spontaneously, they break into a loud wail. Hearing the emotional lament, everyone present at the ceremony is affected by it. Ronnie and Jimmy were carefree kids who innocently played on this land when they were younger, and now they have returned to be together on their traditional territory. Their loud wailing alerts everyone at the gathering of the real significance of the event. On this land, the visible and the invisible pulse with the same life and unseen spiritual forces hold sway.

In the crowd, Archie is surprised to see the fire-engine-red lips of his editor, Sue Barkham. He quickly clutches Alkira by the hand and drags her over to introduce her to Sue.

'Sue, what are you doing here?' he asks.

'I'm here to witness this historic event,' she replies.

'Indeed, it is a memorable moment in our lives,' Archie responds. 'Sue, I'd like you to meet my sister, Alkira Merinda.'

'I'm delighted to meet you, Alkira. Did I hear Archie correctly? Did he say "sister"?'

'Yes, Sue. I'm Kane Stenmark's daughter – so I've recently discovered.'

'Therein lies a tale, I'm sure!' Sue replies. 'Look, I won't keep you two any longer as I realise you are VIPs here today, but, Alkira, if you are accompanying Archie on his return to Sydney, I'd very much like to meet you again to congratulate you in private.'

'I'd like that too,' Alkira replies, before she turns away to greet more well-wishers.

The moment Alkira leaves them, Sue's face switches from charming to severe. She glowers at Archie as she asks, 'When am I going to get that bloody manuscript, Archie Stenmark? You're well past the bloody deadline, you know!'

'I'm nearly done, Sue. I promise you that I'll deliver it to you in Sydney before the month is up, OK?'

'You'd better, sonny boy, because I'm not giving you any more extensions!'

As Archie turns away from Sue Barkham, about twenty native men covered from head to toe in white paint arrive at the commemorative boulder. With goose feathers around their wrists and legs and red bandanas on their heads, the men form a circle, and with knees bent, they dance around the boulder to the haunting sound of Mick's didgeridoo. The dancers skip one way and then the other in perfect unison, joyfully enacting their first ritual dance on their reclaimed land.

When the dancers circle towards Archie, Jimmy proudly points out to him that the two smallest dancers are his sons. Archie nods, glad that they are learning the tribe's traditions. While Archie is watching the boys dance, Kane takes the opportunity to sidle over towards Alkira to congratulate her on her great accomplishment.

'I'm mighty proud of you, Alkira,' he praises, hugging her warmly.

'I couldn't have done it without you releasing the land, Dad,' she replies.

Kane's heart skips a beat. It's the first time his daughter has ever called him Dad.

'I'll never be able to repay you for bringing Ronnie to the ceremony Kane,' Alkira adds. 'It was such a special thing to do. I can't tell you how much I've loved having her here today.'

Alkira looks at Kane with enormous gratitude, and Kane blushes. At last, he has done a few things right!

At the end of the men's dance, some of the indigenous women in the audience join them and together, they dance around the boulder in a joyous celebration to Mother Earth.

Chapter 80

BYRON BAY

In the 1880s, when the government offered a settlement grant to Joseph Stenmark, the gesture extracted all hope from the traditional owners, but after the recent handover ceremony, they now feel they have been brought out from under the shadow of colonial domination. For the first time since the fence went up around Broken Head, the tribe is now able to look forward to a rosy future on their own land.

Determined not to waste another minute, a group of indigenous men rush towards the glitzy Nirvana sign erected at Iron Bark. Keen to remove any vestige of Abel Stenmark's nightmare plan, they drag the sign over to a roaring bonfire and they watch it gleefully as it bursts into flames. Receiving the same fate, the "Strictly No Admittance" sign that was once at the compound gate is thrown on the same fire. Removing the entire boundary fence, however, takes a great deal longer, as it takes a team of indigenous men many weeks of hard yakka before they are finally able to pull the last fence post down.

Jimmy learns that his responsibilities in the national park are wide-ranging, as he must work alongside the Department of National Parks and Wildlife to develop ongoing management plans to reinstate the natural habitat. He soon learns that he must not only remove the introduced plants that have been taking over the native fauna, but also control the feral animals that have been killing the native species. In addition, he is asked to close down the old gold mine so that it is safe, before educational walking tours are introduced. Jimmy is delighted that he has been given the responsibility to promote cultural awareness, and he begins straight away to pass on the message that everyone should respect his country.

Since the historic inauguration, Brett Stenmark's health has made a dramatic improvement and many people believe that his rapid recuperation is a direct result of the disappearance of the curse. After the handover ceremony, there was such a dramatic improvement in his health, that all tubes were immediately removed from his body. The "Nil by Mouth" sign on his bed was taken away the moment Brett began eating semi-solid food.

After noting his sudden improvement, Stephanie made plans to bring him home to Marvell Street, and these days he is recuperating in the gracious family house that Stephanie now owns. Stephanie will have her hands full, however, as she will be on her own with Brett until Abel is released from prison. After being convicted of unlawfully disposing of the three indigenous bodies in the family grave, Abel Stenmark has been informed that he is unlikely to be released for at least another two years.

Their son Jude who is presently residing in a maximum-security prison in Goulburn NSW, has not only been convicted of the double murder of Dingo and Willy, but the abduction and assault of Alkira in the Bangalow barn. As he has shown no remorse for his actions up to this point, Chief Inspector Gallagher anticipates that he is likely to have little chance of parole, and that it is highly likely that he will spend the rest of his life in the maximum-security facility.

Fined for dangerous driving, Abel and Jude's solicitor, Felix Barker, has had to lock up his black Mercedes in his garage, and it is likely to remain there until his license is unrevoked in twelve months' time. Since Kane and Rebecca have excluded him from any further involvement with the Sands Hotel, there are reports that Felix now suffers spates of severe depression.

After his appointment as hotel manager under Kane, Corrie Stenmark is now a popular face who welcomes patrons to the Sands Hotel. In his leisure time, Corrie has been seen entering the ocean, learning how to balance on his surfboard while wearing his new prosthesis. Rebecca is telling everyone that Corrie is hell-bent on getting back out in front of Julian Rocks again to ride the waves.

After being convicted of the manslaughter of Matilda Merinda, Rebecca was given leniency by the judge, because she was a child at the time of the shooting, and was acting under the influence of her elder brother's threats. After a brief spell in jail, Rebecca has returned to the Sands Hotel to take over the reins in the kitchen, and she has recently received rave reviews in the local paper for her healthy modern culinary cuisine.

Since Kane Stenmark took over the running of the Sands Hotel, his relationship with Roxanne Jarvis has solidified, both personally and professionally. No longer suspected of abducting Matilda Merinda, Kane has at last been accepted as a responsible member of the Byron Bay community. The atmosphere at the Sands these days contrasts markedly from when his brother was at the helm, as the new management team is keen to be seen as being inclusive to patrons of all colours and creeds.

Each Thursday evening, the local First Nation people showcase their culture in the beer garden. With Corrie Stenmark as compère, various indigenous youth bands appear with Mick often accompanying them on his didgeridoo. With the Dubay dancers appearing regularly as backup, Thursday evenings sometimes explode into an exuberant celebration of indigenous talent. The tourist guidebooks now tout 'Thursday Night at the Sands' as a night not to be missed by visitors to Byron Bay and its hinterland. As there have been no reports of any mishaps to any members of the Stenmark family since the handover, many observers, including Rebecca, put it down to the end of the curse.

Chapter 81

NORTH SYDNEY

Once the celebrations at Broken Head have died down and the national park has become fully operational, Archie and Alkira decide that it's time they returned to Sydney together, and after flying to Sydney, they decide to make a quick call into Archie's publishing firm. The duo hop out of a taxi in North Sydney and march up the steps of Aston & Irwin, keen to meet Sue Barkham.

Eager to impress the chief editor, Alkira has donned a simple black dress and a perky hat that she wears at a jaunty angle, while Archie wears the same light-blue suit and straw hat that he wore to Abel's luncheon in the beer garden. Proudly carrying his precious manuscript under his arm, Archie guides Alkira towards Sue Barkham's smart office.

'Here it is at last!' he calls, as he strides over to Sue Barkham's desk to hand over his novel.

'Thank you, Archie,' Sue replies, eagerly clutching it in her manicured hands.

While Sue glances down at the title, Archie observes her lips. Her lipstick appears even redder and glossier than the last time he saw her at Broken Head.

'I see you've named it *Pointing the Bone*, Archie.'

'Yes.'

'It's a great title . . . It's simple and to the point.'

After regarding the front page of the manuscript, Sue stands up from her desk and strides over to Alkira. 'How are you, Alkira?' she asks, extending her hand and smiling warmly.

'I'm a very fortunate woman, Sue,' Alkira replies, as she shakes Sue Barkham's hand.

'How's that?'

'I'm fortunate in two ways. First, I'm grateful that my people are free to enjoy their sacred land again, but in the process of getting it back for them, I've managed to snare myself a handsome brother, and what's more, I hear he's a successful author.'

'I haven't read *Pointing the Bone* yet, Alkira, so I don't know about the success of Archie's latest offering, but I'll bet my last dollar on it that you are the contemporary heroine in his story,' she fields.

'I don't know about that, Sue. He hasn't let me read a word of it yet, but I'm hoping that in his life outside the novel I can be an important character.'

'I hear you're a heroine already, Alkira, after your native title success and saving that Stenmark boy from a great white shark.'

'Anyone would have done the same, Sue,' she replies modestly.

'You know, Alkira, I told Archie to go up to Byron Bay to write about the curse, but I didn't expect him to come back with a sister,' she states.

The siblings look at each other and both shrug haplessly.

'He was reticent to go, you know,' Sue confides.

'That's because I was scared of the curse,' Archie defends.

'Well, Archie, you faced up to your demons, you encountered triumph and disaster and now you've come back a man, my son.' Sue applauds theatrically. 'And now that you've finished the damned thing, you can leave it with me. Now both of you go off and have some fun in Sydney.'

'I hope you enjoy it, Sue,' Archie entreats as he clasps Alkira's hand, ready to depart.

'In due course, Archie Stenmark, I'll let you know if you have Australia's next great novel on your hands!'

The End

Acknowledgements

I am grateful to Josie Budge for her guidance in the early drafts of the novel as her encouragement and generous assistance helped me shape the story.

I wish to also thank Mery Stevens who assisted in editing and provided valuable local knowledge.

To my wife Philippa for her enduring love and support.

A

Lightning Source UK Ltd.
Milton Keynes UK
UKHW011210091120
373077UK00012B/1304/J

9 781984 506962